In memory of Sylvester Stein (1920–2015)

THE DEVIL'S WORK

MARK EDWARDS

THOMAS & MERCER

Text copyright © 2016 Mark Edwards

Published by Thomas & Mercer, Seattle

www.apub.com

Amazon, the Amazon logo, and Thomas & Mercer are trademarks of Amazon.com, Inc., or its affiliates.

ISBN-13: 9781503938182
ISBN-10: 1503938182

Cover design by Mark Swan

Printed in the United States of America

Prologue

I lie in bed, scratching at the cold wall, waiting for the sound of footsteps. I knew he would come today, that there was nothing I could do about it. All I could do was hope, pray, that today's treatment would be psychological. A test. Questions. I can't face anything else, not today.

Not the hose.

Not the belt.

Here they come: the footsteps. Slow but steady. He comes into the bedroom and orders me to follow him. We go down one set of steps, then another, through the door and into the damp, frigid air of the basement.

'Take off your robe,' he tells me.

I try to protest but he picks up the belt so I undress as slowly as possible, clinging to every scrap of warmth until I'm naked, shivering, strapped into the chair.

He wheels the metal trolley over, cursing the wheel that has recently started to squeak.

On the surface of the trolley is a leather pouch. He unfolds it and I see what's inside.

Acupuncture needles, handles the colour of dried blood, their sharp tips shining in the artificial light.

'Please,' I say. 'Please.'

He takes the thickest needle from the pouch and moves towards me, licking his dry lips.

PART ONE

Chapter 1
Day one, Monday, 6 April, 2015

Sophie got to Herne Hill station with just enough time to buy a coffee from the stall on the platform and grab a free paper, barely able to believe this was all real, that she was a paid worker again. The last time she'd stood here at this time of the morning she'd been eight months pregnant with Daisy, wearing a little badge that said 'Baby on Board', excited and terrified about being a mother. Now she wore a fitted grey suit, bought in a last-minute panic at the weekend, and the baby in her belly had been replaced by the fizz of nerves and excitement. Today was the day. The first day of her new life.

The first day in her dream job.

The train arrived and Sophie pushed into the throng, fighting for a space between a woman with sharp elbows and a man who clung to the overhead rail, sharing the smell of last night's curry with the carriage. She smiled wryly to herself. She had missed working but she hadn't missed *this*. It would all be worth it, though, she was sure. Wouldn't it? A whirl of conflicting emotions spun inside her as the train rattled and lurched from station to station.

You're starting the job you've wanted your whole life.

But what if I've forgotten everything and am exposed as a fraud?

This is it, your chance to be fulfilled and productive and financially stable again.

But what about Daisy?

She wrestled her phone from her bag, wedged in so tightly against the other commuters that she almost pulled something in her shoulder, and texted Guy. *Everything OK? How was Daisy when you dropped her at school? xx*

He replied immediately. *She was fine! Don't worry :) Have a fantastic first day – you're going to be brilliant. Love you xx*

The train shuddered to a halt at the next station, the doors opened and more people tried to cram on. For a moment Sophie fantasised about getting off, going home. But she immediately told herself to stop being ridiculous. This was what she'd wanted since she was a little girl. She allowed the excitement to take over again, and found herself beaming at the man who smelled of curry, the woman with the pointy elbows. They averted their eyes, clearly thinking she was crazy, but so what? She didn't care. Today, Sophie Greenwood was re-entering the world of work, at the very publishing firm she'd dreamed of joining, and she wanted the world to see how happy she was about it.

———

'Team, this is Sophie.'

The three people at the bank of four desks turned their faces to scrutinise her. The vacant desk on the near right was hers. She would be sitting close to the wall with her back to the entrance. No window view and not much privacy, but she wasn't fussy. She wanted to sit in that swivel chair now, turn on her computer and get to work. She was itching for a chance to prove herself. But first, she had to meet the people she would be managing and spending the majority of her waking hours with from now on. What would they be like? Friendly, helpful, good at their jobs? Would they like her? Would *she* like *them*?

'Sophie, meet Tracey, Cassie and Matt.'

Simon Falstaff, marketing director and her immediate boss, was a few years older than Sophie. He was obviously intelligent; in fact, he reminded Sophie of a mad professor, with his crooked gold-framed glasses and his mousy-brown hair which stuck up in a tuft at the back of his head. Simon had conducted her interview and offered her the job on the spot, telling her he would just need Human Resources to check her references and rubber-stamp her appointment, before going on to tell her about himself. He was part of a new wave within publishing: science graduates who liked books, as opposed to the humanities graduates who had dominated the profession for years.

'This is Tracey Walsh,' he said, gesturing towards a skinny brunette with a bob a shade lighter than Sophie's chestnut hair. Sophie guessed she was in her late thirties and felt herself being appraised back as the other woman's eyes scanned her from boot to crown. 'Tracey's been with us for, how long is it?'

'Forever. Ten years this September. How time has flown.'

'Tracey looks after our social media,' Simon went on.

'So I'm allowed to spend all day on Facebook.'

'I'm Cassandra Said,' said the younger woman who sat beside Tracey, whose eyes had already returned to her screen, fingers fluttering across her keyboard. Cassandra was strikingly pretty with huge dark eyes and caramel skin. She stood and shook Sophie's hand with a feathery grip. 'But call me Cassie. I've been so looking forward to you starting. Since what happened—'

Simon cut her off. 'And this is Matt Hearns. Your senior marketing executive.'

Matt was a black man in perhaps his late twenties, with a pleasant, open face and a tight shirt that showed off his muscles. He had a puppyish quality, his eyes shining with a keenness to please. He grinned at her, accentuating his dimples.

'Welcome to the madhouse,' he said.

'Come on, let me show you the rest of the office.' Simon led her away towards the kitchen. Sophie could feel the eyes of the marketing team on her back.

She still couldn't believe she'd been headhunted for this job at Jackdaw Books, one of the UK's – no, the world's – most successful children's publishers. Sophie had been reading their books since she was Daisy's age. When teachers asked what she wanted to do when she grew up, while her friends said they wanted to be pop stars or doctors or cops, she'd said she wanted to write books. Specifically, books bearing the distinctive purple jackdaw logo – with its short beak that set it apart from a crow – on the cover. When she decided as a teen that she wasn't cut out to be a writer, her ambition shifted. She would create books, work with them, sell them and inspire children to enter magical worlds.

By the time she left university, though, she knew she could never work at Jackdaw. It was tainted. So she had gone to work for another publisher instead, one with which she had no personal connection, and it had been fine. Occasionally, seeing Jackdaw mentioned in the trade press, Sophie experienced a pang, a yearning for what could have been, but that had faded with time.

Then, a few weeks ago, Sophie had been featured in an article that Guy had written for the *Herald* about women who take a career break after having children. They had used a photograph of her at the top of the piece in which she had said that though she loved being at home with her daughter, she couldn't wait to return to work and would love to go back into publishing.

A day later she got a call asking her if she was interested in a position at Jackdaw – and it was the child inside her who reacted, not the adult. *Jackdaw!* By the time she put the phone down, she desperately wanted the job. Regardless of everything that had happened at university, she had to work there.

It was only this morning, pushing through the revolving doors, that she wondered if she was making a huge mistake.

In the kitchen, Simon showed her the fridge, the microwave and the location of the teabags. 'There are usually some communal biscuits and snacks in this cupboard,' he said, fishing out some Jaffa Cakes. 'So help yourself.'

Sophie smiled. 'They seem like a nice bunch. The team, I mean.'

'They are.' He looked towards the door to check no one was eavesdropping. 'Tracey is a little set in her ways, but Matt is excellent at his job – Miranda, your predecessor, certainly spoke very highly of him – and I think Cassie is a future star. She had the highest score in the McQuaig Quick-Thinking Test I've ever seen.'

'Great.'

'Yours was very high too,' he added quickly, moving closer to her. 'But Cassie is a great asset to the team. Hopefully no one will poach her.'

Sophie inched away. The train had arrived ten minutes late and since dashing here from the station, she hadn't had a chance to visit the bathroom. Her armpits prickled with sweat and her bra was digging into her. She was desperate to spray on some deodorant.

As they walked towards Simon's office, which was located in a corridor off the open-plan room where Sophie and her team were based, she began to relax. She took in the banks of desks, the dozens of people hunched over their keyboards or standing chatting. Brightly coloured posters showing some of Jackdaw's bestselling titles adorned the walls.

Bookcases stood between every cluster of desks, stuffed full of picture books and young adult novels and children's encyclopaedias. Books were piled on top of and beneath desks. A few Kindles and iPads lay on tables too, but it was clearly still mostly about print books here. At her interview, Sophie had been told there was a library in the basement containing many of the books Jackdaw had published in its 165-year history, including valuable first editions and original manuscripts. She couldn't wait to visit it.

The sight of the books calmed her. Her inner child pushed her adult fears aside; she was going to love it here. All she had to do was prove she was up to the job.

'OK,' Simon said, 'so we're meeting at eleven to go over your priorities and then Franklin is going to take you out to lunch.'

Sophie stopped walking.

'Franklin Bird?'

'Uh-huh. It's a tradition. He takes all the new starters out on their first day. Don't be nervous. He's not going to eat you.'

'But I thought he'd retired.' She had checked Wikipedia as soon as she'd been offered the job and according to the online encyclopaedia he had stopped work in 2012 at the age of eighty-two.

'Yes. Well, he did, kind of, but he got bored and came back. To be honest with you, he doesn't have a particularly active role these days. He's more of a figurehead, sits up there in his room on the top floor and keeps an eye on us.'

'I . . . I'm just going to pop to the ladies, if that's OK.'

She hurried away before he had a chance to react.

⌣

Sophie studied herself in the mirror and straightened her jacket, then she ran a hand through her hair, sucking in deep breaths. *Franklin Bird!* Shit, shit, shit. She ran her wrists under the cold tap to lower her body temperature. After she'd calmed down, she applied deodorant and checked herself in the mirror again.

Once she was confident she looked normal, that the terror wasn't evident on her face, she left the bathroom and headed to Simon's office. She was astounded that Franklin was still working and cursed Wikipedia, which clearly hadn't been updated. She had known deep down that she was bound to encounter at least one member of the Bird family while she worked here. But she didn't think she'd be having lunch with Franklin Bird himself on her first day.

She paused in the corridor, her heart hammering, and forced herself to calm down.

What was the worst that could happen? He probably wouldn't even know who she was.

Chapter 2
Day one, Monday, 6 April, 2015

'This needs more ice.'

Franklin Bird sent his lunchtime G&T back with the waiter, who smiled indulgently. Sophie was sticking to Diet Coke, even though a drink would do wonders for her nerves. So far, he had given no indication that he remembered her. And why would he? She'd been just one of a large crowd at the funeral. But she couldn't stop imagining him turning to her and saying, 'So . . . let's talk about Jasmine.'

'They never give you enough ice, do they?' Franklin said instead, leaning forward conspiratorially. 'It's not a proper gin and tonic if you can't crunch it, is it?'

He had brought her to a quiet Indian restaurant around the corner from the office, a place where the waiter had sprung into action as soon as they entered, fussing around the old man. Sophie remembered some of the details she'd gleaned from Wikipedia. Franklin was born in 1930, making him eighty-five now, which was hard to believe. He was trim and fit and moved like a man thirty years younger, and though his hair was snow-white it was thicker than Guy's. He had good teeth too, and sharp eyes. All a result of wealth, she guessed, and couldn't help thinking of her own grand-dad back in Wolverhampton, his body knackered after a lifetime spent working at Banks's Brewery.

Perhaps she should tell him who she was, how they were connected. Perhaps he wouldn't see it as a big deal.

Or maybe he would decide he didn't want her working there, stirring memories of what he'd lost.

She was going to keep quiet, for now at least, and wait to see if he brought it up. At the same time, she was trying to reconcile the twinkly-eyed man who sat before her now with the domineering figure Jasmine had spoken of. From what she had seen so far he certainly had a forceful personality, the kind of charisma that made other diners in the restaurant turn and look when he entered. And Sophie knew you needed to be strong and confident to run a large business for so many years. But there was no sign of him being unpleasant, even if he was a little brusque with the restaurant staff.

The waiter returned with a glass filled to the brim with ice and Franklin practically snatched it from him, downing half of it in one gulp.

'Do you have children, Sophie?' he asked.

'One. Daisy. She's four. She's just started school.'

'Ah, marvellous. Children are my passion. Though you can't say that these days, can you? It makes one sound like some kind of pervert. But educating and inspiring children – it's not just the company mission statement, it's my personal mission. As a publisher, we have a responsibility to teach children about right and wrong. About the importance of good behaviour.' He paused. 'No issues with little Daisy, I hope? No misbehaviour?'

'Daisy? No, she's only four.'

'Well, yes, but patterns of misbehaviour can start early. You have to nip them in the bud.' He picked up his knife as he said this and made a cutting motion. Before Sophie, who was taken aback, could respond, Franklin smiled and said, 'I do apologise. It's just something I care about deeply. I'm sure Daisy is an angel. Do you have a photo?'

'I've got hundreds on my phone.'

'Well, come on, let's see.'

Sophie leaned over and flicked through several pictures of her daughter, as Franklin exclaimed how lovely she was. Sophie had to agree. Every time she looked at Daisy her heart swelled with pride. Sometimes she would nudge Guy and say, with wonder in her voice, '*We made that.*' And yes, Daisy could be cheeky and uncooperative and destructive, like every four-year-old in the world. But there was certainly nothing about her that needed nipping in the bud.

'Let's play a little game.' Franklin chuckled to himself. 'Let's find out all about Sophie Greenwood.'

The waiter was just then bringing their food and Sophie noticed his lips twitch with amusement, like he'd seen this game many times before.

'So . . . I'm guessing from your accent that you grew up somewhere in the West Midlands. The Black Country . . . either Dudley or Wolverhampton?'

'Wolverhampton.' She thought all traces of her accent had been rubbed away by a decade in London.

'And I would say that you are . . . thirty-two?'

'A little older – thirty-four.'

'I'm guessing that you were a quiet, shy child. Nose always in a book.'

'Doesn't that describe everyone who works in publishing?'

He laughed. 'True. Apart from the bean counters. But I think you were also driven to do well, always at the top of the class, or maybe next-to-top. And you went to university to read English?'

'That's right.' She braced herself. She had failed to mention that the full name of her degree was English Literature with Publishing.

If he asked her which university she went to, and put that together with her age, he would almost certainly wonder if she had known Jasmine. This was her chance to bring it up.

But he moved on before she could make a decision. 'You love animals and are a vegetarian.'

'That's easy too – I ordered a veggie curry.'

He smiled. 'What do you young people say? "No shit, Sherlock"?'

That made Sophie laugh, and Franklin joined in.

'Let me try to guess something more difficult.' He stared at her until she began to feel uncomfortable. He wasn't smiling anymore. 'You've got a secret – something that hurt you, a long time ago.'

She stared back at him, shocked by this sudden turn in the conversation.

'I can sense that the pain still lingers. It's there, inside you, like a shadow on an X-ray.'

'No. No, that's not right. You're wrong.'

He regarded her, his head tilted. Then the smile returned. 'OK. I apologise for being overly dramatic. I don't get it right every time.'

While she recovered, he said, 'I won't ask you any more silly questions, Sophie. I like you. I can tell you're a bright young woman and clearly devoted to your daughter. I'm sure you will be a wonderful fit for our family.'

'Family?'

'Yes, that's how I see Jackdaw. Like a big family, with all that entails. Welcome aboard.'

He lifted his fork and chewed on a morsel of lamb. 'You probably won't see me around that much, but if you ever need anything please don't be afraid to ask. You'll find my office on the fifth floor.'

'Thank you.'

He popped some more lamb into his mouth and chewed it with his perfect teeth. 'My pleasure.'

Franklin had a meeting nearby so Sophie walked back towards the office on her own, still shaken by what he'd asked her.

Seeking distraction, she called Guy. They had been married for six years now but if they were apart for more than a few hours they usually called or texted each other, even though their main topic of conversation over the past few years had been Daisy or household stuff. At some point their text messages had changed from declarations of passion to reminders to pick up toilet paper. Sophie was delighted to have something new to talk about.

Before having Daisy, she had worked at Lawrence House as a marketing manager in their children's book division. She wasn't intending to take such a long break, but as soon as Daisy was born she decided she didn't want to miss any of her daughter's early years.

But, four years on, she had been starting to go a little stir-crazy at home, in desperate need of adult conversation and greater mental stimulation. And there was another important reason for her to return to work: they needed the money. It had been a struggle over the last four years. Guy's freelance earnings were marginally above average but it was still tough to bring up a child on a single wage in one of the most expensive cities in the world. They had run up debts. Their car was close to death. They hadn't been on holiday for two years. Every month they were getting closer and closer to their overdraft limit. Like many families, they were one unexpected bill away from financial disaster.

Now, though, things would be easier.

'How's it all going?' Guy asked.

'I'm not sure.' She told him about her lunch with Franklin Bird, leaving out the part about the secrets. Guy didn't know about her connection to Jackdaw Books. It had all happened years before they met and she'd felt no need to tell him.

'Sounds like a character. What about everyone else? What are they like?'

She started to describe the people she'd met, Simon and Cassandra, Tracey and Matt, but she could tell Guy wasn't fully paying attention. 'Are you busy?'

'I'm sorry. I have the deadline for today's opinion piece. Claire's emailing me every five minutes asking where it is.' He paused and she could picture him poking at his keyboard. 'You'll have to tell me all about it later, over dinner. I thought we could get a takeaway.'

'The school haven't been in touch?'

'No. Don't worry.'

'And you won't forget to pick her up?'

He made an exasperated noise.

'Guy, it's my first full day away from Daisy since she was born, so I can't help it.'

He sighed. 'I know you worry, sweetheart. It's one of the things that makes you *you*. But I promise not to forget about our daughter. You concentrate on your exciting new job, stop fretting, and when you get home I'll run you a bath, pour you a glass of wine and you can tell me all about everything. OK?'

'Sounds lovely.'

As she ended the call, the Jackdaw building loomed into view, towering above the other buildings on the Holborn street. Victorian Gothic, she believed it was called: red terracotta with arched windows and pointed turrets that stretched towards the clouds that scudded low across the sky. A line of plump cherubs stretched across the facade, crests dotted between them, and mythical creatures peered out from the building's many edges: a unicorn, a fierce dragon with chipped wings, and a pair of gargoyles that had been blackened by pollution.

Inside, though, the building had been modernised with lifts that rose and fell effortlessly around the central atrium, glass-fronted balconies and shiny surfaces. The ground floor was dominated by an entrance hall where a pair of receptionists scrutinised everyone who came through the revolving doors, along with a cafe at the rear that sold salads and health drinks. The next three floors were taken up by the offices of the general staff. The floor above those was mostly used, Sophie had been told, for less glamorous functions: the mailroom and computer servers were located there, along with various storerooms. And on the top floor, the senior managers' offices. Franklin Bird was based up there, of course, as was the CEO and other VIPs whose names Sophie didn't know yet.

She entered the lift and was about to press the button when she heard someone call out, 'Wait for me,' and Matt hurried in.

'Thanks, Sophie.' His smile was a welcome sight. 'Have you been for lunch with Franklin? How did it go? Did he ask if you've got any big secrets?'

'What?'

Matt chuckled. 'He asks everyone. Totally freaked me out. I was racking my brains, trying to work out if they could have found out anything about me. Luckily, I've had a sheltered life.'

She exhaled with relief. 'Oh, thank God.'

'Yeah, it makes everyone paranoid. I don't know if he does it for a laugh or if he's actually trying to get someone to admit to something terrible.'

'Luckily I've led a sheltered life too.'

She pressed '3' for their floor and noticed there was no button for the top floor. Nor was there one for the basement where the library was supposedly based.

'Do you know how to access the library? In the basement?'

His eyes widened like this was a weird question. A forbidden topic. 'I don't know. It's by invitation only. I guess they're worried about people touching all the super-valuable old books.'

'Have you ever been down there?'

'Me? No – I've never been invited. I don't know anyone who has, to be honest. People say it's haunted.'

'You're winding me up.'

'Nah, one of the cleaners apparently saw something one night. She was so freaked out that she didn't come back.'

'That's crazy. It definitely doesn't put me off wanting to go down there.'

'Hmm.'

'What?'

'Nothing.'

'Come on, you have to tell me now.'

'Well.' His voice dropped to a whisper. 'I heard someone died down there. A suicide.'

The lift reached the third floor and the doors pinged open. Matt's phone rang and he mouthed an apology as he took the call.

Sophie headed back towards her desk. Someone had committed suicide in the library? She shivered, no longer keen to go down there. She didn't believe in ghosts but she did believe that tragic events left an imprint on the places where they happened, an echo that lingered in the air.

Her thoughts returned to her lunch with Franklin. Thank God she'd bumped into Matt, because after Franklin's claim to have glimpsed some painful 'secret' in her she had been convinced that he did indeed know who she was and had been testing her openness, a test she would have failed. She'd almost blurted it out and had felt guilty for not doing so before telling herself that she had done it to protect his feelings. That would be her defence if he ever brought it up, anyway. She was reluctant to admit that she was actually protecting *herself.*

She sat at her new desk for the first time, taking a moment to enjoy it, adjusting the height on her chair, switching the monitor on and waiting for the computer to boot up. Someone had left a pile of stationery for her and she sorted through it, writing her name in the front of her notepad, feeling like the new girl at school. She sensed that someone was watching her and looked up to see Cassie staring at her across the bank of desks before quickly snapping her attention back to her screen and continuing to work with a serene expression.

There was a wooden pedestal with three drawers beneath Sophie's desk. She tried to open it but it was locked.

Matt noticed. 'I have a feeling Miranda took the key with her when she left. You'd think Facilities would have sorted it before you started, given you a new one.'

'They're bloody useless,' Tracey said. 'Here, let me call them for you.'

A couple of minutes later, a man in his fifties appeared. He apologised to Sophie and told her that they didn't have any spare pedestals at the moment.

'The spare key is probably locked inside,' he said, scratching his belly. 'That's what most people do. Am I right?'

Everyone around the bank of desks looked guilty, except Cassie, who said, 'I lost my spare key ages ago.'

'Anyone got a paperclip?' the man asked. Cassie handed him a large paperclip and he unbent it, leaving a hook at one end. 'These are the world's most basic locks. I just need to slide this in and . . . lift the catch. *Voila.*' He slid the top drawer open.

'I'll remember not to leave my diamond earrings in my pedestal,' Tracey said.

'And here's the spare key,' said the man from Facilities. 'Humans. They're so predictable.'

He handed the key to Sophie and strode off.

'Is it still full of all Miranda's crap?' Tracey asked, coming round to Sophie's desk. She flapped her hand in front of her face. 'God, it stinks. What did she leave in there?'

Matt got up from his desk too, while Cassie remained in hers. 'I wonder if that box set I lent her is in there,' Matt said.

Sophie slid open the bottom drawer, the deepest of the three, and Tracey gasped as the smell hit them. 'Jesus!' said Matt.

'It smells like something died in there,' Tracey said, her hand over her nose and mouth.

Sophie peered in. She had developed a pretty strong stomach over the last four years, after dealing with copious amounts of dirty nappies and vomit. She could just about bear the stench coming from the pedestal.

'I thought there was a weird smell around here,' Tracey said. 'But I blamed it on Matt's feet.'

'Ha ha.'

'Oh, my God.' Sophie backed away from the open drawer. She closed her eyes for a second but could still see the squirming shapes. The vile creatures.

Cockroaches. The thing she feared most in this world. She thought she was going to be sick, could feel little legs crawling on her skin beneath her clothes. She pulled at her blouse, half-convinced one had got up there.

'What is it?' Matt asked, peering in, with Tracey looking over his shoulder. 'Oh, fuck.' He slammed the drawer shut.

People from across the office had drifted over, wondering what the fuss was about.

'What did you see?' Cassie asked, her words addressed to Matt and Tracey, her gaze fixed on Sophie.

'Somebody call pest control,' Tracey yelled. 'We've got roaches. Feasting on some sandwich that dirty cow Miranda left behind. There are dozens of them. Massive, like this.'

Among the ensuing hubbub, Cassie drifted around the bank of desks and guided Sophie to her chair.

'Are you all right?' she asked.

Sophie couldn't speak for a moment. 'I just . . . I have a phobia of cockroaches, beetles, anything like that.'

Cassie touched her arm. 'Not the kind of thing you expect to find in an office, is it?'

Sophie hugged herself, forcing a laugh. 'I've worked with a few pests before, but this takes it to a new level.'

The man from Facilities reappeared and wheeled the pedestal away, the excitement dying down as people drifted back to their desks and returned to their work.

'That dirty cow,' Tracey repeated. 'I'll make you a cup of tea, with plenty of sugar, yeah?'

'I'm fine, Tracey. Honest. It just gave me a shock. Let's forget about it.'

'All right. You're the boss.'

Sophie stared at her screen, the sensation of insect legs on her skin subsiding, remembering the last time she had encountered a cockroach, fifteen years before.

There are far scarier things, Sophie,' Liam had said, grinning at her. 'I actually think they're quite sweet.'

She rubbed at her bare arms, the hairs standing on end, aware that Cassie was still watching her, as if she was an entomologist and Sophie an interesting bug.

Chapter 3
Monday, 27 September, 1999, Sussex

Sophie walked alone across the lush lawn, passing red-brick buildings where she would very soon be attending lectures, wondering how all the other freshers appeared to have made friends already, strolling or standing in groups or pairs, chatting excitedly and sharing cigarettes. Maybe if I smoked, she thought, I'd have a reason to approach someone, ask for a light, strike up a match and a conversation. She experienced a wave of homesickness, immediately chiding herself for being pathetic. It was ridiculous how much she missed her parents, how cut adrift she felt, when she had been dreaming of this day since she learned of the existence of an amazing place called 'university'. She used to walk to school, down terraced streets where her family had lived for generations, fantasising about how it would feel when she finally escaped into the world. She had built it up in her head, this idyll populated by fascinating people, long discussions about life and literature, revelations and adventures. There would be a boy, of course, a beautiful boy with soft lips and a sharp mind. Most important of all, she would make friends, meet the people with whom she wanted to spend the rest of her life. The fantasy felt so real. But now, less than twenty-four hours after arriving, Sophie was beginning to suspect that a fantasy was exactly what it was.

The previous night she had chatted to some of the girls in her halls of residence before going back to her tiny room to finish unpacking, arranging her books on the shelves, placing Wilbur the teddy bear on her pillow, Blu-tacking a smiling photo of her mum and dad, which almost made her cry, to the wall. And when she returned to the kitchen all the other girls had gone out without her.

They woke her up on their return at two a.m., shrieking and laughing and banging stuff, talking about some lads they'd met and how one of them – Becky, who had the room next to Sophie – had snogged some guy in a band. Sophie got out of bed and, wearing the cotton pyjamas Mum had bought her the week before, went into the communal kitchen, wanting to join in. But as soon as she entered the room Becky shrieked with laughter.

'Nice PJs! Did you borrow them from your gran?'

Sophie tried to laugh it off but Becky came closer, breathing stale alcohol fumes into Sophie's face.

'Looks like we've got ourselves a virgin, girls,' Becky said. One or two of the others gave Sophie sympathetic looks, but they still joined in with the laughter, especially when Becky started dancing around and singing 'Like a Virgin'.

Sophie almost opened her mouth to tell them that actually, she wasn't a virgin, that she'd done it numerous times with her former boyfriend back home, but she feared that would make her seem ridiculous and immature. Instead, she pretended to join in with the laughter, putting the kettle on and making herself a cup of tea, and Becky soon grew bored and moved onto another topic. Sophie studied her from the corner of her eye. She had long blonde hair and a nice body – attractive in an obvious way, though her face was a little pointy and rodent-like. Everything about her reminded Sophie of a girl who had bullied her when she was thirteen.

'I didn't think there'd be any virgins here,' Becky said.

One of the other students, whose name Sophie didn't know yet, said, 'We're not all like you, Becky. Nothing else to do on the Isle of Sheppey except shag boys, eh?'

Becky shot her an evil look, though the remark appeared to have wounded her. Sophie decided now would be a good time to make an exit, before Becky got more vicious.

Somewhere on this campus, she thought now as she neared the Student Union, are my kind of people. New, interesting friends. People who will help me become what I've always wanted to be.

As she climbed the Student Union steps, she paused. A boy in a leather jacket was chatting loudly with Becky and some of the other girls from her halls. Sophie hovered close to the group, hoping they would let her in, but they ignored her until at last Becky turned her head, looked her coldly up and down and whispered to one of the other girls, earning a nasty giggle.

Sophie gave up. What was Becky's problem? She had thought things would be different here, that everyone would be more grown up, welcoming. She clenched her teeth and moved away from the group, sheltering her eyes from the dazzling sun and fighting the urge to call one of her friends back home, maybe even her ex-boyfriend. She longed to hear a warm voice. But at the same time she knew she had to get through this. She wasn't a little girl anymore.

'You look a bit lost.'

Sophie turned around. She hadn't noticed the girl sitting on the grass rolling a cigarette. She was dressed entirely in black, with matching hair cut into a bob and thick eyeliner. Her lips were painted black too and she had a beauty spot on her upper lip, though it was hard to tell if it was real.

The girl finished constructing her cigarette, lit it and blew a plume of smoke into the still air. She patted a dry patch of grass beside her.

Sophie hesitated, then sat down gingerly, shaking her head when the girl offered her the cigarette.

'Please don't ask me the three questions,' the girl said. 'If I have to tell one more person where I'm from, what I'm studying or what I got in my fucking A levels, my head is going to go boom.'

Sophie laughed and the girl in black grinned.

'Friends of yours?' She nodded towards Becky's group.

'Them? God, no.' She lowered her voice. 'I'm not sure they're human. I think they might be robots, the Stepford students, programmed for maximum bitchiness.'

It was the other girl's turn to laugh. 'Jasmine Smith,' she said.

'Sophie Jones.'

'Smith and Jones.' She stubbed her cigarette out. 'We were clearly meant to be friends.'

Chapter 4
Day two, Tuesday, 7 April, 2015

Sophie hadn't spent much time at her desk on her first day and today she was determined to get some work done, even though Simon hadn't actually given her anything to do yet.

Waiting for her team to arrive, she replayed the events of the previous evening, smiling to herself as she waited for her computer to start up. Guy had been in a good mood because he'd hit his deadline and Claire, his commissioning editor at the *Herald*, was delighted with the piece. Daisy had been extra sweet, thrilled to see her mummy. Sophie had read Daisy's bedtime stories, not feeling, for the first time in ages, like it was another chore. When she crept out of Daisy's room, Guy was waiting with a glass of white wine, the takeaway en route, and the flat had felt different, fresher, more like somewhere to come home to than a place where she wrestled a small child, did laundry and cleared up messes. Later, they'd had sex for the first time in two weeks.

'Morning, boss.'

She snapped out of her reverie as Matt chucked himself onto his seat and dug two croissants out of a crinkly paper bag.

At the same time, Tracey arrived, carrying a plate with a half-eaten slice of toast on it and a mug bearing the legend KEEP CALM AND DRINK TEA, a lipstick mark on the rim. There was a crumb next to her mouth, and Sophie resisted the urge to point it out.

'Sorry,' Tracey said, 'I didn't know you were here already or I'd have made you one.'

'It's all right. I bought a coffee on my way in.' Sophie lifted her cup.

'You know the coffee here is free, right? They must be paying you too much,' Tracey said. 'I can't drink coffee, anyway. It makes me go mental.'

'We wouldn't be able to tell the difference,' Matt said.

'Careful. You're not too big for me to put you over my knee. Though keep eating that crap and you soon will be.' She blew out her cheeks.

'Hey, *I'm* young enough to be able to eat as many croissants as I like.' He broke a piece off and offered it across the desk. 'Fancy a nibble?'

'Later, darling.' They both laughed and Tracey changed the subject. 'I had such a weird dream last night. Phil and me were on holiday in Tunisia, where I've never even been, which was bizarre, and there were all these little blokes on bicycles . . .'

Sophie tuned out. Where was Cassie? From what Simon had said, and her initial impressions of the McQuaig-busting superstar, she had expected Cassie to be in bright and early.

'. . . and then I was riding on this camel, stark naked—'

She interrupted Tracey's dream story. 'Have either of you heard from Cassie this morning?'

Matt and Tracey exchanged a look.

'Didn't HR email you?' Matt asked. 'Cassie texted me earlier to ask me if I could send her a couple of spreadsheets to work on at home. She didn't want to come in today because she's got a cold. Doesn't want to spread the germs.'

'Oh.'

'Miranda always told us to stay off if we were sick.'

Sophie wasn't sure about that policy – it seemed like a malingerer's charter – but she didn't want her new team to think she was a hard-nosed authoritarian. As long as Cassie did actually work and not spend the day watching TV it would be fine, but she made a mental note to check with HR if this was company-wide policy.

Yesterday, after the incident with the cockroaches, Sophie had learned that Miranda had left in mid-March, so the pedestal had been locked with food inside for that long. This morning, Sophie had arrived to find a brand new pedestal under her desk, a Post-it note stuck on the front with the single word *Sorry!*

'Do you know why Miranda left?' Sophie asked Tracey.

'No, not really. One morning she just didn't turn up. Then Simon came down and told us Miranda had gone and that he was going to oversee the team while they looked for a replacement.'

So that explained why there'd been no handover. 'Any idea what happened to her?'

Tracey shrugged. 'I heard she moved abroad.'

'Yeah,' Matt said. 'Didn't she meet this Norwegian bloke in a club and fall head over heels for him?'

'I don't know. She wrote this cryptic message on Facebook about making a big decision and then closed her account. It was really weird.'

Sophie waited to see if they would say any more but both Tracey and Matt appeared depressed by the conversation. 'Don't worry,' she said. 'I'm not going to disappear to Norway. I'm not going anywhere.'

'Glad to hear it,' Tracey said. 'Sophie, can you give me a hand with something? I'm having an issue with Twitter.'

An instant message popped up on Sophie's screen. It was from Simon, asking her to come and see him.

'Sorry, can it wait? Simon's just asked for me.' She was secretly relieved. Twitter was not her specialist subject.

'Yeah. Fine.'

As Sophie headed through the double doors, she saw a guy about her age coming down the stairs. She did a double-take.

'*Josh?* Oh, my God, it *is* you!'

'Sophie!'

He threw his arms around her – he smelled of expensive aftershave – before stepping back and looking her up and down, a huge grin on his face.

'I can't believe it,' Josh said.

'Neither can I. Do you work *here* now?'

'Yes. I'm one of the senior designers. So, are you here for a meeting?'

She held up her pass. 'No, I work here too. I just started yesterday. I'm the new marketing manager in the young adult team.'

Sophie and Josh had worked together at Lawrence House. Back then, Josh had been starting out in his career, but he had always been talented and ambitious, so Sophie wasn't surprised that he was now a senior designer. He'd left Lawrence House a couple of years before she had Daisy, taking a career break to go travelling around Australia and New Zealand. With his tan, spiky light brown hair and casual clothes, he looked like he'd picked up a few style tips from the Aussies.

'This is so cool,' he said. 'Listen, I'm going to have to rush off – got a meeting across town. But let's hook up for lunch later in the week and catch up. I'll email you.'

Sophie knocked on Simon's door and went in. He was behind his desk, peering intently at something on his screen. He stood up rapidly when she entered, almost sending his mug of coffee flying.

'Ah, Sophie. How are you settling in?'

'I'm itching for a project to get my teeth into.'

'Marvellous. Because I have something for you.' He took a book from the pile on the desk and handed it to her.

'Brian Mortlake,' Sophie said aloud. The book was called *The Kiss of Death* and the cover showed a pale young woman with black lips and matching eyes.

'Ever read any?' Simon asked. He stared at her so intently that she felt sure she must have something on her face, a crumb or smear of toothpaste.

She recognised the name. 'I'm not sure. Maybe when I was a teenager?'

'Hmm, yes, that's likely. He's been around forever. Sometimes I wonder if he's undead, like some of the characters he writes about.' His burst of laughter was so loud it made Sophie jump. 'He used to write these *Point Horror*-style novels for kids. Then a couple of years ago he wrote a neighbours-from-hell novel based on something that happened in the building where he lives. You've heard of Lucy Newton?'

'The Dark Angel?' Sophie had read about her in the papers. She had been convicted of murdering a number of elderly people in a nursing home where she worked, but had recently been let out of prison after a successful appeal.

'That's the one. Brian used to live in one of the flats above hers.'

Simon went on. 'Brian's book, *One for Sorrow*, did rather well but now he's written something extraordinary. It's about this teenage girl who has the power to kill people by kissing them . . . and to bring people back from the dead with a kiss, too. We're putting a decent budget behind it. And we want you to run it. It will be your first big project.'

Sophie looked down at the book cover in her hand, the girl with the black lips staring back at her. This was exciting. Her chance to prove herself.

'Brian is coming in next Monday so we can talk him through the campaign. I thought we should run through some ideas now, and then you can share them with your team. How does that sound?'

'Fantastic.'

'The book launches in three weeks.'

Three *weeks*? To plan and execute an entire marketing campaign. She opened her mouth to protest but thought better of it.

'I know that's a rather short time frame, but all the work Miranda did on it appears to have vanished from her computer. I'm not sure she even did anything.' He tutted. 'We spent a *lot* of money on the advance for this book and we need to recoup it, so this is extremely important. I'm trusting you, Sophie.' He snatched the book from her hand. 'Do you think you're up to it?'

'Yes. Yes, definitely.' She pulled herself up to her full height.

'Good!' He gave the book back to her and rubbed his palms together. 'I can't wait for you to show us what you can do, Sophie.'

Back at her desk, Sophie asked Matt to pull all the data and biographical information they had on Brian Mortlake and put together a crib sheet. 'Plus, I want a list of similar books that have been published recently and details of how they were marketed.'

'Sure thing,' he said, brimming with enthusiasm, which made Tracey roll her eyes.

'Did you sort out your Twitter problem?' Sophie asked Tracey.

'I just wanted your opinion but, don't worry, I sorted it.'

Sophie knew she really needed to get up to speed with Twitter again. In her last role she had looked after the imprint's Twitter feed but she'd never had her own account and was rusty to say the least. Not wanting everyone to witness her lack of confidence, she took out her phone, downloaded the Twitter app and – deciding it would be quicker and easier to look at an existing account – signed in as Guy. He used Twitter all the time; in fact, his habit of tweeting in bed or when he was supposed to be looking after Daisy had caused a number of arguments between them.

He had three passwords he used for everything online and Sophie knew all of them, just as he knew hers. She logged in, then spent five minutes reading tweets and clicking around till she felt comfortable with it again, relieved that it hadn't changed much in the last four years. She shut the app and put her phone back in the top drawer of her pedestal.

A message from Simon popped up on her computer screen asking her to go to his office. Not again? She'd only left him thirty minutes ago.

She found him with his head in his hands, like he'd just had some terrible news. Or was about to deliver some. She swallowed.

'Is everything OK?'

'You'd better sit down.'

Oh, God. He was going to sack her. Franklin must have found out about her connection to Jasmine and had decided he couldn't live with a constant reminder of what he'd lost wandering around the office. She prepared to plead her case as she took a seat.

'I've just had a disturbing email from Cassie,' Simon said.

'Oh?'

'She's made an accusation about Matt. She says he's been sexually harassing her. Worse than that. Here, let me show you.'

Chapter 5
Friday, 29 October, 1999

The wind whipped sand along Brighton promenade and Sophie pulled her coat around her as she watched Jasmine attempt to light a cigarette. Every time she managed to strike a match and put it to the tip of her roll-up, it would be extinguished. Dead matches lay around her feet and Sophie couldn't help but giggle. A month had passed since she'd met Jasmine and she already saw her as the best friend she'd ever had. She was exactly the kind of person Sophie always wanted to meet. She was funny and interesting and didn't seem to give a damn what others thought of her.

'Fuck it,' Jasmine said, as the wind foiled her eighth attempt to light the cigarette. 'I've had enough fresh air. Let's go to the pub.'

They went into the Bath Arms and Sophie sat at a wobbly table while Jasmine went to the bar, coming over with two large glasses filled with pink effervescent liquid, umbrellas poking out of the top.

'What's this?' Sophie asked.

Jasmine shrugged. 'It's called a Pink Fizzy, apparently.'

'Well, it's certainly pink.' She lifted it to her mouth. 'And exceedingly fizzy.'

'Happy birthday!' Jasmine said, raising her glass. They clinked them together and each took a large swig.

Sophie checked her watch. 'I feel guilty – we're meant to be at our Modern American Fiction lecture now.' They were both studying English Literature with a module in Publishing Studies. That's what Sophie wanted to do when she graduated – work for a publisher in London. When Jasmine let it slip that her grandfather was the owner of Jackdaw Books, Sophie had almost exploded with excitement. It was as if they were fated to meet, and Sophie immediately bombarded her new friend with questions about the company. This, she quickly realised, was a mistake. Jasmine clammed up, her mood darkening, and Sophie assumed Jasmine might think that she would see her as an important contact rather than a friend. So she didn't mention it again, and noticed that Jasmine didn't tell any of the other students.

'Oh, sod that,' Jasmine said. 'You can't go to a lecture on your birthday. It's against the laws of decency. And as your best friend, I am morally prevented from going too.'

As always, Jasmine was dressed entirely in black, with heavy eye make-up that had smudged a little since their walk along the seafront, when the wind had made their eyes water. More black had started to creep into Sophie's wardrobe too, but she still looked very 'normal', in her blue jeans and black sweater, next to Jasmine.

'How long has it been since you last got laid, Sophie? You're going to have to get the WD-40 out soon if you're not careful.'

'Please . . .' She was surprised to see half of the Pink Fizzy had gone already. 'Kevin and I had a farewell, um, shag before I came to uni.'

It was weird. She'd barely thought about Kevin since the first few days here. They'd been boyfriend and girlfriend for over a year, but she'd always known that as soon as she went away to college that would be the end of their relationship. And Kevin, who was off to Brunel to study engineering, had seemed relieved when she told him this.

'I'm so glad,' Jasmine said, finishing her drink and searching through her wallet for more cash, 'that you're not one of those idiots who came to university with a boyfriend at home. Helen spends all week moping around and going on about how much she misses Danny Boy, and then I have to listen to them do it every Friday night when he visits.'

Jasmine didn't live in the halls of residence. She had chosen to live in a house off campus which she shared with Helen, who was from Tunbridge Wells and thought Jasmine was a weirdo. There'd been a big row when Jasmine tried to put a Marilyn Manson poster up in the living room.

Despite this, Sophie was envious of Jasmine's domestic situation. Living in halls was proving to be even worse than she'd anticipated. Becky and the other girls barely spoke to her now. Becky had fulfilled her promise to seduce Lucas, the guy from the band she'd snogged on her first night, and Sophie listened to them having enthusiastic sex most nights, the headboard banging against the wall; their noises reminding Sophie of a pair of mating foxes. She coped with this by putting her headphones on, and she didn't begrudge Becky and Lucas their sex life, but afterwards, they always put loud music on, playing it till three or four in the morning. Sophie had tried to talk to Becky about it but the other girl had sneered at her and told her to get a life. Now Sophie had a dilemma. Should she make a complaint to the university? She could imagine what people would say about her: 'She's the one who was jealous of the girl next door getting laid.' She couldn't do it, so she suffered in silence – or rather, in the opposite of silence – while the rings around her eyes grew darker.

Jasmine came back from the bar with more Pink Fizzies. 'Right, we need to get you some clothes for tonight. Drink up. It's time for Operation Get Sophie Laid. Starting with the clothes. Now, we want something that's going to make you look shaggable but not tarty . . .'

She took hold of Sophie's wrist and Sophie laughed and shook her head, thinking maybe it wouldn't be so bad to go out, get drunk and take a boy home. Give Becky a taste of her own medicine.

⌣

They walked towards the city centre. Halfway up the hill, Sophie stopped and turned, marvelling at how different this city was to the place where she'd grown up. There was something about the sea that made her feel that her horizons were limitless, that she suddenly had access to the whole world, an escape route. With her new friend at her side, she was chewing her way out of her cocoon, at last. She was young and free and, she had to admit it, not bad-looking. Maybe it was the alcohol in her veins making her feel like this, but excitement and anticipation hit her like vertigo. She grabbed hold of Jasmine's hand and said, 'I love this place.'

But Jasmine was distracted, her attention drawn to something on the other side of the road. Sophie followed her gaze but couldn't work out what her friend was looking at.

'What is it?' Sophie asked. Instead of replying, Jasmine took her hand again and dragged her across the road, into the flow of pedestrian traffic. They turned into a side street and trotted up some steps to Churchill Square – a busy plaza surrounded by a collection of high street shops.

Jasmine pointed. 'Look.'

'What am I looking at?'

'Him. There.'

'Who?'

'Oh, for fuck's sake. There, sitting on that step. The guy in the black coat and Converse. Lighting a cigarette.'

Finally, Sophie saw who Jasmine had been so keen to pursue.

He had dark hair that needed a cut and, though he was sitting down, Sophie could tell he was tall, over six foot. He was broad too, with wide shoulders and large hands, one of which held a battered paperback book, the cover folded over so she couldn't see what it was. He read and smoked and beside her Sophie could sense that Jasmine was trembling, a hand held to her breastbone. She could understand why Jasmine was so enamoured. His face wasn't classically beautiful. His nose was slightly too large, his eyes a fraction too small, especially when he squinted at the printed page before him. But he had the kind of lips that were described as 'cruel' in the romances her mum read. His cheekbones reminded her of a Scandinavian pop star's. And there was something about him, the way he held himself, that was appealing. Sitting there on the steps with hordes of shoppers wheeling around, reading a book, still and silent and dark, a crow among pigeons.

'Do you know him?' Sophie asked. They were about twenty feet away and it would have been easy for him to turn his head and see them at any moment.

'His name's Liam,' Jasmine replied. 'Liam Huxley.' She spoke about him as if he were a famous actor or rock star.

'Is he at the university?'

Jasmine nodded, unable to tear her eyes from him. 'He's studying English too. He's in his final year.'

'How do you know this?'

A smile crept onto Jasmine's lips. 'Because I found out.' She turned to Sophie, her eyes shining. 'I saw him in the library a couple of weeks ago and followed him to the counter to see what books he was taking out.'

'And you heard him say his name to the librarian?'

'Uh-huh.'

The boy, Liam, swept his hair out of his eyes and flicked his cigarette away; it danced across the plaza in a shower of sparks. He turned the page of his book and continued to read.

'I'm going to make him mine,' Jasmine said.

'Right.'

Jasmine grinned. 'Just watch. I'm going to have him, all for myself.'

Chapter 6
Day three, Wednesday, 8 April, 2015

Matt was waiting in the corridor outside Simon's office, staring at his phone, apparently engaged in a text conversation with someone. Sophie walked past him, relieved that he didn't look up, and went into the meeting room where Simon and Natalie sat around the table, a jug of water shining between them.

Natalie Evans, who Sophie had met briefly on her first day, was in her forties, with frizzy blonde hair and a North London yummy mummy air about her. Sophie had seen her chaining up her bicycle outside in the morning before coming inside and peeling off her lycra outfit. She had noticed that when people said Natalie's name they did so with a mixture of reverence and fear. As the head of Human Resources, she had the kind of power you didn't want to fuck with.

'Let's get this over with,' Simon said. 'Put the poor bugger out of his misery.'

'What do you mean?' Sophie asked. 'Are you going to fire him?'

Simon didn't reply.

'We're going to give him a chance to tell his side of the story,' Natalie said. 'Sophie, feel free to ask questions, but as you've only been here for three days I don't expect you to lead the meeting. Leave that to me.'

'Is he on his own?' Simon asked.

'I asked him if he wanted a representative with him,' Natalie said. 'But he said no. Come on, let's hear what he has to say for himself.'

Natalie led Matt into the room. When Simon had shown her the email Matt had sent Cassie, she'd hardly been able to believe it. Her first impression of Matt was that he was a nice guy. But she also knew that people, even the ones who seemed pleasant and innocent, were capable of anything. Especially where sex was concerned.

As Matt sat down, Natalie went into a long preamble about the purpose of the meeting and poured glasses of water for everybody.

'What am I supposed to have done?' Matt asked. 'You said Cassie had made a complaint about me.' He seemed genuinely confused, but perhaps he was a good actor.

'Let's have a look at the evidence, shall we? This email was sent to Cassie at nineteen thirty-two on Monday the sixth of April, from your account.' That had been Sophie's first day at Jackdaw. Natalie opened a folder and produced several A4 sheets of paper from a manila envelope. She laid one carefully on the table before Matt and passed copies to Sophie and Simon.

Sophie scanned the text, shocked again by what she read. *Every day I imagine coming round there to your desk and bending you over it, pushing up your little skirt and pulling your panties aside, and I know you'll be so wet, so ready for me. You groan my name as I push my thick hard . . .*

She stopped reading as Matt barked out a laugh. 'This is a joke, right? A wind-up? You're pranking me for some new TV show or something.'

'It's not a joke, Matt,' Natalie said.

He stared at her until all hope that this *was* a joke drained away. 'I honestly didn't write this.' His voice was quiet and shaky. 'I just wouldn't. It's like . . . terrible porn.'

'Your name is clearly in the email header, Matt,' said Simon. 'IT have checked. It was sent from your work email address. And Cassandra tells us that she wasn't terribly surprised to receive it. Disgusted and upset but not surprised.'

'She told us that you are always staring at her,' Natalie said before Matt could respond, her tone even, impassive. 'Making inappropriate comments. Talking about sex and giving her meaningful looks.'

'That's a lie!' He sounded desperate now.

Simon waved the printout. 'I think the evidence speaks for itself.'

Silence filled the room, until Matt finally whispered, 'I didn't write this.'

'So you deny everything?' Simon asked.

'Yes.' Matt had the look of a condemned man. 'I would never write something like this. Not even to my girlfriend.'

'You have a girlfriend?' Sophie asked.

Matt seemed surprised that she'd spoken. 'I mean, if I did have one.'

'Do you talk about sex at your desk?' Simon asked.

Matt glanced over at Sophie. 'A bit, I suppose. But only having a laugh with Tracey. I wouldn't talk about it with Cassie.'

'Why not?' Natalie asked.

He blew out some air. 'Because she doesn't have a sense of humour.'

'You think she should have found this email amusing?' Simon asked.

'I told you! I didn't send it.'

Natalie put her hand up like a cop stopping traffic. 'Let's move on. Do you have anything else you want to tell us at this point?'

Matt's face was hard to read now. He was upset and angry, but defiant too. He was silent for a long moment before he finally spoke. 'I really love working here. And I promise I'm telling the truth. I don't want to lose my job. I honestly didn't send that email. On my mother's life.'

'Matt,' Natalie said softly. 'You understand that we simply cannot tolerate sexual harassment in the workplace. We have no choice but to suspend you pending further investigation.'

'But I'm innocent!' Matt thumped the table. 'I've been set up.'

'Calm down,' Simon said.

There was no emotional conflict on Matt's face now. He was all anger. He stood and pointed a finger at Simon, then Natalie. 'Cassie has made it all up. And she, or somebody else, must have accessed my email account. That little bitch.'

'Matt!'

'Oh, fuck this. I'm wasting my breath.' He screwed the email into a ball and dropped it on the table. 'I quit. You can shove your job. And I'm going to do you for constructive dismissal.'

'You don't have a leg to stand on,' Simon said.

Matt ignored him and headed towards the door, then paused and turned.

'Thanks a fucking lot for sticking up for me, Sophie.'

Simon stood up. 'For God's sake, man. I'm going to call Security.'

Matt glared at him then stormed from the room, slamming the door behind him.

Natalie sighed and scribbled in her notebook while Simon followed Matt, presumably to ensure he left the building.

'That went well,' Natalie said without looking up.

'It was horrible.'

'Well, at least it's over now. You don't need to worry about it.' She flipped through her notepad. 'For me, it's just one of a dozen issues I have to deal with every day. You know the old joke about the schoolteacher who says school would be lovely if it wasn't for the kids? That's what this place is like. It would be great if it wasn't for the bloody employees.'

'Do you think he actually sent it?' Sophie asked.

'Of course he did. The computer system doesn't lie. Sitting next to Cassie for months, trying to get her to take an interest in him – it probably drove him mad with lust, and one night he got home, had a couple of drinks, and decided to tell her what he wanted to do to her. Poor girl. I mean, I'd be shocked if I received an email like that, and I'm a woman of the world.' She sighed. 'Shame, eh? He was a good worker. He didn't take a single sick day last year.'

When Sophie got back to her desk she found a man on his knees under Matt's desk, his cheap patent shoes sticking out. Cassie and Tracey were at their desks. Tracey said, 'We've got a visitor from IT.'

'Hello?' Sophie said, and the owner of the patent shoes crawled out backwards. He was clutching a snake's nest of cables. 'What are you doing?' she asked.

'Taking this machine away.'

The man, who looked like he might be related to the man from Facilities Management who'd unlocked her pedestal, bent and lifted the tower from Matt's PC, wincing as his knees creaked.

'Why is there such a big rush?' Sophie asked. 'It's only just happened.'

Cassie and Tracey stared at the IT guy. Tracey looked utterly confused but Cassie seemed excited – or perhaps satisfied was a better word.

The man would have shrugged if he wasn't cradling the computer with both hands. 'Just doing what the powers-that-be ask.'

'Which powers?'

'The gods of Jackdaw Books,' he said in a reedy, sardonic voice. 'Inhuman Resources.' He snickered to himself as he staggered off with the computer.

Sophie stared after him.

'What's going on?' Tracey asked. 'Where's Matt?'

She wanted to talk to them separately, so took Tracey into one of the little meeting rooms first and told her what had happened.

Tracey was shocked. 'No way. No *way*. I can't believe he'd be that stupid.'

'I'm afraid it's true.'

'That horny little bastard.'

Sophie sensed that Tracey was desperate to get out of the meeting room so she could tell everyone.

'What did he say?' Cassie asked when it was her turn. The sky beyond the windows was as blue as it ever got in London and it was warm in the office, but she was wearing a cashmere scarf and knee-high boots. She was perfectly turned out, hair sleek and shiny, skin glowing with health, fingernails perfectly manicured. Sophie couldn't help but feel envious. Even in the days before Daisy she had never looked immaculate.

'I can't really discuss that. But he has resigned.'

Cassie nodded. 'Good. Because there was no way I was going to be able to work with him after that.' She wrapped her arms around her tiny frame. 'It made me feel violated.'

'I understand. Well, he's gone now. You don't need to worry about it anymore.'

'Thank you.' Cassie bit her lip and appeared reluctant to say what was on her mind.

'What is it?' Sophie asked gently.

'I was wondering . . . Could I have Matt's old desk? It's bigger than mine. I can arrange it with facilities and IT myself.'

'I . . . I guess so.'

A smile lit up Cassie's face. 'Thanks, Sophie.'

Chapter 7

Day six, Saturday, 11 April, 2015

Sophie pushed the swing until her muscles ached, her daughter kicking her legs with excitement and calling out to be pushed ever higher.

'I think that's high enough, sweetheart. You might fall off.'

She had an image of Daisy losing her grip, tumbling to the ground, and even though the floor was soft and rubberised, Sophie pictured her little girl hitting concrete, gravel embedding the tender flesh of her knees, blood and screams and tears.

'You worry too much,' Guy said for the thousandth time since Daisy was born. 'She's not going to fall off the swing, and she's not going to vanish if you take your eyes off her for a second.'

'She might.' But Sophie was in too good a mood to argue. They'd had sex again last night. Twice in a week! That usually only happened on holiday.

As she pushed, Sophie looked at Guy in a way she seldom did these days. Her handsome husband, with his blue eyes, sandy hair and strong jaw, though that sandy hair was thinning and his stubble had started to come through grey in patches. She liked that, though. It made him look distinguished. Other things she liked about him:

his height; the way he still got enthusiastic about new music, books and TV shows; how seriously he took his career; the easy way he had with Daisy. Keeping a marriage going when you had a small child and you were both so busy that you barely had time to look at each other was far more challenging than she'd ever imagined. But they were doing OK, Guy and her.

'I read your article while you were in the shower. Loved it.'

He grinned. 'You're biased. Most of the people who commented below the line don't agree with you.'

Guy's article on the *Herald* website, which was also printed in the paper, was about a famous comedian who was urging young people not to vote in the upcoming General Election. This – politics with a dash of celebrity and popular culture – was Guy's speciality, and he was making a name for himself with his articles bringing in increasing amounts of traffic and comments.

'You don't still read the comments, do you? You mustn't.'

'I can't help it.'

'They're all nutters and trolls. I've stopped reading below the line on your articles – it makes me too angry. I want to leap in and defend you.'

He laughed. 'Please don't do that or they'll come after you. But thank you.'

Sophie continued to push the swing, ignoring her daughter's pleas to go higher, higher.

━━━━━

Daisy needed new shoes so Sophie took her into Brixton while Guy headed home, promising to have lunch ready when they got back.

After getting Daisy's feet measured and handing over an extraordinary sum for a tiny pair of school shoes, they waited at the bus stop, Daisy chattering non-stop.

'Maisie was *ridiculous* yesterday, Mummy, she told Celso that she is going to marry him but Celso pushed her over and then she was crying and . . . Mummy, are you listening?'

She put her phone away, feeling guilty for checking her work emails. There were two new messages from Cassie containing ideas for marketing Brian Mortlake's book.

'Mummy, Jack got a lizard for his birthday and he's going to call it Daisy.'

While Daisy went on about the annoying Jack, Sophie wondered why a woman in her early twenties was sending work emails from home on a Saturday morning. She should be out having fun, or sleeping off a hangover. Doing something with her friends.

'Mummy, Jack got a lizard for his birthday and he's going to call it Daisy.'

Sophie wished she didn't feel so irritated at Cassie. She should welcome her ideas, encourage them, be pleased she was a workaholic. She would send an enthusiastic response when she got home.

'Mummy, Jack got a lizard for his birthday and . . . *Mummy, are you listening to me?*'

'Yes. Jack got a lizard and wants to call it Daisy.'

'That's *mean*, isn't it, Mummy?'

'I suppose it depends how cute the lizard is.'

Brixton High Street was teeming with people. They poured out of the Tube station, jumped on and off buses, streamed forth from shops. Sophie held Daisy's hand tightly as passers-by jostled them, trying to work out whether to wait for a bus or head to the train station. As she was scrutinising the laughably unreliable electronic display at the nearest bus stop, a man in a long, filthy coat lurched across the road towards them, drivers sounding their horns angrily as he dodged the traffic. He appeared to be a homeless man and Sophie felt simultaneously sorry for him and desperate to keep him away from her and Daisy. But it was as if her thoughts called out to him. He paused before them and gawped at Daisy as the crowd parted.

'It's the Little Mermaid!' the man boomed. He took hold of Sophie's sleeve and tugged at it. 'Can you spare me some change? For the bus fare.' He displayed his black teeth and blasted her with fetid breath. 'Beautiful little girl. Look . . .'

Before Sophie could pay him off or whisk Daisy away, the man reached into one deep pocket of his flapping coat and produced a decapitated doll's head. 'Lovely baby,' he growled, thrusting the head at Daisy, who burst into tears.

Sophie grabbed her daughter and picked her up, just as the bus arrived. She shoulder-barged her way through the crowd and just managed to squeeze on to the double decker. It lurched away, leaving the man and his dolly's head standing in the road. He pointed a filth-encrusted finger at her and she shivered as if she'd just been cursed.

Chapter 8
Day eight, Monday, 13 April, 2015

'Cassie, can you come round here a moment?' Sophie said. She was working on her presentation, ensuring she was ready for that afternoon's meeting with Brian Mortlake. Most of the marketing plan was done and Sophie was ninety-nine per cent happy with it. She was greatly relieved to realise that she still remembered how to put together a good campaign.

The younger woman moved gracefully around the bank of desks.

'Can you cast your eye over this one last time?' Sophie asked, showing Cassie the overview of the campaign. 'I still feel like there's something missing. Some kind of X factor.'

Cassie's face was blank. 'I don't know, Sophie. What about an advertorial?' She named a popular magazine.

'No, teenagers don't read magazines anymore. How about an app of some sort? Something that teens will engage with, that will help the book go viral. I was thinking about something that plugs into social media . . .' She drummed her fingers on the desk. The book was about a girl who kills or revives people with her kiss. 'What about something based on that game – snog, marry, kill?

The app could pull up people from your social media contacts and ask if you want to snog them, marry them or give them the kiss of death.'

From across the desk, Tracey said, 'That's a bloody great idea.'

Sophie asked Cassie, who was now sitting at Matt's old desk, to pull up a chair. Tracey came round too and the three of them discussed Sophie's idea. Finally, a week into the job, Sophie found herself slipping into a higher gear, doing what she was good at: brainstorming ideas, refining them, quickly figuring out what was worth pursuing and what could be discarded. Her boss at Lawrence House had told her that she had an unusual brain, both the left and right sides equally developed, capable of creative thought and statistical analysis. It felt great to be using that brain again.

She had finished reading *The Kiss of Death* the night before. Guy went out with a friend for a few drinks so she had the flat to herself, and she settled on the sofa with a glass of wine and entered the creepy world Brian Mortlake had created. The main character was feisty yet tragic, unable to kiss the boy she loved because it would kill him. There were hints of *The Monkey's Paw* in the terrifying sequence in which the protagonist's little brother is killed in a hit and run and his sister brings him back to life, keeping his undead body hidden in an old bunker. When Guy came back at midnight, banging the front door as he reeled into the flat, Sophie jumped out of her skin.

Then, at two a.m., after she had finally slipped into sleep, Daisy had woken up crying.

Sophie ran into her room, leaving Guy snoring in bed.

'What's the matter, sweetheart?'

Daisy looked at her with those big green eyes, clutching the pink rabbit she'd had since she was a newborn. Her pyjamas were damp with sweat and her brown hair tangled like she'd been thrashing about on her pillow. 'I had a bad dream, Mummy.'

Sophie put her arms around her, inhaling her sweet scent, alarmed by the heat coming from Daisy's little body. 'Do you want to tell me about it?'

Daisy's eyes were wide, scared, tears brimming. 'Someone was trying to get us. A man. A bad man.' She trembled and Sophie guessed Daisy was thinking about the homeless man they'd encountered in Brixton. She had already explained to Daisy that he was merely a normal man who'd had some bad luck, that they should feel sorry for him. But it was hard to get that across to a four-year-old, especially when she herself had found the man so chilling.

'Do you want to come and sleep in Mummy and Daddy's bed?'

Daisy nodded. 'It will be safe there, won't it? From the man?'

Sophie stroked her daughter's forehead. 'Nobody's going to hurt you, sweetheart.'

So Daisy had slept between her and Guy, taking up most of the space in the bed, periodically kicking Sophie in the thigh. By morning, haunted by *The Kiss of Death*, with Daisy's nightmare seeping into her own dreams in the short snatches of sleep she managed, Sophie felt wretched. But her tiredness was forgotten as she and her little team thrashed out the details of what Sophie was certain was going to be a hit.

'I reckon this could win an award,' Tracey said, as they finished the discussion and she and Cassie returned to their desks.

'Let's not get carried away.' But Sophie believed Tracey might be right.

Cassie didn't say anything. It was crazy, but Sophie had the feeling Cassie was unhappy that *she* hadn't come up with the idea.

⌣

The meeting with Brian Mortlake was a success. He seemed delighted that they were doing any marketing at all and loved all their ideas. Brian was in his mid-fifties, with glasses and a neat grey beard. When Sophie began to run through their plans for marketing *The Kiss of Death* he said, 'It's all about computers these days, isn't it? I'm useless with the things. I lost an entire work in progress once because of a virus.' His eyes took on a faraway look for a moment before he laughed. 'Still, I got a new, much better book out of it.'

He was clearly taken with Cassie, his eyes twinkling whenever he looked at her. Cassie was solicitous and flattering during the meeting, even flirting a little with this man who was thirty years her senior. Watching Cassie turn on her sex appeal, Sophie found herself wondering if she had done the same with Matt. But he hadn't claimed that Cassie had led him on, as many desperate men would have done. He had flat-out denied the charges.

After their meeting with Brian, having shaken his hand and watched him bumble out to the lift, Sophie said, 'Cassie, you didn't make any notes.'

'Don't worry, I'll remember it all,' Cassie said. 'I've got an eidetic memory.'

'Really?'

'I never forget anything.'

'Wow. If I don't write everything down in my notebook it vanishes out of my head the moment I leave the meeting.'

'I guess I'm lucky,' Cassie said. And Sophie watched her glide elegantly back to her desk.

———

'You look like you just won the Lottery – or had an amazing orgasm,' Josh said, pressing dry lips to her cheek when she met him in the lobby downstairs. They had arranged to go out for lunch to catch up.

She laughed. 'Neither of those, unfortunately. Just a successful meeting.'

'Oh. A meeting with someone hot?'

'Stop it, you. You're looking very smart.' He was wearing a trendy suit and his hair had been cut since she'd last seen him. He smelled of expensive cologne.

'Oh, I'm going to a party tonight, straight after work – you should come. Bring that handsome husband of yours.'

'If only.'

'Oh, yes. You're a mum now. Well, why don't you come? Let . . .'

'Guy.'

'Yes, let Guy babysit. Anyway, how do you feel about Japanese? I know a noodle place that's cheap but cheerful.'

Cheap was good. Sophie had spent a couple of hours at the weekend doing life admin and paying bills. Despite her new earnings, it was going to take them a year to pay off their debts, and that was only if they stuck strictly to their budget, cutting down on nights out, takeaways, presents for Daisy, but still allowing a small amount for an inexpensive holiday.

'So I hear you're working on the Brian Mortlake book?' Josh said when they reached the restaurant and slid onto benches either side of a high table. 'I designed the jacket for that.'

'Really? It's a great cover. Very creepy.'

He basked in the praise. 'I channelled my inner goth. So how was your first week at Jackdaw?'

'Yeah . . . it's been good.'

'You don't sound too sure.'

'No, it has been. I really like it. But there's been all this stuff with a member of my team.'

'Cassie?'

'No. Well, she was involved, but I meant Matt.'

'Ooh, yes, I heard about that.' Josh leaned forward. 'What did the email say? Was it really dirty? Someone told me he wrote that he wanted to tie her up and lick her till she screamed for mercy.'

The waitress plonked their food in front of them: a bowl of ramen for Josh and yasai yaki soba for Sophie.

'I think I just lost my appetite.'

Josh laughed. 'Oops, sorry. I won't tell you the other thing I heard he'd written.'

'Josh . . .'

'Sorry. I shouldn't make light of it, should I? I don't want you to report me to Natalie.' He mock-shuddered.

'When I said there'd been stuff with a member of my team, why did you assume I meant Cassie?'

'Oh. No reason.'

She waited, knowing he would feel the need to fill the silence. It was an interrogation technique she'd learned when Daisy had done something naughty and was reluctant to confess.

'It's just,' Josh said, 'that I heard your predecessor had some trouble with her.'

'Miranda? Did you know her?'

'Not well. Chatted to her in the kitchen a couple of times. Had a dance with her at the Christmas party. She was nice. But I'm glad she left because here *you* are.'

'Do you know why Miranda left, though? Tracey on my team thinks she might have moved to Norway with some bloke she met.'

Josh's eyes shone with the pleasure a gossip feels when he has something juicy to share. 'That's what I was going to tell you. Apparently' – he looked left and right, checking there was nobody else from Jackdaw in the restaurant – 'she disappeared.'

'Disappeared?'

'Yeah. As in, nobody knows where she went.'

The temperature in the restaurant seemed to dip. 'Were the police looking for her?'

'I don't know. To be honest, I don't really know any details, just rumours I've heard.'

Sophie waited for him to go on.

'She left all of a sudden. Updated Facebook with some message about making a big decision and that was it.'

'Tracey told me about that.'

He nodded. 'I know someone in IT who said he got a call one morning from Natalie asking him to remove Miranda's PC. And that was it. No leaving card, no collection. Quite weird, isn't it? To leave like that without saying goodbye to anyone. I know a few people tried to get in touch with her but she shut down her Facebook account and didn't answer any emails.'

'Did anyone go round to see her? To check she was OK?'

'I don't think so.' He shrugged. 'Maybe she did go to Norway.'

'You mentioned Cassie. Do people think she had something to do with her leaving?'

Josh's eyes shifted from side to side again. But then his expression altered, as if he'd had a change of heart. 'Listen, I'm sure it was pure gossip and speculation. From the encounters I've had with Cassandra, she seems nice enough and she's clearly very clever. But I heard she made Miranda's life difficult, constantly questioning her, going directly to Simon to complain about things she thought Miranda was doing wrong.'

Josh shoved his plate to one side. 'Again, it may be a load of rubbish. Just gossip. But I'd keep an eye on Cassie if I were you.'

Sophie poked at her noodles. 'I intend to.'

'Brian just emailed me to say thank you,' Cassie said after Sophie sat down. 'He seems really happy with our plans.'

'He emailed *you*?'

'Yes. Didn't he send it to you too? He must have forgotten.'

Sophie checked her emails. No, nothing from Brian. 'Can you forward it to me?'

She didn't want to seem like a control freak, but she also didn't want Brian to think Cassie was in charge of the project. She emailed him, telling him how excited she was about his book and asking him, politely, to send everything to her in future, as she was leading the project and she 'wanted to ensure nothing slipped between the cracks'.

He replied almost immediately. *Sorry, Cassie asked me to email her. But you're the boss!*

She would have a word with Cassie later. But exchanging emails with Brian reminded her of something she needed to do. Remembering what Josh had said about designing the jacket of *The Kiss of Death*, she emailed him to thank him for lunch and ask if he could create some banners to help promote the book on social media. When he replied saying *Of course!*, Sophie forwarded the emails to Cassie, asking her to liaise with Josh.

'Sophie, can I have a word?' Cassie said a little later.

'Sure.'

'I mean in private.'

She led Cassie into the little meeting room. 'Everything OK?'

Cassie was wearing a white silk blouse and a beige skirt that Sophie had seen in the fashion charts in the previous week's *Grazia*. It was a Victoria Beckham. Sophie had looked at it and imagined being able to afford it. She glanced down at the younger woman's feet. She wore black shoes with heels with the distinctive Louboutin red strip. If they were real, they would have cost Cassie a month's salary.

'I was wondering,' Cassie said. 'Are we going to hire someone to replace Matt? A new senior marketing executive.'

'I'm not sure yet.' It was something she needed to raise with Simon and was high on her to-do list.

Cassie's gaze was unwavering. 'I would like to be senior executive. I think I deserve it.'

Sophie was taken aback. Had *she* ever been this confident, this self-assured?

'I'll have to talk to Simon about that.'

'Thank you, Sophie.' The sweet smile returned. 'Can you do it soon?'

'I . . . Yes, of course. I don't want us to be short-staffed either.' She paused. 'Another thing. It's great that you and Brian have struck up a rapport, but I should be his first point of contact. Otherwise things might fall through the cracks.'

'Sure, Sophie, I understand.'

Cassie left the room. Sophie was a big fan of young women being ambitious and she respected her for being so direct, and she would have a word with Simon. But it felt as if Cassie was trying to jump into Matt's grave.

Sophie laughed at herself. Why was she being so uptight? All Cassie had done was ask to move to a better desk and put forward a request for promotion. If Matt had died or left due to some tragic circumstance, Cassie's actions would be insensitive. But that wasn't the case, was it? Sophie emailed Simon as soon as she got back to her desk, asking if they could meet to discuss the vacant position on her team. She felt Cassie watching her as she typed out the message, but when she looked up, Cassie was concentrating on her work, that butter-wouldn't-melt expression on her pretty face.

Chapter 9
Wednesday, 8 December, 1999

This was the first time Jasmine had visited Sophie's room. Usually, they hung out on campus or went to Jasmine's house. But the weather was foul and neither of them wanted to trudge through the rain to Jasmine's so they'd come here to kill a couple of hours between lectures.

'Have you got any coffee?' Jasmine asked. 'I'm shattered. I was up most of the night.'

Sophie held up a hand. 'Please. I don't need to hear any more details.'

Jasmine was seriously loved-up and hadn't talked about anything except Liam since doing exactly what she'd said she'd do. She'd hung around the library until he came in, striking up a conversation about the book he was carrying, *Crime and Punishment*, which Jasmine had, fortunately, read. Then she'd asked him out for a drink. Sophie had witnessed all this, impressed by her friend's confidence. Liam had been, too, it seemed. Later that night, Jasmine had called her, almost purring, to tell Sophie what Liam was like in bed.

They went into the kitchen. It was busy, half a dozen girls making lunch, sitting around drinking tea and chatting or reading magazines.

Sophie's heart sank when the fridge door shut to reveal Becky, peeling cling film from a bowl of pasta. Jasmine hadn't met Becky yet, apart from that glimpse of her on their first day, though she had listened to Sophie's stories about her with horror, shaking her head and exclaiming over what a cow the other girl obviously was.

Becky turned and spotted Jasmine, looking her up and down, a curious expression on her face. She was wearing a long-sleeved top and leggings, plus black boots with a low heel, and her face was fresh today, devoid of make-up. She was actually very pretty when she wasn't tarted up, though she was too skinny. This was the first time Sophie had seen Becky eat anything.

Jasmine ignored Becky and went over to a table on the other side of the kitchen, keeping her back to her. Sophie made coffee and watched as Becky stared openly at Jasmine's back while forking cold pasta into her mouth.

Sophie took Jasmine's coffee over to her and sat down. A minute later, Becky came over, her head cocked as she addressed Jasmine. 'Do I know you?'

'I don't think so.' Jasmine didn't glance up as she replied, continuing to leaf through a celebrity gossip magazine that Sophie knew she had no interest in.

There was a weird tension in the air, like two cats had been thrown into a room together.

'Where are you from?' Becky asked, continuing to stare at Jasmine.

'London.'

Becky narrowed her eyes. 'I could have sworn I've seen you around Sheppey. Have you ever been there?'

Sophie was taken aback to see Jasmine's hand tremble as she turned the next page of the magazine. 'No, I haven't.' She gathered herself and looked up at Becky for the first time. 'Why, is that where you're from?'

'Yeah.'

'Explains a lot.'

The other girls in the kitchen were watching now.

'What the fuck do you mean by that?'

'Oh, nothing. I've just heard it's a bit of a backwater. Lots of people marrying their cousins, stuff like that.' She smiled sweetly.

Sophie expected Becky to erupt, but instead a little smile bloomed on her lips. 'I know who you are now. You never used to dress like this, that's why it took me a minute.' The smile became a smirk.

Jasmine stood up. 'You must be mistaking me for someone else. Come on, Sophie. I'm starting to feel sick. Let's get out of here.'

She grabbed Sophie's hand and pulled her towards the door.

'Rich bitch,' Becky said as they left.

'What was all that about?' Sophie asked as soon as they got into her room.

Jasmine had gone even paler than normal and refused to meet Sophie's eye, focusing instead on the CD collection, pulling cases from the shelf and looking at most of them with distaste. 'Robbie Williams? Urgh.'

Sophie refused to be diverted. 'Does she know you?'

'I don't want to talk about it.'

'But—'

'Oh, my God, you've got the first Kenickie album. I love this. Let's put it on.'

She put the CD in the player and turned it up loud, dancing around the tiny space and singing along. Sophie gave up. She would save it for another time.

A few days later, they were back in her room, this time with Liam. Sophie's entire body was tense with discomfort. She fiddled with the stereo, trying to decide which CD to play, while Jasmine and Liam sat on the single bed behind her, kissing noisily. What she needed was some music that would dampen their ardour, the musical equivalent of one of those machines that drives cats out of your garden by emitting a terrible noise. She loved Jasmine, and Liam seemed – well, she wasn't sure how she felt about him yet. He was charming and different and charismatic. But however she felt about him, she hated being a gooseberry.

She put the Robbie Williams CD on and made a noise in her throat, turning around to see Jasmine and Liam coming up for air.

Sophie really didn't want to imagine the two of them in bed together, though it was hard not to, especially here, with Liam's hand high on Jasmine's thigh, pushing her skirt up so her underwear was almost on display. Maybe she should leave them to it, make her excuses, but she really didn't want them having sex on her bed. She needed to get them out of here.

'Shall we go to the Union, get a drink?' she asked.

'What time is it?' Jasmine asked. 'I've got a lecture at four.'

Liam checked his watch. 'It's two-thirty. Time for a quick one before your lecture.'

'Mmm.' Jasmine leaned into him, kissing him, her hands on his broad chest.

'A quick drink, I meant.' He looked up at Sophie, one thick eyebrow arched. 'I apologise, Sophie.'

Liam stood up. His height and broad shoulders made him seem too big for this room, but he carried himself lightly. In his black clothes, with his sharp eyes, he reminded Sophie even more of a crow than when she'd first seen him. Or something sleeker, more dangerous; a hawk perhaps. He seemed older, more worldly, than the other boys here. Sometimes, when he looked at her, she felt that he was looking right into her, seeing her thoughts. It scared her in an unfamiliar way.

As they left the room, Becky waltzed past, carrying a pile of textbooks. Her hair was shiny and blow-dried and she wore a black hoodie bearing the university logo. As she passed them, Becky gave Jasmine and Liam what could only be described as a dirty look.

'Who was that?' Liam asked, as they headed out into the crisp December air.

'That was the lovely Becky,' Jasmine replied.

Liam's face darkened. 'Really? The one who's been telling everyone about you?'

A couple of days after Jasmine's encounter with Becky in the kitchen, a guy on their course had approached Jasmine and told her that he was a big fan of Jackdaw Books and that her granddad, Franklin Bird, was a hero of his. The shock on Jasmine's face had been almost comical. When they entered the lecture hall, half the people in the room had gawped at Jasmine, as if seeing her for the first time. Suddenly, she was a celebrity. Everybody here knew how important it was to have contacts, and now they knew that a direct link to a major publisher walked among them. All the people who had ignored Jasmine suddenly wanted to be her friend. Even the lecturer, an aspiring children's author, gave her an obsequious smile when he entered the hall.

'You're the only person I told,' Jasmine hissed afterwards.

'I didn't tell anyone, I swear.'

'I believe you. Then how the hell did everyone find out?'

'Becky?'

The look on Jasmine's face told Sophie she was right. So Becky *did* know Jasmine. Sophie tried to ask her about it but she refused. She stalked away and Sophie had to run to keep up with her. As they neared the edge of the campus, Becky, who had missed the lecture, passed them, smirking this time.

Jasmine stopped and pointed a painted fingernail at her. 'Keep your mouth shut,' she said.

'Or what? Don't tell me, you'll shut it for me. How original.'

Jasmine took a step towards her, glowering. 'No. I'll cut out your fucking tongue.' She wheeled away and marched on, leaving Sophie standing beside Becky for moment. The other girl actually appeared scared. Then she regained her composure.

'I've already told everyone what I know. She's Franklin Bird's granddaughter. Big deal. I don't know why it's such a big secret.'

'How did you know?' Sophie asked.

Becky shrugged. 'Everyone on Sheppey knows the Birds. They've got a massive house there, down on the marshes.'

'What, like a holiday home?'

'Why don't you ask your friend? Fucking psycho.' Becky winced, like she'd been stung by her own words, then marched on towards the nearest building.

Jasmine had stopped at the edge of the lawn and stood immobile, her black coat flapping around her, smoking furiously. Sophie headed over to her, knowing that asking Jasmine anything else would be futile. Worse than that, she sensed it could ruin their friendship. And Jasmine was still her only friend here. She wasn't going to do anything to risk losing her.

Now, leaving the halls of residence, Jasmine said, 'I hate her.'

'Are we still talking about Becky?' Liam asked, putting his arm around his new girlfriend. 'Don't worry, babe. You're a hundred times the woman she is.'

Sophie studied Jasmine's face, expecting her to agree, to make a contemptuous remark about Becky. But instead she frowned, a glimmer of anxiety in her eyes. It struck Sophie then that Jasmine wasn't as tough as she liked to make out. And seeing this vulnerable side made Sophie like her even more.

They reached the Student Union bar, which was decked out with tinsel and streamers, a droopy Christmas tree in the corner. Apparently some second year rugby players had poured a large amount of beer into its bucket, trying to get it drunk.

Sophie had a lime and soda, while the other two had pints.

Liam spent the next ten minutes telling them about a gruesome book he was reading. 'And then he gets the rat and—'

'I need the toilet,' Sophie said, escaping to the ladies. She took her time, wishing she could have Jasmine to herself for a little while. She felt on edge in Liam's company. He was so intense. The way he looked at her when she was talking. Some men's eyes would stray downwards when they talked to her, but Liam always looked at her lips as she spoke. It was disconcerting. It made her heart beat extra hard.

'I was just asking Jasmine what she's going to do when she graduates,' Liam said, when Sophie returned.

'That's, what, two-and-a-half years away.'

'True. But I was asking Jas if she's going to go and work for her granddad.'

Jasmine pulled a face. 'I'd rather take a bath in a gallon of sick.'

Sophie was shocked to hear her dream job slandered so viciously. Who *wouldn't* want to work at Jackdaw Books?

'One day,' Jasmine continued, 'I'm going to set up my own publishing company and call it . . . Raven Books. Bigger and badder than stupid jackdaws.'

Liam put his arm around her and winked at Sophie. 'Family issues.'

'Have you fallen out with them?' Sophie asked. 'Is that why you don't want anyone to know about your family?'

Jasmine made an exasperated noise. 'Listen, "falling out" doesn't touch it. I don't want to talk about it, all right? I'm not going to. Let's just say I don't get on with my granddad, how's that?'

'All right. I'm sorry—'

'Everyone thinks he's this great, benevolent figure, but they don't have any idea what he's really like. And my parents are so weak they do whatever he tells them to do.' She rubbed her arms as she spoke, her shoulders hunched. Her eyes had been fixed, burning, on the floor, but now they blazed up at Sophie.

'When I started here I was happy because nobody knew who I was. I could be a new person. My own person, not the granddaughter of the great Franklin Bird. And now it's wrecked. That stupid Sheppey bitch has ruined it.'

'She's not going to get away with it,' Liam said with a frown. 'Don't worry.'

She kissed him, then snapped at Sophie, 'I told you I don't want to talk about it.'

'But I didn't—'

'Would you forget it?' She started throwing her things together. 'I need to make a move.'

Sophie watched Jasmine march away across the Student Union, feeling unjustly accused. She hadn't been prying, or hadn't meant to, anyway. Jasmine lost speed and seemed to deflate as she went, her chin dipping. By the time she slipped out of sight, some of the spirit Sophie loved so much had been wrung out of her, like Tinker Bell without her fairy dust.

'Do you think she's all right?' Sophie asked Liam.

'She will be,' he said. 'Want to stay for one more?'

'I don't know . . .'

'Go on, I'll pay.'

Sophie twisted her hands together. She hadn't been on her own with Liam before and, for reasons that weren't clear to her, it made her uncomfortable.

'You haven't told me much about yourself, Sophie,' Liam said.

'There isn't . . .'

He was sitting close to her and she inched away. She could smell him, a slightly acrid, mannish smell. To his credit, he noticed and moved discreetly away from her too.

'Don't say there's nothing to tell,' he said with a big smile. 'Everyone has a story.'

'Mine's pretty boring.'

'Can I be the judge of that?'

Apart from Jasmine, no one else had shown any interest in her personal history since starting here.

'Do you have any siblings?'

'No. I'm an only child.'

He nodded. 'I thought so. You have that air about you. I don't mean spoilt, I mean – well, you seem shy. And comfortable being on your own. Did you have a boyfriend back home?'

She had to sip down the last drops of her drink to open her throat. 'Not a serious one. A guy called Kevin. We broke up just before I came here.'

'So now you're free and single? A wise move. It's much better that way.'

'But you're with Jasmine . . .'

'Yes, of course. Jasmine is very special. But' – he leaned closer, the smoke from his cigarette stinging her eyes – 'at the end of all this, this life, we're all alone, really. No one ever knows what's going on inside someone else's head. No one can fully rely on anyone else. It's tragic, but it's true.'

'That's a pretty depressing way of looking at things.'

He smiled. 'Maybe I've been reading too much Russian litera-ture and am talking rubbish. But "talking nonsense is the sole privi-lege mankind possesses over the other organisms".'

'*Notes from Underground*?'

His eyes widened. 'You've read it?'

'I'm not a complete philistine, you know.'

He laughed. 'I never thought you were, Sophie.' He lit another cigarette. '"We sometimes encounter people, even perfect strang-ers, who begin to interest us at first sight, somehow suddenly, all at once, before a word has been spoken."' He leaned back and looked into her eyes and she found herself growing hot, like the glowing tip of his cigarette.

'What's your favourite book?' he asked.

She thought about naming something by Kafka or Camus. But she knew how pretentious that would sound. So she answered truthfully. '*The Phoenix and the Carpet*.'

'Really? What, the old kids' book? Interesting choice.'

'I love it,' she said. 'The idea of this magical creature turning up and taking you on loads of adventures while your parents are com-pletely oblivious. We had this ancient, dusty rug in our house and I used to stare at it for hours, imagining a phoenix emerging from beneath it and whisking me away.'

'The great yearning for escape from the humdrum.'

'Exactly. Listen, I need to go. I have an assignment I need to finish.'

'Of course.' He exhaled a plume of smoke and she found herself staring at his lips. 'I'll see you soon.'

Two days later, Sophie left her room, where she'd been re-reading *Notes from Underground*, and found Becky in the kitchen, surrounded by two of her friends, one of whom had her arm around Becky's skinny shoulders. Becky's loud sobs rang out from their corner of the kitchen.

She considered heading straight back to her room but, sod it, why should she? Sophie crossed to the kettle, trying to look like she wasn't interested in what was going on, but Becky and her friends were talking so loudly that she couldn't help but overhear. They were talking about Becky's boyfriend, Lucas.

'He says he never wants to see me again,' Becky said, sniffing.

'I'm sure he'll come round,' said her friend, a Liverpudlian girl with a fake tan.

'He won't! He said – he said that his last girlfriend cheated on him and he forgave her, and then she did it again, breaking his heart. He says he won't be put through that again. Oh, God, I really loved him.'

'But how did he find out?' asked the Liverpudlian.

'I don't know. I mean, I barely even remember doing it. I was wasted . . .'

'I know. I was there.'

'I've never been that out of it before. I'm sure someone spiked my drink. And that guy, I don't even know his name, he came on to me, told me I was the most beautiful woman he'd ever seen. I didn't know what I was doing.' She made a keening noise.

'Did you say there were photographs?' asked the third girl. She had a Birmingham accent, similar to Sophie's.

'Yeah,' she sobbed.

'You were actually shagging him behind the Student Union?'

Becky nodded miserably.

'What, up against the wall?'

'Do the details matter?' Becky snapped, before the sobs came again. The other two waited for her to calm down. 'All that matters is that someone followed us out there and took photos.'

'Don't you remember, like, seeing a camera flash?' asked the Liverpudlian.

'No. Well, maybe. I had my eyes shut, didn't I? We both did. Hey, what the fuck are you smirking at?'

Sophie realised Becky was talking to her.

She smiled sweetly. 'Oh, nothing. Just wishing my life was as sordid as yours.'

She walked out of the kitchen, taking her tea with her, shocked by her own behaviour. And not a little pleased. She would never have dared to speak up like that before. She imagined herself telling Jasmine what she'd said. She'd be so impressed. And Liam too. For some reason, she found herself even more eager to tell him than her best friend.

Chapter 10

Day twelve, Friday, 17 April, 2015

Cassie was already at her desk when Sophie arrived at work. A bowl of cereal with chopped bananas and strawberries sat beside her keyboard, untouched, as Cassie concentrated on her screen, brow furrowed, frowning like someone had pissed her off. Sophie was still tense after the scene at home that morning. Daisy had thrown a massive tantrum about going to school, clinging to Sophie as she tried to leave, sobbing and pleading, 'Mummy I don't *want* you to go to work.' Daisy had refused to cooperate, fighting against Sophie's attempts to get her dressed, chucking her breakfast on the floor, the hurricane of her tantrum escalating from category three to four.

Guy had texted her when she was on the train to say that Daisy had calmed down minutes after Sophie left and was happily watching *Dora the Explorer*. She'd had another bad dream last night, another dream in which 'a bad man' was trying to get Mummy.

She stuck her phone in her drawer, not wanting to be distracted by it.

'Morning, Cassie.'

No response, just furious tip-tapping at the keyboard.

'Everything OK?'

Cassie looked up, flustered. 'Yes. All fine. Just working on *The Kiss of Death*. I'm having a few issues with the banners. I've briefed Josh, like you asked, but he's being really slow. We need them now.'

'I'll talk to him.'

'No!' Cassie's vehemence jolted her. 'You delegated it to me, so let me deal with it. I'll have to use my charm on him.'

'Fine. If you're sure. But let me know if he keeps delaying, OK?'

Cassie said she would. 'How was the meeting with Skittle yesterday?'

'It was great – I'll send my notes round to the team later.'

Sophie had been to see the team at Skittle, the agency who were developing the *Kiss of Death* app, the day before. Simon was expecting her to brief him later. It was absorbing a large chunk of the marketing budget and Simon was anxious about using this untested method.

Cassie scowled. 'I wish you'd let me come with you. It would have been good experience for me.'

'We've been over this, Cassie. I needed you here in the office. You know we're short-staffed.'

'Yes, but I never get to do anything exciting.'

'Going to a meeting with app developers is hardly exciting.'

'It would have been for me.'

Sophie sighed. 'Well, it's too late now. Maybe you can come next time.'

Cassie made a non-committal sound. 'Brian emailed me overnight, asking how it was all going.'

'Oh.' Sophie dug her fingernails into her palms. He hadn't sent the email to *her*. 'Can you forward it to me and I'll update him?'

'Don't worry, I've replied already. He's over the moon. And that's what it's all about, isn't it? Keeping the authors happy.'

'Cassie, do you remember how we talked about how I should be Brian's main point of contact? I'm managing this project, so I need to know everything that happens.'

'But I just told you.'

'That's not the point.'

Cassie blinked at her. 'I'm sorry, Sophie. It won't happen again.'

Sophie needed a cup of tea. Actually, she wanted something cold, something to take away the stickiness in her armpits, the fever of irritation that scratched at her skin.

'It's ridiculously hot in here. Why isn't the air con on?'

Cassie looked at her with those big, beautiful eyes. 'I don't know, Sophie. If I put it on, Tracey complains and sits there in her woolly hat shivering.'

'Did I hear my name?' Tracey had arrived, sneaking up behind them. Or that's how it felt, anyway. 'It's not my fault if I feel the cold. I've got sensitive skin. And the air con unit blows straight onto my desk. It's like sitting in a wind tunnel.'

'Maybe you could move to Cassie's old desk.'

Tracey looked horrified.

'Or not,' Sophie said.

'I don't really like change.'

Sophie was about to head to the kitchen when Cassie scooted closer to her. 'Have you had a chance to talk to Simon about my role?'

'Not yet.'

'Maybe I should talk to him.'

'No. I said I'd do it.'

In the kitchen, Sophie downed a pint of water, wishing she hadn't snapped at Cassie like that, even if it was justified. She was over-tired, worried about Daisy and anxious not to mess up the launch of Brian's book. She breathed in deeply through her nose and exhaled slowly through pursed lips, urging herself to relax.

Maybe she should book a massage. Her shoulders were hard with tension and the breathing exercises weren't working.

Simon came into the kitchen.

'Sophie! Just the woman. I . . . are you all right? You look like you're about to faint. Have you had any breakfast?'

'No, I didn't have time. Daisy was—'

'Go and get yourself something to eat from the cafeteria. Then I'll see you in my office for an update meeting about Brian's app. Can't wait to hear what the guys at Skittle have come up with.'

He left the kitchen before Sophie could respond.

⌣

In the cafeteria she grabbed a cereal bar and a banana. She hadn't had time to prepare for the meeting with Simon. All the important information was in her notepad.

As she left the cafe, she noticed Franklin, distinctive with his white hair, standing with his back to her in the corner of the reception area, half-concealed by a stand of books. He was leaning forward, talking to someone considerably shorter than him, and when Franklin moved to one side, Sophie realised it was Cassie. She couldn't read her expression from where she was, but the younger woman nodded several times, not spotting Sophie watching her. She guessed Franklin was giving Cassie a pep talk. He was, apparently, well known for it, going around the building, singling out individuals and telling them some inspirational anecdotes.

Sophie hurried back to her desk. Where was that notepad? She had definitely brought it back from the meeting with Skittle. She remembered taking it out of her bag and putting it here, on the desk.

Sophie opened each of her drawers in turn, flinching as she imagined cockroaches crawling out of the darkness. She'd heard they could fly and she pictured them launching themselves at her, getting tangled in her hair. She told herself to get a grip – this was a new pedestal, she hadn't even thought about cockroaches for a week – but opened the drawers fully before putting her hand inside. There was no notepad. She checked her bag. Not in there.

'Have either of you seen my notebook?'

'What does it look like?' Tracey asked.

'It's an A4 Pukka Pad, green.'

'No, sorry.'

Where the hell was it? It contained not only the notes about the app but several important to-do lists and notes from other meetings. Her phone rang. It was Simon.

'Coming?'

'Yes, hang on.'

On the way to Simon's office she searched inside her head for facts from the meeting with Skittle, but it was like trying to fish without a rod.

'How are you feeling?' Simon said as she sat on his sofa.

'Much better, thank you.' She hoped he couldn't tell she was lying. 'Before we start, there's one thing I need to ask you about.'

'Oh yes?'

'Yes . . .' The way he was staring at her made her uncomfortable. 'I wondered what we can do about finding a replacement for Matt? We could really do with another pair of hands.'

Simon sat back. 'I do sympathise. The only issue is that recruiting someone is expensive and we haven't budgeted for it.'

'But—'

He waved a hand. 'You might have to muddle along for a little while. I'm sure you'll be fine. I have every faith in your abilities, Sophie. And I know you're not afraid of hard work, are you?'

'No, of course not.'

So he was expecting her and the rest of the team to work harder, and probably work longer hours, to fill the gap.

'Good. Was there something else?'

'Well, Cassie has been asking about being promoted to senior executive.'

'I see. And she wants a pay rise?'

'I think she just wants the job title. For her CV.'

'What? Is she thinking of leaving?' He said this as if Sophie had just told him there was a gang of angry Hell's Angels in reception, asking for him.

'Not as far as I know.'

He puffed out air. 'I really don't want to lose her. She's too good. Did you know she got the highest—'

'Score ever in the McQuaig Quick-Thinking Test. Yes, I remember.'

'Of course, of course.' He paced around the office, tapping his lower lip with his finger. 'Listen, tell her we are looking at the structure of the team but will keep her . . . desire for the position in mind. In the meantime, if there's any hint that she's looking for another job, let me know ASAP, OK?'

'OK.'

He checked the time again. 'Do you mind if we take a rain check till later? Actually, just email me all the stuff about the app. I'm sure you've got it all in hand.'

───────

She'd had a reprieve, but she still needed to find that notepad. Maybe she'd taken it home absent-mindedly and left it there. Guy would be at home now. She took her phone out into the corridor and called him.

He sounded flustered when he answered.

'Hiya, it's me. Can you do me a favour? I think I might have left a—'

'Can it wait? Is it life or death?'

'No it's not . . . What's up? The school haven't called to say something's wrong with Daisy, have they?'

'What? No, no . . .' He made a groaning noise. She could picture him rubbing at his little bald patch, the way he did when he was fretting about something.

'What is it, then?'

'Hopefully it will all blow over. But something really fucking horrific has happened.'

Chapter 11
Day twelve, Friday, 17 April, 2015

'What is it?'

Guy made that groaning noise again. 'It's Twitter. A thing on Twitter. It's a total nightmare.'

Sophie leaned against the wall between the lifts, the tension in her shoulders dissipating a little. 'Twitter? I thought it was going to be something serious.'

'Sophie, it *is* serious. Or – it could be. I don't know.'

'What's that constant pinging sound?'

'That was an alert telling me someone's replied to my tweet.'

'But it's gone off about twenty times during this call.'

'I know! My phone's going fucking mental.'

The sudden increase in the volume of his voice shocked her. 'Guy, what exactly have you done?'

Another ping. Another groan. 'Nothing. I haven't done anything, Sophie. It wasn't me. You believe me, don't you?'

This was exasperating. 'Believe you about what?'

The lift arrived and the doors slid open with a sound not unlike the noise from Guy's phone. Simon emerged, along with Franklin Bird.

'Good morning,' Franklin said. 'Simon's been telling me all about some marvellous thing you're doing with apps.'

She lowered her phone. She was painfully aware of the sounds coming from it and Guy babbling away between pings.

'It's all Greek to me,' Franklin said. 'But this company has always prided itself on moving with the times. We evolve and survive, like a cockroach.'

Franklin grinned at her and for a moment she thought he must have said this deliberately to freak her out. Had he heard about the cockroaches in her desk?

No, she was being silly. It was a common analogy, that was all.

'Anyway, better let Sophie get back to work,' Simon said.

The three of them drifted away. Sophie raised her phone to her ear. Guy had stopped talking and was breathing heavily like he'd just sprinted a hundred metres.

'Are you still there?' he asked eventually, his voice flat.

'I need to go,' she said.

'Me too.'

'I'll call you at lunchtime.'

What a morning. Back at her desk, she found Tracey shaking her head at her computer.

'What is it?' Sophie asked.

'Oh, some journalist on Twitter tweeted something really offensive and now everyone's piling on, giving him a proper shaming. I can't believe anyone could think domestic violence is funny. In this day and age. My sister's ex-husband was abusive, before she finally kicked the bastard out. And it was on the news this morning – that poor woman who fled her house because her husband was beating her, and then he murdered their children before killing himself. Those poor mites. And this idiot journalist thinks it's something to joke about on Twitter.'

Sophie's legs were heavy as she headed around to Tracey's desk.

'What did this journalist tweet?'

Out of the corner of her eye, Sophie was aware that Cassie was staring at her. Was that a smile on her lips? She turned her head and Cassie swiftly looked away.

'A stupid joke,' Tracey replied. 'It's not even funny. A link to that news story with the comment, *Don't talk to me about domestic violence – I get enough of that at home.* Then an emoji of someone with a bandage.'

Sophie lay her hand on the back of Tracey's chair and leaned forward so she could read the words on the screen, see the username of the person who had sent this tweet.

She knew before she saw his name. Of course it was him. Guy.

By the time Sophie got home that evening, Guy's 'joke' had been retweeted more than ten thousand times, and a similar number of people had tweeted him to tell him what a callous bastard he was, echoing Tracey's words. Domestic violence was nothing to laugh at. He was a disgrace. They felt sorry for his wife. Did he beat *her*? Then there were hundreds of messages from men sticking up for him, saying that the 'crazy feminists' bitching about the tweet needed a sense of humour and a good seeing to. Some of Guy's self-appointed supporters had taken this further, threatening to rape or kill the women who were condemning Guy.

This sort of thing happened on Twitter all the time. Sophie remembered the young woman who had tweeted a stupid, misjudged joke about AIDS before boarding a plane to Africa. By the time she got off that plane her life was ruined.

Guy was half-drunk, an almost-empty bottle of wine beside him at the kitchen table. Daisy was running riot, toys everywhere, pages torn from a colouring book and scattered around, chocolate all over her face where she'd raided the kitchen cupboard and gorged on Cadbury's buttons. Sophie sniffed the air.

'Have you had a cigarette?'

His eyes were pink. 'That's the smoking ruins of my career you can smell.'

'Daddy smoked out the window,' Daisy said. 'And told me not to tell you.'

'Thanks a lot, sweetheart,' he said. 'Sophie, me having a cigarette out the bloody window is the least of our worries.'

She sat down heavily and poured herself half a glass of wine. She allowed the alcohol to hit her and calm her down before saying, 'Tell me.'

'Have you seen the tweet?'

'Yes.'

'It wasn't me. I didn't write it.'

'You mean it was a fake account. Someone pretending to be you? Then it's not a problem, surely?'

He shook his head. 'I wish. It was my real account. But I didn't send the tweet. I must have been hacked. Someone logged in as me and sent it.'

'Right. So can't you simply tell people that?'

He went into the little kitchen. He took a long time and Sophie suspected he was checking his phone, unable to leave it alone, to resist the pain. Daisy came over for a hug, leaving a smudge of chocolate on Sophie's blouse, before bouncing across the room, buzzing on E-numbers. There was no way Daisy was going to go to sleep before midnight.

Guy finally came back with another bottle of red. He refilled his glass.

'You haven't answered my question.'

He rubbed at his little bald spot. Sophie wanted to grab his hand away, tell him to stop making it worse. At the same time, he looked so wretched that she wanted to put her arms around him, salve the pain.

'Yes, I wrote a tweet denying that I'd sent the offensive one. And I've told Claire I didn't write it. Whether she believed me or not, I have no idea. But the public won't,' he said. 'Maybe a few people will, but the majority will think I'm lying, trying to cover it up. They'll ask how anyone could get my password.'

A horrible thought struck Sophie. 'I logged in to your Twitter account last week, on my phone.'

'What? How did you know my password?'

'I know all your passwords, Guy. Just like you know mine.'

'But what were you doing?'

She explained how she needed to be familiar with Twitter for work and had wanted to take a look at a live account. 'But I didn't do anything. And I'm sure I logged out straight away.'

'How sure?'

She thought back, tried to picture the screen as she'd exited the site. She took out her phone and navigated to Twitter then held the screen up to show Guy. 'See, it's logged out. And no one else has had my phone anyway.'

He nodded. 'Oh, God, it's a nightmare. When the first offended tweets started coming in I made the mistake of arguing with some of the people who were slagging me off. I might have made it worse.'

'Oh, Guy.' She sighed.

'I have to go and see Claire tomorrow.'

'But tomorrow's Saturday.'

'I know. She still wants to see me. The *Guardian* have put a story about it on their homepage. They're combing through everything I've ever written and tweeting quotes about women and sex and violence and every stupid joke I've ever made. Even some pieces I wrote about the challenges of raising a daughter. All out of context, of course. Making me look like the most misogynistic arsehole on the planet.'

'Daddy said a swear.'

They both turned to see Daisy staring at them, wide-eyed.

Guy slapped his own hand. 'I'm a bad daddy.'

Daisy scrambled onto his lap.

'You smell funny.' She wrinkled her nose and Sophie was able to smile for the first time in hours.

'Come on, Daisy-Doo, it's past your bedtime.'

'But I'm not tired. And the owl hasn't hooted yet.'

Guy went, 'Tu-whit tu-whoo.'

They spent the next hour getting their daughter through the bath and bedtime routine, which finished with Guy reading *We're Going on a Bear Hunt*, acting out the story, stomping around Daisy's bedroom as she giggled and hid her face from the scary bear. Sophie stood outside the room, listening and trying not to think about what had happened. By the time he emerged from the sleeping Daisy's room, Sophie had convinced herself it would all blow over. It would all be a big fuss about nothing.

'They've suspended me.'

Sophie stared at him, standing there in his best jacket, unshaven, hair sticking up. She had been on Twitter most of the morning, unable to tear herself away from the storm that was still raging on. She half hoped someone else would write something stupid to take the heat off Guy. But nothing else seemed to be going on. Today, with the story about the abusive husband who'd killed his children then himself all over the papers, everyone on social media wanted someone to kick, and that person was Guy.

'What?'

'Well, I'm a freelancer, not an employee, so they can't actually suspend me. But they are not going to run any more pieces by me for the foreseeable future.'

'That's crazy.' She approached him to give him a hug but he stepped away.

'She wants me to apologise on Twitter and in the paper. And make a public donation to a charity that helps victims of domestic violence.'

'That sounds like a good idea.'

'But I didn't send the tweet! If I apologise it will look like an admission of guilt.'

'If you apologise, will they give you more work?'

'Probably. Assuming the apology and donation are received positively, whatever that means.'

'Then you should do it.'

His mouth dropped open. 'I expected you to be on my side.'

'Guy, I am. But—'

'But what?'

'I believe you when you say you didn't send it.' At least, she thought she believed him. He had been known to flatly deny wrongdoing in the past. She knew he had told his ex-wife plenty of lies. 'But you need that work. We need the money.'

He stalked off into the kitchen, rifling through the cupboard and cramming half a chocolate bar into his mouth.

'*You're* working now,' he said once his mouth was empty. A smear of chocolate remained on his lip. She stared at it, irritated and wishing he'd wipe it away. He looked like a kid. He was acting like one, too. 'We'll be all right for a while. I'll approach a few other editors. But this will all have blown over in a week or two. Just wait and see.'

He bit off another chunk of chocolate and spoke with his mouth full. 'In a couple of weeks we'll look back at this and laugh.'

Chapter 12
Day fifteen, Monday, 20 April, 2015

It was chilly in the corridor and Sophie pulled her cardigan around her. It always felt like this in the older, less modernised parts of the building – the corridors and storerooms. It was as if the walls sucked all the warmth out of the air. She wondered what it felt like down in the basement, if she would ever get an invite to the library. She remembered Matt telling her about the ghost. Nonsense, but it was easy to believe, standing here now, chilled to the bone while the sun shone brightly outside.

This morning, the damp and cold suited her mood. She was scared about what was going to happen if Guy's 'suspension' from the *Herald* became protracted, but he was going to make some calls today, try to get some more commissions. He was well known, had lots of contacts. She was sure it would be all right.

As she neared Simon's office, the door opened and Cassie came out, wearing a trouser suit and a satisfied smile. She held a green notepad under her arm, just like the one Sophie had lost, and when she noticed Sophie she paused for a moment before heading off in the other direction.

Sophie knocked on Simon's door.

'Come in,' he called.

It was frigid in here too, but Simon was in his shirtsleeves, perched on the edge of his desk munching an apple.

His fly was unzipped, his red underpants clearly visible.

Sophie focused on his face as he talked to her, asking her to fill him in on Skittle's plans for the app. She'd managed to drag the information out of her head over the weekend and was confident she had memorised all the important details now. He nodded and chewed his apple as she recited the information.

As she spoke, she wondered: was there something going on between Simon and Cassie? It seemed unlikely. Cassie was young and beautiful and, as everybody knew, not afraid to bring up the topic of sexual harassment. Simon was both socially awkward and physically in a lower league to her, with his pudgy face and weak chin. The apple he was eating had left juice-marks on his chin, which drew attention to his shaving rash. But he had power. The world of work was full of men having affairs with beautiful younger women. It was one of the biggest clichés in the book. Was that why Simon praised Cassie at every opportunity? Why he was so desperate to hang on to her? She had a mental flash of Simon leaning back against his desk, Cassie standing on tiptoe to kiss him, her hand inside his pants.

'What was Cassie doing here?' she asked once she'd finished her report, hoping she didn't look as sick as she felt.

'Cassie?' He turned away towards the window and she realised he was discreetly trying to fasten his fly. He must have seen her eyes flicker downwards. Sophie cringed.

'You were asking about Cassie,' he said in an irritated tone.

'Oh. Yes. She was coming out of your office just before I got here.'

'That's because I asked her to pull together some stats for me on Friday. *You* had already gone home.'

There was disapproval in his voice. She cast her mind back. On Friday she'd hurried out of the office at bang on five thirty, when the working day officially ended, needing to get home to talk to Guy. Was Simon expecting her to apologise? He folded his arms and tapped his foot. Well, sod that.

He gave up waiting. 'Regarding Cassie, I think we *should* promote her to senior executive,' he said. 'It's only a tiny bump in salary but it will make her happy. We really don't want her to move elsewhere. I've already told Natalie, so she's going to send you a copy of Cassie's new job description.'

'Do we have the budget for this pay rise?' Sophie asked.

He waved a hand dismissively. 'Yes, yes – it's certainly a lot cheaper than hiring a whole new person.'

'But about that new person—'

His phone pinged, allowing him to evade the question. He tapped out a reply then looked up. 'You're still here?'

'I thought—'

He waved a hand. 'I want you to keep me informed about what's happening with this app. It's costing a lot of money. You know I'm trusting you with this, Sophie? Like you said I could.'

'Of course.' She was still confident the app would be a success.

'Good. Well, have a productive day. I'll leave it to you to give Cassie the good news, yes?'

She left Simon's office, whispering, 'Dickhead' under her breath. So, Cassie was being promoted. She wished Simon had consulted her first, but it was fine. Really, it was. Giving staff members good news was never a chore. And Cassie would be thrilled.

Braving the chilly corridor again, Sophie vowed to forget her misgivings about Cassie. It was all so stupid and irrational. She hadn't done anything wrong, had she? She'd been confident about putting herself forward. She was respected by senior managers. She got on brilliantly with their authors. She had been sexually harassed and had stood up to it with grace and guts. Sophie experienced a pang of shame for her misgivings, and especially for suspecting Cassie of having an affair with Simon. *This isn't you*, Sophie told herself. *You're not one of those narrow-minded, suspicious people.*

She was lucky to have Cassie. And from now on, she vowed, she was going to try to be wholly positive and supportive.

When she got back to her desk, her phone was ringing. It was Josh.

'Can you come down to my floor? Meeting room two.' He hung up.

What now? She headed down to the second floor where the design department was based. She found Josh pacing around the little meeting room. She could almost see steam coming out of his ears.

'Everything all right?' she asked.

'No. It is not. That girl of yours is lucky she hasn't been shoved out of a window.'

Sophie was confused. 'Daisy?'

'No – Cassie! You delegated that design work to her, didn't you? Well, she has been on about it to me non-stop. She was even emailing me over the weekend.'

Sophie attempted a smile. 'She does that. She told me there was some delay.'

'What? I finished it the day you asked, because it was you. And she's been on at me ever since, asking me to change it, tweak it, then completely change it again. She keeps messing with the brief, being vague and then telling me it's not what she wants. She was here when I got in this morning, waiting by my desk.'

Cassie must have headed to the design department straight after her meeting with Simon.

'She started to berate me in front of my team, telling me my work wasn't good enough.'

Sophie felt torn. Cassie was doing what she thought was right, trying to ensure the work was perfect. She had just gone about it the wrong way.

Josh's face was pink with fury. She had never seen him like this before. 'I don't want you to apologise, Sophie. I want *her* to. I've never been spoken to in such a condescending way before.'

Thinking back longingly to the days when she'd only had to deal with a toddler's tantrums, Sophie picked up the phone. 'Cassie, can you come to meeting room two on the second floor, please?'

'What are you doing?' Josh asked.

'What you wanted. Getting her down here now. So we can sort this out.'

He pulled a face like he hadn't expected this to happen. But then he folded his arms and said, 'Good.'

Cassie appeared a minute later, calm and collected. 'Hi, Josh,' she said. 'Thanks for those banners. They're perfect.'

Josh's eyes bulged. He addressed Sophie. 'That's not what she said twenty minutes ago.'

'I don't know what you're talking about, Josh.' Cassie sounded so reasonable, so unflustered. Compared to the raging, bright red man before her, any passive observer would have thought Cassie was wholly in the right here. 'I told you the banners were just what we were after. Tracey has started tweeting them out already.'

Josh took a step towards Cassie, his finger pointed an inch from her face. 'You're insane. Not only that, but you're a lying little—' He bit his tongue.

Cassie turned to Sophie. 'Can you tell him to stop, Sophie? This is workplace bullying.'

Sophie stepped between them, fearing that Josh would thump Cassie. His eyes were almost coming out on stalks now.

'Is that your strategy, huh?' Josh shouted. People passing the meeting room turned their heads to watch the show. 'The moment someone does something to upset you, you go running to Natalie. Well, I've got your number, Cassandra. *I know your game.*'

Sophie held her hands out. 'OK, I think we should stop this now. Let's all go back to our desks, cool down—'

But Josh hadn't finished. 'You're going to regret crossing me.'

'I doubt that,' said Cassie. Her expression remained impassive. Sophie was willing to bet that if she took Cassie's pulse now, it wouldn't have increased at all since she entered this room. 'Can I go now, Sophie? I'm not prepared to tolerate this bullying behaviour.'

'You little—'

'Verbal abuse is a breach of the staff code of conduct,' Cassie said in an even voice. 'According to page twenty of the company handbook, using derogatory terms based on a person's gender, race, religion or sexuality are considered to be gross misconduct which can lead to instant dismissal. You called me a bitch, Josh. I believe that's a sackable offence.'

'I did *not* call you a bitch.'

'He's right, Cassie.' He had just stopped short.

'But you did accuse me of having an affair with Matt, of leading him on. Which you wouldn't have done if I were male.'

He stared at her, nostrils flaring. 'Don't even try it. I'm familiar with prejudice. You don't know anything. Look at you, swanking about in your Louboutins and your cashmere sweater. Why do you need a job anyway? Why don't you just piss off and live on the allowance Daddy gives you?'

'Josh.' Sophie tried to put her hand on his arm but he pulled away. 'I think you need to calm down.'

He glared at Cassie again. 'You had better watch out. I'm valued here. And I'm going to be watching you.'

Cassie didn't blink.

As he stormed out of the room, she said, 'Thanks again for the banners.'

Chapter 13

Day sixteen, Tuesday, 21 April, 2015

Sophie stopped off at Starbucks on her way to the office. She was tired again and desperately in need of coffee. She had stayed in the office till seven p.m. the night before, Simon's words about her leaving early on Friday ringing in her ears.

The scene between Cassie and Josh had put her on edge for the rest of the day. After the confrontation, Cassie had told Sophie she didn't feel well and asked if she could go home. Sophie had gladly agreed, telling Cassie that they would talk about it in the morning. She already knew what she was going to say. She would tell Cassie about her promotion and use that to explain to Cassie that she needed to be more careful, more professional. Not to antagonise people. That you certainly shouldn't berate people in front of their colleagues.

As she entered the coffee shop, she saw several members of the design team huddled together around a tall table. She paused, unsure if she could face Josh right now, before she'd spoken to Cassie, but then realised he wasn't with them.

One of the designers, a tall guy with a goatee called Chris, spotted Sophie and waved her over.

'Did you hear about Josh?' he asked in a hushed voice.

She thought he must be talking about the argument with Cassie and was formulating an answer when Chris said, 'Somebody attacked him on the way home last night. He's in hospital.'

She put her hand to her mouth and stared at Chris as he filled her in on the awful details. Apparently, Josh had gone out drinking the night before, 'because he was so stressed out and needed to let off steam.' He'd stayed at a bar in Soho till about one a.m. before heading off in search of a night bus. The other people from Jackdaw had already gone home.

'We don't know exactly what happened after that.'

A pretty redhead from the design department whose name Sophie didn't know added, 'He's unconscious.'

'Oh, my God.'

The redhead had tears in her eyes. Another member of the team, a skinny guy wearing a red T-shirt and matching Converse, put his arm around her. Sophie felt like she was at a wake.

'We're going to go to the hospital later to see him, if they're allowing visitors in.'

'Was it a mugging?' Sophie asked. 'I mean, did they take anything, like his phone or wallet?'

'We don't know.'

They dispersed, heading back to the office, leaving Sophie standing there on her own, commuters buzzing in and out of the shop, pushing past her with their takeaway cups and their briefcases, focused on the working day ahead. Sophie couldn't remember why she was here, what she was meant to be doing. She left without buying a drink and stood outside next to the smokers and vapers loading up on nicotine before the working day began.

Unconscious. Did that mean he had serious head injuries? What if he never fully recovered? A selfish thought hit her: he was her only friend at work, assuming he still wanted to be friends after she'd told him to calm down yesterday. If he wasn't there, she had no one else to confide in. But that wasn't what mattered, was it? What mattered was that Josh was OK.

———⌣———

She could hardly concentrate all day. After lunch, she spoke to Chris, who told her that Josh had regained consciousness and that he was allowed visitors. Sophie exhaled with relief.

When Sophie told Cassie what had happened, she seemed concerned but not hugely surprised. 'I suppose he's always going to be a target,' she said.

'What do you mean?'

'You know. Being gay. There are a lot of homophobes out there, aren't there? Gay men being attacked in the street. You hear about it all the time.'

Sophie didn't know if this was true anymore. In 2015? Really? Maybe she was out of touch, living in a liberal bubble. She looked on Google and saw that she was indeed naive. Hate crimes against gay men had actually increased in recent years.

'Cassie, the meeting with Josh yesterday . . . I need to talk to you about it.'

'I'm sorry, Sophie. I was out of order. I shouldn't have spoken to him like that.' And just like that, Sophie had once again been wrong-footed. 'Maybe I was a bit pushy over the banners, but it was only because I wanted to do a good job. Because I want to help sell Brian's book. I'll apologise to Josh as soon as he comes back.' She stared at the floor. 'I feel terrible now.'

'It's OK, Cassie. I understand you're trying to do a good job. But you have to be careful how you communicate with people.'

'Yes, Sophie. And I want you to teach me.' Her eyes were wet with sincerity. 'To be like you.'

Taken aback, Sophie smiled. 'I'm sure you'll go a lot further than me, Cassie. Actually, I've got something to tell you. We've decided to promote you to senior marketing executive.'

'Really? Oh, my goodness. Thank you so much, Sophie.'

'You should be thanking Simon.'

Cassie frowned and Sophie immediately regretted saying it. 'Oh? You didn't want me to be promoted?'

'Of course I did. But it was his final decision.'

'Right. Well, I'll be sure to thank him.' She smoothed down her hair and changed the subject. 'Can I be in charge of the *Kiss of Death* app?'

The book was due to be published the following week and the app was launching on the same day. Brian's tour of schools would start a week later and he'd been in earlier trying on the ludicrous gothic outfit that Rebeka Venters from PR had put together after deciding Brian needed an image. 'It worked for Terry Pratchett,' she said.

With a top hat, black gloves and a cape, Brian looked like some kind of crazed magician. Sophie couldn't believe the outfit would impress teenagers or make them want to buy his books, but Cassie and Rebeka had gushed about it and, exhausted and worried about Josh, Sophie had given in.

'I don't know,' Sophie said in response to Cassie's request. 'It's so important we get it right . . .'

'And you don't trust me?'

'Of course I do.'

'Then trust me with this, please.'

Sophie hesitated. After spoiling things by telling Cassie that Simon was responsible for her promotion, she felt the need to show the other woman that she had faith in her.

'OK. Fine. I'll put everything you need to know in an email and you can talk to Skittle.'

Finally, Cassie's smile returned.

_____

Five thirty arrived at last. Sophie rushed down the stairs towards the exit, slowing when she saw a familiar figure slowly climbing the steps.

'Mr Bird.'

He stopped and looked up at her. She was impressed that he wasn't out of breath. 'Didn't I tell you to call me Franklin?'

She couldn't remember if he had.

'I'm just on my way to the hospital,' she blurted, filling the awkward silence.

'You're not sick, are you?'

'No. A friend of mine who works here, Josh Barker, was attacked.'

Franklin's eyes widened, but only for a second. 'The chap in design? Oh dear.' He leaned closer and gripped Sophie's forearm, shocking her. 'You know who did this, don't you?'

'No. Who?' Did he really know who had attacked Josh?

'Whomever he may be as an adult, I can tell you precisely who he was as a child. The son of foolish, irresponsible parents. The pupil of lax, head-in-the-clouds educators. The product of a coddling, corrupt society. The man who committed this crime was himself the victim of every adult who failed in his duty to effectively, *memorably*, discipline him as a child. You mark my words – that's the root of all criminal behaviour.'

Sophie didn't know what to say. Where had *that* come from? All of a sudden Jasmine's words came back to her. *Let's just say I don't get on with my granddad, how's that?*

Franklin let go of her arm and, disconcertingly, flashed a broad smile.

'How are you liking it here, Sophie?' he asked. 'Feel like a member of the family yet?'

'The family?' His sudden transformation back into twinkly old Franklin had left her disoriented. 'Oh, the Jackdaw family. Yes, yes I do. Thank you.'

'And how's your daughter? Daisy, was it?'

She was impressed that he'd remembered. 'She's great, thanks. A handful, you know but . . .'

'Misbehaving, is she? Maybe as a reaction to her mummy going to work?'

He was obsessed. 'No, she's fine about that. Usually.' He raised a white eyebrow. 'She's just a typical four-year-old.'

His hand returned to her arm. 'Remember, I have a lot of experience with children. I am your resource, to be made use of. If you ever need any advice, you know where I am.'

'I . . . thank you.'

'I suppose you'd better hurry if you're going to make visiting time.'

As she went by him on the stairs, Franklin patted her shoulder.

'You take care,' he said.

She continued to the foot of the stairs. At the bottom, she turned. Franklin hadn't moved. He stood immobile, staring into space, like a robot whose batteries had run out. But before Sophie could call up to ask if he was OK, he lurched into life, continuing his patient ascent, back to his room on the top floor.

Sophie reached the ward where Josh was recovering just as his other visitors, including Chris and the pretty redhead, were coming out. There was a man with them too, wearing a navy suit with threadbare elbows. He was about five foot ten, with spiky hair and five o'clock shadow.

He nodded goodbye to the other visitors then turned to Sophie.

'Detective Constable Darren Paterson,' he said. 'You're here to visit Mr Barker?'

She nodded and introduced herself.

'I'd like to talk to you after you've seen him.'

'What for?'

'I'll explain when you come out.'

She hurried to Josh's bed, slowing down as she approached him, the shock of seeing him turning her limbs to lead.

He was propped up in the bed, a bandage wrapped around his head. His eyes were circled with purple and grey bruises. There was a gash on his cheek, stitched up but horribly painful-looking. A scrape on his chin. Lips swollen and bruised. He was sipping a drink through a straw and she saw that one of his hands was injured too, three of his fingers on his right hand wrapped in bandages with splints keeping them straight.

'Jesus,' she said, as she reached the bed.

He could only open one eye and it was apparently too painful to smile, but he said, 'No, Josh.' His voice was thick, like his tongue was swollen.

'You look like you were run over by a truck, not beaten up.'

He winced.

'I'm sorry, I was in a rush so I didn't bring you anything . . .'

He made a circling gesture with his good hand. The bed was surrounded by flowers in vases, more bouquets still in their wrappers lying on every surface. 'Take some,' he said, his voice slurred. She guessed he must be on strong painkillers. 'Why does everyone think gay men like flowers? They play havoc with my allergies.'

Speaking seemed to exhaust him. She shouldn't have come here. Should let him rest.

'Anyway, I just wanted to see you. I'll come back when you're feeling a bit better.'

He stared at her with his one open eye.

'Do you want me to get the nurse?' she asked.

He shook his head, the pain making him gasp.

'OK, I'll come back. I promise not to bring flowers.'

An attempt at a smile.

She turned to go and heard him whisper her name.

'He was going to kill me,' he said, so quietly she could hardly hear.

She stooped so her ear was close to his mouth. 'Sorry, what did you say?'

'The man who beat me. He told me he was going to kill me. But someone came by, disturbed him.'

'Oh, my God. Have you told that detective?'

'Of course. He wanted to know if I recognised the guy, but he was wearing a balaclava.' He sucked in a rattling breath.

She left the ward and found Detective Paterson waiting on a chair outside.

'Let's walk,' he said. 'It's too quiet here.'

She followed him along the corridor, noticing that his trousers were a little too tight, like he'd recently put on weight.

'Josh said the guy who attacked him was going to kill him. Like they knew who he was. Do you think that could be true?'

'It's certainly something we need to look into. Do you know if Josh has any enemies? Any people who hate him? Who've threatened him?'

'No. Everyone loves him.'

'Why did you just pull that face?'

'What face?'

'When you said "Everyone loves him", it seemed pretty clear you didn't believe what you were saying.'

'Oh. It's nothing. I was just thinking about an argument he had at work yesterday.'

Paterson produced a notepad. 'Who was that with?'

Sophie hesitated. She didn't want to get Cassie into trouble with the police.

'It was nothing major. Just a disagreement over something stupid. It was between Josh and a girl on my team, Cassie.'

'Big girl, is she, this Cassie?'

Sophie laughed despite herself. 'No, she's tiny. Like a little doll.'

'Hmm, well whoever beat Josh up was six foot and built like a brick shithouse, excuse my French.'

They parted outside the hospital, the detective heading to his car while Sophie crossed to the bus stop. There was hardly anyone around and Sophie felt ill at ease, eyeing a sportswear-clad teenager as he came towards her up the hill, wondering if he was the kind of miscreant Franklin had talked about, the street suddenly feeling far less safe than usual. She was glad when the bus arrived to take her back to the safety of her home.

Chapter 14
Sunday, 9 January, 2000

Sophie disembarked from the train at Brighton's London Road station, two stops before Falmer, where the university was based. This was where Jasmine lived with her housemate Helen and, after almost three weeks back home, Sophie was desperate to see her best friend.

The Christmas break had been boring. Although it had been lovely to see her mum and dad again, she quickly became stir-crazy at home. Her bedroom, with the posters of Suede and Placebo and all the trinkets and detritus of her teen years scattered around, seemed childish. Their street was too small; the horizon too close.

To get away, she went on long bike rides through the south Staffordshire countryside, invigorated by the cold, heading for a pasture where a group of overweight horses stood grazing. As she propped her bike against the hedgerow, a pair of chestnut mares would make their way languorously towards her, happy to be petted and whispered to. She told the horses all her secrets and desires, asked them questions, glad they couldn't talk, could never tell. Happy that neither of the horses could lift the phone and tell Jasmine what Sophie had confessed about Liam. About the things he did to her in her dreams. The way she would wake feeling excited but dirty and confused.

They were just dreams, though. She didn't really fancy him. And even if she did – which she didn't, she reminded herself – nothing could ever happen between them.

'Happy new century!' Jasmine cried as she opened the door of her terraced house. She threw her arms around Sophie, who noticed that Jasmine reeked of cannabis. She was pale and appeared to have lost weight, but she was smiling, her eyes bright.

She ushered Sophie into the house. Jasmine's housemate, Helen, was on the threadbare sofa with a bowl of soup, staring at the TV. The electric fire glowed orange and the smell of burning dust filled the air. Helen raised a hand in greeting as Jasmine led Sophie into the kitchen and produced a bottle of white wine from the fridge.

'We need to have a New Year toast. What did you do at the stroke of midnight? Sit around terrified that the millennium bug was going to send planes hurtling out of the sky?'

'I went to the pub with my mum and dad.'

Jasmine laughed. 'I spent mine at home, in my bedroom, watching TV.'

'Oh, God, really? Why?'

Jasmine shrugged. 'I don't really have any friends back home.' Jasmine lived in west London with her parents. Sophie would love to see inside Jasmine's house, imagining it to be full of books, people talking about books, famous authors dropping by for tea. She wished she could press to find out more, but knowing how Jasmine felt about her family she had to be content with the scraps of information she occasionally let slip. For example, she mentioned her brother, Sebastian, a couple of times, though Sophie – an only child, always fascinated to hear about others' siblings – had no idea if the two of them were close.

'I was kind of hoping I'd be able to spend New Year with Liam,' Jasmine said. 'Except he went back to *his* family.'

'That sucks.' Sophie didn't tell Jasmine that she'd had to fight the urge to call Liam at midnight to wish him a happy new millennium.

'Let's go upstairs,' Jasmine said. She passed Helen without a word and led Sophie up the narrow staircase. 'After you.'

Sophie entered the room and stopped dead.

Liam was sitting up in the bed, propped up against some pillows, the sheets gathered about his waist, exposing his naked upper body.

'Happy New Year, Sophie,' he said, flicking cigarette ash into a mug he held on his lap.

She needed to play it cool. She mustn't look at his body, but she couldn't help but glance at him. She couldn't believe how toned he was, muscular and brawny, like he worked out in secret. Biceps and pecs and even abs, a hint of a six-pack. There was a tattoo on his right shoulder, which she caught a glimpse of as he twisted to put the mug on the floor. It was a bird but she couldn't quite make out what kind.

'Jasmine didn't tell me you were here,' she said.

'Really? I hope it's not an unpleasant surprise.'

'We were just getting reacquainted after the break, weren't we?' Jasmine said to Liam, sitting on the bed and kissing him. Sophie almost groaned. Not again.

'Listen,' she said, 'I was just dropping by. I have to get my stuff back to the halls and I'm knackered after the journey down.'

'But we haven't given you your present yet,' Liam said.

'Oh! Yes!' Jasmine jumped off the bed, spilling wine on the sheet. She rummaged in a drawer and brought out a large white envelope. She handed it to Sophie. 'This is your New Millennium present.'

'But I didn't get you anything.'

'Oh, it doesn't matter. Go on, open it. It's exciting.'

'Go on, Sophie,' Liam said from the bed.

She tore her eyes away from his chest and ripped the envelope open. She blinked at the card inside, a single A5 sheet with pictures of hearts and skulls and naked women all over it.

'It's a fifty-pound voucher,' Jasmine said.

'For a tattoo parlour?' Sophie couldn't hide the shock in her voice.

'I got one too.'

Liam lit another cigarette. 'I paid for them. I thought it would be something nice for you both. Jas hasn't got any tattoos either so you could go and lose your tattoo virginity together.'

'I don't know. I've never really thought about getting a tattoo. It's the permanence of it . . .'

'Don't be stupid,' Jasmine said. 'It will be so cool.'

She thought about it. There *was* something exciting about the idea of a tattoo. The idea was kind of . . . sexy.

'Doesn't it hurt?' she asked.

Liam shrugged, his pecs contracting so Sophie had to avert her eyes again.

'A bit. But a little pain—'

Sophie interrupted. 'Don't tell me – Dostoevsky has a quote about that too.'

She meant it as a joke, humour to mask her nervousness about the idea of being tattooed, but Liam's eyes flashed with anger. Or perhaps she imagined it, as a blink later he was smiling.

'So, what do you say? Do you accept the gift?'

If she said no she would look like a chicken, and ungrateful to boot. And the way Liam was looking at her, the challenge in his eyes. What else could she do?

'How about tomorrow?' she said. 'I'd really better get going.'

'I'll see you out,' Liam said, getting out of bed. He was wearing nothing but boxer shorts and Sophie felt her cheeks turn pink.

She waited until he'd pulled some clothes on before looking at him. From the way he was grinning, she was certain he knew how he made her feel. Jasmine was concentrating on rolling a cigarette, apparently oblivious.

Downstairs, Helen had dragged herself off the sofa. She crossed her arms when she saw Liam.

'Has Jasmine talked to you about getting the pest control people in?' Helen asked.

'Yes, don't worry. We'll pay our share.'

'Pest control?' Sophie said.

Liam yawned. 'Yes, apparently we have mice.'

'And cockroaches,' Helen said.

'Cockroaches?' Sophie shuddered. 'Oh, God. You're joking, right?'

'Why would I joke? It's the filthy state this place is in, because only one of us ever does any cleaning round here.'

'You're so bourgeois,' Liam retorted.

Helen glared at him. 'Fuck off, Liam,' she said, before stomping up the stairs to her room.

Sophie looked around the room, sure she could see creatures darting about in the corners.

'Are you all right?' Liam asked.

'No. I can't believe you have roaches. They're vile.' She hugged herself. 'Ugh.'

'You're not scared of them, are you?' He seemed to find the whole thing amusing, watching her with a little smile on his lips. He really could be a dickhead sometimes. 'There are far scarier things, Sophie. I actually think they're quite sweet.'

He opened the door, letting in a blast of cold air.

'Well. Bye,' she said.

'Wait.' He went back into the house, leaving her wondering what was going on, and reappeared a minute later with a small brown paper bag. 'I got you something else. A Christmas present from me.'

He handed it to her, grinning at the surprised expression on her face. She reached into the bag and pulled out a yellowed hardback.

'I found it in a second-hand bookshop. It's a first edition. You told me it was your favourite book as a kid, so I couldn't resist.'

It was a copy of *The Phoenix and the Carpet*. She opened the cover to see that Liam had written a message inside.

For a girl who's really going places. Liam Xx

'I can't accept this.'

'Don't be stupid. It didn't cost much. I just thought you'd like it.'

He was standing very close to her so she could smell him. Cheap soap and cigarettes. In years to come, whenever she detected this smell she would be thrown back to this moment and be reminded of how confused, scared and aroused she had felt.

'I do like it.' She was whispering, afraid Jasmine would appear at any moment. 'But it's not . . . appropriate. You're Jasmine's boyfriend.'

He frowned. 'Come on, Sophie. Just fucking take it.'

'No. I can't. Thank you, but I really can't.'

She turned away, leaving him on the doorstep clutching the battered paperback.

Back in her room, she was about to start unpacking her suitcase, trying hard not to think about Liam or the gift she'd turned down, when a scream came from the room next door.

Sophie jumped up, yanked the door open and peered out. Several other girls had done the same.

Becky stood outside her room, both hands held to her mouth, eyes stretched open in horror, fingers clawing at her head like the character in that painting, *The Scream*. All the blood had drained from her face. Her bulky pink suitcase lay at her feet. She was staring at the room like there was a monster inside. Or a corpse. She made little gibbering noises, unformed words, like the sound of her sanity shattering into tiny fragments.

Sophie reached her first. 'What is it?' she asked in a soothing voice. 'What's happened?'

'My. Room.' That was all Becky could say. She pointed a shaking finger at the closed door then sank to her haunches. She stared up at Sophie, her eyes empty. What had she seen in that room? Sophie didn't want to know.

Two other girls had reached them, Jenny and Ameera, the latter crouching and putting an arm around Becky, who was making the awful noises again, noises that penetrated Sophie's skull, made the inside of her head itch. Sophie guessed that not many people had returned yet or the whole corridor would be filled with gawping, concerned students.

'Go on,' Jenny said. 'Take a look.'

Sophie turned to her. 'Me?'

When she realised no one else was going to make a move, she approached the door, gripped the handle and pushed it open slowly, sticking her head inside then immediately withdrawing it.

'Oh, God, it stinks in there.'

'What of?' Jenny asked, clamping her hand over her nose as the smell escaped the room and reached them.

It smelled like a cut she'd once had that became infected, sweet and rotten.

'What did you see?' whispered Ameera.

Sophie had been hit so hard by the stench that her other senses hadn't kicked in. She moved back towards the door and pushed it open.

'Oh, my God,' said Jenny, as Becky began to wail.

All the clothes and possessions that Becky had left behind were strewn around the room – clothes and underwear on the floor, CDs and books smashed and ripped and scattered. A large cuddly rabbit lay in the middle of the floor, its belly slit open, stuffing bulging out. Its eyes had been pulled out and there was a vibrator stuck into one of the holes, still buzzing. Photos of Becky which were stuck to the wall had been defaced – devil's horns drawn on her head, red pen slashes across her face. A family photo had been torn to shreds and a picture of a woman who was clearly Becky's mum had been rendered obscene, saggy breasts and a dense pubic triangle drawn over her clothes, a crudely rendered penis spurting close to her lips.

That was far from the worst of it.

A washing line had been strung across the room, tied to the wardrobe handle at one end and attached to a nail in the wall at the other. Dead mice had been attached to it by their tails, their plump white bodies hanging motionless, little black eyes open, staring sightlessly. Their stomachs had been slashed open like the rabbit toy beneath them. Stepping closer, forcing herself to confront the horror, Sophie could see that wire had been wrapped around the tails and the washing line to pin them to it. There were seven of them.

'I'll call Security,' Jenny said quietly from the corridor.

Sophie looked back. Becky sat on the floor, arms wrapped around her legs, rocking back and forth, her expression glazed and slack. Her sleeves were pulled up and Sophie was shocked to see scars criss-crossing Becky's forearms. She realised she had never seen Becky in short sleeves. There were no fresh cuts but the scars were evidence that Becky had, at one point, self-harmed.

'Take Becky to the kitchen, give her something to drink.'

The other two girls nodded and led Becky away, leaving Sophie on her own in the room, trying not to look at the dead mice, focusing on the bed.

Photos of Becky and Lucas lay on the pillow, ripped in two. A used condom lay unfurled on the quilt, apparently still containing sperm. She turned her head away. Someone had scrawled words on the mirror in red lipstick.

SLUT. BITCH. SLAG.

DIE IN PAIN.

Small words designed to cause maximum pain.

Next to them were more photos, dim and underexposed, of Becky pressed up against a wall, face screwed up, a man entering her from behind.

Sophie left the room. Her head felt light, legs shaky. The urge to be sick bubbled up through her but she fought it. A minute later, one of the caretakers arrived along with a security guy. Sophie drifted away towards her room. She wasn't going to be sick. She wasn't. She had a horrible feeling about who had done this. She remembered hearing Liam say that Becky needed to be taught a lesson, recalled Jasmine's threat to Becky after she revealed her identity.

No. Surely not. Liam was a self-proclaimed rebel, but she couldn't believe he would do something this hateful. Beneath the pose, he was a nice guy. She had to believe that. Jasmine too. She could be hot-headed, had told Becky she'd cut her tongue out, but there was no way she would do this, surely?

It had to be Lucas, Becky's betrayed boyfriend. Apart from seeing his band play once at the Student Union she didn't know him very well, but he came across as pretty intense on stage, his lyrics all about S&M and suicide. She had thought that was just him playing at being a rock star but maybe it went deeper. And besides, jealousy could turn the mildest people into monsters. The room was full of vile sexual imagery, including the shots exposing Becky's betrayal of Lucas, plus naked photos that had probably been taken for Lucas's benefit. Everything in the room spoke of revenge for Becky's betrayal of her boyfriend. It had to be him.

Chapter 15
Day twenty-four, Wednesday, 29 April, 2015

'Here's to *The Kiss of Death*,' Sophie said, raising her glass of wine. 'May it sell millions.'

'Billions,' said Cassie.

Tracey clinked her glass against the others'. 'I haven't even read it yet. Is it any good?'

'It's a work of genius,' said Cassie, her voice so earnest that Sophie couldn't help but laugh.

At five thirty, confident that they were fully prepared for the launch of Brian's book the following day, Sophie had told the others she wanted to take them for a drink to celebrate the climax of their first marketing campaign.

The wine tasted good: dry and strong, easing the tension in her shoulders a little more with every sip. She was trying not to worry about the launch but it was hard not to. She was still in her probation period – meaning Jackdaw could get rid of her at any point – and with Guy still *persona non grata* in the newspaper world she really couldn't afford for that to happen. If she allowed herself to think about it – both of them jobless with no income – a cold panic squeezed her insides. They had enough money in their current account to pay the mortgage and buy groceries for a couple of months, but that was it. They had debts that they would be unable to pay off while Guy wasn't working. And if Jackdaw sacked her, it certainly wouldn't be easy to walk into another job.

It's not going to happen, she told herself. *Even if Brian's book is a flop, they won't fire me.*

'I can't believe this is the first time we've all been to the pub together,' Sophie said.

'You usually have to get home to your daughter,' said Cassie.

'True.'

Cassie looked thoughtful. 'What's it like having a child? Are you constantly worried that something awful is going to happen to her?'

'Yes. Terrified.' She paused. 'My husband, Guy, tells me I worry too much. But I can't help it. Whenever I'm out with her I have visions of her vanishing or being snatched. Or wandering off and hurting herself.'

'I'm never going to have kids,' Cassie said. 'My career is too important.'

'You can have both,' Tracey pointed out.

Cassie shook her head. 'Not really. Women lose so much ground if they go on maternity leave. And how can you put sufficient energy into your job if you're always worrying about your children?'

Tracey rolled her eyes and said, 'You'll change your mind when your biological clock starts ticking. That's what happened to me. I thought having kids would totally cramp my style, but I love 'em to bits.'

'I won't change my mind.'

Cassie had jabbed Sophie in both of her most sensitive spots. The fear she was neglecting Daisy by working full-time and the worry that what Cassie said was true. But . . .

'That's such sexist bullshit,' Sophie said. 'Men don't worry about having it all. Women should be able to do both, even if it isn't easy. I think I do a pretty good job here and at home.'

She sounded a lot more confident than she really felt.

'Sorry, Sophie. I didn't mean you. I just don't think I'd be very good at doing both.' She smiled disarmingly and Sophie felt her anger drain away.

She went to the bar to get another round of drinks and texted Guy to tell him she'd probably be late.

I'm getting used to it, came his reply.

She stared at her phone. For God's sake. She'd only been late home two or three times. How many times had he gone out, leaving her to do the bedtime routine on her own? She started to compose an angry reply. But before she could hit send her phone pinged again.

Sorry didn't mean to sound passive aggressive. You deserve a night out. Have fun xxx PS Will give Daisy a kiss goodnight from you.

She deleted her text, resisting the urge to reply and point out that his line about giving Daisy a goodnight kiss was also slightly passive aggressive. She headed back to the table. The second glass of wine slipped down as easily as the first. Tracey was drinking quickly too, but Cassie was still nursing her first glass. 'I'm not a big drinker,' she said. 'I don't like the way it makes me lose control.'

'What, of your bladder?' Tracey laughed.

Cassie smiled sweetly. 'Actually, I do need to visit the bathroom. Excuse me.'

When she'd gone, Tracey's expression became serious. 'I hope she's all right. It was awful, wasn't it? The email from Matt, I mean. Even I would have been shocked to get a message like that, and Cassie's such a sensitive little flower. I don't think she's ever had a boyfriend.'

Sophie looked round to check Cassie wasn't on her way back.

'Did you ever witness him harassing her? Or hear him say anything inappropriate?'

'No, not at all. He could be a little bit patronising towards her, especially when she first started. But when he realised how clever she is I thought he basically treated her with respect. But, you know, nothing surprises me anymore. In my last job, a bloke in accounts was caught masturbating at his desk by one of the cleaners, watching a video of women going to the toilet. Turned out he'd put a little CCTV camera in the ladies and was recording us all doing our business.'

'God, that's so creepy.'

'What have I missed?' Cassie had returned from the ladies.

'Not much,' Tracey replied. She winked at Sophie. 'I hope you checked the cubicle for cameras.'

'Huh?'

Tracey laughed and said, 'Oh, nothing.'

'What was Miranda like?' Sophie asked.

'She was too fragile to be a leader,' Cassie said after a thoughtful pause.

That was a curious response. 'What do you mean by that?'

'She was weak. Couldn't cope with the pressure. She ran off before she was sacked. We had a string of bad results last year, loads of books that failed to sell. Miranda said it was bad luck, or tried to blame the books. But she wasn't up to the job.'

'Hey,' Tracey said, deliberately changing the subject. 'Have you seen that outfit they've come up with for Brian? It's hilarious. He looks like the Child Catcher from *Chitty Chitty Bang Bang*.'

Tracey laughed and Sophie found herself studying Cassie, who didn't join in but sat there, running a finger around the rim of her wine glass. What was going on inside that head? Sophie would kill to find out.

Two hours passed. Sophie had lost count of how many glasses of wine she'd consumed. Four? Surely not five. She had lost track of time too, had been ignoring the buzzing of her phone for ages, knowing it would just be Guy trying to find out what time she was coming home. She didn't want him dampening her mood – she was having the best time she'd had in ages. When was the last time she went out and got drunk?

Then her phone began to ring. Why couldn't he leave her alone? She never did this to him when he went out with his journalist colleagues. Or former colleagues, she should say.

'That your husband, trying to find out where you are?' Tracey asked. 'Mine used to do that before he stopped caring. Now he likes it when I go out because he's hoping I'll come home horny. He lies in bed waiting for me with his erec—'

'Too much information!' cried Sophie, putting her hands over her ears.

'How did you meet Guy?' Cassie asked.

Sophie grinned. Should she tell the story? She felt an uncontrollable urge to share. 'It was a bit scandalous, actually.'

'Ooh, this sounds good,' Tracey said.

'Scandalous?' said Cassie.

'Yeah . . . We met at a book fair. He was writing something about the publishing business and I was there with my old company.'

'And your eyes met across a stand of books?' Tracey said.

'Something like that. It was like, well, a thunderclap. Instant attraction, you know. The kind you only experience once or twice in a lifetime.'

'I remember that.' Tracey sighed.

'When you met your husband?' asked Cassie.

115

'Oh, God, no.' She screeched with laughter. 'So why was it scandalous?'

'Because he was married. A newlywed, in fact. He'd only got married a few months before but he said he knew he'd made a mistake while they were still on their honeymoon.'

Sophie glanced up to check the reactions on the other women's faces. Tracey was enrapt but Cassie looked like she had a piece of lemon in her mouth.

'But he felt the thunderclap too, when he met you?' Tracey asked.

'Yeah.' She fell quiet. It seemed like such a long time ago, but she could still, if she concentrated, feel the knot in her stomach, the way her blood seemed to pump harder, the longing, the sickness and the excitement. Meeting in secret, kissing for hours, all the texts that they exchanged expressing their love and lust for one another. He promised he would tell his wife and Sophie's friends warned her he never would.

But then he did.

'The worst bit was when Amanda, his ex-wife, turned up at my office with a bag full of his stuff: clothes, CDs, even a teddy bear that she'd bought him on their wedding day. She dumped it in reception, called me a bitch and ran off crying. It was horrible. I still feel sick with guilt when I think about it.' She was starting to regret telling this tale already. She knew how it made her look, betraying another woman. All the lies Guy had told Amanda when he was sneaking off to meet Sophie. She tried to imagine how she'd feel if he did that to her.

'But you loved him,' Tracey said. 'What else could you do?'

Her phone vibrated again. 'I still love him,' she said. She checked the text. Guy, telling her that Daisy wouldn't sleep, that she kept getting up saying she was having the dream about the 'bad man' again. He was going to let her sleep in their bed, so Sophie might need to spend the night on the sofa.

She stood up, the sudden movement making her head spin. 'I need to go.'

As soon as the cold air hit her face she realised how drunk she was. Disorientated, she took a wrong turn and ended up walking in a circle before she found the bus stop.

As the bus rumbled through Brixton she became sure she was going to throw up so she disembarked. Home was thirty minutes away but the walk should sober her up a little, make the world stop spinning.

As she neared Brockwell Park she became aware of footsteps behind her. She turned but couldn't see anyone there. Jesus, now she was hearing things. Since Josh – who was still in hospital, recovering slowly – had been attacked she'd felt more wary walking by herself. That must be what was happening now. She was jumpy because of what had happened to Josh. There wasn't really anyone following her.

She crossed the street so she was close to the shops, where she felt safer. The jolt of adrenaline had sobered her up a little and she no longer felt like she might vomit. Soon, she was turning in to the street where she lived. She paused to rummage through her bag for her keys – and heard footsteps behind her.

Somebody *was* following her.

She started walking again, quickly, casting a look back over her shoulder. It was a man, featureless in baggy clothes, a hood obscuring his face. At least, she assumed it was a man – it was hard to tell.

The man started to walk faster too.

She found her phone and decided not to call Guy, in case it made the man run at her, so she punched out a short text instead, her fingers shaking, praying Guy would see it immediately.

On our road. Man following me. Come out!

She further increased her pace, scrabbling in her bag for her keys, unable to find them. The man behind her increased his pace too.

She panicked, running towards her flat, abandoning the attempt to find her keys. She would hammer on the door. But what if Guy had already gone to bed? He was probably sulking because she'd stayed out so late. He'd be in bed, Daisy beside him, with his earplugs in. He'd already told her she'd need to sleep on the sofa. Oh, God, the man was jogging behind her, so close, just twenty feet away now. He was going to grab her, pull her into the alleyway, rape her . . .

She reached the door and raised her fist to bang on it.

It opened.

She threw herself inside, a sob breaking in her throat as Guy stepped past her. The man, whose features were still cloaked by darkness, stopped moving.

'I've called the police,' Guy yelled, going out onto the front step. 'They're on their way.'

The man stood still and silent for a moment, then turned and jogged away, back up the road. The darkness swallowed him.

'Have you really called the police?' she asked, after Guy closed the door.

'No. Do you want me to?'

She shook her head. 'What's the point? He'll be long gone by the time they get here.'

The next morning, Guy went outside to put the bins out. He came back in almost immediately, looking like he was going to throw up.

'Those bins smell rancid, don't they?' Sophie said.

'No, it's not that.' He rummaged beneath the sink and found the Marigolds and a carrier bag.

'What are you doing?'

She went to follow him as he headed back outside but he said, 'Wait there.'

She hesitated, then decided she had to see what it was. She heard a cry of disgust come from Guy, who was by the front door. She reached the doorway and clapped her hand to her mouth.

A large white mouse had been superglued to the front door, its nose pointing to the ground, tail stiff with rigor mortis. Its eyes were closed, front teeth protruding, a look of pain frozen on its face. Guy had tried to remove it from the door and part of its fur had pulled away, exposing raw flesh.

Sophie couldn't take her eyes off it, even though she was sure her breakfast was going to come back up. Her mind flashed back to that time at college, in Becky's room, the dead mice hanging there among the trash and the stink. She could hear the terrible gibbering noises Becky had made.

'Do you think it was the man who followed me?'

He shook his head. 'It's got to be something to do with me. Because of the Twitter thing. I've been getting loads of emails from this hard-core feminist action group. They call themselves Sisters in Blood.'

She stared at him.

'They want me to apologise for that tweet, to confess that I'm a misogynist and to repent for what I supposedly said. But I can't, because it wasn't me.' He hung his head. He looked faintly ridiculous, standing there in his pink Marigolds. 'I tried to engage with them, to explain that I'd been hacked, that I'm totally opposed to violence against women. But that just made it worse.'

'Why didn't you tell me?'

'Because I didn't want to worry you. I thought they would just keep emailing me and slagging me off on social media until they got bored and moved on. But they do have a reputation for taking direct action.'

'Maybe it was one of them last night. I couldn't see if it was a man or woman. I assumed it was a he but maybe I was wrong.'

'Mummy, what are you doing?'

Daisy appeared in the hallway, wandering towards them. Sophie quickly ducked through the doorway and swept their daughter up in her arms, carrying her into the living room. She kissed her and put her down on the sofa as Guy appeared behind her.

'Who are you calling?' he asked as she got her phone out.

'The police.'

He grabbed her phone. 'No. Don't.'

'Why shouldn't I?'

'Because if you send the police round to them it will end up in the papers and put the spotlight on me again. We need to starve the situation of oxygen, let it die. That's the only way I'm going to get work again.'

'Or you could apologise.'

'But I didn't do it!'

'I know. But we can't have a group of maniacs supergluing dead mice to our front door! What if Daisy had seen it? I'm going to call the police.'

'No. Let me do it. You need to get to work. Your book is launching today isn't it? *The Kiss of Death*.'

He was right. Reluctantly, she put her phone back in her pocket. 'You promise you'll call them?'

'I promise. As soon as I've cleaned up the mess.'

Chapter 16
Monday, 10 January, 2000

'So have you heard?' Jasmine asked, as soon as she and Sophie met outside the lecture hall. 'Lucas is being kicked out for what he did to Becky's room.'

Sophie stopped walking. The two of them had been in separate lectures and tutorials all day and this was the first time they'd spoken since Sophie had discovered the scene of devastation in the halls of residence. The sight of the seven mice hanging with their bellies slit open kept returning to her, penetrating her dreams.

'Has he confessed?' she asked. It was a bitterly cold afternoon, black clouds rolling in from every direction. The damp and cold crept beneath her clothes and burrowed into her pores.

'No. But he got back a day before Becky, so he had plenty of time to do it, and he had a key to her room which she'd given him.'

'Couldn't they, I don't know, test the condom for DNA?'

'Apparently it wasn't really semen. It was cream.' Jasmine linked her arm through Sophie's and led her towards the campus exit and the train station. Sophie felt nauseous but Jasmine was in good spirits.

'It was horrible,' Sophie said, picturing the scene.

'Yeah. Poor little mice. Hey, apparently there's a line in one of Lucas's songs about "seven blind mice". Maybe he meant to cut out their eyes but—'

'Please. I don't want to think about it. Don't make it even worse.'

Jasmine laughed. 'All right, sorry.'

Sophie didn't tell Jasmine that she was relieved that Lucas appeared to be the guilty party. And a little ashamed. How could she tell her that she had initially suspected Liam or Jasmine herself of doing it?

But, she thought, what about the photographs of Becky having sex with that other guy? Who had taken and sent them to Lucas? Liam had initially acted as if he had nothing to do with it, had said he'd like to shake the person responsible by the hand, but now Sophie wondered. Would he admit it? Knowing him, she would have thought he'd enjoy taking the credit for it. And now she felt too embarrassed to ask him.

Besides, she had something more imminent to worry about.

⌣

'Are you absolutely sure you're up for this?' Jasmine asked for the tenth time as they left the train at Brighton Station.

'Yes. I want to do it. I'm actually really excited about it.'

'You look remarkably pale for someone who's excited.'

'So do you, Jasmine.'

'Really? That's just my make-up.'

Sophie smiled. Jasmine *did* seem a little nervous.

They walked through the underpass and down a steep hill towards the North Laine. The tattoo parlour for which they had vouchers was only a fifteen-minute walk away.

'I thought I'd just wait and see what they have,' Sophie said. 'I assume they have books you can look through?'

'Yes, but we want it to be symbolic, a tattoo that says something about us. And we don't want anything tacky.'

'Like an anchor with Mum written across it.'

'Or a devil. Or Chinese characters. A girl I knew at school had some Chinese characters inked on her lower back and later found out it was the symbol for a gents' toilet. My brother, Sebastian, has a tattoo as well. An evil eye.'

'How come Liam couldn't make it today?'

'He's got a tutorial he can't miss. He skipped quite a few at the end of last term and got into shit, so he's got to be on his best behaviour for a while. I don't want him to get punished.'

'You really love him, don't you?'

The words surprised Sophie as they emerged from her mouth, staining the bitter air.

They clearly surprised Jasmine too, as she stopped walking, pushing her hair out of her face then repeating the gesture as the wind blew it straight back over her eyes.

'We haven't used that word. I don't . . . It makes me uncomfortable.'

'Sorry.' Sophie wished she hadn't blurted the question out. What had she been thinking?

'I can't imagine him saying that he loves me,' Jasmine said. 'He's too cool. I know he likes me. That he desires me. He says amazing things about me, poetic things. The words he uses when we're in bed. The way he looks at me. It's like he wants to eat me.'

She drew her hand across her sternum as she said this, pupils enlarging. Sophie squirmed with awkwardness.

'But, yeah. I do love him.' Jasmine fixed her eyes on Sophie's, a look of uncharacteristic sincerity. 'Don't tell him I said that. Please. Do you promise?'

'I promise.'

Other people pushed past them in the narrow lane but it felt like they were the only two people in the city.

'The way he makes me feel, it's fantastic, but horrible too, you know? I don't just mean when we're having sex, I mean the way he makes me feel in here.' She thumped her chest. 'And here.' She touched her stomach.

Sophie nodded.

'When we were apart at Christmas I felt lost. Lovesick – that's the only way I can describe it. I didn't know what to do with myself. I kept imagining him with other women, girls he knows back home.' She took a deep breath and behind the smile Sophie could see a woman who was losing control. A woman who had got in too deep.

'He's going to hurt me, isn't he?' Jasmine said. 'I know it. And I won't be able to bear it. I couldn't stand the thought of him being with someone else. No, worse than that – I can't stand the thought of him not being with me. This wasn't part of the plan, you know? I swore I'd never fall in love and let anyone have that power over me.'

'I think he really likes you,' Sophie said, aware of how weak that sounded.

Jasmine gave a sad smile. 'He does like me, yes. I know. But not enough. Not forever.'

'Forever's a long time,' Sophie said.

Jasmine stared into a shop window where a T-shirt of Sid Vicious and Nancy Spungen was displayed on a mannequin. Jasmine nodded at the picture of the dead punks. 'They'll be together forever. Even if it's in hell.'

As they entered the tattoo parlour, Sophie's stomach lurched as if she was going over a bump in the road. A woman with long black hair sat behind the counter. Her entire left arm was a sleeve of tattoos: roses and skeletons and ornate playing cards. The Joker and the Ace of Spades. Sophie felt like a little girl as she and Jasmine approached the woman and showed her their vouchers.

'I'm Daphne,' the woman said, her name somehow making Sophie feel more at ease. Daphnes weren't scary, were they? 'Do you know what you want?'

She handed them a thick black book and told them to take a seat. At that point a large man, six foot and fat with a wiry beard and dozens of interlinking tats on every visible part of his flesh except his face, came out through the curtain that divided the area from the back room. He nodded at them and whispered something into Daphne's ear.

Sophie tried to concentrate on the book. She had no idea what she wanted. Her eyes wouldn't focus on the images before her. The mythical creatures, the cartoon characters, the squiggles and, yes, all the Chinese characters. She knew she didn't want a topless lady or the Tasmanian Devil. She didn't want a tiger or a mermaid. Like Jasmine said, she wanted an image that held meaning for her, something symbolic.

'I know, why don't you get a picture of Jasmine, the Disney princess. From *Aladdin*.'

'What? That's a terrible suggestion. Do you really think I'm the kind of person who likes Disney princesses?'

Surprised by Jasmine's anger, Sophie said, 'Sorry. It was only a suggestion.'

'Yeah. Well. I fucking hate having the same name as a Disney princess. I'd rather be named after one of the bad girls. Like what's-her-name from *The Little Mermaid*.'

'Ursula?'

'Yeah. Maybe I should change my name to that. Ursula Smith. It's got a ring to it. Anyway, let's decide what you're going to have first. What about this?' She pointed at a picture of a scorpion, its tail held high. 'You're a Scorpio, aren't you?'

'Yes, but I want something that symbolises escape. New beginnings. Becoming a new person.' Becoming a mature, confident woman.

'A phoenix?'

Sophie loved that idea and wondered why she hadn't come up with it herself.

'We have some great phoenixes,' Daphne said. Sophie hadn't realised the woman was listening to them. Daphne took the book and turned the pages till she found what she was looking for. 'I really like this one.'

It was a picture of a phoenix, wings outstretched, flying upwards, its tail feathers alight like it had just emerged from the flames. Its face was proud, determined. Just like the creature from her favourite book.

'That's beautiful,' Sophie said. 'Now I need to decide where to have it.'

'I'd recommend here.' Daphne touched the back of her shoulder. 'It will look great, trust me.'

Sophie swallowed. She was really going to get this done. It was exciting. Her dad would be horrified. 'OK,' she said. 'That's the one.'

'What about you?' Daphne handed the book back to Jasmine.

'I want the same.'

'The same?'

'Yeah.' She put her arm around Sophie. 'We're sisters. And my boyfriend has a tattoo of a bird too, though it's not a phoenix, just a regular old bird. It will be cool if we all have them.'

'All right,' said Daphne, taking the book back. 'Wait here and Jason will call you through in a minute. Who's going to go first?'

Sophie looked to Jasmine, whose paleness definitely wasn't just down to her make-up. She really was scared.

'I'll go first,' Sophie said.

'If you have any doubts, you know once it's done, that's it. This isn't a henna tattoo. It's permanent. It will be there for the rest of your life.'

'Yes, yes, I know that. I want it done. I want it to be forever.' Sophie crossed her arms.

Daphne retreated behind the counter, a knowing look on her face, and Sophie and Jasmine sat in silence, waiting. Jasmine was surprisingly quiet.

After ten minutes, Jason, the large man with the tattoos all over him, poked his head through the curtain and said, 'Sophie?'

She stood up and, without hesitating, followed him through into the back room. He confirmed which tattoo she wanted and where, then told her to take off her top and sit on the chair, facing the backrest.

'Do I need to take my bra off?' she asked, feeling awkward.

'Just pull the strap down.'

She leaned against a soft cushion and a moment later heard the buzz of the needle, felt a gloved hand rest on the bare flesh of her back.

'Hello, Sophie,' a voice said.

She swivelled round.

'Liam? What the hell—'

He touched his finger to his lips. 'Ssh. I want it to be a surprise for Jas.' He grinned at her. Behind him, Jason sat watching, a smile on his lips.

'Are you qualified?' she asked in a low voice.

'Oh, yes.'

'I didn't know that.'

'There are a lot of things you don't know about me, aren't there? Now, turn around. Let me get closer . . .'

She did as he asked and felt his hand on her back, the buzz of the needle starting up again. Even through the glove, his hand was warm, and she tried to fight the wave of feelings that cascaded through her, the desperate tug of arousal, and she heard Jasmine's words, telling her how much she loved this man, how she couldn't bear to lose him. She wanted to tell him to stop, she didn't want him to do this, it was too intimate, too personal. She couldn't bear for him to be this close to her. But at the same time, she wanted this more than anything, wanted his hands on her flesh, wished he would remove the glove and touch her with his bare fingers. She closed her eyes, praying he couldn't sense how she felt. Couldn't read her mind.

'Hold still,' he said in a soft voice. 'This is going to hurt.'

Chapter 17
Day twenty-nine, Monday, 4 May, 2015

Four days had passed since *The Kiss of Death* had launched; four days since Guy had scraped the remains of the mouse from the door. But, he said, as soon as he'd done this he realised it would be a waste of time reporting it to the police because there was no longer any evidence. Sophie was certain he'd done this deliberately and they'd argued about it, a dark cloud hanging in their flat all weekend until they had a drink together and made up on Sunday night. Perhaps Guy was right: it was best to ignore the incident and wait for the whole thing to blow over. She only hoped it would happen sooner rather than later.

Sophie arrived at her desk on Monday morning to find a Post-it note stuck to her screen.

'Simon was looking for you,' Cassie said, looking up at Sophie through her lashes. As always, she looked perfect, like a box-fresh Barbie.

Little cold fingers of dread fluttered down Sophie's spine as she read the note. *Please come to my office.*

'Any idea what it's about?'

'He didn't say. But he asked me to show him the stats from Skittle.'

Cassie was referring to the *Kiss of Death* app. The strategy had been to get as many teenagers as possible to download the app and share it with their friends. The app then linked through to a page where they could either purchase the ebook or a physical book. Everybody agreed that the 'snog, marry or kill' app was excellent and there was talk of nominating it for an industry award.

'And what do the stats show?' Sophie asked.

'I'd better show you.'

Sophie went round to Cassie's desk and peered at the computer. Cassie pointed at a high number on the screen. 'This shows how many times the app was downloaded.'

'Wow. That's fantastic!'

Sophie brightened. Maybe Simon wanted to congratulate her. Give her a bonus! A fantasy flashed through her head in which Simon handed her a payslip showing a fat sum that would clear her debts and ease her financial worries.

'And this is the other important stat – the number of users who went on to purchase the book.'

Cassie pointed to a glowing zero and the fantasy evaporated.

'Oh, my God.' The fingers of dread turned into fists, punching her in the gut. 'But . . . that's not possible.'

Tracey arrived. 'What's up?'

'Looks like there's a problem with the app,' Cassie said.

'Uh-oh.'

Cassie smiled sweetly at Sophie. 'Don't worry, I'm sure it's a mistake. Maybe you should call Skittle, ask them to check everything's set up correctly.'

Sophie felt ill. 'What about first week sales? Have you checked the system?' She had already checked the ranking on Amazon over the weekend, numerous times in fact. It wasn't great but they had expected to sell most copies on the high street and via the app, so she hadn't been too concerned.

Cassie showed her the number. They'd sold 236 copies. Sickeningly short of their target.

'I'd better go and see Simon.'

'Good luck,' said Tracey.

'It's a disaster,' Simon said the moment Sophie sat down opposite him.

'It must be a mistake. A problem with the reporting.'

He sighed dramatically. 'I've already spoken to Frankie at Skittle. The reporting is correct. We haven't sold *any* copies via the app. Meaning we've just wasted ten thousand pounds.'

Sophie's insides went cold. 'I don't understand.'

Simon picked up his phone and opened the *Kiss of Death* app. He went through the motions of choosing whether to snog, marry or kill someone – he chose snog – then held up the screen. 'Look.'

'What am I looking at?'

'Why don't you try to buy the book?' He handed the phone to her. She pressed the 'Buy Now' button, feeling a mixture of confusion and nausea. It was supposed to take her through to Jackdaw's website, where the customer could order the book at a special price.

'The purchase button doesn't work.'

'Exactly.'

Sophie was glad she was sitting down. 'I don't understand. I'm sure I checked it before it launched. And how could they have missed it out in the first place?'

'They're developers. You should know that developers only do exactly what you tell them to do. Frankie was very apologetic but he said they were waiting to get the link from us before they activated the button. It obviously wasn't checked properly.'

She opened her mouth to say that she thought Cassie was going to check it. *She* had taken on responsibility for the app, at her own insistence. But that would make it look like Sophie was trying to pass the buck. She was the manager. The ultimate responsibility was hers.

'I'm so sorry.'

He sank back into his chair. 'I should have done it myself. You're new. I just thought . . .'

She waited.

'I thought that you were experienced enough not to make such a fundamental error.' Another of his big sighs. 'Skittle are going to contact you to get the link and will fix it straight away. It's such a shame though. The first week is so important.'

'I know,' she said quietly. 'But I promise I'll find a way to fix this. We'll make the second week big.'

'I hope so,' Simon said, studying a printout of the sales report. 'You know we've sunk a lot of budget into this campaign, not to mention the advance we gave the author. Let's just hope nobody tells him about the cock-up, eh?'

Sophie stood up quickly. Cassie was probably emailing Brian right now.

'I'll report back later, and tell you how we're going to turn this around.' She paused by the door. 'I'm really sorry, Simon.'

He waved her out, not looking up from the printout on his desk.

⌣

She almost ran back to her desk, desperate to stop Cassie before she revealed all to Brian. Whenever Brian called to see how things were going, he still asked to talk to Cassie. Sophie had given up, deciding to be more relaxed about it. But if that led to Cassie telling him about the error . . . It was never a good idea to be too honest with authors. They tended to overreact.

Cassie wasn't at her desk.

'I think she went to the ladies,' Tracey said.

But there was nobody in the ladies on their floor. Sophie decided to try the cafeteria, heading down in the lift. Surely they wouldn't fire her for this? It was a stupid mistake, yes. But it was just one mistake. And they didn't know how many books they would have sold via the app anyway because it was an experiment, though she had no doubt Simon was imagining thousands of lost sales.

She felt sick. She hated screwing up, couldn't bear the idea that her boss didn't think she was good at her job. But if they fired her, decided that she hadn't passed her probation, it wouldn't be just her professional pride that suffered. She cursed herself and Cassie. Why hadn't she checked the other woman's work? Because she trusted her not to make basic errors like this. Why hadn't Cassie checked it properly?

She tried to figure out the chain of events that had led to the disaster.

In the meeting at Skittle's office, they had told her everything they would need from her. She had written it all down in her notepad – including the need to send the purchase links to Skittle. When she'd lost the notepad and typed up her notes from memory and sent the instructions to Cassie, she must have forgotten that step.

But Cassie must have known Skittle needed it. Why hadn't she checked it?

Cassie wasn't in the cafeteria, which was almost empty, either. While she was there, Sophie decided to take five minutes out to calm down. She bought a coffee and took it to a quiet table in the corner of the cafe, concealed behind a pillar.

Two women were sitting a few tables away. She recognised their voices. Carla and Gisele were from the other marketing team, the one that looked after books for pre-school children. They hadn't noticed Sophie.

'I'm so glad it wasn't me,' Carla said.

Gisele replied. 'I know, right? Maybe this will bring her down a peg or two.'

'What do you mean?'

'Well. Have you seen the way she swans about, like she's God's gift, thinking all the men in the office are looking at her? I'm glad Michael doesn't work here anymore.'

'She's married though, isn't she?' asked Carla.

'Yeah, to that journalist. The wife-beating one from Twitter.'

Sophie had been about to take a sip of coffee. Her hand froze. They meant Guy. They were talking about her.

'You know how she met her husband, don't you?' Gisele went on. 'He was married when they met. She stole him off his wife.'

How the hell did they know that? But of course, she knew. That evening in the pub with Cassie and Tracey.

'She's not even all that,' Gisele said. 'Though I've heard she's dirty. You know, in bed.'

'Really?'

'Yeah. I heard that when she was at—' The next part of Gisele's sentence was drowned out by the hiss and grind of the coffee machine. Before they could say any more, they got up and left, still not noticing Sophie seated in the corner, gripping her cup of coffee, hands shaking and wondering what else was going to go wrong today.

Who had spread the gossip about her? There were only two candidates. But she had a horrible suspicion she knew which one it was.

She marched back to the office and found Cassie at her desk. She couldn't accuse Cassie of spreading gossip about her – not here, now – so focused on the thing she knew Cassie was definitely responsible for.

'You forgot to send Skittle the purchase link, Cassie.' She explained the consequences of this.

'What? No I didn't.'

'I'm afraid you did. Perhaps I should have checked your work, not trusted that—'

Cassie interrupted her. 'But I didn't forget. I sent them the link the day before the book and app launched. I remember clearly. I'll show you.'

Cassie opened her 'sent items' folder and scrolled down, looking for emails to Frankie at Skittle. There were a few covering other aspects of the app. But the email containing the purchase link wasn't there.

'I don't understand.'

'Check your drafts,' Sophie said.

Cassie clicked into the drafts folder, where emails that had been composed, or started but not sent, were stored. And there it was: the email to Frankie.

'I'm certain I hit send,' Cassie said, her voice quiet.

'Well, you clearly didn't.' Cassie appeared so genuinely stricken that Sophie felt her anger dissipate a little. 'Like I said, I should have checked. It's an unfortunate mistake, that's all.'

'But I don't make mistakes.'

'We all make mistakes, Cassie. Even you.'

Cassie continued to stare at the screen as if she couldn't believe what she was seeing. 'It wasn't my fault,' she said eventually. 'I definitely clicked send. I told you, I've got a photographic memory. I clearly remember doing it. It must have been a system error.'

Sophie sighed. 'Let's move on. There's no point dwelling on it, is there? We need to fix it.'

She went back to her desk. Did Cassie really believe she'd clicked send or was she trying to cover her back? She was either lying or had finally shown she was fallible. Sophie hoped it was the latter. And she still had to deal with the matter of the gossip. She was pretty certain if she asked Cassie about it now she would deny everything. It would have to wait.

Chapter 18
Day thirty-one, Wednesday, 6 May, 2015

'Guy, are you actually listening to me?'

'Sorry, what?'

She leaned closer to him, not wanting the other commuters to overhear, not that any of them would be interested. Even her husband was bored of the topic, would rather flick through Twitter on his phone to see if anyone had insulted him on there this morning than pay attention to her.

It was weird travelling to work with Guy, let alone Daisy, who was kneeling on the seat, nose pressed against the window, watching London whoosh by. Last night Daisy had crept into their bed at two a.m., crying because she'd had the bad dream again, and it had taken ages to get her back to sleep. At four a.m. Sophie had found herself propped on an elbow, while Guy clung to the edge of the mattress and Daisy twitched and grimaced in her sleep. At one point she made a whimpering noise and Sophie pulled her against her, waking three hours later soaked in both their sweat.

Today was Bring Your Daughter to Work Day at Jackdaw. The official day for taking your daughter to the office had been two weeks before, but Natalie – who had control over such things – had been on holiday at the time so had rescheduled it. Sophie wasn't keen on the idea, but Guy had insisted that it would be interesting and educational for Daisy and had asked the school if she could take the day off. He then announced he was going to come too so he could take Daisy home if she got bored. Miraculously, all three of them had found seats on the train.

'I was telling you about Cassie.'

He rolled his eyes.

'Will you please listen to me, rather than acting like you're bored?' She tried to ignore the other commuters whose ears pricked up, suddenly interested, especially a middle-aged woman wearing a red blouse that was too tight across her boobs.

'Sophie, come on. I'm not bored. Honest.'

'Please don't fight, Mummy, Daddy.'

Sophie pulled Daisy onto her lap and said, 'We're not fighting, sweetheart,' as Guy reached across and stroked their daughter's hair.

'I don't like it when you have an argument.'

Sophie wished the woman in the red blouse would stop staring. She inched closer to Guy and gave him a kiss on the cheek to show Daisy and the spectators that she wasn't mad at him.

'She *did* call Brian and tell him about the disaster,' Sophie said, as quietly as she could. 'She actually claims that he rang her, asking how everything was going, whether the sales figures were in yet, and she said she didn't realise it was a secret.'

'Nightmare,' said Guy.

'So now Brian's really pissed off, though he believes Cassie's story about the unsent email. I've come up with a way of rescuing the situation though, touch wood.' She explained her idea briefly, knowing he'd zone out if she went into too much detail. 'You know, I'm starting to wonder if Cassie actually did it all deliberately, to undermine me.'

Following the incident in the cafeteria with Gisele and Carla, Sophie had become increasingly sure that Cassie had spread the gossip. Really, the number one suspect should be Tracey, firstly because she was a motormouth and secondly, she was always chatting with the other two women. But Tracey had thought Sophie's story was funny, romantic even, and Sophie couldn't imagine her reporting it in a negative way. Conversely, she could tell Cassie disapproved, had seemed faintly appalled by the whole thing.

And this had made her think more about the app disaster, arriving at the suspicion that Cassie had deliberately sabotaged her. She had been unreasonably upset about not being allowed to go to the first meeting with Skittle, acting as if Sophie had deliberately wronged her. Could Cassie have hidden her notepad as the first step in this act of revenge, before knowingly screwing up the purchase button, writing an email and saving it to her drafts folder 'accidentally'? Cassie had seemed genuinely surprised, but it did seem unlikely that she could have mistakenly saved it to her drafts instead of hitting send.

She knew that she was thinking like a crazy conspiracy theorist. *She* had fucked up. It was her responsibility. She imagined how Simon would react if she told him she thought she'd been sabotaged.

'Why would she want to undermine you?' Guy asked.

'I don't know! Maybe she thinks they'll promote her again, make her the manager if she gets rid of me.'

'That wouldn't happen though, would it? She doesn't have enough experience.'

'I don't know. She doesn't have enough to be senior executive either. But Simon thinks the sun shines out of her perfect little bottom.' She put on a stupid voice. '*Did you know, she got the highest ever score on the McQuaig?*'

Guy laughed. 'Tell me more about this perfect little bottom.'

'Ho ho.'

She hadn't told Guy about the gossiping women in the cafeteria. She knew he would ask her why she'd been crazy enough to tell her colleagues about the origins of their relationship.

'Sorry. Honestly, Sophie, this Cassie person does sound like a bit of a nightmare.' She wished he'd stop using that word to describe anything negative. He'd been doing it for years but recently it irritated her to an irrational degree. 'But they're not going to fire you, she's not going to get your job.'

She opened her mouth to thank him but stopped when he added, 'And you really can't afford to get fired. We'd be totally screwed.'

She narrowed her eyes at him. 'Yeah. That would be a *nightmare*.'

Sophie held Daisy's hand as they approached the Jackdaw building, with Guy on the other side of their daughter.

'Wow, I didn't realise it would be so grand.'

Daisy tugged at her hand. 'Mummy, they're scary.' She pointed up towards the gargoyles that stared across the street from the terracotta brickwork, grotesque expressions on their faces. Daisy screwed her eyes shut. 'Their horrid faces . . . they look like the man in my dreams.'

'It's not scary inside, poppet. Come on.'

There were seven or eight other girls waiting in reception with their parents, a mix of mums and dads, though no couples, which made Sophie a tad embarrassed. She recognised a few of the other parents, but there was no one else from the marketing department.

Most of the other girls were aged between nine and eleven. At four, Daisy was the youngest by a long way, which made Sophie wonder if she'd made a mistake agreeing to this. Perhaps she should tell Guy to take Daisy out for the day instead, to the Natural History Museum or something.

But she didn't get a chance, as Natalie arrived with a scowling fourteen-year-old in tow. Sophie was amused to see that Natalie's daughter was an emo, dressed all in black, slouching and clearly allergic to public displays of affection from her mother, as she flinched like she'd been stung by nettles whenever Natalie touched her.

Natalie did a quick head count. 'Marvellous, we're all here. Let's see the girls.' The parents pushed their daughters out in front. Lots of keen, pretty, middle-class girls.

'Everyone excited?' Natalie rubbed her hands together like a Girl Scout leader. Most of the girls nodded but Natalie's own daughter stared at the ground like she wished it would turn into quicksand and suck either her or her mother into it. Daisy put her arms in the air and Guy picked her up.

'We're going to learn all about what your mums and dads do every day, how they earn the money that buys you all your lovely things,' Natalie said. 'This is my own little girl, Roxanne.'

Sophie had never seen anyone look so mortified. But as she looked at Roxanne, she realised she reminded her of someone she'd known a long time ago, which sliced the edge off her amusement. Jasmine. She was a younger version of Jasmine.

'Does everyone know what we do here at Jackdaw? We make books – lovely books for children and teenagers.'

Natalie went on in this vein for five minutes, before explaining how the day would work. Each parent would take their daughter to their own office, introduce her to their colleagues and show her what working for the famous children's publisher actually entailed. They were due to convene in the cafeteria at eleven for snacks and drinks. After a tedious run through health and safety points, Natalie clapped her hands and they dispersed.

'I can't wait to see where you work,' Guy said, as they waited by the lift.

'Mummy, I need a wee.'

'OK, I'll take you when we get to my floor.'

'I'm going to wet myself.'

As soon as the lift doors pinged open, Guy said, 'I'll wait here,' while Sophie headed to the restrooms with Daisy.

'Mummy, that lady was funny. The one with the big voice.'

'Her name's Natalie. And please don't tell her she's got a big voice.'

'But she has. If I'm good, can we go to the Rainforest Cafe afterwards?'

Sophie groaned. Guy had promised Daisy this 'treat' but Sophie could think of few things worse than going to that place and sitting among the fake topiary eating mediocre food which appeared to have had some vast jungle tax applied to it. They couldn't afford to throw money away like that, though she had been meaning to have a word with Guy about how much of their dwindling cash reserves he was still frittering away entertaining Daisy.

'We'll see.'

'But Daddy said so.'

'I said we'll see.'

Daisy pulled a face and Sophie had a glimpse of what she'd be like in ten years, a moody scowling teen like Roxanne. 'Meanie.'

When they got back to the lifts, Guy was nowhere in sight. She walked over to her desk, holding Daisy's hand. Tracey made a fuss of Daisy, telling her how pretty she was and trying to engage her in conversation about *Dora the Explorer*. At the next bank of desks,

Gisele raised her eyebrows and swivelled her chair to whisper in Carla's ear.

'I've lost my husband,' Sophie said with a smile. 'Probably wandered off in search of food.'

'I think he's in the kitchen,' Tracey said. 'With Cassie.'

'Can you look after Daisy for a minute while I find him?'

Sophie entered the kitchen to find Cassie leaning back against the work surface. The first thing Sophie noticed was the minuscule skirt Cassie was wearing. Her bare legs were like something off a billboard, lean and smooth and the colour of honey. Cassie could only have been five foot five or so but her legs seemed to make up two-thirds of her body. She was halfway through a laugh, unlike any laugh Sophie had ever heard her emit before, and her eyes sparkled. She had her hand to her mouth as if Guy, who was sitting on a chair gazing at Cassie in a way that made Sophie feel very small, had just said something outrageous.

'Oh, hi, Sophie,' said Cassie. Was it Sophie's imagination or had Cassie had some kind of voice transplant overnight? She sounded like a movie vixen. There was a purr in her throat. 'I found your husband looking all lost and alone by the lifts.'

'Cassie offered to make me a cup of tea,' Guy said, holding his mug aloft.

'Did she?'

'Your husband's very funny,' Cassie purred, running a hand through her shiny hair.

Sophie turned her back on the younger woman. 'Darling, you're not planning on hanging around here all day, are you? You'll get terribly bored.'

'I can look after him,' Cassie said.

'Don't you have a lot of work to do?'

Cassie smoothed her skirt over her slim thighs. 'Yes, you're right. Sorry, Sophie. You're going to be busy with Daisy, aren't you?

And we can't slack off if we're going to turn things round with the *Kiss of Death* app.'

Snog, marry, kill. Sophie knew which one she'd choose right now if Cassie's face appeared on her screen.

Unfortunately, she knew which one Guy would choose too.

Cassie sashayed from the room and Sophie watched Guy's eyes follow her all the way to the door. Following that perfect bottom.

'Is that the one you were telling me about?' Guy said. 'She seems nice.' He stopped when he saw the expression on Sophie's face. 'Yeah, I'd better go. I'll find a coffee shop, send some emails. I'm trying to set up another meeting with Claire.'

'Good. You do that. I'll show you out.'

At the exit, he said, 'Let me know when you want me to pick up Daisy.'

'OK.'

'I love you,' he said.

She felt too annoyed to reply.

In the lift, she pressed the button to hold it, needing a minute to compose herself. Was she being unfair to Guy? A young, attractive woman with gorgeous legs had shown him attention for a minute, laughed at his jokes. It wasn't as if he'd leapt across the kitchen, hoisted Cassie onto the work surface and pulled her knickers off. She just wished he hadn't stared at Cassie like a dog eyeing a steak. Why couldn't he have ignored her, shown more loyalty to her, his wife?

A phrase ran through her head. *Once a cheater, always a cheater.* She pushed it aside. She didn't believe it.

She released the hold button and let the lift ascend till it reached her floor, then headed across the office where Cassie and Tracey stood together by Cassie's computer looking at something on the screen. As Sophie approached, Cassie grinned at her and said, 'Great news. Orders have started to come in from the app.'

'That's . . . Where's Daisy?'

Tracey looked over at her chair.

'She was sitting right there a minute ago, playing a game on my computer.'

Sophie jumped up onto her desk, surprising herself and everyone around her, and turned 360 degrees. 'Daisy?' she called, her voice rising an octave, the name of the person she cared about most quivering in her throat. '*Daisy?*'

Her heart immediately began to thump. Daisy was nowhere to be seen.

Her daughter was gone.

PART TWO

PART TWO

Chapter 19
Day thirty-one, Wednesday, 6 May, 2015

'Daisy?' Sophie shouted again, louder this time. She jumped down from the desk. She needed to stay rational. Daisy had probably wandered off to look for her mum and dad. Sophie sprinted off across the office and checked the kitchen.

Daisy wasn't there.

Sophie gulped down air. *Don't panic.*

Tracey explained that Daisy had been sitting at her desk, playing something on the CBeebies website. The jaunty music was still audible and Sophie experienced a terrifying vision of a future in which every time she heard the *Postman Pat* theme tune she would be plunged into sickening despair, wondering why she had let her little girl, her only child, out of her sight. She would be one of those hollow-eyed mothers you see on the news, appealing to a stranger, asking them to return her child. She would be a husk, zombie-walking through what remained of her life.

She hardly ever let Daisy out of her sight when she was with her. And this was why. She had been right to be scared. If Guy was here she would grab him and say, See? *See?*

'It can't have been long,' Tracey said in a defensive tone. 'We were looking at the sales figures on Cassie's PC.'

Natalie appeared. 'Sophie, I need you to bring . . . What's going on?'

Sophie battled to keep her voice calm. 'My daughter, Daisy. She's disappeared.'

'What?' She glanced around, as if they were all useless and simply weren't looking hard enough. 'Well, she can't have gone far, but I'll call reception, make sure they don't let any little girls wander out on to the street.'

While Natalie talked to reception, Sophie found herself staring at Cassie. *You did something with her*, she found herself thinking. *You.*

She stopped. What was wrong with her? Cassie had been in the kitchen, then here with Tracey. It was physically impossible for her to have done anything with Daisy. Sophie cursed herself. She shouldn't have gone off to find Guy, shouldn't have paused in the lift. She was the one who had been absent. No, worse than that – neglectful.

But there would be plenty of time to beat herself up afterwards. Right now, she needed to find Daisy. If only she could think straight. All she could do was turn in circles, dash from point to point, peering hopelessly beneath desks. She ran over to the stationery cupboard and yanked it open, expecting to see a pair of green eyes blinking out at her. But the cupboard contained nothing but notepads, pens and printer paper. While she was searching, Simon arrived.

'What's going on here?' he said.

Sophie wanted to scream, but Natalie stepped in and told Simon what had happened.

'Oh, yes, it's Bring Your Daughter to Work Day. Well, let's all stay calm and rational.' He flicked his eyes at Sophie as he said this.

Oh, God, he thought she was crazy. Well, maybe she was. She had a right to be crazy at this moment in time, didn't she? She became aware of a hand on her arm. Tracey's.

'We'll find her,' Tracey whispered.

'Where could she have gone?' Simon asked. 'Let's think. One, she could be hiding somewhere in this room—'

'The windows!' Sophie blurted. 'Are any of the windows open?'

Everybody looked. No one was allowed to open the windows when the air conditioning was on. Emails were always being sent around about this issue. But a few rebels who sat on the edges of the office had been known to open them, complaining the room was too stuffy, that they needed fresh air to stop them falling ill. Sophie had witnessed at least one blazing row about it since she'd been here.

The window closest to the kitchen was open now. Sophie ran across the office – and collided with Carla.

'Careful where—'

'Fuck off,' Sophie hissed, pushing past.

Gisele mouthed something at her teammate, a look passing between them that told Sophie she had just confirmed everything they already thought about her. Well, she really didn't give a flying fuck what they thought of her right now, the poisonous, gossiping, lazy . . . She took a deep breath and counted to three as she stormed across the office.

Simon and Natalie followed Sophie and as she reached the window, peering through the crack at the ground far below, Simon caught hold of her.

'Sophie. No child could fit through that gap. You need to calm down.'

She turned to him. She mustn't cry. Not yet. Afterwards, when she was safely holding Daisy in her arms, she could let the tears flow. But not now. Now she needed to do as he said. But first . . .

'What are you doing?' Natalie asked.

'Calling the police.'

Natalie gently took hold of Sophie's wrist and lowered her arm. 'There's no need to do that yet. Come on, she's got to be in the building.'

'But—'

'By the time they get here, we'll have found her. Tell you what, if we don't find her in the next ten minutes, I'll call them myself.'

Natalie led her back across to her desk. Everybody was staring at her. Why were they sitting still? Why wasn't everyone looking for Daisy? She wanted to yell at them, tell them to get off their butts and search for her missing daughter.

'Right,' Simon began as they reached her bank of desks, putting his phone away. 'Two of the reception staff are going from floor to floor looking for her. Natalie, why don't you take all the other kids to the cafeteria to avoid any confusion? I've asked Facilities to send around an email asking everyone to search their immediate surroundings.'

'An email?' Sophie couldn't believe it. 'Some people take forever to read their bloody emails.'

'And an instant message which will pop up on every screen. We've disabled the lifts too so if she goes from floor to floor she'll have to use the stairs. Sophie, you stay here with Tracey so we know exactly where you are and can reunite you with Daisy as soon as we find her. Cassie, you come with me.'

'Cassie? I don't want—' The words came out of her mouth before she could stop them.

Both Simon and Cassie blinked at her. Simon touched her lightly on the shoulder. 'Sophie, don't worry. We'll find her. She's probably found a book she likes the look of and is holed up somewhere reading it.'

Simon and Cassie headed towards the stairwell. Cassie glanced back at Sophie, her expression inscrutable. But Sophie could have sworn she was enjoying this.

Sophie chewed her fingernails, trying to decide whether to call Guy to let him know what was going on. Why should she suffer alone? He should feel this anxiety too.

She shook her head, castigating herself. The worry and fear were curdling her emotions, making her irrational. She would leave it. She'd tell him about it later. Once Daisy was safe.

'Are you OK?' Tracey asked, peering at her.

'It's my heart. I think it's going to burst out of my chest.'

'I'll get someone to make you a cup of tea.' She yelled across the office to a guy at a nearby desk. 'Oi – fetch her a cuppa, will you? With two sugars.'

'I don't want a fucking cup of tea.'

'Don't worry. By the time it's brewed Daisy will be back here and you'll be giving her a cuddle.' She paused. 'I remember when my youngest, Jamie, got lost in the supermarket once. I went mental, was convinced some pervert had abducted him. There are so many paedophiles out there, just waiting for their opportunity to . . . I need to shut up, don't I?'

Sophie could hear the tremor in her own voice as she spoke. 'I'm not so worried about her being snatched by a paedophile, here at work. I'm terrified she's had an accident, is lying hurt somewhere. Or she managed to sneak out the building.' She took a deep breath. 'She's got good road sense though. I've always taught her to wait for the green man, not to wander into the road.'

'I'm sure you're a great mum.'

'I shouldn't have let her out of my sight.'

Tracey frowned. 'It's my fault. I was supposed to be looking after her.'

Sophie checked the time on her phone. 'How long have they been?'

'Just five minutes.'

But a trace of doubt had entered Tracey's voice now. Sophie pictured Daisy lying beneath a fallen cabinet, her little bones crushed, crying weakly to her mummy to save her, nobody there to help.

Sophie got up. 'I can't stand this. I can't wait here. I need to do something.'

'But Simon said—'

'Screw Simon. I'm going to look for her.'

She ran to the doors before Tracey could stop her, narrowly avoiding the young man who'd been sent to fetch her a cup of tea. She left the office and looked up and down the stairwell. Which way would she go? Given a choice, Daisy always gravitated *up* stairs, ever since she was a toddler and learned to climb them on her hands and knees. Sophie ran up the stairs to the fourth floor. This was where the mailroom and computer servers were based, along with several storerooms. She'd only been up here once before, to deliver some books to the mailroom. Surely, if Daisy was hiding (*injured*) anywhere, this was the most likely place.

She headed to the mailroom first. It was dominated by two large franking machines and an enormous plastic bin which was already overflowing with outgoing parcels. The mailman wasn't here. Maybe he was helping to look for Daisy. She scanned the room. Nowhere here for a child to hide, unless she was buried beneath the pile of parcels in the plastic bin. Impossible – but she looked anyway, before heading to the computer server room.

The door to the server room was locked. Was it always locked? Could Daisy have gone in there, hidden and got locked in? She knew these rooms were kept cold, and she pictured her little girl trapped inside, shivering. Turning blue. Dying of hypothermia.

She needed to find someone from IT to unlock the door, suddenly convinced this was where Daisy was.

'Sophie?'

She jumped, clutching her chest. 'Jesus.' It was the man from Facilities, the one who'd unlocked her pedestal and revealed the cockroaches. Dave, that was his name. He looked almost as anxious as she felt. 'I've searched through the storerooms,' he said, trying to keep his voice light.

'I need to get someone to open this door. I think she's in here.'

'I've already checked it, Sophie. She's not in there.'

'Then where the hell is she?' Her voice cracked.

Dave didn't move and Sophie found herself suspecting him for a moment. He had sweat patches under his arms and he was breathing deeply, the classic image of a predatory paedophile. What if he was lying about the server room? What if he was keeping her locked in there till later, when he would sneak Daisy out and take her somewhere.

'Why are you looking at me like that?' he asked.

'I want to see inside the server room.'

'What? I already told you, she's not in there.'

'I want to see for myself!' she yelled, unable to keep her voice down.

He was clearly shocked, muttering, 'Fine, see for yourself.' He unlocked the door and held it open so she could go in. It was freezing inside the little room and, apart from banks of computer equipment, empty.

'See? I told you.' He panted. 'There's no need to be so rude. I was only trying to help.'

She brushed past and headed back to the stairwell. She was pretty sure she heard Dave call her a rude bitch, but she really didn't care right now.

She looked up towards the fifth floor where Franklin and the other powers that be were based. She reached a door at the top of the stairs and tried it.

Locked. For a moment, all her energy deserted her. She leaned against the door, fending off the panic and despair that were trying to consume her. Again, she had a glimpse of life without Daisy, and she found herself staring into a black hole. It would destroy her, destroy her marriage. Life as she knew it would be blown away. She felt the black hole drawing her in, sucking her towards its core. But as her knees threatened to buckle she caught her elbow on the door handle and the jab of pain pulled her out of her fugue state, snapped her back into reality. Daisy wasn't gone yet. She was going to find her. She *had* to find her.

There was a keypad above the door handle. She stared at it for a moment, wondering what the combination might be. Six six six? She almost laughed. Then she heard Simon's voice, growing louder as he ran up the stairs calling her name. When he reached her, he was panting.

'We've found her!'

She followed Simon down the stairs.

'Natalie's got her in her office. Her daughter found her.' He led a dazed Sophie down to the second floor, then along a cold corridor towards Natalie's office.

'I knew there was nothing to worry about,' he said, pushing the door open and ushering her inside. 'See you later, Sophie.'

He strode away – and there she was. Daisy. Sitting on the sofa, wide-eyed and clutching a book to her chest. Natalie's daughter, Roxanne, sat beside her, talking to her in a voice so soft Sophie couldn't hear the words.

She scooped Daisy up and wrapped her arms around her, squeezed her, buried her face in her soft hair, inhaling her, that lovely scent, her favourite smell in the whole world.

'Mummy. You're hurting me.'

'Sorry. Sorry, sweetheart.' She loosened her grip. 'I'm just so happy to see you. I was so worried.'

'Why are you crying?'

Sophie put Daisy down and wiped her eyes with the back of her hand. She felt almost hysterical. She looked up to see both Natalie and Roxanne staring at her.

'Where was she?' Sophie asked, sitting on the sofa and lifting Daisy onto her lap. She glanced down at the book Daisy had been holding. A picture book with an elephant on the cover.

Roxanne answered her question. 'In the library.'

'The . . . library? In the basement?'

Roxanne shrugged. 'Yeah. I got bored listening to Mum bang on about all the important work she does—'

'Roxanne!'

The girl ignored her mother and carried on. 'So I went for a wander. I thought it was weird that the lift wouldn't go down to the basement even though there was a button for it so I went down the stairs. There's, like, a keypad on the door.'

Just like the top floor, Sophie thought.

'But when I tried the door it wasn't actually locked.'

'Somebody must have accidentally left it open,' Natalie said, tutting. 'Roxanne, you shouldn't have gone down there. No one is supposed to go into the library without permission. It's full of rare volumes. Some of the books in there . . . there's only one copy in the world.'

'It was amazing,' Roxanne said, wonder in her voice. 'There were just, like, thousands of children's books. Shelf after shelf, all these books I remember from when I was a kid. And a lot of them were *ancient*. I could have stayed down there all day. But then I found Daisy.' Roxanne looked at the little girl. 'She was sitting in the middle of the floor, reading a book.'

'How did you get in there, sweetheart?' Sophie asked quietly. Her heart hadn't fully recovered yet, and the adrenaline was draining from her body, leaving her feeling queasy and light-headed.

Daisy looked up at her with those big eyes. 'The man took me.'

The breath got stuck in Sophie's throat. Everyone in the room was staring at Daisy.

'What man?'

That was when Daisy began to cry, reacting to the alarm in Sophie's voice. She buried her face in her mum's chest. 'I don't know,' she wailed. She was inconsolable, hyperventilating and clinging to Sophie, digging her sharp little fingers into Sophie's arms.

'Let's leave them alone for a minute,' Natalie said, gesturing for Roxanne to follow her from the room.

Sophie was finally able to calm Daisy down, drying her eyes and cuddling her until her breathing returned to normal. At least being forced to deal with Daisy's upset had made her own trauma recede.

She stroked Daisy's hair.

'The man said—' Daisy broke off, and Sophie feared she was about to start sobbing again.

'It's OK, sweetheart.'

'He said he was your friend, Mummy.'

'My friend?'

'Yes. But when he said it he made this face.' She stuck her bottom lip up in an exaggerated frown.

'What else did he say, Daisy?'

The little girl shook her head. 'Nothing.'

'Are you sure?'

'Nothing' was what Daisy said if you asked her what she'd done at school, or to recount anything she didn't feel like talking about.

Daisy nodded vigorously then looked at Sophie with wide eyes. 'I don't like it here, Mummy. I want you to come home and live with me and Daddy *all* the time. I don't like you doing work.'

This was the first time Daisy had voiced this opinion.

'Come on,' Sophie said. 'Let's go and find Daddy now.'

'And then . . .' She struggled for the words. 'Then you'll leave here forever? Never come back?'

'I have to work, Daisy. Mummy has to earn money to pay for all our nice things.'

Daisy burst into tears again. 'But Mummy. I don't want you to *die.*'

Chapter 20
Day thirty-one, Wednesday, 6 May, 2015

Rain beat against the windscreen as he drove over the bridge, wipers working fast, the lights on the other cars coming on, shining white and red. As he reached the island he experienced that little tingle of excitement, the one he always felt when he knew he was getting closer to her. He was young again, like a teenager heading into the city, his entire life ahead of him.

He licked his lips and turned the radio up.

The land here was flat, almost featureless. There was a kind of beauty to it. An *ugly* beauty, if that were possible. He had been thinking about this a lot recently, how the two things could exist together. When he looked at her face, at the smoothness of her skin, he marvelled at how beautiful she was, how glorious. Making love, that was beautiful too. But some of the things she whispered to him when he was inside her – they were ugly. Cruel and wicked and violent.

Maybe that was why he liked it so much, why he wanted to please her, make her happy.

He was a bad boy.

And she was a bad girl.

His bad girl.

It was dark when he reached the house. He parked the Land Rover by the gates and walked up the long path. A single light burned in an upstairs bedroom. Their room. The place where all the good things happened.

She came to the door wearing a red robe and flung her arms around him, kissing him on the lips. Pressed herself against him, soft breasts against his chest. He felt a stirring below, a frustrating stirring, but he pushed that frustration away, knowing it would be OK.

She took him by the hand and led him inside, and as he took off his coat he felt himself transforming, turning into the real him. She handed him a glass of red wine and they sat together in the sitting room. A candle burned on the mantel and the soft light made her seem even more stunning.

What would he do, where would he be now, if she'd never come into his life?

'Tell me about today,' she said, leaning forward, revealing her shadowy cleavage as her robe fell open. He swallowed. Her eyes were bright, eager. 'Did it work?'

'Yes. It went perfectly. She was going absolutely mad.'

'Oh, God, I wish I could have been there.'

'I have some of it recorded. I'll show it to you.' He produced the memory card containing the video from his jacket pocket and she clapped her hands together.

'And the little girl? Did you deliver the message?'

'Yes.'

She jumped onto his lap and kissed him, taking the memory card from his hand. With her other hand she plucked a little blue pill from the pocket of her robe and held it out on her palm. He wished he didn't need it but said a silent prayer to the scientists who had discovered this miracle. This medicine that made him feel vital, his body doing what it was supposed to. He popped the pill onto his tongue and washed it down with a mouthful of wine.

'Let's watch this while we do it,' she said. 'Can you see her face?'

'Oh, yes.'

'See her suffering?'

'Yes.'

'Brilliant.'

She kissed him deeply, her tongue slipping into his mouth, and he put his hand under the silk robe, caressing her skin. It would take a while for the blue pill to kick in, but that was all right. They had plenty of time. He wouldn't have to leave till the early hours of the morning. And if he got tired at work, he could take another little pill, a white one, to perk himself up. Everything could be controlled. She'd taught him that.

'Let's go upstairs,' she said after a while.

Chapter 21
Day thirty-one, Wednesday, 6 May, 2015

Sophie's body was still knotted with tension hours after Daisy had been found. Not just tension but unease. What Daisy had said had chilled her.

Natalie had told Sophie to take Daisy and go home early. She'd found Guy in the Starbucks near the office and she knew she would never forget the way his expression shifted when he saw her and Daisy standing there: surprise, then a smile, then shock as Sophie crumpled into a tearful heap.

Now he stood before her holding a glass of wine to match the one she'd almost finished. Daisy was in bed, worn out by her adventure.

'So, this man,' Guy asked. 'You have no idea who he might be?'

'No.'

'Did you ask around?'

'I told you, we left straight away. Natalie said she will try to get to the bottom of it. But I think Daisy must have been making it up – you know how imaginative she is. You remember the man in Brixton? With the doll's head?'

'Of course. The one she's been having bad dreams about.'

'Yes. She told me the other day that she was looking for her 'dolly without a head'. She searched her room for it and started crying when she couldn't find it. I think she confuses her dreams with reality. Maybe that's what happened. She felt tired and crept off to find somewhere to take a nap, found her way to the library and fell asleep.'

'And had a dream about a man saying he was your friend?'

'Exactly.'

Guy nodded. 'I guess that makes sense. Four-year-olds, eh? I bet she thought she was in paradise when she found all those books.'

'I know. I'm a little jealous. I'd love to spend some time in that library.' She grew serious again. 'I hope she wasn't too scared. I think it's all connected to me going back to work. I thought she was fine with it, but after what she said today, I'm not so sure. I feel horribly guilty, Guy.'

'She'll get used to it,' he said.

'I don't know. I mean, I know she's at school most of the day. But I hate not being here when she gets home.'

'I'm here.'

'Maybe I should quit.'

Guy sat down beside her. It struck her how tired and scruffy he looked, unshaven with bloodshot eyes, his lips already stained by the wine. Had he sneaked a glass when she was reading Daisy her stories?

'You know that's not an option. And besides, you like work. You need to work, don't you? It's important for you.' He lay his hand on her thigh.

'It is, but not as important as Daisy.' She took a large mouthful of wine, fidgeting until he removed his hand. 'This job isn't turning out how I imagined, anyway. There's all this stuff with Cassie . . .'

She stopped, remembering how Guy had behaved in the kitchen with Cassie before Daisy had vanished. She really didn't want to go there. Not now. She made a conscious decision to let it go.

'Every job's like that when you start, isn't it?' he said. 'You need time to settle in.'

'I guess so.' She paused, aware that what she was about to say would probably sound crazy. But she'd been thinking about it all the way home. 'There's something not right about that place.'

'What do you mean?'

'I don't know. It sounds mad, but it's as if it's cursed. Bad things seem to happen to the people who work there.'

Guy pulled a sceptical face. 'What are you talking about, Sophie?'

'Like . . . like Josh getting beaten up. And my predecessor – apparently she disappeared and nobody knows what happened to her. Also I heard that someone hanged himself in the library. Years ago, but still.'

She took another glug of wine. 'Then there was you losing your job. And what happened with Daisy today.'

She shuddered as she remembered Daisy's words. *I don't want you to die.*

She disappeared into her thoughts for a minute. When she emerged she saw that Guy was looking at her like she had said something crazy, just as she'd feared.

'It's all coincidence, Sophie.'

'I know. I'm sure you're right.' She attempted a smile. 'I guess I'm feeling a little overwrought after what happened today.' She leaned forward and placed her empty glass on the coffee table. 'I think I'm going to go to bed and read.'

'Do you want me to come with you?' Guy leaned towards her. 'I thought maybe . . .'

Now it was her turn to stare at him. 'Guy, I can't believe you think I'd be in the mood. Not after today. I feel emotionally exhausted. Maybe tomorrow.'

She stood up. Her entire body ached, the blood heavy in her veins. She doubted she'd be able to read five pages of her book before she fell asleep.

'Shall I put it on the calendar?' Guy asked. 'Sex, question mark.'

'For God's sake.'

Since he'd lost his job, they always seemed to be hovering on the brink of an argument. Actually, that wasn't fair. It wasn't only Guy; everything that had been going on at Jackdaw was making her tense, too, more irritable and snappy. She hated this version of herself. If she got a decent night's sleep she'd feel better, more normal.

Guy looked contrite. 'I'm sorry, Soph. I was being an idiot. Talking of tomorrow, I'm meeting Claire at eight-thirty in the evening. Will you be able to get home by eight at the latest?'

'I promise.' She walked towards the bedroom, her legs feeling heavier with every step.

As she put her PJs on, she caught a glimpse of herself in the full-length mirror in the corner, her eye drawn to her tattoo. It had been there so long now that she barely noticed it, like a picture that's been hanging in a hallway too long. Actually, that wasn't quite true. The truth was that she didn't want to look at it, because of the memories it brought back. She had considered laser treatment but decided against it, and not because of the pain and cost. The tattoo would remain, a permanent reminder of what she'd lost.

———

She fell asleep and immediately dreamed about the man with the doll's head. He was shuffling through Sophie's office, unnoticed by anyone else. He had something around his neck and Sophie knew exactly what it was. A necklace of dead mice, strung together by their tails. Something moved on his head and she looked closer to see cockroaches, scuttling in and out of the greasy locks of his hair, antennae waving, emitting a ghastly clicking sound.

When he reached Sophie's desk he held up the doll's head like he had in the street. Except it wasn't the doll's head, it was Daisy's. And the old man had morphed into Liam, and he whispered – the same words the man had spoken in Brixton – as blood dripped from Daisy's decapitated neck onto the gleaming surface of Sophie's desk.

'Lovely baby.'

Sophie jerked awake.

Chapter 22
Tuesday, 11 January, 2000

Sophie sat in her room at university, her hand drawn to the sore area on the back of her shoulder like a tongue to a wobbly tooth, constantly wanting to touch the gauze that protected the tattoo. Waking up this morning, the white pulse of nausea had hit her like she'd drunk a bottle of whiskey the night before. *Liam's hands on her skin. The tattoo, with the word 'Forever' etched beneath the burning phoenix.* What had she done? She grabbed her dressing gown and ran out into the hallway, barging past Jenny and locking herself in a cubicle, head bent over the bowl, dry retching.

Tea, toast and sunlight made her feel a little more human. She'd dreamed of flying and falling, and as the morning progressed the echoes of those dreams, the sensation of swooping and plummeting, Icarus-like, receded. The only thing she couldn't shake was the feeling of something, or somebody, by her side as she moved through the air. A dark shape, a shadow just beyond her line of sight. She drank more tea and told herself there was nothing to be gained from wishing. *Je ne regrette rien*, she whispered to herself, giggling.

The important thing was to do nothing else she might regret.

'I can't believe you chickened out.'

Jasmine sat opposite her in the coffee shop, fiddling with a sachet of brown sugar, a sheepish expression on her face. Her black nails were chipped, the cuticles bitten and bloody.

'It was when I saw the needle,' Jasmine said. 'I completely freaked out. Liam said I went completely white and my eyes rolled up into my head.' She laughed. 'He said I'd make a lousy heroin addict.'

Sophie wasn't sure what to say to that. After her tattoo was finished, Sophie had headed home, saying goodbye to Jasmine in the waiting room.

'Did you know Liam was going to do the tattoos?'

'Yeah.' Was Sophie imagining it or did Jasmine's face darken for a split second? 'But he asked me not to tell you. He wanted it to be a surprise.'

'Where did he learn to do it?'

Jasmine shrugged and sipped her coffee. 'He won't tell me. Maybe he grew up in a tattoo parlour.' Liam still hadn't told Jasmine anything about his past and the two women loved to speculate about his childhood when he wasn't around.

'Or a circus.'

Jasmine's face lit up. 'Yes! Wouldn't that be cool? His dad's a strongman and his mum's one of those bendy contortionist women. They taught him to walk the high wire when he was three and his best friend growing up was a circus pony.'

'Maybe *I* should ask him,' Sophie said, when they'd stopped laughing.

'Huh?'

'Ask him about his background, where he's from, etcetera.'

Jasmine's eyes narrowed. 'What makes you think he'd tell *you*?'

Sophie was speechless for a moment. 'I just thought, maybe he's being deliberately mysterious with you because you're his girlfriend. He thinks it makes him more alluring. But he might tell a friend.'

Jasmine was still giving her that look. 'Why is your face going pink?'

Sophie touched her cheek, surprised by how warm it felt.

'Do you fancy him?'

'Jasmine! Of course I don't.'

'Now your face is bright red.'

'It's because you're making me really uncomfortable.' She was aware of people at nearby tables staring at them. 'You're my best friend and he's your boyfriend. Maybe I shouldn't describe him as a friend – I only know him because of you. I wouldn't be his friend otherwise.'

'Why, what's wrong with him?'

Sophie made an exasperated noise. 'Jasmine, this is ridiculous.'

Jasmine rubbed her face. 'You're right. I'm sorry.' She leaned closer. 'Liam and I had a big fight last night. I guess I'm still feeling fragile. Especially after everything I said to you yesterday about, you know.'

About being in love with him.

'Do you want to talk about it? The fight, I mean,' Sophie asked.

Jasmine sighed. 'Not really. But it was about him being so secretive. I accused him of not trusting me.' She shook her head. 'You'll never guess what he said.'

'That you can't trust anyone?'

Again, her eyes narrowed, making Sophie wish she hadn't said anything. 'How did you know that?'

'No reason. It's just . . . it's part of his pose, isn't it? That you can never really know another person. And I suppose trust is part of that.'

Jasmine stared at the tabletop, tracing patterns in the sugar she'd spilled. 'It's not a pose.'

They sat in silence for a moment, surrounded by the clatter of crockery, the babble of the students around them. Then Jasmine nodded to Sophie and whispered, 'Look.'

It was Becky. As she entered the coffee shop a hush fell. Becky stopped and almost retreated from the room.

'She's coming over here,' Jasmine hissed.

Becky glided across to their table like a ghost. She was as pale as the mice Sophie had seen hanging in her room, with a dazed demeanour, like she was on heavy antidepressants. She stared at Jasmine, who refused to look at her. Eventually, Becky's attention turned to Sophie.

'You.'

'Hi. How . . . how are you feeling?'

Becky blinked at her. Her hair was lank and she had no make-up on, revealing the dark circles around her bloodshot eyes. She wore a long coat and slippers that had blades of damp grass stuck to them. Had she been lying on a lawn somewhere? Was she on drugs? It was only two days since the incident. Shouldn't someone be looking after her?

For the last couple of nights, Sophie had lain awake remembering what she'd seen in the room next door. Becky was staying temporarily in an empty room in halls and Sophie wondered why she hadn't gone home to her parents. She glanced across the table at Jasmine, who was once again refusing to meet Becky's eye. If Liam or Jasmine were responsible for taking the photos that had exposed Becky's infidelity, then they had set in motion the events that had turned Becky into the wreck that stood before them now. Sophie was shocked by how traumatised Becky was, how fragile the girl she'd seen as her college nemesis had proven herself to be, and felt a twinge of guilt for her role in bringing Becky into

Jasmine and Liam's orbit. She also hoped she never got on their bad side.

Becky shuffled closer and lay her hands flat on the table, leaning into Sophie's face. Her breath was stale, fetid, teeth coated with plaque. Everyone in the coffee shop was watching them.

'You win,' she said, her eyes shifting sideways to Jasmine.

She leaned even closer, her stale breath making Sophie flinch.

'Becky, I think you should be resting. Do you want me to—'

'I'm going home.'

Jasmine finally looked at Becky. 'Best place for you.'

Becky pulled herself upright and pointed a trembling finger at Jasmine. Her voice was so quiet Sophie could hardly hear it. She thought she said, 'I know all about you.' Then she turned away and glided out of the coffee shop, shuffling across the campus till she vanished from sight.

A week later, Becky was gone.

Sophie was heading to a lecture when she bumped into David, a tall, popular guy from her course. He had the university scarf wrapped around his neck, his nose pink from the cold. Sophie usually sat next to him when Jasmine wasn't around. David was taking drama as well as English and was always trying to persuade Sophie that she should be an actor because she had what he called a memorable face.

He looked her up and down. 'Let's see it,' he said.

'Huh?'

'Your tattoo. I heard all about it.'

'It's a bit cold to start taking my clothes off out here.'

'Your *entirely black* clothes. I'm concerned about you, Sophie. You're turning into them. Your weirdo friends.' His eyes flicked left and right. 'You need to be careful of that bloke. He's a psycho.'

'What are you talking about?'

'He was in a club in town, just before Christmas, wasted and acting like a dickhead. It's amazing he didn't get into a fight. He was going on and on about how he and his girlfriend had a suicide pact, how they were too beautiful to live, too special for this shithole.'

Sophie was too shocked to respond.

'It was clearly all bullshit. And I know they're your friends so you probably don't want to hear it but you're a nice girl, Sophie. I wouldn't want you to be tainted because of your association with those two.'

'You're right,' she said. 'They are my friends. They stuck up for me when other people were horrible to me.'

His eyes shone at the chance to impart gossip. 'Becky, you mean? Have you heard?'

Sophie hurried back to Becky's room and found the door standing open, the room emptied of Becky's possessions. She'd done what she'd said in the coffee shop: left college and fled home to her parents.

Later, she went to see Jasmine and Liam, still angry about what David had said. They'd had the pest control people round, putting down traps and spraying some noxious substance around. Sophie was afraid to go into the kitchen in case she encountered a fleeing cockroach.

Liam smiled when Sophie told him the news. 'Good riddance,' he said. He held a glue trap in his hand, a cockroach stuck to it, legs waving feebly. Sophie recoiled.

'If only,' he added, poking at the roach, 'all pests were that easy to get rid of.'

Sophie stared at him. 'What do you mean by that? Was it you? Did *you* do that to her room?'

If he said yes, Sophie knew that their friendship would be over. She held her breath.

'Of course I didn't. Jesus, Sophie. Do you really think I would do something like that?'

She realised she believed him, and exhaled with relief. 'But you did take the photos of Becky having sex with that guy outside the Union? And sent them to Lucas?'

He touched the tip of one of the cockroach's legs and Sophie shuddered. 'Maybe.'

'That means yes.'

A little smile. 'Well, the opportunity was too good to miss. I saw her sneaking out with that guy and followed. Luckily, I had my camera with me. I thought Lucas should know.'

'Come off it, Liam, that wasn't your real motivation. You wanted to get back at her for telling everyone about Jasmine.'

He shrugged. 'You got me, detective. But it wasn't just that. I was thinking of you. She was a bitch to you too, wasn't she? And I know you hated having to listen to her partying in her room every night. Becky never thought about other people. She got what she deserved. Though I had no idea Lucas would do anything other than dump her. I'm quite impressed, actually. Who'd have thought he'd have such a baroque imagination?'

Sophie sat down and rubbed her face, the image of Becky gibbering outside her room coming back to her. 'You wouldn't say that if you'd seen her. If it had been me, I would be horrified, sickened, feel violated and upset, but I'd get over it. Becky, though . . . it was like something broke inside her. Like she had no mental defence against it. She wasn't strong enough to cope.'

'If you're not strong, you shouldn't pick fights.'

Sophie turned as Jasmine entered the room.

'I'm happy she's gone,' Jasmine said.

Sophie got up from the frayed armchair. 'Because now she can't tell anyone anything about you?'

Jasmine, who had gone over to stand beside Liam, didn't respond.

Sophie swallowed. Her tongue was dry. 'What did Becky mean, when she said she knew about you?'

Jasmine took the glue trap from Liam's hand and stared at the wriggling cockroach like she was trying to set it on fire with her eyes. Then her demeanour changed in an instant. She laughed, handed the trap back to Liam and put her arm around Sophie's shoulders. 'She didn't know anything, Sophie. She was just trying to freak me out.'

'But—'

'She couldn't know anything. Because there's nothing to know. Now, why don't we go out, get some lunch? My treat.'

'Her granddad sent her some money,' Liam said.

'I'd say it was guilt money,' Jasmine muttered, 'if I thought he were even remotely capable of it.'

'What do you mean?'

But Jasmine had moved on, acting as if spring had just arrived. Indeed, bright winter sunshine poured through the window, lighting up the room. 'Where shall we go? I heard there's a new veggie cafe in the Lanes. Or we could go for an Indian.' She pulled Liam into her arms and pressed herself against him. 'I've got a big appetite.'

Liam looked at Sophie over Jasmine's shoulder, a broad smile on his face, a smile that told Sophie that she was part of this group, that they loved her. In that moment, she cast aside her unease and reminded herself that these were her friends, her best friends, the only people who really understood her, who had taken an interest in her.

She loved them too. And, she admitted to herself with a twinge of guilt, she was glad Becky had gone.

Chapter 23
Day thirty-two, Thursday, 7 May, 2015

At lunchtime, Sophie bumped into Chris from the design department in the cafeteria.

'Josh went home yesterday,' Chris said. 'Back to his parents' place in Teddington.'

'That's great news!' But then she noticed the scowl on Chris's face. 'What's the matter?'

'I just think it's a bit off that you haven't been to see him since that first day.'

She recoiled as if he'd slapped her. 'Chris, I haven't had time. I've been so busy.'

'Yeah. Being busy – the great modern disease. But you've known him longer than anyone else here, and most people have made the effort. Even Cassie went to see him.'

'You're kidding?'

'No. She went to apologise for what happened between them. I thought that was pretty big of her, actually. And now Josh knows how much pressure she was under—' He glared at Sophie. 'He understands why Cassie acted like she did.'

Sophie shook her head. 'You've lost me.'

'Yeah.' He swallowed, his Adam's apple bobbing. 'I think you've lost a friend too.'

He walked away, head held high. Sophie watched him go, wondering what the hell had just happened. She tried to unpick what Chris had said, to make sense of it. Firstly, why was Chris so angry with her? She could only assume that he and Josh were more than colleagues. Secondly, what had Chris meant when he said Josh understood why Cassie had acted like she did? Did they think Sophie had put Cassie under so much pressure to get those stupid banners made that her behaviour was Sophie's fault?

Is that what Cassie had told him?

Walking back to her desk, she slowed down and watched Cassie at her desk, tapping away at the keyboard. Unaware that she was being watched, Cassie tucked some loose strands of hair behind her ear and picked up her mobile, smiling at the screen. She tapped out a message then replaced it on her desk. When she noticed Sophie watching her she reacted like she'd been caught stealing. A moment later, Cassie had composed herself and was gazing serenely at her computer again.

Sophie wondered what to do. Confront Cassie and ask her what she'd said to Josh? No, Cassie wouldn't be honest. It was better to ask Josh himself. At her desk, she sent Josh a long message, telling him that she hoped he was OK and if he needed anything she was there for him, that he should give her a ring. She added: *Chris told me you're upset with me but I don't know what I've done. Can we talk? Maybe I could come and see you? x*

As soon as she sent the message, an IM popped up on her screen. It was Simon, asking if she could pop in to see him at 3.30. He wanted to run through some preliminary ideas for the next big marketing campaign, and 'have a little look' at the budget. He also wanted to discuss the campaign for Brian's book and 'lessons learned'. She told him that was fine.

At three twenty-five he called her again and asked if she minded putting the meeting back to four thirty as something had come up. Actually, it might be closer to five, if that was OK. He'd call her as soon as he was ready.

'No problem,' she said. She knew that she needed to leave the office by seven at the latest so Guy could make his meeting with Claire. But she didn't want to tell Simon that, not after the Skittle fiasco, not after she'd left the office before lunch the day before.

'Don't worry,' Simon said, displaying an uncanny ability to read her mind. 'It won't take long. Just a quick chat.'

'Oh, I'm not worried.'

She absorbed herself in her work, not noticing the time until Tracey stood up and said, 'See you tomorrow.'

Five thirty. Where was Simon? As Tracey walked off, Sophie's phone buzzed. It was Guy.

Hiya. You haven't forgotten about tonight, have you? Xx

She replied. *No of course not. I'll be leaving soon. Just got a thing to finish off. Hope Daisy's OK xxx*

'Come on, Simon,' she said aloud.

'Everything OK?' Cassie asked.

'Absolutely fine.'

'Guy's got his meeting with Claire tonight, hasn't he?'

'How—?' Sophie's desk phone rang before she could complete the sentence. It was Simon, apologising and asking if she could come to his office now, promising it would be a quick chat.

How did Cassie know about Guy's meeting? She had no memory of telling her. But maybe she had, absent-mindedly. Or maybe Cassie had overheard her telling someone else. She didn't have time to worry about that right now.

She reached Simon's office and found him sitting on his little sofa, feet on his coffee table, an inch of hairy white ankle on show. A manuscript rested on his belly. This was the next big book they were going to be working on, a novel called *The Devil's Work*.

'Come in, come in. I've just been reading this. It's a masterpiece.'

Sophie sat down at the desk.

'What's it about?'

He smiled. 'You'll have to read it to find out. But I think this could be the next *Hunger Games* or *Twilight*.'

She picked up the manuscript. There was no name on the front sheet. 'Who's the author?'

'I don't know. They've chosen to remain anonymous,' he whispered, as if they were in a crowded room. 'I think it's a famous author, a big name. But they want the book to succeed on merit, not because of who they are.'

'Wow.' This was exciting.

'I've started to work on the budget for it.'

He swivelled the laptop on the desk so she could see a spreadsheet that was filled with numbers, and listened as Simon started to talk through the different columns, asking for her opinion about newspaper ads, billboards, advertorials and deals with newspapers. Fifteen minutes in and they were still only on the second column of this spreadsheet, which stretched beyond the edge of the screen.

She tried to keep her answers short and not ask too many questions. This was maddening. She was interested but needed the meeting to finish as quickly as possible so she could get home. Simon strode about the office making notes on his whiteboard and showing absolutely no sign of wanting the meeting to come to an end. Sophie sneaked a look at her phone and saw that it was already six fifteen. Oh, God, she should tell him she needed to go, but she couldn't. After the fiasco with the app, she needed Simon to believe she was fully committed to this job. She *was* fully committed. Despite everything, she loved it here. If only this meeting didn't have to take place on an evening when it was crucial for her to get home by eight.

Stay calm, she told herself. Plenty of time. She might have to run to the Tube but it would be fine.

Half an hour later she hoped her twitchiness wasn't visible. Simon was still at his whiteboard, working out projections for how many units they could shift. Halfway through he told her he needed the loo and left the office, not coming back for ten minutes. Finally, at six fifty, he put his marker pen down and threw himself onto the sofa.

'Well,' he said. 'I think we've made some great progress here. Good stuff. Sorry it took a little longer than expected.'

'That's fine.'

She went to stand up.

'Before you go . . .'

She sat back down, trying to keep her face blank, her breathing even.

'I was thinking about your staffing issues.'

'Oh?'

'Yes. I tried to persuade the powers that be that we need to hire someone new to join your team. But I'm afraid they said no.'

'Oh.'

'Times are tough at the moment, Sophie. Now, if Brian's book had done better . . .' He sighed. 'Still, I am sure this one, *The Devil's Work*, will be a big hit. And then we'll be able to hire that new assistant. Perhaps we should have a chat now about how you, Tracey and Cassie can manage your workload effectively.'

Inside her head, she was screaming. She was going to have to tell him she needed to go.

His phone chirped and he glanced at it. He slapped himself on the forehead.

'Oh, holy cow – I didn't realise how late it is. I need to get going. I'm meant to be meeting someone.'

Thank God.

'So I can go?'

But he was ignoring her now, gathering up his things, throwing them into his briefcase.

She walked at top speed back to her desk. Cassie had gone, as had everyone else in the office. It was 7.05. If she was really lucky with the Tube connections and got a cab from Herne Hill station to home, she *might* just make it. Her phone kept vibrating, and she knew it would be messages from Guy asking her where she was.

She badly needed the toilet so popped into the ladies, even though she knew it would delay her by a few minutes. Then she half-ran towards the exit and pressed the button to call the lift. She could hear it whirring and clunking somewhere in the shaft. She pressed the button again, stabbing at it repeatedly. If anyone had been around she was sure they would have been able to hear her heart. There was a pain in her chest. She cursed Simon and the technology that was ganging up on her and headed to the stairs, running down them as fast as she could, one shoe almost falling off, causing her to stumble and jar her ankle painfully. She took a deep breath and finally reached the bottom of the stairs.

The reception area was empty and dark.

She headed over to the revolving doors and pushed at them. They wouldn't move. She pushed harder. No, they were locked. Trying to stay calm she tried the other door. It wouldn't shift either. There was no emergency exit button or bar.

Don't panic, she told herself. But she couldn't help it.

She was locked in.

Chapter 24
Day thirty-two, Thursday, 7 May, 2015

Sophie headed over to the reception desk. There had to be some way of opening the doors. She groped around in the half-light but found nothing. She sat on the receptionist's chair for a moment, to calm down, ignoring the constant buzzing of her phone. She knew she needed to let Guy know she was going to be late, really late, but before that she needed to figure out what to do.

First, she should check there was no one else stuck in the building. She walked up to the next floor, her ankle tender as she climbed the stairs. All the lights were off. She called, 'Hello? Anyone here?', feeling foolish and unable to get any volume into her voice. As she turned she caught sight of somebody, a ghastly pale woman with wild eyes. She jumped, then realised it was her own reflection. She looked half mad.

The second floor was empty too. Soon she was back on the third. The lights were on but it felt eerie, silent, apart from the faint electric buzz. She really wanted to get out of here. But . . .

'Of course,' she said aloud. The fire exits. The door that led to the fire exit was over by the kitchen. She remembered being talked through the fire procedures on her first day, though there hadn't been any drills since then. She carried her bag over to the door and pushed it, expecting it to open and lead her into the emergency stairwell.

The door, like those downstairs, was locked.

She couldn't believe it. How could this door be locked? Surely that was illegal. She shoved harder, in case it was stuck, but there was no give.

Feeling light-headed, she headed up the stairs to the fourth floor and located the corresponding fire door. This one, too, was locked.

Heart fluttering, she did the same down on the second floor with the same result.

That was it. She was going to have to call someone. She had been delaying calling Guy because she knew he would be furious with her and she didn't want to have that conversation until she knew exactly when she'd be home.

She called Guy on her way back up to the third floor. The phone rang seven, eight times then went to voicemail. She ended the call and tried to ring him again. As she waited for him to pick up, the phone chimed to let her know a message had arrived.

Where are you? Don't forget you need to be home by 8. Xx

What should she do? It was seven twenty. If she could get out now there was a chance she could make it home. Even if she was ten or fifteen minutes late, she was sure Guy could make his meeting. If she told him she was locked in the office, he would start freaking out. And it was so embarrassing.

She sent a reply. *Just got held up. Don't worry, I'll be there. Xx*

Bang.

She raised her face to the ceiling tiles, her heart echoing the noise that had come from above. She hadn't imagined it, had she? It sounded like somebody had dropped a heavy object somewhere above her head.

183

Someone was here, in the building. This was good news. She wasn't alone. Whoever it was would probably be able to let her out. Maybe it was the guy who worked in the mailroom. She'd heard he often worked late. Imagine how astonished he'd be when she knocked on his door.

She was surprised how rubbery her legs felt when she got to her feet and walked out to the stairwell. The lift was here on the third floor, the door standing open. She pressed '4'. As the lift ascended she tried to imagine what the mailman could have dropped to make such a noise.

It was dark on the fourth floor. Silent. She peered out of the lift before leaving it, then pushed open the door that led to the mail and storerooms.

'Hello?' she called.

No response. There were no windows in this part of the building and it was pitch black, a darkness that threatened to swallow her whole. There couldn't be anyone here. She must have imagined the noise. Or perhaps it was something electrical, the server making a loud noise. Did servers do that? She shut the door and was about to head down when she heard it again.

Bang.

The noise had come from above her head again, but even louder than before. The fifth floor. Was somebody up there?

This is crazy, she told herself, as she found herself treading up the stairs to the fifth floor. *You should go back down to your desk, call somebody to let you out.*

She found herself confronted by the locked door that kept the hoi polloi off the top floor. She pressed her ear to the door and felt it move a fraction. She gave it a speculative push – and it opened.

She stepped through into a dark corridor lined with closed doors. Using the torch on her phone to provide light, Sophie walked slowly past the offices of the CEO and several of the directors. Then a pair of doors with no names on and finally a door at the end bearing Franklin Bird's name.

There was a light coming from beneath it.

Sophie hesitated. Should she knock? Breathing deeply, she put her ear to the door. The wood was cold against her face.

She thought she could hear something, a sound like somebody moving around slowly. She knew she wasn't supposed to be up here, but she had a good reason. And Franklin had said if she ever needed anything . . .

She knocked. And waited.

No one came to the door. She forced herself to knock again, but again nobody answered. She pressed her ear against the cool wood again, was certain she could hear movement.

Sooooo–phie.

She spun round, her insides flooded with cold. Someone behind her had whispered her name. But there was no one in the corridor and the door to the stairwell was closed. Her heart thudded and the rubbery sensation had returned to her legs.

'Get a grip,' she muttered to herself. Maybe there was someone downstairs, someone who realised she was here, locked in. The person who'd made the banging noise, calling her.

She hurried to the end of the corridor, through the door that was normally locked and back out into the stairwell, then headed down to the third floor, pausing by the double doors of her office.

'Hello?' she called, but there was no reply. 'Is anyone there?'

There was no one in her office, no sounds of anyone moving around. Had she imagined it?

Oh, God, she thought. *I'm going crazy.* She had a flash of herself sitting in a corridor, rocking back and forth, making a terrible gibbering noise. She shook her head and sweat dripped into her eyes. When had she started sweating? She gulped down air, telling herself to calm down, wiping her wet brow with her forearm.

Walking away from the doors towards the lifts, she checked the time on her phone. It was eight o'clock. How the hell had that happened? Instantly, a text arrived from Guy.

I've cancelled the meeting. Thanks a lot. Daisy is fine, in case you're wondering.

She swallowed. She didn't blame him for being angry, but once he knew why this had happened, he'd understand. And how did he know she hadn't had an accident? She began to tap out a reply as fast as she could, but she was tense and clumsy and only got as far as *I'm so sorry* before hitting send accidentally. As she typed the second half of the message, explaining what had happened, another message arrived.

I'm so mad I don't want to talk to you so I'm switching off my phone. See you later.

Fuck. She tried to ring him but it went straight to voicemail. He really had turned off his phone.

She leaned against the wall, trying to think straight. She needed to get someone to come and let her out. But who? This was Simon's fault, but he'd said he was meeting someone. She didn't have Natalie's number. She was going to have to call the police. She looked up the number for her local station on her phone and called them, explaining what had happened to the amused-sounding police officer who picked up.

'OK,' he said. 'Do you know who manages the building?'

'I think it's owned by the company. I don't know.' She was aware that her voice sounded shaky, panicky. She babbled something about trying to find out but he interrupted.

'It's all right, madam. Sit tight and we'll find someone to come and let you out.'

She hung up, feeling relieved and embarrassed.

'OK, Sophie,' she said to herself. 'You'll soon be out of—'

She heard a thump from somewhere beneath her and dropped the phone. She quickly scooped it up but the police officer had gone. She remembered Matt telling her about the ghost in the library and her stomach flipped over before she had time to remind herself that she didn't believe in such things.

So who was that sobbing?

The noise drifted up the stairwell, chilling Sophie to the core. A woman, sobbing.

She stuck her head through the door into the stairwell and called out, 'Hello? Who's there?'

The sobbing continued, and then changed to something else. Something worse. A woman, begging. 'Please, please don't hurt me. I'll be good, I'll be good, I swear. Not the needles, please . . .'

And then the woman screamed, a cry of pain and anguish. A scream of despair.

Sophie darted out of the stairwell and shoved through the double doors into her office, her legs almost giving out beneath her, her heart thumping like the footsteps she'd heard. She looked around, trying not to panic. Who was the woman being tortured? What could she do to stop it? What kind of weapon can you find in an office? She ran to her desk and picked up a hole punch, the largest item she could find. That was no good. A fucking hole punch? She giggled hysterically as a shadow appeared beyond the double doors.

Another blood-chilling scream.

What had Matt said about the ghost? Someone had committed suicide in the library.

Was that what Sophie was hearing now? The ghost of that suicide victim?

All rational thought left her. She shoved her swivel chair aside and dropped to her hands and knees, crawling beneath the desk – and coming face to face with a cockroach.

It stood motionless, little antennae or feelers or whatever the fuck you called them waving. She was frozen, unable to move or make a sound. The only part of her still moving was her heart, which banged against her ribcage. The roach shot away, moving at an incredible speed, under Cassie's pedestal.

Peering into the dark space beneath the pedestal, she could see an object hidden in the shadows. She pushed the wheeled drawers forward a couple of inches to reveal a key. Now she remembered Cassie telling her that she'd lost the spare key, back on Sophie's first day.

She slipped the key into her pocket and waited, cowering. Time seemed to fold in on itself, so she had no idea how long had passed until a noise snapped her out of her trance.

Behind her, she heard the door to the office open, then footsteps. Someone was in the office. The ghost. The woman who had been begging and screaming. Whoever had been torturing her. Or it could be the man from her dream, the man with roaches in his hair, Daisy's head in his hands. She shook uncontrollably, convinced she was going to die. This was the end.

She peered out from her hiding place and saw the shadow grow larger, taking human shape. She could hardly breathe.

The shadow came towards her.

Chapter 25
Day thirty-two, Thursday, 7 May, 2015

'Sophie?'

She slumped to the floor. It was Natalie. Oh, thank God. Thank *God*. Sophie crawled out from beneath the desk.

'The police got hold of my number and told me there was someone locked in the office, so . . . What are you doing?' The HR woman watched Sophie get to her feet.

'I heard something. Someone . . . a woman . . . she was being hurt.'

'What?'

'Out there. In the stairwell.' She sat down in her swivel chair, all the strength gone from her legs.

Natalie gave her a curious look. 'Wait here.'

'No, don't leave me—'

But it was too late. Natalie had left the office, leaving Sophie alone for a few minutes, convinced she was going to hear a scream, that whoever was out there was going to attack the other woman. But Natalie returned unharmed.

'There's no one out there. No one else in the building.'

Sophie stared.

'Maybe you heard a radio. Or a TV from one of the adjoining buildings.'

Sophie clung to this rational explanation. Yes, that must be it. Someone in one of the buildings nearby watching a horror movie. She'd taken Daisy to a science museum recently and had been struck by an exhibit that showed how sound could carry and be amplified if the conditions were right. If that was the reason, it meant no one had been here. It meant she wasn't hearing things, going crazy or seeing ghosts.

'Maybe you should take a couple of days off,' Natalie suggested in a gentle voice as she escorted Sophie from the building and called her a taxi.

'I can't. I'm too busy.'

'Well . . . you do seem a little . . .' She trailed off, clearing her throat. 'Is it the after-effects of Daisy going missing?'

Sophie nodded helplessly but assured her she would be fine. 'I heard a weird noise, that's all, and it freaked me out a little. Like you said, I'm still a little highly strung after what happened with Daisy.'

'There's definitely no one else in the building,' Natalie said, studying her. 'If you ever want to talk about anything, Sophie, you know that's what I'm here for.'

'Oh, look, the taxi's here.' Sophie scuttled away and jumped into the back of the cab, waving at a bemused Natalie as it pulled away. The driver had Capital FM on, the latest Taylor Swift track playing, and Sophie asked him to turn it up. Anything to drive the lingering echo of what she'd heard from her mind.

'At least she didn't have one of her bad dreams last night,' Sophie said as soon as Daisy left the breakfast table. *Unlike me.*

'Hmm.' Guy didn't look up from his phone. His toast lay half-eaten on the plate.

'Are you still not talking to me? I've explained what happened, Guy. And I've told you I'm sorry.'

When she had finally got home, Guy had been in bed, asleep or pretending to sleep. She whispered in his ear but he didn't respond. She had been tempted to wake him, but she couldn't face a big argument. Didn't want to have to deal with his anger. Instead, she had run a bath and sat in the water for an hour, trying to shake the images that had pummelled her as she hid beneath her desk, convinced the man from her nightmare was coming to get her.

Now, as Guy stared at his phone, probably checking Twitter for his daily dose of abuse, Sophie asked, 'Did you talk to Claire?'

Sophie's bowl of muesli sat untouched. Only Daisy, who normally had to be nagged half to death before eating any breakfast that didn't involve chocolate, had been hungry this morning.

He finally looked up from his phone but didn't meet her eye. 'Yeah. She's pissed off. She had to cancel a date to make our meeting, and only agreed because I pestered her about it. Begged, practically. I don't blame her for being angry.'

'But you shouldn't blame me, either.'

She went over to him, lay a hand on his arm. His body was stiff, unforgiving. She should tell him how scared she'd been last night, but she knew how it would make her sound. And here, in daylight, it all seemed like something she'd seen in a film, not something that she'd actually lived through.

'You should have told Simon that you had to come home,' Guy said.

'I wanted to. But I'm on probation. I knew he'd frown upon it. And I need—'

His eyes flashed. 'Yes, you need that fucking job because I'm an unemployed layabout. Well, maybe I wouldn't still be unemployed if you hadn't made me miss that meeting.'

She counted to three before responding. Don't rise to it. 'Can't Claire reschedule your meeting?'

He scowled. 'She's saying she hasn't got another slot for two weeks. At *least* two weeks. I can tell they want shot of me. I'm damaged goods.' He rubbed his head, the self-comforting gesture she knew so well. 'It's a total nightmare. I'm going to call everyone I know today, try to get some work somewhere else.'

'Maybe you should write an article about what it's like to go through a public shaming.'

'What? Are you stupid? I don't want to keep reminding everyone about it.' He stalked out of the room, calling, 'Daisy? Have you cleaned your teeth?'

He had never called her stupid before. She fought the anger and counted to five, persuading herself he didn't mean it. He was angry, disappointed, under a lot of stress. Everything he'd worked so hard to build up over the last few years – his name, his reputation – was crumbling around him. He was lashing out at her and she understood why he was angry. She should have told Simon she had to leave. He would have understood. Maybe. But she was under pressure too. Under pressure and exhausted. And why couldn't Claire be more flexible? She had a good mind to call her herself, explain why Guy had missed the meeting.

As she was thinking about this, Guy's phone, which he had left on the table beside his plate, chirruped. Maybe it was Claire. Or someone else with an offer of work. Sophie was so keen to be the bearer of good news that she picked up the phone – and found herself looking at a familiar name.

Cassie.

How are you feeling this morning? x

It felt like all the blood had drained from her body. She dropped into her chair and held Guy's phone with a shaking hand. Although she could only see this one message, she knew there would be more messages between Guy and Cassie beyond the locked home screen. She tapped in the passcode.

It didn't work.

Guy's passcode had always been Sophie's birthday. Maybe she had mistyped it. Checking that he wasn't coming, she tried again. The phone remained locked. He must have changed it. When did he do that? *Why* did he do it?

Then she remembered Cassie yesterday, mentioning Guy's meeting with Claire. She'd wondered how Cassie knew about it. Well, now she had the answer.

She made her way to Daisy's bedroom, trying very hard to remain calm. Daisy was dressed for school, sitting on the floor playing with two of her Barbies. One of them, the blonde, was saying to the other, a brunette whose hair had been cut short at some point, 'You're very stupid.'

'No, you are,' said the brunette.

Sophie left the room, the choppiness in her stomach growing worse as she neared the bedroom. Guy was standing by the back window, staring out, seemingly at nothing.

'Guy.'

He turned. If, in that moment, he hadn't looked so surly and unhappy to see her, the next words might have come out differently.

'What the fuck is Cassie doing texting you?'

'What?'

She held up his phone and he went to take it off her, but she snatched it away.

'*How are you feeling this morning? Kiss.* What the hell's going on, Guy?'

193

His expression shifted several times in a second. A frown, a tiny smile, then indignation. 'What do you mean, what's going on? I only met her two days ago. Nothing's going on.'

'She knew you were meeting Claire yesterday. She mentioned it at work. And now, first thing in the morning, she's texting you. Something's going on.' She held up the phone. 'I want to see the other messages between you. What's your passcode? And why did you change it? To stop me seeing the messages, I bet.'

'Sophie, you're being crazy.'

'Oh! Stupid *and* crazy, eh? I think any woman would want to know what was going on in this situation. Any woman who witnessed her husband staring at a much younger woman with his fucking *tongue* hanging out—'

'I wasn't.'

'—and then, two days later, imagine if that woman discovered the little slut was sending her husband messages with a big *kiss* on the end. Oh, and that he'd changed the passcode on his phone.'

'I did that after the Twitter hack. I changed all my passwords on everything.'

'Stop changing the subject. I want to know about you and Cassie.'

He shook his head angrily. 'For fuck's sake. When I met her in your office she told me she had a friend who's a magazine editor so I gave her my number to pass on.'

She waited.

'And that's it. Cassie texted me to check she'd got the right number. I replied and told her hopefully I wouldn't need her to talk to her friend because I had the meeting with Claire. I guess Cassie texted me this morning to find out how it went. That's it.'

Sophie breathed. It sounded reasonable. Plausible. And yet . . .

'So why the kiss?'

He sat down on the bed. 'I don't know. That's what all young women do these days, isn't it? She probably puts a kiss at the end when she emails her frigging bank manager.'

'She doesn't put kisses on her messages to me.'

'Yeah, well, she doesn't like you.'

Sophie was stunned into silence.

'I didn't mean that,' he said.

'Is that what she told you? That she doesn't like me?'

'No, it's what *you* told me. It's pretty much all you've talked about this week. How Cassie is out to make your life a living hell. How she is trying to sabotage you so she can have your job. Well, do you know what? Apart from upsetting Josh I can't think of a single thing she's actually done wrong, and now the two of them have made up and it's *you* he's pissed off with. She seemed nice to me. I liked her. And if I want to exchange the odd text with her, there's nothing wrong with that.'

She threw the phone at him. It struck him on the shoulder and he swore as it bounced off.

'Jesus, Sophie. That hurt.' He rubbed his shoulder.

'Why don't you get Cassie to come and kiss it better?'

'Fuck you.'

'I wouldn't let you fuck me again if you were the last man on earth.'

'I wouldn't *want* to.' He was standing up now, in her face, his greater size and physical strength suddenly scaring her, making her step back. She had never seen him like this before: his face pink, the veins in his neck standing out, a look of abject hatred in his eyes.

'Back off,' she said.

He didn't move. She looked down at his fists. They were clenched and for a moment she was sure he wanted to hit her.

Instead, he took a step back.

'You've changed since you started at that place,' he said.

She wanted the argument to stop. But she felt out of control, unable to stop the words. There was a whole boiling lake of tension and frustration inside her. And here it came, hissing and spitting as she let it out.

'You just don't like me working. You want me to be the little woman, sitting at home looking after your daughter. A house-wife who'll have your dinner on the table and a blow job ready at bedtime.'

'Is that *really* what you think of me?'

He was standing up again now, too close.

'What are you going to do?' she said, barely able to believe she was saying these words, that she wasn't watching someone who looked like her performing on the stage. 'Are you going to hit me? We all know – everyone knows – that you think domestic violence is funny. The whole fucking world knows. I bet you did write that tweet really. Hacked, my arse. It was you. And you're not man enough to admit it.'

His fists clenched and unclenched and the part of her that believed this wasn't real thought how ironic it would be if he hit her now. She also knew that it would be over, a huge part of her life, that the man she had adored would be gone forever. And she wanted to scream.

He didn't hit her. Instead, he pointed a shaking finger at her and hissed, 'How do I know it wasn't you who sent the tweet? After all, you logged in to my account. Another reason I had to change all my passwords.'

'Oh, my God. How could you accuse me of that? Get out.'

His smile was sickeningly smug. 'And what? You're going to take the day off from your precious job to take Daisy to school?'

She was trembling. Sick with anger and fear and horror as the words they'd both spoken echoed around the bedroom. She prayed Daisy hadn't been listening, though she must have heard at least part of it. She was probably re-enacting it right now with her Barbies.

'Fine,' she said, after taking a slow, deep breath. 'I'm going to work.'

'Good.'

She brushed past him, not wanting to touch him. As she went, she was tempted to ask him if he wanted her to give a message to Cassie. But she managed to resist. She kissed Daisy goodbye and went out of the door, unable to believe what had just happened. But unable, too, to shed the anger.

Maybe he was right. Maybe she had changed since starting at Jackdaw. But it wasn't her fault. And she couldn't leave. She wasn't going to quit.

But she needed to figure out what to do about Cassie. Guy's explanation was plausible. Stepping back from her emotions, she could see that he was probably telling the truth about the texts. But Cassie had definitely been flirting with him in the kitchen at work, and put together with the kiss at the end of the text message, she had crossed a line. The question was one of intent: were Cassie's actions innocent, unknowing, or was she deliberately trying to wind Sophie up or, worse, damage her marriage?

Why would she do that? Mischief or something worse? Sophie thought it through as she walked to the bus stop. Was Cassie behind the gossip about Sophie being a 'homewrecker'? Had she really sabotaged the *Kiss of Death* campaign?

A new suspicion entered her head. Matt had protested his innocence vehemently, said that he'd been set up, that Cassie had faked the email. Such things must be possible. All Cassie would need to do would be to log on to Matt's computer and send the email to herself. The only problem with that idea was that Cassie would have needed Matt's password, but that didn't make it impossible. Had Cassie decided that Matt stood in the way of promotion and resolved to get rid of him? Would anyone be that ruthless, destroying a colleague's reputation and causing him to lose his job? Cassie had certainly been quick putting herself forward as Matt's replacement – and she'd got what she wanted.

Was she planning to do the same to Sophie? To get her to quit so she could take her place?

Her mind leapt. If Cassie had faked the email from Matt, was she also responsible for the tweet that had wrecked Guy's career? Sophie often left her phone in her pedestal drawer, and she was lax when it came to locking it. Could Cassie have taken it out and sent the tweet from Sophie's phone? The phone was protected by a PIN but maybe Cassie had got past it somehow. Sophie had told Guy that she had logged out of his Twitter account but the truth was she couldn't be one hundred per cent sure she had. She'd only checked after the offensive tweet had been sent. Cassie could have sent the tweet, then logged out before putting Sophie's phone back.

But why would she do that? It had led to Guy losing his regular source of income, making Sophie more reliant on her job at Jackdaw, meaning she was more likely to stay. If Cassie wanted to get rid of her, the last thing she would do would be to create a situation where Sophie was forced to stay.

When Daisy was a baby, just about able to sit up, Guy had left her on her own in the living room and gone into the bedroom to tell Sophie something. They had heard a loud thump and rushed in to find Daisy lying on the floor, screaming. Sophie knew that he had left Daisy unsupervised on the sofa, but he denied it, making increasingly bizarre claims about what must have happened. It was as if he was so ashamed of what he'd done that he'd convinced himself he was telling the truth, that he wasn't to blame. His refusal to accept responsibility was maddening, but Sophie had no proof. She had no proof that he'd sent that tweet either, but she was becoming more and more convinced that he had.

So Cassie was almost certainly innocent of that, but Sophie couldn't shake the feeling that Cassie had something to do with Daisy's trip to the library. Logistically, it seemed impossible, but maybe she had an accomplice, a male friend in the office who was helping her in her aim to destabilise Sophie. And she had told this friend to scare Daisy, to talk to her about Sophie being in danger at work, knowing it would freak Sophie out.

Had she done the same to Miranda, her plan spoiled when Sophie was quickly recruited to take her place?

Sophie imagined herself going to Simon with this, telling him her suspicions. It all sounded so nebulous. He would laugh her out of his office. Worse, decide she'd lost the plot and fire her. She could go to Natalie, but the HR woman would probably tell her that Cassie hadn't breached any of the rules in the company handbook. And then she would phone the men in white coats.

Sophie knew only one thing: she didn't trust Cassie.

Chapter 26

Day thirty-six, Monday, 11 May, 2015

Sophie hoped she would never have to endure another weekend like the one that had just passed. She had come home the evening after the row half expecting Guy to have gone. Perhaps, if it wasn't for Daisy, he would have packed his bags. But he'd been there, the dark cloud on his face telling her all she needed to know the moment she entered the flat. He didn't want to make peace. He was still angry and wounded.

Well, so was she. And whenever they'd had a big fight in the past – not that there had been many – she'd been the one to make the first conciliatory overtures. Why should it always be her? Yes, she regretted most of the things she'd said, like him wanting her to be an oppressed housewife, but he had yelled equally hurtful words.

On top of that, she couldn't help but still feel suspicious about the texts between him and Cassie. She had watched Cassie closely all day on Friday, twitching with suspicion every time the younger woman picked up her phone. And she'd watched Guy all weekend, wondering if he was texting Cassie whenever he went to the bathroom. She was desperate to talk to him about this whole mess, but felt a constriction in her throat whenever she tried.

How long was it going to go on? How long would he insist on sleeping on the sofa? If she backed down she could fix this. If she dragged him into the bedroom it would break down the barrier between them. She wanted him to apologise and to mean it, but he stayed silent and, consequently, the atmosphere in their flat was like that moment before a storm, when the air is thick and dark, and only a cloudburst and the crackle of lightning can blow that suffocating closeness away. The storm wouldn't break, the air wouldn't clear, because neither of them was willing to make the first move.

Now, here she was, back in the office on Monday morning, trying not to think about it, to lose herself in her work, going over the budgets that Simon had discussed with her last week. Cassie and Tracey were busy too, and the three of them barely spoke all morning, until at just after eleven Tracey gasped, 'Oh, my God!'

Sophie looked up. 'What is it?'

'Check your email.'

Sophie saw what had made Tracey gasp straight away, and as she opened the email she heard a murmur, a growing babble of excitement, wash across the office, bouncing from desk to desk.

The email was from a woman in the HR team called Amy Douglas and titled *That info you requested*. Attached was an Excel file containing the salary details of everybody at Jackdaw. And Amy had erroneously sent it to 'All Staff'.

Across the office, people were squinting at their screens, ignoring the instant message that popped up from Natalie, instructing them not to open the file, to delete it immediately. On the other marketing team, Gisele stood by Carla's desk, tapping the screen and exclaiming noisily.

'I'm not going to look,' Cassie said. 'It's wrong.'

'Me neither,' said Sophie, even though she would love to know how much certain people, like Simon, earned.

But Tracey was whizzing through the document, muttering and shaking her head.

'Tracey, you need to stop now,' Sophie said.

But the other woman ignored her. 'Bloody hell. Robert in Accounts earns three times what I do! And . . . oh, my God.'

Tracey's eyes met Sophie's, and at the same time Sophie was aware of other people across the office looking at her.

'What is it?' Sophie went round to Tracey's desk, who at least had the decency to appear embarrassed. She leaned forward and saw her name in the first column, then a high five-figure number. 'That's not right! I don't earn anywhere near that much.'

'Really? Well, *my* salary is correct.'

Cassie peered across. 'So's mine.'

'Glad to see we both earn a pittance.' Tracey smiled at Sophie. 'Still, you are a manager. I knew you'd earn substantially more than us. I just didn't think it would be that much more.'

Sophie opened her mouth to protest, and then it dawned on her. The figure was right, but it included her maximum on target earnings. When she had started at Jackdaw, they had explained that they were trialling a new bonus scheme. Her total salary for the year could be sky-high, but only if she exceeded all her sales targets to a degree that would involve having more than one huge *Fifty Shades of Grey* style breakout hit, the kind of thing that only happened once in a blue moon. Her actual salary was modest, even by publishing standards.

'It's not right,' Sophie said. She was about to explain her bonus system but did she really want her team to know the ins and outs of how much she earned? It was private. Or, at least, it had been.

'If you say so. Oh, shit, it's Natalie.'

The HR woman stormed through the double doors into the office and stalked towards them, her eyes sweeping across the desks like a Martian's death ray. Tracey quickly closed the Excel document and deleted the email. Sophie hadn't seen Natalie like this before, in full-on scary mode; now she understood why people always checked over their shoulders before talking about her. She dreaded to think what had happened to poor Amy Douglas who'd sent the email.

After completing her tour of the office, Natalie stomped off to check on the next floor, leaving a nervous silence in her wake until someone said, 'Well, at least no one can be jealous of my salary.'

Laughter broke the tension, but when it was over Sophie felt eyes on her back, could almost hear people whispering about her. Why was *she* earning so much? What made her so special? She could hear Gisele and Carla carping about her. *She thinks she's God's gift and she earns more than us put together.* She could try to explain, but they'd probably feel resentful of her bonus scheme. As she closed her emails and opened a spreadsheet to begin work, she heard Cassie say, 'I guess it's a good job you earn so much. What with poor Guy being unemployed.'

Sophie stared at Cassie, sitting there in another designer skirt, expensive shoes, diamonds in her ears.

'It must be so hard for him,' she said. 'He seems like such a nice guy.'

'If you'll excuse the pun,' Tracey said.

Cassie didn't laugh. 'You didn't meet him, did you, Tracey? He's lovely. I can understand now why you couldn't resist stealing him away from his first wife, Sophie.'

Sophie stood up. 'Cassie, a word.' She marched over to the small meeting room and waited, not counting to ten, not trying to control the fury that burned in her chest.

'Everything OK, Sophie?'

She looked so damned innocent, standing there with those big brown eyes, hands clasped in front of her like a lady-in-waiting.

'Whatever's going on between you and my husband, it has to stop.'

She had expected Cassie to act shocked, or be immediately defensive. Instead, she laughed, and then suddenly stopped.

'Are you joking, Sophie?'

'No, it's not a joke. I know you've been exchanging texts.' She was breathing hard, her heart pulsing so loudly in her ears that it was like being underwater.

'I only texted him about his work. I was going to put him in touch with an editor I know.'

'Did he tell you to say that?'

Cassie's face hardened. 'Oh, Sophie. You shouldn't tar me with your own brush. Just because you encouraged Guy to cheat on his first wife. Just because you betrayed another woman. *I'm* not like that.'

Sophie was speechless. Cassie was right. She, Sophie, was the one with the track record. She went back on the offensive.

'What about you and Matt? Did he really send you that email? The more I think about it, the fishier it seems.'

Cassie narrowed her eyes.

'What happened between you and him, Cassie? Were you having an affair that went wrong? Did he hurt you so much that you decided to destroy him? Or did you decide you wanted him out of the way so you could have his job?'

Cassie took a step towards her and, for the second time in recent memory Sophie thought she might be hit. But she would welcome it. If Cassie slapped her, it would be instant dismissal. It would be well worth a second of pain. *Do it*, she urged silently.

Cassie held herself rigid. 'You're losing it, Sophie. Just like Miranda before she vanished.'

She headed to the door, stopped and turned back.

'Maybe you should quit too. If you can't handle the pressure.'

'What the hell do you mean by that?'

Cassie waved the question away. 'I have no interest in your husband. He's old and he's not even a good writer. I was trying to do him and you a favour. Next time, I won't bother.'

She slipped through the door, as graceful as ever, shutting it quietly behind her.

Sophie stayed in the meeting room for five minutes, trying to calm down and decide what to do next. She couldn't simply go back to her desk, sit down and carry on working. She was Cassie's manager and she needed to sort this out, now. Sophie had no experience of dealing with a conflict like this. She had always got along well with her colleagues. She realised she had acted unprofessionally by aiming accusations at Cassie. She had made herself vulnerable. Oh, God, Cassie was probably composing an email to Simon right now, telling him she wanted to make an official complaint, that Sophie was bullying her.

Her stomach went cold. They could fire her for this, or at least suspend her while they investigated.

She needed to get her version of events in first. Explain the situation. She hurried down to the second floor and knocked on the door of Natalie's office.

'Come in!'

'Natalie, can I have a—' The expression on Natalie's face made Sophie freeze.

'I'm *exceedingly* busy trying to sort out this *clusterfuck*,' Natalie said. 'Is it life or death?'

'Well . . .'

'Will someone actually die in the next five minutes if you don't talk to me right now?'

'I'll come back later.' She closed the door. Shit, she was going to have to talk to Simon. The man who thought Cassie was God's gift to marketing. She flashed back to the time she'd caught Simon with his fly undone and prayed that he and Cassie weren't really having an affair.

Luckily, Simon was in his office and seemed pleased to see her.

'Sophie! Great work on those budgets.' He cleared his throat. 'Natalie told me about the incident the other night. So sorry about that. I thought you'd already left and told reception I'd lock up. I did pop my head into your office to see if you were still around and there was no sign of you.'

That must have been when she was in the loo.

'It's fine,' she said. She had wondered if he would ever apologise. 'I need to talk to you about something else. I've got a bit of a problem.'

She explained what had happened, accentuating her sense of guilt, admitting up front that she'd acted unprofessionally. She didn't tell him that she suspected Cassie of trying to make her life hell, concentrating solely on Cassie's flirtation with Guy.

'I feel terrible,' she said. 'I shouldn't have accused her. I should have come to you first. But I lost my temper, which is something I never do.'

Was it her imagination or did Simon appear to find the situation amusing? He must have read her face because he said, 'Sorry, Sophie. It's just the thought of Cassie seducing your husband. It seems a little far-fetched.'

He meant crazy, didn't he? Oh, God, now her boss thought she was losing it too.

'Let's get Cassie up here now for an open conversation, iron things out.'

While they waited for Cassie, Sophie gathered her courage and asked, 'Simon, what happened to Miranda?'

The smirk disappeared entirely. 'What do you mean?'

'Well, people seem to think she left in mysterious circumstances, that she disappeared and no one knows what happened to her.'

Simon headed to the window, talking with his back to her. 'It's true that she left very suddenly. But there was nothing mysterious about it. She met someone and fell madly in love with him. I heard he was Danish or Swedish, something like that, and she decided to move over there to be with him.'

'You know that for a fact? You've heard from her?'

'No. It was extremely unprofessional of her.' He coughed. 'I hope she never comes looking for a reference. But she updated her Facebook status, said she had made a big decision, that she was going away. That's what I was told, anyway.'

Cassie arrived before Sophie could ask any more. The younger woman's demeanour was very different to how it had been in the meeting room: sheepish, refusing to meet Sophie's eye.

'Cassie, Sophie has told me that she and you had a little *contretemps.*'

Now Cassie looked directly at her. 'I'm so sorry, Sophie. I was out of line.'

Sophie was speechless.

'I should never have spoken to you like that. And I realise it was inappropriate of me to contact your husband, even if it was completely innocent. I should have passed the messages through you. I promise not to contact him again. But if you want me to resign I will completely understand.'

'Let's not be hasty,' Simon said. 'There's no need for you to resign. It sounds like this is going to be very easy to resolve. Perhaps you'd like to apologise too, Sophie? As one colleague to another.'

'I . . .'

'Sophie doesn't need to say sorry. I understand why she felt worried about her husband.'

Sophie bit her tongue so she wouldn't say something else she'd regret. She realised Simon was waiting for her to say something.

'I'm sorry, Cassie. I shouldn't have spoken to you the way I did. It was highly unprofessional of me.'

'Right,' said Simon. 'That was easy.'

'I'd better get back to work,' Cassie said. 'I'm so busy.'

'Yes, me too,' Sophie added.

They left Simon's office. Cassie walked a little way ahead and Sophie eyed her back. Why did she get the feeling she'd just been played?

'I still don't trust you,' she said under her breath.

———

'I'm heading home now.'

Sophie looked up from her work. She had been completely absorbed and had lost track of time. Was it really six o'clock? 'OK. See you tomorrow, Cassie.'

The younger woman hesitated as if she wanted to say something, but headed off without speaking. As the doors swung shut behind her, Sophie realised she was alone in the office. Everybody else had gone home. She felt a flutter of panic, but quickly got hold of herself. She wasn't going to get locked in again. Natalie had assured her that the receptionist had been given strict instructions to ensure everyone was accounted for before they locked up. The fire officer, who was responsible for the fire escapes, had been given a bollocking too, though they swore they had no idea how the escape doors had been locked.

Sophie touched her pocket and felt the spare pedestal key she'd found when she was locked in the office. She thought about her missing notepad. What if it was in Cassie's drawer? That would be proof that she wasn't being paranoid, going crazy. She needed to know, felt it like an itch that had to be scratched.

Before she could change her mind, she scooted round to Cassie's desk and unlocked her pedestal. Of course, she could have done this before – she knew how to pick one of these locks with a paperclip – but she hadn't thought about it till she found the key. Her pulse accelerated as she slid the shallow top drawer open, glancing around to check no one was coming. She had no idea what she would say if she was caught doing this.

There was nothing but stationery in the top drawer. She opened the second drawer and found a number of books that Cassie had been working on, including *The Kiss of Death*. Sophie checked behind them, at the back of the drawer, and spotted a green notepad. She grabbed it, sure it was hers – but it had Cassie's writing in the front. Disappointed, she put it back then opened the final, deepest drawer.

It was full of A4 dividers, each containing printouts and sheets of paper, filed neatly. Cassie's contract was in the first divider, the company handbook in the second. Sophie flicked through them, realising that she wasn't going to find her missing notepad or any other evidence that Cassie had been trying to sabotage her. One divider contained printouts of emails, including a recent one from Simon telling her what a marvellous job she was doing and congratulating her on her promotion.

In the next divider, she found the email from Matt. She guessed Cassie had printed it so she would have physical evidence in case the email itself was accidentally deleted. The next divider contained a brown manila envelope. Turning her head sideways so she could read the headers, Sophie saw a single word written on the front:

Miranda.

She checked the coast was still clear then took the envelope out, laying it on Cassie's desk. It was unsealed. Sophie pulled out a wad of A4 paper and a small notepad. Flicking through the printouts Sophie realised with horror what she was looking at.

The first email in the pile read: *Hi Cassie – thanks for pointing out that mistake earlier. It would have been a disaster if that had slipped through :) What would I do without you, eh? M.*

Next to this, Cassie had written by hand, 'Miranda forgot to clean up email list, 7/11/14'.

The next email was also from Miranda to Cassie. *Hiya – here are those files you'll need. Thanks a lot for this! See you tomorrow. M.*

Cassie had written, 'Miranda off sick as "she had too much to drink last night". Said she told Simon she has stomach bug. 2/12/14'.

There were a dozen more notes like this, all of them revealing something Miranda had done wrong, a rule she'd bent or broken. Cassie had been keeping a file on her manager. She opened the slim notepad that had been inside the envelope and found a kind of diary detailing conversations she'd had with Miranda, things she'd overheard Miranda say ('Whoever designed this cover must be blind; it's the worst jacket I've ever seen' – 17/12/14) and details of when Miranda had made personal phone calls or taken longer than an hour for lunch.

Sophie stuffed the notepad and printouts back in the envelope and bent to flick through the remaining dividers, her heart thudding against her ribcage, convinced there would be a similar file on her. She checked through twice but couldn't find a thing. That didn't necessarily mean anything, though. Cassie could have taken it home. Shit, she was probably updating it *right now* with details of their so-called *contretemps* today.

She locked the pedestal and sat back in her chair, trying to process what she'd seen. Why had Cassie been keeping a file detailing everything Miranda did wrong? And had she done anything with all the information she gathered? Simon had seemed convincing when he was talking about Miranda earlier. Surely he would tell her if Miranda had been fired. He had no reason not to. He wouldn't need to mention Cassie's role.

So what had Cassie done with her file? Had she blackmailed Miranda, told her she would go to Simon and get her fired if she didn't resign? She heard Cassie's words from earlier. *Maybe it's time you quit too.* What exactly was Cassie planning to do?

There were so many questions. And only one way to get the answers.

She needed to find Miranda.

On the bus home, she took out the manuscript Simon had given her the evening she was locked in the office, the one by the anonymous author, *The Devil's Work*. Simon kept asking her if she'd finished it yet but she was only halfway through. She liked it but didn't share Simon's optimism about it being a bestseller. It was short, dark and extremely grim. It was set in a big house in the middle of nowhere where a girl was kept prisoner. She was kept locked up in a tiny room with nothing but books for company. And every day she was taken to what they called the improvement room, where she was forced to endure terrible punishments.

Sophie turned to page fifty and read on.

He came for me early this morning while I was still rubbing the sleep from my eyes. There was a storm last night that kept me awake, thunder rolling in from the mainland, rain crashing against my window.

As always he didn't speak as he led me to the improvement room.

As I stood in the doorway, waiting to see what today's treatment would be, I found myself wishing he would hug me, pull me to him and tell me this was over, that I have been a good enough girl and can go home. But he gestured for me to enter the room and sit down, told me to take off my robe so I was naked, goosebumps rippling across my skin so I looked like an uncooked turkey. I shivered and wondered what today's treatment would be.

Would he make me scrub the concrete floor with a tiny cloth, crawling about until my knees bled?

Would he fire questions and accusations at me till all I could do was scream and cry?

Would he make me lie in an ice bath till I turned blue again? Use the hose on me?

I hadn't eaten for twenty-four hours and I wondered if he would feed me or lock me in the room with a plate of sausages and eggs and bacon and forbid me from touching it. My mouth watered at the thought.

He gestured towards the chair, the one with the leather straps.

'Sit down,' he said. 'Here. That's a good girl.'

'Please. You're not going to hurt me, are you?'

He stroked my brow and for a moment I felt like a very small child again, the child I was before I turned Bad. I felt loved. But then he said, 'It's for your own good. You know that.'

He wheeled the trolley towards me and I wondered if I would ever get out of this place, this dank basement, this living hell. All I want is to be normal. To be a good girl.

All I want is to be loved.

Chapter 27

Day thirty-six, Monday, 11 May, 2015

Sophie got home to find Guy hunched over his laptop at the kitchen table. She stood in the doorway, taking off her coat; waited for him to turn to her, to smile, to allow a chink of light through and give her something to work with.

She kept waiting.

Eventually, unable to bear the silence, she said, 'Hi.'

He ignored her and she felt herself deflate, all her hopes for the evening vanishing. His black mood was infectious, creeping across the room like dark matter. She opened her mouth to speak, to say something bright and positive, but a wave of exhaustion hit her and now all she wanted to do was open a bottle of wine and take it to bed.

She fought it. She needed to see their daughter. That would cheer her up. Guy might hate her but Daisy still thought she was the best, most important person in the world.

'Where's Daisy?'

He jerked his head towards their daughter's room.

'Hi, sweetheart,' Sophie said, standing in Daisy's doorway. 'What are you doing?'

Daisy looked up at her and said, 'Being a good girl.'

She had the brunette Barbie with the chopped hair in her hand. It had been stripped naked. Crouching beside her daughter, Sophie noticed the doll had something drawn in marker pen on its shoulder.

'Can I see?'

It was a crude representation of Sophie's phoenix tattoo. Sophie ran her thumb over it lightly. It didn't smudge so must have been there a little while.

'Is this me?' Sophie asked.

'Uh-huh.' Daisy looked around, seemingly bored of this conversation. Sophie's eyes filled with tears. Was Daisy playing with a doll replica of her because she missed her and it was the closest she could get to her when she was at work?

She kept her voice light. 'What happened to my clothes?'

'I threw them away. Because of what the man said.'

'What man?'

Daisy huffed, like it was obvious. 'The man from the library.'

Sophie shuffled closer to Daisy on her knees, keeping her voice low and soft. 'Is that the same man who was in your dreams?'

'No. That man is scary. This man is kind.'

'So why did you throw the clothes away?'

Daisy shrugged. 'Because angels don't wear clothes.'

'Angels?'

'Yes. When you go to heaven you'll be an angel.'

Guy appeared in the doorway. He appeared to be making an effort, the sullenness absent from his voice as he asked, 'What's going on?'

Sophie looked up at him. 'Daisy says I'm going to heaven.'

He came further into the room and sat on Daisy's little bed. 'Not for a long time.'

'No,' Daisy said, her eyes wide, her own voice dropped to a whisper now. A shudder rippled up Sophie's spine. 'The man said you'll be going soon. Unless you're very, very careful.'

⌣

After Daisy had gone to bed, Sophie opened a bottle of wine and poured a glass for Guy, who was on his laptop again. He accepted the wine with a grunt and she waited to see if he would say anything.

She gave up. 'What are you doing?'

'I've started a blog,' he said. 'I need to keep writing, even if I'm not getting paid for it. And maybe it will lead to something.'

'Good idea.' She hesitated. 'Anything from Claire?'

He scowled. 'She's ignoring my emails. And I can't say I blame her.'

'How many times do you want me to apologise?'

He shrugged, still refusing to look at her. She resisted the urge to shake him. Instead, she downed half her glass of wine and sat in the chair opposite him.

'I'm worried about Daisy,' she said.

Finally, he looked up and she let it all pour out, words tumbling over one another, not knowing if she was being coherent but ploughing ahead anyway: her theory that Cassie had got her accomplice, whoever that was, to take Daisy to the library and give her a scare – with the ultimate aim of frightening Sophie. She told him all of her other suspicions about Cassie, finding the file she'd kept on Miranda, her fear that Cassie was doing the same to her.

He shut the lid of his laptop. 'You went in her drawer?'

'Is that all you can say?'

'Well, I don't know what else to say, Sophie. It all sounds completely nuts.' He reached across the table to take her hand. 'I'm worried about you. I think maybe the pressure is getting to you. I mean, you've been out of work for a while and you're not used to dealing with stress.'

She was aware of her face growing hot.

'Maybe you should go to see the doctor, see if he can give you anything.'

'What? You think I'm going crazy? That I need medication?'

'Just something to help you cope.'

She stood up, the chair toppling behind her. 'Make me all nice and passive and docile, you mean? Maybe I can ask the doctor if he has any pills that will make me feel horny too. Not used to dealing with stress? My God! Do you really think being at home with a baby or a toddler all day isn't stressful? You're unbelievable. Unbelievable!'

'I didn't mean—'

'Shame we don't live in Victorian times, when a husband could make a phone call and have his troublesome wife committed. You'd probably love that. Cassie could come round here and comfort you.'

'Sophie, for fuck's sake. Listen to yourself. And you're going to wake Daisy up.'

She stared at him, her breathing ragged, feeling very close to losing control. She wanted to pick up the chair she'd knocked over and throw it at him, smash it to pieces. She counted to ten but got there too fast and had to start again, then again. Guy was standing now too, clearly unsure of what to do, not used to seeing her like this.

'I just thought,' he said, 'that going to the doctor might be a good idea. I mean, you told me that when you went through a dark period before, when you were at university, that the doctor put you on antidepressants and it helped you.' He paused. 'Maybe you should look for another job.'

'No! I'm not going to be driven out. Not by her. This is the job I've wanted since I was a little girl, you know that.'

'Yeah, but it's not exactly working out how you imagined, is it?'

'But it will. It can. I just have to—'

'What?'

'Deal with Cassie.'

He shook his head. 'Sophie, you're acting like she's some kind of devil. But the problem is here.' He tapped the side of his skull. 'It's all in your head. Please go to see the doctor. For me. For Daisy.'

She laughed. 'I wondered how long it would take you to play that card. It's a shame you didn't think about our daughter when you sent that disgusting tweet.'

'I told you, I didn't do it!'

'Whatever.'

She grabbed the bottle of wine by the neck and strode towards the door of the living room. She turned and pointed at him with her free hand. 'I thought I could talk to you, that you'd help me figure it out. But I'm going to have to do this on my own, aren't I?'

She left the room, slamming the door behind her.

***

She sat on the bed, a pillow propped against the headboard, hugging her knees and trying to ignore the howling noise inside her head. Her cheeks were wet, eyes stinging with the aftermath of tears.

She hadn't felt this alone since the final days of the first year at university, and those first months of the second year when her tutor, Lance, noticed the deterioration in her work and advised her to seek help. The doctor had prescribed Prozac, and it had made her better, if sleepwalking through life with a little smile on your face could be described as better. Eventually, she had flushed the pills away and found she could get by without them if she threw herself into her studies and forgot about everything else. She became the student who spent all her spare time in the library. She stopped going out and led a hermitic, academic existence. Work and learning replaced everything else.

It would be so easy to go back to the doctor, to tell him she was feeling down, anxious, having trouble sleeping. The anger would go away and Guy would be happy. It would be better for Daisy too. Nothing was worse for a child than living in a marital warzone. And maybe things would be easier at work as well. She could drift through the days, get on with her job, not worry about Cassie or whether people were whispering about her, all those gossips who thought she was a homewrecker who was being paid too much. She knew she shouldn't care about them, but how could she not? The stress was justified, wasn't it, *because somebody was out to get her.*

Last time she'd felt like this, struggling to cope, she'd given in, let loneliness consume her, allowed regret to beat her. She should have fought against it. She had been passive when she should have taken action. She should have gone looking for Jasmine and Liam.

Maybe she could have found them.

Maybe they'd still be alive.

She got down from the bed and knelt on the carpet, reaching beneath the bed and pulling out a box file that was furry with dust. Here were mementoes of university. The prospectus that originally prompted her to apply to Sussex. Her degree certificate. A CD-ROM containing her dissertation. Postcards that had once graced the walls of her room, with scraps of Blu-tack still on the corners.

Beneath this lay a white envelope, and inside that was a photograph she hadn't looked at in a long time, the only picture she had of her, Jasmine and Liam. Helen had taken it one evening before the three of them went out. Sophie looked impossibly young, like a fourteen-year-old, reminding her of how naive she had been back then, how – what was the word? – *gauche*. Wet behind the ears. Beside her, Jasmine was smiling, though it was a sardonic smile, as if posing for a picture with her friends was an exercise in irony.

Liam was next to Sophie on the sofa, his hair flopping over his eyes, cigarette burning between his fingers. He appeared to be sucking in his cheeks, pouting and scowling at the same time. A poseur, but so beautiful. He was pretentious too, with his Dostoevsky quotes, but like Sophie, he had been so young, typical of many students. Back then, Sophie had seen Liam, who was a few years older than her, and Jasmine, with her metropolitan background, as sophisticated, worldly. That had been a large part of their appeal. Sophie had come to university desperate to find out who she really was, to create a new version of herself, and she had thought Jasmine and Liam could help her. They showed her a darker side of the world, and it had been seductive, exciting. Now, she felt ashamed of how malleable she had been, how foolish. She knew most people looked back at their younger selves and cringed, but she had real regrets too. The way they had treated Becky, Liam taking those photos that made Becky's boyfriend go psycho.

She flashed back in time and found herself standing outside Becky's room, saw Becky in that *Scream* pose, the terrible gibbering sounds coming from her.

Liam had admitted to taking those photos, but denied destroying Becky's room. At the time, she had believed him, but thinking about it now, she wondered. Had she, Sophie, believed him purely because she wanted to? Because she knew that she couldn't be friends with someone who could do such a thing? Had she been a sucker? She would never know. But she wished she had asked more questions, not been so trusting. After all, Liam was the one who was always saying how you couldn't trust anyone.

Sophie's attention returned to the photograph. She could hardly remember what they'd done that evening, where they had gone, but she knew that she would have spent much of the evening stealing glances at Liam, wishing he was hers, and no doubt she and Jasmine would have danced together, laughing and embracing and telling each other they were best friends forever, guilt coursing through Sophie's veins as she looked over Jasmine's shoulder at her boyfriend.

Months later, they were gone.

Two years after that she knew they were never coming back.

She took the other item from the envelope. It was a folded newspaper cutting, dated 6 October, 2002.

AMID THE WRECKAGE, MYSTERY OF MISSING STUDENTS SOLVED

The fates of two young people who went missing from university have been tragically revealed after DNA and possessions belonging to the pair were discovered among the wreckage of a boat that caught fire off the coast of the Isle of Sheppey in North Kent.

Liam Huxley and Jasmine Smith were 22 and 19 when they went missing from Sussex University in June 2000. Police believed the couple had run away together and despite efforts by both families to find them, their whereabouts were never discovered – until now.

Coastguards were alerted to a boat on fire three miles from Queenborough in the early hours of 1 September. No bodies were found but forensic investigations have since discovered DNA that matched Huxley and Smith along with their passports and other possessions.

'We believe they jumped from the boat when it caught fire and that they subsequently drowned,' said Detective Sergeant James Wheeler of Kent Police.

Huxley's father, Clive Huxley, a dentist who lives in Slough with his wife, Mary, said, 'It's dreadful news, but at least we finally have closure.'

Jasmine Smith was the granddaughter of Franklin Bird, the owner of children's publisher Jackdaw Books. Mr Bird issued a statement asking that the family be left alone to absorb the tragic news.

Chapter 28
Day thirty-seven, Tuesday, 12 May, 2015

Josh was recuperating at his parents' end-of-terrace in Teddington. Sophie rang the bell and waited, taking in the neat little garden and well-tended flowerpots that lined the path, hopping impatiently from foot to foot, about to press the bell again when the door opened.

Josh's mother had grey hair, an anxious expression and a well-to-do accent. She was wearing a mauve cardigan and grey slacks.

'Can I help you?'

'I'm a friend of Josh's, from work.'

'Oh, how lovely. Come in. He's in his room.' She lowered her voice. 'He's stayed in there pretty much the whole time since he came, like he's afraid to even come down to the living room. But you're the third person from Jackdaw to visit him now. And Franklin Bird himself sent a card.' She frowned. 'Though the message was a little odd, I thought. And harsh, really. It said something about how little boys hide in the dark, but real men aren't afraid to face the world. What do you suppose he was on about?'

'He's a great one for self-improvement, I think,' was all Sophie could think to say.

Josh's mother made a face. 'I'm sure he's quite an inspiration.' She gave her head a shake. 'Listen, I was making a cup of tea. If you wait a moment, you can take one up to Josh.'

Sophie said she'd be glad to.

'They still haven't caught the bastard who did it.'

Sophie was taken aback. 'Have you heard anything from the police?'

'Hardly a bloody thing.' She poured water into a teapot. 'I warned him about walking around on his own late at night. People think that just because gay people are able to get married these days that everything is rosy for boys like Josh. But there's still so much hatred out there. You know, a year or so ago, he was walking down the street with his boyfriend in broad daylight and someone spat in his face.'

She handed Sophie two mugs of tea. 'It's the second room on the left at the top of the stairs.'

'Thank you.'

She knocked lightly on Josh's door and went in.

Josh was visibly startled when Sophie appeared. He was sitting on his bed in the gloom, headphones on, a laptop on his thighs. He removed the headphones and lay them aside. The bruising had faded around his eye and his lips were no longer swollen. The cut on his cheek was healing, though it looked like it would leave a scar. His left hand was still bandaged but, physically, he looked much better than he had in hospital.

The psychological damage, though, had clearly deepened. His eyes were haunted, and he held himself in a permanent flinch, as if Sophie was about to leap across the room and attack him.

'Your mum said it was all right to come up.'

'She could have asked me first. Why aren't you at work?'

'I took a sickie.'

He raised an eyebrow. 'That's not like you.'

'I know. But, well, I'll explain in a moment. I'm so sorry that I haven't been to see you before. Chris told me that you were pissed off with me.'

He waved a hand. 'Did he? I can barely remember half the conversations I've had recently. Maybe I mentioned something about how you hadn't been to see me, but . . . whatever. It's not a big deal.'

He said this without much conviction, then stood slowly like an old man, and crossed to the window, parting the curtains to peek out. 'He could be out there now. Waiting for the chance to finish what he started.'

Sophie was shocked by how scared he sounded. 'Josh, that's not going to happen. I know this might not make things better, but surely the attack was opportunistic. You were in the wrong place at the wrong time.'

He turned from the window. 'No, he knew who I was. And he said he was going to kill me.'

'He was trying to scare you. Josh, it wasn't personal.'

'Sophie, you're wrong.' He moved slowly back to the bed and picked up his laptop, tapping at the keys then rotating it so she could see the screen. 'I got this a week ago.'

It was an email, from someone called A Friend. It consisted of a single line.

Next time, I'm going to finish the job.

'Have you shown this to the police?'

'Yeah, of course. But it's from an anonymous Gmail account,' he said. 'No way of tracing it.'

'It might not actually be from the guy who attacked you. It could be someone who read about the attack in the paper, some idiot who thinks it's funny to scare people. A troll.'

'That's what DC Paterson said.' That was the policeman Sophie had met at the hospital. 'He thinks it's highly unlikely someone has a personal vendetta against me, that I should talk to a counsellor, get over my fear and go back to work. I think that's what Franklin was saying too, in his card. How I ought to man up. But I'm just not up to risking it.' There was a long, awkward pause. Eventually he said, 'My God, I'm sick of talking about this, of thinking about it. Tell me what's going on with you.'

She hadn't meant to go into so much detail, but she found herself sharing the whole story of what had been happening at work and home. Being followed home after the pub. Daisy's temporary disappearance. Making Guy miss his meeting and the consequent falling out with him. The argument with Cassie about Guy.

'She came to see me at the hospital,' Josh said. 'I couldn't believe it. But she was really nice, apologising for the way she'd acted.'

'She does that. But, Josh, I don't trust her. You have to swear you won't tell anyone this, but I looked in her pedestal.' She told him what she'd found.

'Wow. The thing is, it doesn't really surprise me. It's exactly the kind of thing I'd expect her to do. You know, this might sound crazy, but after I was attacked it went through my mind that Cassie had something to do with it, that she set it up as revenge following our argument. But I can't see her doing that, can you?'

They looked at each other.

'No,' Sophie said. 'I guess not.'

'She'd have to be an actual, certifiable, grade A psychopath to do that.'

Sophie shook her head. 'I need to track down Miranda.' This was one of the reasons she'd come to see Josh today. 'Do you know where she lives? Or lived? I need to find out if these stories about her moving to Europe are true.'

'So you can ask her about Cassie?'

Sophie nodded.

'You've tried to find Miranda online, I assume?'

'Yes. She deleted her Facebook account after she left Jackdaw, apparently. I found her on Twitter but she hasn't tweeted since then either. And I found her on LinkedIn and sent her a message but she hasn't replied. I thought if I could find out her address I could go round, talk to her neighbours.'

'I don't know her address,' Josh said.

'Shit.'

'But I know someone who might.'

A cat dashed across the pavement as Sophie got out of the taxi on Palace Road, a wide, leafy street which stretched between Tulse Hill and Streatham Hill, just ten minutes from Sophie's own home. Josh had called the design department and asked Chris, without explaining why he needed it, if he could look up the address. Apparently, Chris had once arranged to have some work couriered to Miranda's flat. She'd been working from home and they needed her to sign off on some advertising designs. The email from Miranda containing her address was buried deep in Chris's inbox.

The building was a huge mansion block, beautiful, but in need of a lick of paint or three. Sophie found the buzzer for flat twenty-three but no one answered, so she tried the next-door neighbour. A minute later she found herself face-to-face with a woman who appeared to be in her sixties. She introduced herself as Hettie.

'I'm trying to track down your neighbour, Miranda Singer.'

Hettie squinted at her suspiciously. 'What's it about?'

Sophie thought on her feet. 'Well, I'm not really supposed to say, but it's about an inheritance.'

That piqued Hettie's interest. 'Really? I haven't seen her in a *long* time. Two months, something like that. Her post is piling up downstairs.'

'So there's no one living there.'

'Uh-uh. Quiet as the grave, it is.'

'Did she say anything about going away? Leave a forwarding address?' Hettie shook her head. 'What about the other neighbours? Anyone she was close to?'

'I don't know. She kept herself to herself, you know. That's what it's like around here. No sense of community, everyone wrapped up in their own troubles.'

'So she just disappeared?' Sophie studied Miranda's front door. 'Has anyone been here to look for her?'

'Not that I know of.'

'Do you know if she was renting?'

Hettie seemed to be growing impatient of Sophie's questions. 'No, she owned it. I think she owned it outright, you know. Bought it before the prices round here went crazy.'

Sophie thought about the rumour that Miranda had vanished to Norway. Would she really do that without arranging for her post to be forwarded on? Leave the flat that she owned unoccupied and unloved? She was starting to get a bad feeling in the pit of her stomach. Two other people had disappeared suddenly from her life, and look what had happened to them.

'Have you noticed any bad smells coming from inside Miranda's flat?'

Hettie's eyes widened. 'Bad smells? You mean she might be *in there*?' Her voice dropped to a whisper. 'Sweet Jesus. You know, I haven't smelled anything, but sometimes my dog runs out here and sniffs around the door. I read in the paper about some woman dying in her flat and no one finding her for six months. Oh, Lord, I'm going to call the police.'

Sophie realised that perhaps she shouldn't have pretended to be here about an inheritance. But it was too late now. She was going to have to brazen it out.

By the time two police officers, a man and woman in uniform, turned up, Hettie had convinced herself that Miranda's body was rotting next door and the stench had been seeping into her own flat for the past two months. While the male officer went round the back onto the fire escape, the policewoman, PC Marsons, asked Hettie the same questions Sophie had already asked.

'Has she been reported missing?' Sophie said, glad the police officers assumed she was another concerned neighbour.

'I'm going to check that now,' Marsons replied, walking a little way down the hallway and speaking into her police radio.

The male officer, PC Drake, came back and told his colleague he couldn't see any signs of life and was going to try to break through the back window. By this point, half a dozen other neighbours had gathered outside Miranda's, including a red-headed woman of about Sophie's age with a baby on her hip. Sophie recognised her: most parents in this area went to the same venues, hung out at the playground, attended the same mother and baby groups.

'You've got a four-year-old son, haven't you?' Sophie said, suddenly remembering that they had both gone to the same birthday party of a little friend of Daisy's.

'Yes, Henry. He's at school now. And you've got a little girl? I thought I recognised you.'

The woman's gaze returned to Miranda's door, just as PC Drake opened it and Marsons went through into the flat. 'This is worrying, isn't it? Were you a friend of hers?'

Sophie hesitated then said quietly, 'A colleague.'

The police came back out.

'Well?' Hettie demanded. 'Is she in there?'

Sophie realised she was holding her breath, until Marsons shook her head. 'The flat's empty.' The police conferred in quiet voices and the neighbours drifted back to their own front doors, disappointed by the anti-climax. Sophie was desperate to see inside Miranda's flat, to take a look around, but it was impossible.

The police started to walk away but Hettie called after them. 'Hey, what are you going to do about the back window? I don't want squatters moving in.'

'We'll send someone round to fix it later,' Drake replied.

'What are you going to do about finding her?' Sophie asked.

Drake shrugged. 'No one has reported her missing. There's no sign of foul play in the flat. The fridge is empty and the bins have been cleaned out. She's probably gone on a long holiday. It happens all the time.'

'But what about the mail stacked up downstairs?'

'I guess she forgot to have it forwarded. It happens all the time.'

Once they'd gone, Sophie turned to the woman she recognised. What was her name? She looked like a typical, exhausted stay-at-home mum, wearing a baggy shirt over leggings, her baby gazing about with wide eyes. Hettie had gone back into her flat.

'Do you want to come in for a cup of tea?' the woman asked. 'I could do with some adult conversation.'

Sophie followed her into her flat, which was next to Miranda's on the other side to Hettie. A hallway led to a kitchen; beyond that, Sophie could see the back door. The living room was unsurprisingly messy, plastic Marvel figures and dinosaurs scattered about, finger marks on the TV screen, dozens of children's books crammed onto a miniature bookcase.

'I'm Joanne,' the woman said as she settled on the sofa with the baby on her lap, 'and this is Millie.' The baby smiled gummily at Sophie.

'I'm Sophie. Did you know Miranda?'

'Yeah, quite well. She gave me some of those books – brought them home from the office. So that's where you work?'

Sophie nodded. 'There's a rumour at work that Miranda met a guy from Norway or some other part of Scandinavia and moved abroad to live with him.'

'Really? She never said anything about that to me. The last time I saw her she was talking about how she was going to try Tinder. I'm pretty certain she hadn't met anyone. In fact, she was saying how she wished she had a man about the place. She said she might need someone to protect her.'

Sophie sat up straight. 'When was that?'

'Right before she disappeared.'

'And you didn't tell the police?'

'I thought she was joking. She said immediately afterwards that she was.' She looked worried. 'I'm trying to remember. We were talking in the corridor, out there. She was on her way in, from work I assume. She told me she was joking and went inside before I could press her. That was the last time I saw her.'

Sophie tried not to betray her despair. 'Did she ever mention someone called Cassie? Cassandra?'

'I don't think so. I mean I'd remember that name. Cassandra. I studied the Classics at college and . . .' She smiled, clearly realising she was about to go off on a tangent.

'Do you know anything about Miranda's family? They must know where she is.'

'Her parents died,' Joanne said. 'That's how come she owned the flat – she bought it with her inheritance. She was an only child too.'

'What about close friends?'

'I think she was a bit of a loner, to be honest. I felt sorry for her. She was always really good with the kids, said she'd love to have some of her own.'

The baby let out a cry, almost drowning out Joanne's last words, and the crying grew louder until she said, 'I'm going to have to feed her.'

'I'd better go anyway,' Sophie said, getting to her feet. She found a business card in her pocket and handed it to the other woman. 'If you think of anything else, anything that Miranda might have said that would help me find her.'

Joanne unhooked her bra and tried to get the baby to latch on, but she refused, continuing to cry.

'I'll see myself out,' Sophie said, heading back into the hallway. But instead of exiting the flat, she headed stealthily to the back door. Masked by the sound of Millie crying, Sophie opened the door and stepped out onto the fire escape.

Chapter 29
Day thirty-seven, Tuesday, 12 May, 2015

There was a jagged hole in the window where PC Drake had broken into Miranda's flat. Sophie checked over her shoulder at the communal garden two storeys below. A woman sat in the garden reading a book, facing in the other direction. Sophie slipped her hand through the hole in the window, opened the back door and let herself in, closing it quietly behind her.

She found herself in a small kitchen. It was, as Drake had hinted, immaculately clean. She opened the fridge. As the policeman had said, it was empty; no food rotting in the vegetable trays, no out-of-date butter or eggs. This surely indicated that Miranda had planned to go away.

Either that, or someone had come into the flat and cleaned up.

Sophie paused, feeling dizzy suddenly and leaning against the counter for support. Because if she thought someone had been in here to make it look like Miranda had gone away voluntarily, what else did she think?

That Miranda had been murdered?

The moment Joanne had told Sophie that Miranda had felt the need for protection, even if it was supposedly a joke, a chill had spread through Sophie's insides. And Joanne was certain – or as certain as she could be – that Miranda hadn't run off to be with her mysterious Scandinavian lover. Then there was the fact that Miranda had left her flat empty. Hettie had mentioned squatters, a common fear in London. Leave a property standing empty for too long and someone could move in. Finally, Miranda hadn't arranged for her mail to be forwarded. In isolation, the police didn't think this was suspicious, but taken along with everything else, it clearly was.

Miranda had no family, no close friends. No one to persuade the police, with their many thousands of missing persons cases, to look for her.

Sophie didn't know Miranda, had never met her. But she had done the job that Sophie was doing now. She had sat at her desk, in the same chair. She had clearly clashed with Cassie too. But whether or not Cassie had something to do with Miranda's disappearance, Sophie felt a connection to this stranger, a compulsion to find out what had happened to her. Because what if it happened to Miranda's replacement too?

What if Sophie suddenly disappeared?

She knew, again, that trying to explain her fears to someone else would make her sound crazy. In need of medication. But what about all the strange things that had happened recently? Had they happened to Miranda too? Was that why Miranda felt the need for protection? Hopefully, somewhere in this flat, there would be something that would lead Sophie towards the answer. Something she could take to the police.

She started by going through the drawers in the kitchen, but found nothing except the usual junk people keep in their kitchen drawers: old batteries, boxes of matches, pizza delivery leaflets, packs of napkins. There was nothing in Miranda's kitchen that showed her personality. No photos on the fridge, no chalkboard with scrawled reminders. The room was purely functional, and Sophie could imagine her predecessor in here, microwaving a meal for one, washing up a single plate, a knife and a fork. She had a flash of what her life would be like if Guy left her and took Daisy after persuading the court that Sophie was mentally unstable. She shuddered and went into the next room.

The living room was spacious, with tall bookcases full of neatly arranged hardbacks, a small TV and a cream Ikea sofa. There were several framed photographs on the mantelpiece, including a picture of Miranda at her graduation ceremony, wearing a gown and mortar board, clutching a scroll and smiling in an embarrassed way at the camera. She was pretty, with mousy hair, a round face and intelligent eyes. There were no recent photos of her around; again, this room told Sophie little about the woman who lived here, except that she loved books.

Apart from the bathroom, there were two more rooms: the master bedroom and a small second bedroom which Miranda had turned into a study. The master bedroom was at the front of the flat, the study at the rear, next to the kitchen, with a window overlooking the garden. Sophie decided to check this room first.

A computer stood on an uncluttered desk. Miranda was certainly a tidy, organised person, a detail that made it seem even less likely that she would do something wild and impetuous like run away to Norway. Sophie opened the top drawer of the desk and pulled out a handful of papers, telling herself it was OK to do this, that if something terrible had happened to Miranda she would want someone to look for her.

The drawer was full of bills and paperwork that had yet to be filed. Gas, electricity, a reminder to register to vote, a credit card statement showing a small outstanding balance. Nothing illuminating. She checked the second drawer with similar results, and was about to open the third when she heard a scratching noise at the front door, then the sound of the door opening.

Somebody was coming into the flat.

She froze. It must be the police, returning to fix the back window. She swore under her breath. She hadn't expected them to come so soon. What if they found her here? What was she supposed to say? Would they arrest her? At the very least, it would look like another example of crazy behaviour.

As quietly as she could, she crouched on the floor behind the door, listening as footsteps went past the study into the kitchen, pausing for a few seconds before heading back towards the front of the flat. She tried not to panic. There was no reason for them to come into the study. All she had to do was wait here till they'd gone, then let herself out the front door.

The person in the flat – she wasn't sure if it would be a police officer or the maintenance person they'd sent round – seemed to be walking around the flat. The footsteps receded and she realised they had gone into the front bedroom. What were they doing in there? Oh, shit, maybe they had decided to look into Miranda's disappearance and were investigating the flat. Surely they would come into the study at any moment. It was unlikely she'd be able to get to the back door and out onto the fire escape without being spotted. And what was she supposed to do then anyway? Knock on Joanne's back door and tell her she'd got lost on the way out?

There was a door on the far side of the study, behind another stuffed bookcase, and Sophie crept across the room to open it, relieved to find that it was an almost-empty broom closet. She squeezed herself inside and pulled the door to, crouching in the darkness. All she could hear was her own heart and the blood rushing in her ears.

Almost as soon as she shut the door behind her she heard someone come into the room. Her whole body tensed and she held her breath. If she got caught now she would really have some answering to do. The person in the room stood still for about twenty long seconds, then she heard them leave the study.

Sophie allowed herself to breathe again.

Who'd have thought, when I took the job at Jackdaw, I'd end up here, she thought, suppressing a wild giggle. She was supposed to be at her desk right now, planning campaigns, analysing data, getting to grips with social media. Instead, she was hiding in the broom closet of a woman she'd never met. She pressed her hand to her mouth.

She heard a bang. It sounded like the front door closing. Had the person left already? She got up into a crouching position again and pushed the door open a crack to listen.

Immediately, she smelled smoke. She pushed the door open another couple of inches and sniffed. It wasn't the familiar scent of cigarette smoke. This smell was thicker, more acrid. She pushed the closet door fully open and emerged into the study. The smell was growing stronger and a part of her brain was screaming at her to get out, to run. Tentatively, she poked her head out of the study.

Flames rushed towards her along the carpet.

Chapter 30

Day thirty-seven, Tuesday, 12 May, 2015

Acting on pure instinct, she stepped back into the study and slammed the door, trying to make sense of what she'd seen. Smoke was pouring from the open doorways of the master bedroom and living room, gathering like an evil cloud at the ceiling, and the floor was on fire. That was the strangest thing, the way the flames had rushed along the carpet towards her, as if following a trail.

The toxic smell she'd detected when she was in the closet, that was so much stronger now she was standing in the study, wasn't a cleaning product. It must be some kind of fuel: kerosene or turpentine. And they had splashed it in here too, and not just on the floor. The desk and computer were shining where liquid had been thrown over them. Thankfully, the arsonist had neglected to leave a trail from the hallway into the study. The fire had rushed past the closed door, presumably into the kitchen. But Sophie knew it wouldn't be long before the flames reached beneath the door and ignited the liquid around her feet.

Her head was telling her to do two things at once. Call the fire brigade. Find a way out. The fire brigade would have to wait. She might only have seconds.

There was a large sash window behind the desk. She pushed the desk aside and unlocked the window, then tried to push it upwards.

It was stuck. She tried again. Smoke had entered the room and her eyes watered, blurring her vision. Panicking, she grabbed the computer and threw it at the window. It bounced off the frame. Screaming with frustration and fear, acting almost purely on instinct now, she climbed onto the desk and tried to push the window down from the top. It wouldn't budge. She yelled at it, calling it every foul word she could think of it, and it moved. Just half an inch, but it gave her hope. She worked her fingers into the gap and pushed down with all her strength.

The window slid down like it was greased with butter. Now the top half of the window gaped open.

She stuck her head through the gap and shouted, 'Fire!' at full volume. The woman who was reading in the garden turned to look and jumped to her feet, running over towards Sophie, who was convinced the flames were going to burst into the room and kill her at any moment. There were terrible noises coming from outside the study, crackling and rushing, the sound of items collapsing. She prayed Joanne and baby Millie had got safely out of their flat, and Hettie on the other side.

She peered down at the garden. It was too far to jump, even if she could get out of the window. The edge of the fire escape was perhaps a metre and a half to her right, outside the kitchen. There was no way she could manoeuvre herself through the top half of the window with any hope of doing anything beyond plummeting head first to the garden below. She looked around desperately. Miranda had an old-fashioned stereo system with a record player and two bulky speakers which sat on a table next to the desk. She jumped down from the desk, grabbed a speaker, yanking the lead from the back of the stereo, and smashed it against the window.

The lower half of the window had four panes, the heavy wooden inner frame creating a cross. The pane she'd struck shattered and glass rained onto the garden below. Sophie rammed the speaker into the second pane, then the remaining two. Now most of the glass was gone but the stout wooden cross still barred her exit.

It was growing hotter in the room, the fire pressing against the outside of the door. Smoke poured into the room, blinding her, burning her eyes. With a scream of fury, she swung the speaker at the frame. It cracked, giving her hope. She slammed the speaker into it again, and the wood splintered. One more heave, one more scream, and the wood broke apart, revealing a large enough gap for her to squeeze through onto the window ledge.

She climbed out, clinging to the edge of the window, till she found herself on her knees on the ledge. Carefully holding on to what remained of the frame, she pushed herself into a standing position. At that moment, the door of the study blew open and flames and a great cloud of black smoke rushed into the room.

Pushed back by the wall of heat, Sophie almost toppled backwards, but managed to cling on, trying not to look at the burning carnage inside the study. She needed to focus on the fire escape. It had appeared so close to the window from the inside, but now she saw that she'd need to leap to the left, twist in the air and seize the railing. There was nothing for it, though. Broken bones, disfiguring burns – all she wanted was to survive. She wanted to see Daisy again, to hold her in her arms and kiss her hair. She wanted to see Guy too, to have a chance to make things right between them. And she wanted to live for herself. She wasn't prepared to die.

Not now. Not here.

She inched along the windowsill to the left as far as she could, aware of the woman in the garden shouting at her. Other people were there too now, their voices blending together. She could hear sirens and a baby crying.

She bent her knees as much as she dared, glanced to the left, twisted her body and leapt for the fire escape.

———— ————

Ten minutes later she sat in the back of an ambulance on Palace Road, a blanket around her shoulders, paramedics checking her over. She had a bruise on her chest where she'd struck the fire escape and her lungs were sore, her throat irritated by the smoke she'd inhaled. She was dizzy and light-headed, adrenaline draining from her body, and the paramedic told her she needed to watch out for signs of shock: feeling weak, clammy skin, a slow pulse.

A policewoman stood outside the ambulance, waiting to talk to her. When the paramedic finished checking Sophie over, the policewoman stepped up into the vehicle.

'I need to ask you a few questions, if that's all right.'

Sophie rocked back and forth, hugging herself.

'What were you doing inside the flat?'

Sophie coughed. She was exhausted, couldn't blink without seeing herself suspended in mid-air, the moment before she hit the railing on the fire escape. She knew she would revisit that moment many times, would picture herself falling to the hard ground beneath, bones breaking, darkness swallowing her.

She turned her face towards the policewoman who was looking at her warily, like she was a dog who might bite. She thinks I'm unhinged, Sophie thought, suppressing a giggle.

'Sophie?'

She remembered the detective who had spoken to her at the hospital when she visited Josh. She was now certain that everything was connected.

'I want to talk to DC Darren Paterson,' she said.

Sophie sat opposite Detective Paterson in an interview room at Paddington Green Police Station. She had washed her face, brushed her hair and reapplied make-up, but her clothes still stank of smoke.

She found she liked it. It gave her strength.

Made her feel reborn.

Paterson sipped from a can of Diet Coke, scepticism in his blue eyes.

'So, let me get this straight. You think Cassandra Said murdered Miranda Singer? And that she came back earlier this afternoon to set fire to Ms Singer's flat? You also think she is responsible for the attack on Josh Barker?'

'That's exactly right.'

'I see. All right, let's start with Josh. What's Cassandra's motive?'

'They had a huge falling out that day in the office, which I told you about at the time. He said some pretty strong words to her. They've made up now, apparently, but that's probably all an act. And I think . . . I think she'll do anything to further and protect her career. It's why she accused Matt of sexually harassing her, so she could have his job.'

'You've lost me.'

Sophie explained about the email. 'But I think she set him up. I bet she logged on to his computer and sent the email herself.'

Sophie coughed, eyes watering. She tried to ignore the dizziness that made the room tilt from side to side for a moment before righting itself. Paterson apparently noticed.

'Are you sure you're up to this conversation?'

'Yes. I'm strong, DC Paterson.' She lowered her voice to a whisper. 'I am a phoenix.'

'What?'

'Have you checked where Cassie was this afternoon?' Sophie was aware that Simon and co would know now that she hadn't really been sick. She had broken an important rule. But she didn't care right now; she'd deal with that problem later.

'I have indeed,' Paterson replied. 'Cassandra was at her desk, working. There are dozens of witnesses who can attest to that. And we already established that Josh's attacker was male, about six foot, "built like a brick shithouse", to use Josh's words. So unless Cassandra turns into the Incredible Hulk when she gets angry . . .'

Sophie didn't smile. 'She has a male accomplice. The same man who took my daughter to the library in the basement and told her I was going to die.'

Paterson's sceptical expression became one of outright disbelief. This was so frustrating, but not surprising. She knew it sounded crazy. But she was also convinced she was right.

'So her "accomplice" works at Jackdaw too. Any idea who it might be?'

She leaned forward. 'I'm guessing it's a secret boyfriend of hers, someone who's in thrall to her. She's very attractive. She could twist any man around her finger. She tried it on my husband. I'm guessing she sent her accomplice round to Miranda's flat too.'

'I . . . see. Why today? How come it happened while you were there?'

'I don't know. Somebody must have tipped them off, let them know I was there. One of the neighbours, maybe.'

Paterson narrowed his eyes and it struck her: maybe they thought *she* had started the fire, messing it up so she only just got out alive.

'Oh, my God, you don't think it was me, do you?'

'I don't know, Mrs Greenwood.'

'What possible reason would I have for burning down Miranda's flat?'

'You tell me. You're the only person who we know for a fact was in the flat, a place where you shouldn't have been.'

'What? I know I shouldn't have gone in there, but your lot, the police, won't do anything to try to find Miranda. I told you, I was in the study when someone came in, so I hid in the closet. Stop looking at me like that! I'm not crazy. And I'm not an arsonist.'

He sat back and stretched out his legs, accidentally kicking her under the table and apologising.

'All right. Let's rewind. I admit Miranda Singer's sudden disappearance does look unusual, and I understand your concern about her. But you have to understand, thousands of people go missing every year and the great majority of them do so voluntarily. For a number of reasons they decide they want a fresh start somewhere new. Perhaps they are running from something—'

'Like persecution at work.'

He ignored that. 'Or they could be suffering from mental health problems. Depression, for example. The chances are Ms Singer has gone off on an extended holiday. Or maybe she is holed up with some fella she met. It's possible that she has committed suicide, that her body is at the bottom of the Thames – that, sadly, happens a lot too. Of course we need to find out who set the fire in the flat, but there is no evidence that it was Cassandra Said.'

Sophie wanted to scream. 'You don't really think it was *me*, do you? I don't see you arresting me. She was scared of someone. Joanne next door said that too, that just before Miranda had been talking about wanting protection. Have you spoken to her?'

'Not yet. It's on my list.' Paterson took another sip of Coke.

Sophie leaned forward across the table and put her head in her hands. 'This is maddening. There's a murderer out there. I've pointed you straight at them and you're refusing to believe me. You're going to regret it when I wind up dead. Or maybe I'll disappear like

Miranda. And you'll say, *Well, she did seem mentally unstable. She's probably at the bottom of the river. What a shame.*'

'Mrs Greenwood, Sophie, calm down. *Sit* down.'

Sophie, who had stood up during her outburst, reluctantly sat back in the uncomfortable chair.

'Let me spell it out for you,' Paterson said. 'Josh was attacked by a random thug. It was what is commonly referred to as a gay-bashing. Your issues at work with Miss Said are exactly that – common work problems. Yes, she does sound like a troublemaker, but it's something your management needs to sort out.'

'So what are you going to do?'

'We – by which I mean the Metropolitan Police's fire investigators – are going to find out the cause of the fire at Ms Singer's flat. They will no doubt want to talk to you. And then they will follow the evidence. If that evidence leads them towards Miss Said, then we will interview her. And, of course, I will report what you've told me.'

Sophie got back to her feet, the chair scraping against the hard floor. 'And what about me? Cassie must know I'm on to her. That puts me in danger.'

'Sophie, I really don't believe—'

She left the room without letting him finish and hurried out of the police station, ignoring him when he came out of the interview room and called her name. Outside, she ran across the road, narrowly avoiding a bus, and into a little alley between two shops. She leaned against the brick wall, catching her breath and fighting the dizziness that threatened to topple her. The fucking police. They were useless. Maybe, eventually, they would find evidence that led them to Cassie. But how long would that take?

She tried to get her thoughts straight. If Cassie knew she was on to her – and she badly wanted to know how the younger woman had known she was at Miranda's – what would she do? It would be risky for Cassie to act now. If Sophie suddenly perished in an 'accident', Cassie must be aware that was a coincidence too far. If she was Cassie, she would wait, bide her time and see what happened next.

Which meant Sophie had time too. Time to prove to the police that she was right. As long as she was careful and didn't allow herself to go anywhere she would be in danger, she was confident she would be fine.

Cassie might think she was clever, but Sophie was going to prove she was cleverer.

Chapter 31
Day thirty-seven, Tuesday, 12 May, 2015

'Let's get you out of those clothes,' she said. 'You stink of kerosene, or whatever it was you used.'

He unbuttoned his shirt and saw her wrinkle her nose as he passed it to her. Such a pretty nose. He noticed his hand was trembling as he unbuckled his belt and pushed his trousers down, stepping out of them so he stood before her in his underpants. He felt embarrassed. He knew he needed to go underwear shopping, get some things she would like. Calvin Klein or something. He didn't know much about clothes, though she always seemed to like the presents he bought her: the satin chemises and skimpy underwear. She liked the schoolgirl outfit he bought for her too, though she drew the line at dressing as a policewoman; said it was too close to some of the things she'd had to do for *him*.

'I need a drink,' he said. 'What have we got? Any whiskey?'

'He's got some,' she said. 'He won't notice if we take a little.'

She went into the study and came back with a tumbler. He swallowed most of it down in several large gulps, gasping as he sat down in an armchair, still wearing only his underpants. He wondered when she was going to offer him a blue pill, wished his stupid penis would work without it.

'I had no idea she was in there,' he said.

She sat opposite him, her face solemn. 'It would have ruined everything. All our planning.'

'Though wouldn't a part of you be happy if she were dead? If it were all over? At least she would have, you know, died in pain.'

He grimaced as he took another swig of whiskey. It was good stuff, unsurprisingly.

'No!' The look she gave him, as if he were stupid, made him feel small. 'You know I don't want her to die. Not until she's suffered. That's the whole point. She can't die until she knows how it feels . . . How I felt.'

'I'm sorry. Of course, I understand.' They'd had this conversation before. 'But you know I won't be fully happy till it's done and we can get on with our lives. Our new beginning, where nobody knows us.'

She was lost in thought and didn't respond. In moments like this he feared she didn't love him, that she was too locked up in the prison of her own pain, that what had happened to her meant she would never be free. He leaned in to kiss her, sucking in his belly as he did so. To his relief, she responded and kissed him back.

When they drew apart at last, he said, 'All the evidence that might have been in Miranda's flat will be gone now. It should have bought us the extra time we need. It won't be much longer now.'

She nodded then got up and took his hand. 'Come on, let me show you the room. It's almost done. I've got it all set up.'

He followed her, finding a robe and slipping it on. He watched her bottom as she left the room in front of him, felt a little twitch down below and wondered if something might happen, but the moment he thought about it he dwindled. Just like always.

Thank God she understood. For years, he had been terrified of relationships. The idea of getting into bed with another woman, after the last few humiliations, made him go cold inside.

She was so good to him. So good for him.

He would do anything for her. *Anything.*

She opened the door that led to the basement and led him downstairs.

He shivered. It was a beautiful day outside, but in here, entering this dim room beneath ground, it felt like a damp February morning.

'Welcome to the new improved improvement room,' she said with a smile.

He looked around, impressed. It was really coming along. The grubby, lumpy mattress on the floor. The chair with leather straps to hold the subject in place. The metal trolley and all the glinting instruments. The hose pipe attached to the wall. There was a little glass case in the corner in which cockroaches wriggled and squirmed, fighting to get out. Speakers had been set in the walls so loud, discordant music could be blasted into the room.

He walked over to the trolley and picked up a little leather pouch, unfolding it to reveal a row of acupuncture needles in varying lengths and thicknesses. He slid one out and held it up, examining it as it glinted beneath the strip light.

He thought about the things his beloved intended to happen here and something clenched inside him. But seeing the happiness on her face, he relaxed. She deserved this. And he would do everything he could to make sure she got what she deserved.

Chapter 32
Day thirty-nine, Thursday, 14 May, 2015

'Sophie, can you help me with this?'

Cassie came round to Sophie's desk with a printout of some marketing copy she'd written for the forthcoming Jackdaw catalogue. Cassie was acting as if nothing had happened and Sophie was forcing herself to be completely normal too. In fact, Cassie appeared so relaxed that for a fleeting moment Sophie wondered if she'd got it all wrong, but then she reminded herself that Cassie was a brilliant actor, that she was somehow able to remain utterly calm under pressure.

The previous evening, Sophie had read an ebook about psychopaths, prompted by Josh's comment. They were able to disguise themselves as normal people, adapting behaviours that allowed them to pass through life with their true nature undetected. Remaining extremely cool under pressure, convincingly manipulating people, feeling no remorse or regret – Sophie was certain these were all traits that Cassie shared with the subjects in the book. According to the author of this book, many CEOs and high-powered people were psychopaths who had climbed to the top, ruthlessly treading on anyone who stood in their way, leaving a trail of ruined lives and careers behind them.

She looked at Cassie, who was wearing a black crepe mini-dress that Sophie was pretty sure was from Stella McCartney's new collection, and thought, *I've got your number.*

'That's great, Cassie,' she said, after making some suggestions, hoping the insincerity didn't show in her voice. 'Good work.'

'Thanks, Sophie.'

At that moment, Simon appeared, barrelling into the office with a look of wide-eyed excitement on his face. He headed over to Sophie and Cassie.

'Just the people I was looking for. You've heard about the PR event we're running next week?'

'The zombies?' Cassie asked.

'That's the one!'

Sophie tried not to groan. The event Simon was referring to was the brainchild of Rebeka Venters in PR, with the aim of building up excitement about a new young adult book called *Consumed*, a zombie novel in which a group of teenagers hole up in a mall while the undead pound at the doors. Rebeka had invited a group of journalists and bloggers, along with a number of 'key influencers', including a popular YouTuber and a guy who ran a digital radio station for younger teenagers. They, along with a group of PR and marketing people from Jackdaw, were going to take part in a simulated zombie survival experience.

'We need a couple more volunteers,' Simon said.

'I'll do it,' Cassie said immediately.

'That's the spirit. Sophie?'

How could she say no now? 'Sure. Sounds fun.'

Simon grinned broadly then bounced off across the office like Tigger. Who'd have thought Simon would be so excited by the prospect of dressing up and pretending to kill the undead?

At lunchtime, Sophie headed towards the exit. She had a couple of phone calls to make and didn't want anyone to overhear her. As she walked through the office she was certain people were watching her, whispering about her. She didn't think anyone, apart from Cassie and her accomplice, whoever that was, knew she had been at Miranda's flat on Tuesday. Her name hadn't appeared in the tiny newspaper report about the fire. It seemed that when the police called to check whether Cassie had been at work when the fire broke out, Paterson hadn't revealed to whoever had taken the call – presumably Natalie – that Sophie had accused Cassie of being responsible. So nobody knew that rather than being off sick, Sophie had almost died on Tuesday.

Almost died. She was still waiting for the shock the paramedics had warned her about to kick in.

She hadn't told Guy about the fire either. He was collecting Daisy from school when she got home from the police station and she'd stuck her smoky clothes straight in the washing machine and jumped in the shower so she smelled fresh and clean when her little family came in. She had wanted to tell him. She knew he would be horrified, would insist that she didn't do anything else to put herself in danger. And it wasn't just that: she also knew he would see it as further proof that she was losing her mind. He would drag her to the doctor, try to persuade her to get a prescription for antidepressants. It would all be ammunition he could use if he decided to leave her; if they ended up in a custody battle.

Thinking about the state of her relationship with Guy almost brought her to tears. She prayed their marriage was repairable, that they would be able to get back on track once this was all over, and then she would tell him what had happened. But for now, she couldn't risk it. She needed to stay mentally sharp.

In fact, she felt sharper than ever. The fire had burned away her remaining doubts. She really did feel like a phoenix, reborn among the flames. She knew she shouldn't have said that aloud to DC Paterson – another person who thought she was crazy. She needed to be more careful.

If only all these people would stop staring at her, stop whispering and giving her dirty looks. As she passed through reception, she noticed a tall man with broad shoulders staring at her. She met his gaze. Was he Cassie's secret boyfriend? But as she stared back he turned away and stalked off towards the lifts. Then she caught the woman on the reception desk watching her. What was wrong with all these people? She pushed through the revolving doors and stood blinking in the warm sunshine beneath the gargoyles.

Settled on a bench in a courtyard behind the main thoroughfare, Sophie made the first of the two phone calls she'd been planning all morning.

She was quickly put through to the HR department at Goldfinch Books.

'Hi, I'm calling from Lawrence House. I'm after a reference for a Cassandra Said. I believe she used to work in your marketing department and I was wondering if it was possible to have a word with her former manager.'

The woman at the other end tapped at her keyboard. 'That's Diana Silver. Let me transfer you.'

This was easy. People were so trusting.

Trust no one, she heard Liam say.

A woman with a cut-glass accent came onto the line. 'You're after a reference for Cassandra? I thought she went to Jackdaw. Can't you get one from them?'

'We will. But, ah, Cassie, Cassandra, doesn't want her current employer to know she's looking for other jobs. And I'd appreciate your discretion, of course.'

'Hmm. I bet.' The other woman paused. 'Listen, I don't really feel comfortable doing this.'

'Going behind Jackdaw's backs, you mean?'

'No. Well, there is that as well.'

'You mean you don't want to give Cassandra a reference?'

Another long pause. This was very interesting. Diana Silver said, 'I don't feel in a position to, to be honest with you.'

'But you were her manager, weren't you?'

'I was, but . . .' She made a strangled noise in her throat. 'I'm sorry, but I simply don't feel comfortable doing it. Goodbye.'

'Wait—'

But Diana Silver had hung up. That really *was* interesting. What had happened at Goldfinch? She racked her brains, trying to remember if she knew anyone who worked there . . . publishing was such a small world. But she couldn't think of anyone.

She made her second call, following up on a contact she'd established the day before.

After speaking to the man, she remained on the bench for a little while. Was she wasting her time doing this? She knew she wouldn't be able to prove that Cassie killed Miranda. She couldn't follow her around everywhere. Yes, she could keep an eye on her, but the best she could do at the moment was to find evidence of psychopathic behaviour in Cassie's past. She would follow up with Goldfinch later, maybe go to see Diana Silver in person, be honest with her. In the meantime, she was going back further. To Cassie's school days.

⌣

She called Guy to tell him she was going to be a little late home. He grunted and asked if she wanted to talk to Daisy, which she did as she was walking to the bus stop. An hour later, she disembarked in Dulwich Village in south London, just a few stops past where she usually got off.

Sophie passed the entrance to the park where she had come on many occasions before Daisy started school as a change of scene from Brockwell Park. In the distance, she could see Dulwich College, one of London's oldest and best private schools, a cathedral-like building set within huge grounds with immaculate lawns where schoolchildren played cricket and rugby. Cassie hadn't attended the College, but had gone to a private school nearby. William Abbott's Girls School. Or Wags, as everyone called it.

As Cassie's manager, it was easy for Sophie to get access to Cassie's CV and learn that she had attended Wags between 2002 and 2009. Half an hour on Facebook and she had been able to make contact with several of Cassie's former classmates, telling them she was planning a surprise for Cassie and needed them to be discreet. But none of them wanted to help. Finally, Cassie had contacted the man she was meeting today. Not a former student but the school caretaker, who was a member of the school's Facebook group.

She walked till she reached a small field with a children's playground. Wags was still five minutes' walk away, but the caretaker had asked if they could rendezvous here, away from his place of work.

Sophie shaded her eyes with her hand and scanned the area. Several mums and a dad were watching their small children running around the playground. A little further back were some benches. A man wearing a brown cap sat on the bench that was furthest to the right. He stood up as Sophie approached.

'Mr Headley?'

'That's me.'

He was in his early sixties, weathered, with a bulbous nose and deep frown lines. He seemed nervous, peering over Sophie's shoulder to check no one was behind her. He gestured for Sophie to sit beside him. She eyed the blob of bird shit on the bench and chose to remain standing.

Sophie asked, 'How long were you the caretaker at Wags?'

'I'm still the caretaker.' His voice was gruff. 'One more year till I can retire.' He coughed and produced a pack of cigarettes from his pocket. He lit one and coughed again, his eyes watering. He didn't look like he'd last far into his retirement.

'So can you tell me what happened with Cassandra?'

'It was a tragedy, that's what.'

Sophie waited.

'She was to blame for that girl's death. One of the boarders. Pretty girl.' He coughed. 'They found her in the bath, with her wrists slashed. She'd done it properly too, you know. Length-wise.'

He traced a line from his wrist to his elbow with the butt end of his cigarette.

'And how do you know Cassandra was involved?'

'Because of the suicide note. They were both in the running to be Head Girl. Straight A students, prefects, immaculate academic records. Except Nadine was popular and Cassandra – well, she didn't have many friends. I'm not sure if she had any, to be honest.'

Sophie nodded, enrapt. 'What did the note say?'

'Well, before poor Nadine topped herself, Cassandra accused her of being a bully. She reported her to the principal, said Nadine had made a racist remark, which was utter rubbish according to the other kids. I mean, we have kids from all over the world here. All the colours of the rainbow.' He shook his head. 'They were talking about suspending the poor girl, even expelling her. Her note said that's why she topped herself, because no one believed her. And because of the shame.'

'And you're sure Nadine was innocent?' Sophie asked.

'That's what everyone said. I mean, no one witnessed her saying anything racist and from the amount of crying and hysteria that went on afterwards she was a popular lass. The kids said Cassandra accused Nadine of being a racist to sabotage her chance of being Head Girl.'

Removing anyone who stood in her way, just as she'd done with Matt. And Miranda.

'So what's she done now?' Headley asked.

'I can't tell you, I'm afraid.'

Hadley grunted. 'Well, whatever it is, I hope you bang her up. I never liked her. She was condescending. A spoilt little rich girl.'

'How rich?'

'Filthy rich. Her dad owns some big accountancy firm in the City.'

So that explained the expensive clothes.

Sophie said goodbye to Headley and headed down the hill towards home. At one point she heard a noise behind her and went stiff, certain she was about to be attacked, instantly regretting walking home on her own. But it was a jogger, thundering past her. By the time she reached her street her legs were shaking and she felt like she might faint. Perhaps this was shock, arriving at last.

She neared her flat, desperate to lie down in a dark room. But nearing the building she paused. There was something attached to the front door. Oh, Jesus, not again.

It was another dead mouse, superglued by its tail, its guts sliced open, innards hanging out. There was something wrong with the rodent's face. Peering closer, fighting nausea, she saw that someone had cut off its snout, exposing its tongue and its yellow back teeth.

Chapter 33

Day forty-six, Thursday, 21 May, 2015

London glimmered in the sunshine. Perched on the edge of the fold-down seat in the black cab, Sophie wished she could relax and enjoy the view of the city as it stretched out before her. Canary Wharf and its gang of less-famous friends casting a moneyed glow over the East End. The former Millennium Dome, now a cavernous music venue. The Shard towering imperiously over all of them. She had no idea what today was going to be like. It really wasn't her kind of thing. Zombies, for God's sake.

The black cab turned into a car park ringed by chain fences, weeds busting through the tarmac, litter and abandoned supermarket trolleys scattered about. At the far edge loomed what had once been the Fresh Fields Shopping Centre, a mall that had closed down three years ago. Sophie took in the boarded-up windows, the graffiti, the huge banner strung across the entrance – WELCOME TO THE ZOMBIE-POCALYPSE – and wondered what she'd let herself in for.

The cab pulled up near the entrance and Cassie put her hand on the door handle. Sophie reeled, having a sudden flash of those fingers wrapped around the handle of a knife, plunged deep in

Miranda's chest. Or the same hands, shoving Miranda into the dark, nocturnal waters of the Thames.

Cassie hopped down from the cab and caught Sophie's eye. She gave a little smile and Sophie tore her eyes away, terrified that Cassie could see what she was thinking. That she would know Sophie knew what she'd done. As she exited the taxi, she moved round to the other side of the vehicle, keeping it between Cassie and herself. Again, she wondered who Cassie's accomplice was. Could he be here today? She wasn't yet sure which other members of staff were coming, but she needed to be vigilant, didn't she? It was safe in the office – as long as there were other people around, anyway – but being here, in this alien environment, Sophie felt newly afraid.

Did Cassie suspect that Sophie was on to her? She had originally thought that Cassie, or her accomplice, had followed Sophie to Miranda's flat, had set the fire to get rid of her. But the more she thought about it, the more she realised it was more likely they had been trying to destroy evidence. Perhaps they had murdered Miranda at the flat and were worried there would be DNA evidence there. Sophie still didn't know why Cassie felt the need to act now. Did she know Sophie was looking into Miranda's disappearance? Had someone tipped her off?

The police weren't exactly treating this as a high priority. According to Paterson, they were still waiting for the report from the fire investigator, though they had spoken to Joanne next door, who confirmed that Miranda 'might have' been afraid of someone. This was maddening, but Sophie guessed Joanne was terrified someone was going to come looking for her and set her flat on fire if she said too much to the police.

Simon clapped his hands together, snapping Sophie back to the present moment. 'I cannot wait for this.'

Sophie forced herself to smile. It was important to keep up appearances in front of her boss. Thinking logically, it was surely more likely that Cassie would try to get rid of her through legal means, driving her out or getting her fired, rather than risk trying to get away with another murder. So Sophie had set about making herself bulletproof, working late into the evening, delivering reports and plans to Simon that showed her to be an invaluable member of staff, the perfect hire. She put her head down and ignored the gossips and the misguidedly jealous looks. She didn't make any personal phone calls or look at the Internet. She ate lunch at her desk every day. She did all this to ensure Cassie wouldn't have anything negative to write in her file. And when Sophie spoke to Cassie she was professional, polite, friendly, teeth gritted, wondering if Cassie could see through her act.

It had been agony. Because all the while, she could sense Cassie watching her, waiting for her to slip up. She liked to think that Cassie was confused, like a chess player whose opponent starts making erratic moves. And the more confused Cassie was, the more likely she was to reveal her true nature, give Sophie something she could use to prove what she knew to be true.

It just hadn't happened yet.

She wanted to visit Diana Silver but hadn't had time. And the situation at home hadn't improved. Guy was still angry and Sophie knew his fury wouldn't dissipate until he found work. He had been mortified when the second mouse was glued to their door, taking it as a sign that Sisters in Blood were still after him, that they wanted him to keep quiet, to stop blogging.

Sophie didn't tell him she was unsure whether the feminist group was really responsible. Because the real culprit was right here, walking across the car park with her. The mouse, with its snout cut off, was a message for her to keep her nose out. To stop talking to the police. It, and the other one, had been put there by Cassie or her unknown accomplice. And that accomplice had to be the person who'd followed Sophie home after that night in the pub.

A young man, a hipster with a handlebar moustache greeted them beneath the ZOMBIE-POCALYPSE banner. Another young man, this one in a sweatshirt with a large orange Z zigzagging across the front, joined him.

'Welcome,' the first young man said in a loud voice, 'to Apocalypse Z!'

'Some of your group are already here,' the man in the sweatshirt announced, leading Sophie, Simon and Cassie along a corridor lined with Missing posters, faces of early victims of the zombie outbreak, including several children, which Sophie averted her eyes from. He introduced himself as Alex then took them into a back room where Rebeka sat with half a dozen other members of the PR team – glossy young women who could have come off a production line. There were a couple of other men from Jackdaw: a large Indian guy from the web development team and a blonde boy with pipe-cleaner arms who also worked in marketing. Neither of them seemed like they could be Cassie's accomplice.

Sophie was surprised to see Natalie, poking at her BlackBerry with one finger.

'I didn't know you'd be here,' Sophie said, sitting beside her.

'Believe me, I didn't intend to be. But someone from PR dropped out at the last minute and muggins here was asked to take their place. Like I have nothing else to do.' She sighed and returned her attention to her BlackBerry.

Cassie sat down opposite and smiled at Sophie, who found it impossible to smile back.

'You all right, Sophie?'

Simon was giving her a curious look. Oh, God, she hoped her emotions hadn't shown on her face.

'I'm fine. Just thinking about taking down some zombies.' She laughed weakly. 'Let me at 'em.'

'I never knew you were so aggressive,' said Simon.

'There's a lot we don't know about Sophie, I bet.' Cassie delivered the words along with her trademark sweet smile.

Simon laughed. 'You'll have to tell us all your secrets in the pub afterwards.'

Sophie changed the subject. 'How's Roxanne?' she asked Natalie. 'I didn't thank her properly for finding Daisy.'

'She wouldn't acknowledge you anyway, so don't bother.'

'But maybe you could give me her number so I can text her to say thanks?'

While Natalie forwarded her daughter's number, the two guests of honour, the YouTuber and the guy who ran the radio station, arrived and the room erupted in a flurry of air kisses and declarations of delight. Then Alex called for quiet.

'I hope,' he said, 'that you are all prepared for the experience of your lives.' He paused dramatically. 'Before I go on, we have to check if anyone has any health issues that will prevent them from taking part, so my colleague here is going to hand round some forms that I need you to answer honestly. We also have a legal disclaimer form for you to sign, just in case a zombie eats your brains.' He guffawed.

After the forms had been collected, Alex led them into what had once been a shop, where several more members of staff waited, dressed as soldiers with replica machine guns hanging from their hips. The room was dark, illuminated only by the soldiers' Maglite torches and whatever light had crept in from outside. The ceiling was covered with plastic sheeting and there were warning posters on the wall. *What to do if you become infected.*

'OK, listen up,' Alex said. 'This is not a drill. London has been wiped out by a deadly virus that transforms its victims into the living dead. And these zombies have a taste for flesh.' Somebody giggled. 'You have somehow managed to survive and are holed up in this shopping mall, guarded by a small group of soldiers. Their task is to keep you alive.'

Sophie felt Cassie staring at her. She turned her face and Cassie quickly looked away, pretending to be listening intently to the briefing.

'These are the rules,' Alex went on. 'If you get caught by a zombie, you will be marked like this.' He produced an ink stamp and demonstrated it against his arm, leaving a vivid red Z on his skin. 'If you are marked, you join the other team. That's right. You become one of the undead.'

'Awesome,' breathed Simon.

'The zombies cannot be stopped. You cannot fight them. All you can do is dodge them or attract the attention of one of the soldiers and hope they can shoot them in the head before they bite you. Understood? Good. Your aim is to stay alive and complete the mission you will be given. This is Sergeant Major Colin Blackman, who is going to explain your mission.'

He headed towards the door and turned back before exiting.

'Good luck. I hope to see most of you again.'

Sophie listened to Alex's footsteps echo through the empty corridor. There was a moment of eerie quiet before the sergeant major started yelling at them.

'This is your mission,' Blackman shouted, the redness of his face indicating he took his job very seriously indeed. 'What remains of the government has air-dropped a crate of supplies – food and water – at the far end of the mall. We need everyone to head towards this area.' He pointed at a map, indicating a large room on the upper level. 'The undead are attracted to heat, and large groups of human bodies generate what?'

'Body heat,' replied Simon.

'Correct. So we are going to split into small teams. Each team will be escorted by one of my soldiers. Your job is simple – do what you're told and don't get my troops into danger. Got it?'

One of the PR women laughed and Blackman turned on her. 'Think this is funny, do you?'

'Um . . . No.'

'No what?'

'No, sir.'

'Good.' He divided them into teams. Sophie was put into a group with a blogger called Alice, a guy from the PR department called Vince, and Natalie. To Sophie's relief Cassie was put in a team with the YouTuber and the radio guy, while Simon, who seemed like he might combust from excitement, joined another.

Sophie watched Cassie and Simon's teams head off into the corridor towards the heart of the mall, followed by the third team.

'I have no idea why I agreed to this,' she said to Natalie as their soldier, a woman who introduced herself as Jackson, led them into the corridor. Strip lights, no doubt powered by a generator in this fictional set-up, flickered above their heads.

'Me too,' Natalie said. 'Roxy would love it. She's into all that horror stuff. Personally I find real life scary enough. How's Daisy?'

They chatted about their kids as they passed the gaping facades of a number of shut-down shops. Sophie had never visited this place when it was open, but the shops were the same as those found on high streets and in malls all over the country, making this experience feel worryingly real. They passed what had once been a Build-A-Bear Workshop. Sophie peered inside. A teddy bear lay on the floor, stuffing spilling from its ripped belly. She shivered and Natalie lay a hand on her arm.

'It's not real.'

'I know.'

Natalie studied her. 'Are you sure you're OK, Sophie? You've seemed a little intense recently. Simon's not working you too hard, is he?'

'No. Well, I'm busy, but I'm fine.' She longed to be able to tell Natalie everything that was going on. Maybe she could. Natalie might be able to help her.

But before she had time to make up her mind, someone ahead of them screamed and suddenly the corridor was filled with shouting and running footsteps, more shrieks, the drumming of gunshots. Jackson yelled at them. 'The undead! Come on!'

Jackson sprinted into a side passageway, shouting at them to follow. Sophie tried to see what was happening up ahead but the lights went out and they were plunged into darkness. Jackson's torch came on, illuminating the passageway with a thin stream of light.

'Come on, if you don't want to be dinner!'

Sophie, Natalie and the others ran at full speed after Jackson, while screams and shouts echoed behind them. They stopped outside what was once the parents' room.

'Team one were attacked,' Jackson informed them, producing a walkie-talkie which crackled to life. 'We need to take an alternative route.'

Sophie was out of breath, heart thumping. In this moment, she really believed this 'soldier' was their only hope of survival.

'Follow me,' Jackson barked.

They went up a staircase onto the next floor, which looked very similar to the one below: rows of vacant shops with familiar names. It was silent here, nothing but the faint hum of electricity. Sophie found herself hunched over with tension.

'Boo!'

Sophie jumped, clutching her chest.

'Jesus, Natalie!'

The HR woman's eyes widened. 'Wow, Sophie. You're taking this seriously. Are you all right?'

Sophie didn't answer the question. When her pulse had returned to normal she said, 'Natalie, can I ask you something?'

'Sure.'

'Before Miranda left, did she and Cassie have any issues? Like, did Cassie ever complain about her? Or vice versa?'

Natalie checked over her shoulder. 'Why, are *you* having issues with Cassie?'

The other three members of the team were busy watching out for zombies. Sophie said, 'I take it you know about the situation with Cassie and my husband?'

'No! What situation? What's going on?'

Sophie was surprised Simon hadn't told the HR woman. She quickly said, 'Oh, it was nothing in the end. We sorted it out.'

'OK. Well, that's good. I mean, I'd be shocked if there was something going on between Cassie and *anyone*.'

They kept moving through the still, silent corridors of the mall. This really wasn't the time and place for this conversation, but Natalie was always so busy Sophie knew she might not get another chance.

'What do you mean by that?'

'Well. I've always thought Cassie seems kind of asexual. Like she's just not interested in the opposite sex. Or other women, for that matter.'

'Unless it suits her,' Sophie said.

Natalie cocked her head. 'What do you mean?'

Sophie waved it away. She'd been thinking about something she'd read in her book about psychopaths, that they were not capable of love but often formed relationships for convenience's sake: for sex, to keep up appearances or because they got something from the relationship. Sophie had also read that sometimes two psychopaths teamed up to create a killer team. The 'dark angel' Lucy Newton and her husband, Chris, were mentioned in the book as a perfect example of this.

'I don't know what's going on,' Natalie said, 'but if you're having a particular problem with Cassie you can come to me. You know that.'

Jackson motioned for them to stop by an abandoned cookie stall, the front of which was splattered with fake blood.

'What is it?' Sophie asked.

'I heard something. Coming from in there.' The soldier nodded towards what had once been a sports equipment shop.

They all turned to look – and a zombie shuffled out through the door, groaning loudly, followed by another, then another. Becoming aware of them, the zombies' heads jerked up and their groaning intensified. Blood ran down their chins towards their filthy, ragged clothes. Even though Sophie knew they were actors, they looked terrifyingly real, their faces caked in make-up that rendered them unrecognisable.

Jackson yelled 'Run!'

Chapter 34
Day forty-six, Thursday, 21 May, 2015

Sophie sprinted after the soldier. Her heart was pounding, lungs burning.

'There are more of them up ahead,' Jackson said, as several more zombies shuffled into view. 'Runners.'

'What?'

'These ones can run. Oh, shit.' She lifted her machine gun and let off a volley of realistic-sounding shots towards the runners. One of them fell writhing to the ground, before dragging itself back to its feet. Jackson fired again then shouted, 'This way.'

She sprinted past the cookie stall towards a department store.

'OK, now I'm feeling the tension too,' Natalie panted, as they headed through the dark store. Sophie noticed that Alice the blogger was shaking. She tripped over something and shrieked. It was a mannequin, lying on the floor, its head missing.

'Quiet,' hissed Jackson. 'We should be OK in here. But stay alert.'

Sophie walked down the deserted aisle, shoulder to shoulder with Natalie, Jackson taking point, the other two not far behind. Sophie thought she could see someone watching them from the shadows at the edge of the room, but when she peered closer the shape disappeared. What the hell, she asked herself again, was she doing here when her nerves were already so shot?

'So, are you having issues with Cassie?' Natalie asked.

Sophie hesitated. 'Maybe we should talk about it back at the office. Because you're going to think it sounds outlandish.'

'Really?' Natalie paused. 'You know Simon thinks she's the bees' knees.'

'I know. But that's because . . .' She hesitated. 'I'm sure he fancies her.'

Natalie laughed. 'I'm pretty sure Simon is spoken for.'

They reached a motionless escalator and began to tread up it, following Jackson.

'Really?' But Simon's love life was the least of her concerns right now. 'I'm not denying that Cassie is good at her job. It's everything else about her.'

Natalie stopped walking, so Vince and Alice almost bumped into her. Sophie stopped too and the other two carried on, catching up with Jackson.

'What's going on?' Natalie asked.

'Can we talk about it in the office tomorrow?'

Natalie was wearing the stern expression that made people so fearful of her and Sophie regretted saying anything. She should have stuck to her original plan, to deal with Cassie herself without involving any of their colleagues. But now the cat was scrabbling out of the bag and it was going to be hard for her to pretend nothing was wrong.

'OK,' Natalie responded. 'But I should warn you; if you're going to accuse Cassie of anything, you need to be absolutely sure you can back it up. Like I said, Simon thinks she's a superstar and you're still on probation.'

'Are you saying that if I make any kind of complaint against Cassie I could be fired?'

'No. I'm just saying be careful. Don't rock the boat unless you're certain it's not going to capsize. Because it won't be Cassie who drowns.'

For the second time, their conversation was interrupted by an outbreak of activity as two zombies burst through a side door near the top of the escalator, growling and snarling, and one of them grabbed Jackson. She dropped to the ground, playing dead, and the zombies, a man and woman, swivelled towards the others.

'Run!' shouted Natalie, grabbing Sophie's arm and pulling her back towards the escalator. Vince and Alice followed them. But halfway down, two more zombies appeared at the bottom of the steps. Sophie froze. She wanted this game to be over, was happy to surrender so she could get out of here, abandoning her plan to talk to Cassie so she could retreat and think about what Natalie had said.

But Natalie's competitive streak had come out. She grabbed Sophie's arm. 'Stay close to me.'

Natalie led Sophie slowly down the escalator towards the zombies, still holding her forearm. The zombies stayed rooted to their spot at the bottom of the escalator, swaying and growling hammily. They had almost reached them now, the outstretched arms of the *faux* undead almost touching Sophie's chest.

'OK,' Natalie whispered, her lips close to Sophie's ear. 'On the count of three. One, two . . .'

On three, to Sophie's astonishment, Natalie vaulted over the side of the escalator and jumped six feet down to the ground, landing like a cat. 'Come on.'

Sophie hesitated.

One of the zombies, a woman with stringy hair matted with clumps of fake blood, took a step onto the escalator. Sophie propelled herself over the edge, leaping down to the floor. Natalie caught her and stopped her from falling.

'Let's go,' Natalie urged, and they fled towards the exit.

Sophie glanced over her shoulder to see the zombies complete their pincer movement on the remaining two members of the team, taking them out of the game. As soon as they were out of the department store, Sophie drew to a halt, gasping for breath.

'What should we do now?' she asked.

'I've had enough excitement. I'm going to get a cup of tea.'

'Good idea.'

'Then maybe we can chat more about Cassie,' Natalie said.

As they neared the exit, after dodging another herd of zombies, Sophie said, 'I'll meet you out there. I just need to go to the loo.'

Coming out of the bathroom a few minutes later she found a large group of the undead blocking the exit. She hesitated. She could let herself get caught, exit the game, but maybe they would force her to dress up like a zombie and carry on playing. She cursed, and headed back into the mall.

As she turned a corner she found herself confronted by a scene from Dante: lights flickering wildly, some kind of fake smoke, possibly dry ice, filling the corridors. Through the mist, Sophie could make out the silhouettes of zombies, soldiers and civilians, could hear the crackle and pop of machine gun fire. Somebody screamed and Sophie's nerves rattled again, imagining Miranda screaming as she was murdered.

A zombie peeled off from the pack and shuffled towards her, a hand outstretched, snarling at her. It wore a torn soldier's uniform, its face smeared with what looked like dried blood. It opened its hideous mouth.

Sooooo-phie.

She gawped, horrified. The zombie was saying her name. She backed up against the wall, unable to make her legs work. She was going to get bitten. She could feel its teeth tearing at her flesh, hear herself crying out, begging for her life, eyes screwed shut as fantasy and reality flipped and flipped again, so she had no idea that this wasn't real.

'Sophie?'

Slowly, she opened her eyes. The zombie was smiling at her.

'Simon?'

He laughed. 'Yeah. I got bitten. Can you believe it? Ten minutes in and I ran into a trap, got turned.' He studied her. 'Are you OK? You look very pale.'

She felt foolish but couldn't stop shaking. 'I need to get out of here.'

'Come on. Let's get you some fresh air.'

He led her behind the shops to a fire exit. He pushed at the metal bar on the door and, to Sophie's relief, it opened. After two steps out into the open air, Sophie collapsed onto her knees.

'That's right,' he said. 'You get some rest.'

She peered up at him. He looked ridiculous, caked with greenish make-up, which had smeared where he had sweated. He stank of sweat too. He still exuded that air of wild excitement, like static electricity.

'Bit much for you, eh?' he said.

She nodded. Her mouth was too dry to speak. She was kneeling on the pavement beside some wheelie bins, the sun shining above her. She was spent, all the anxiety and stress of the past weeks catching up with her.

'There's a little cafe at the front,' Simon said. 'Maybe we should get you a cup of tea.'

'Yes. Thank you.'

He helped her to her feet. His hand was hot and slippery.

'Listen, Simon, I need to talk to you about something. About Miranda and Cassie and—'

She stopped. Something on the ground beyond the wheelie bins had caught her eye. A shape on the asphalt that she at first assumed to be bags of rubbish. But something about it didn't look right.

She took a few steps forward to get a better view. And realised what it was.

'Oh.' Sophie's hand went to her mouth. 'Oh, Jesus.'

She moved closer, Simon behind her, breathing heavily as the sun beat down on them.

Someone was lying on the pavement in what had once been a pick-up point at the edge of the car park. A small woman, on her back, one arm bent behind her head, black hair covering her face, stirred by the wind that was gentler down here. One leg was twisted beneath her, snapped, with bone sticking out through the skin. There was blood too, pooled around the woman's head and, worse, fragments of bone and brain, where the back of the woman's head had split open as it struck the concrete. Sophie looked up. High above them was the edge of a roof, with a rusting sign that read THE TERRACE GARDEN.

Sophie dropped to her knees, unable to believe what she was seeing. Behind her, she heard Simon say, 'Oh, my God.'

The woman was dead, there was no question.

Cassie was dead.

PART THREE

Chapter 35
Day forty-six, Thursday, 21 May, 2015

'Talk me through it again,' Detective Paterson said, back in the interview room where they'd spoken before. This time, Sophie could already feel the effects of shock: the dizziness, the cold clamminess of her skin. Paterson seemed weary and suspicious, even more sceptical than before. Beside him sat his colleague, DC Angela Lockwood. She had ash-blonde hair and was in her early thirties, a sporty-looking woman with an East London accent.

'Again? Please, I want to get home to my daughter. I've been through it twice already.'

'I just need to check a couple of details.' Paterson consulted his notebook. 'Natalie Evans told us you were meant to be going to the cafeteria with her. Then you disappeared.'

'I told you. I went to the toilet and the exit was blocked by a group of zombies.'

'Well,' said Lockwood. 'Pretend zombies.'

'Of course, I know that! I'm not crazy.'

The detectives' faces were difficult to read, but she bet Paterson was remembering how she'd acted last time they'd met.

'We're just trying to figure out what happened,' Paterson said. 'We need to know if there was anyone else up there with her.'

'You don't think she was pushed off that roof terrace, do you? I never went up there. I didn't even know it existed until afterwards.'

'Is that what you think happened, Sophie?' Lockwood asked.

'I don't know. I assumed it was an accident.'

She refused to entertain the third option – that Cassie had jumped. Cassie was not the kind of person who would commit suicide. That idea seemed ludicrous.

'Oh, my God. You don't think I pushed her, do you?'

Neither of the detectives responded.

A vision of Cassie's corpse, the blood spatters around her shattered head, flashed in Sophie's mind's eye and a cold wave washed over her. 'I can't believe you think I could have killed her.'

Paterson jotted something in his notebook. 'Sophie, a week and a half ago you sat here and told me that you believed Cassandra Said was responsible for the disappearance of Miranda Singer. You told me that she, along with some mysterious accomplice, murdered her, then set fire to her flat, while you were there, in order to cover up what they'd done.' He glanced down at his notes, then up again at her. 'You also referred to yourself as a phoenix.'

DC Lockwood smirked as Paterson went on. 'We know you were in Ms Singer's flat when it was set on fire. And now you were at an event at which Ms Said fell to her death.'

He fell quiet and the two of them just looked at her.

Sophie knew they were waiting for her to fill the silence, that if she was guilty this would be the point where she would blurt something out, incriminate herself. But she had nothing to say. Instead, she covered her face with her hands. They were cold against her skin. 'I don't feel well.'

'You want to see a doctor?' Paterson asked.

She put her hands in her lap and looked from one detective to the other. 'I just want to go home.'

There was a knock at the door and another police officer peered into the room. 'Darren, can I have a word?'

'Interview suspended.' Paterson paused the recorder and stepped out of the room. A couple of minutes later he came back in and gestured for Lockwood to join him. Sophie waited, taking deep breaths, trying to push away the image of Cassie. Because she knew she was innocent, she found it hard to believe the police could really believe she had murdered her. She had a flash of herself in prison, Guy bringing Daisy to visit her, their little girl asking why Mummy wasn't coming home while Guy glowered at her. Or maybe he wouldn't bring Daisy. He'd say he didn't want their daughter growing up with a murderer for a mother. He'd find a new wife, a stepmum for Daisy, somebody nice and harmless who didn't argue, who would never make him miss an important meeting. She was close to tears. She wanted things to go back to how they were before she started this fucking job. She knew Guy didn't really want an insipid housewife. He wanted her, his strong, spirited Sophie, the woman he'd exploded his life to be with. And she missed him, she missed *them*. She needed to get out of this, to persuade the police she was innocent, so she could go back to Guy and talk to him, start to make things right.

Paterson came back into the room, Lockwood at his heels. They took their time sitting back down opposite her.

'Would you like us to call a taxi for you?' Paterson asked.

'I can go?'

He nodded. 'We will probably need to talk to you again, but Natalie Evans has confirmed that you were with her the entire time, and Simon Falstaff also confirms that you were with him for the last fifteen minutes, that he saw you coming out of the ladies, as did a couple of your other colleagues. We know you didn't have time to go up to that terrace.'

Sophie exhaled.

'We're going to want to talk to you again, Sophie, once we've finished interviewing everyone else who was there. Don't leave the city.' He cleared his throat. 'Now, would you like us to call that cab for you?'

Sophie watched London roll by in her second taxi journey of the day. The driver had taken one look at her pale, drawn face and said, 'Better get you home before you throw up, love. You're not going to, are you?'

She assured him that she wasn't, hoping that wouldn't turn out to be a lie. She was relieved that he wasn't trying to make conversation. She didn't feel capable of talking anymore.

She felt numb. That and something else, something unexpected. A sense of loss, of bereavement. Looking at Cassie's tiny, shattered body it had been hard to believe that this woman was responsible for the misery she'd endured these past weeks. Sophie had believed Cassie was a psychopath, something not fully human, but hadn't she bled like any other person? Hadn't her bones broken like anybody else's would?

And did the police believe Cassie had been murdered? Sophie's first instinct when she'd found the body had been that Cassie must have had an accident: gone up to the roof terrace, probably because she wanted to escape the mayhem, walked to the edge and fallen. She imagined crumbling brickwork, Cassie feeling dizzy after running through the smoke and flashing lights inside the building. A dreadful, unfortunate accident. Who would want to push her?

Someone else Cassie had clashed with at work, something Sophie didn't know about?

Or – and this thought made Sophie sit upright, jerking against her seatbelt – could it have been Cassie's accomplice, whoever that was? Had they fallen out? Argued about what the two of them were doing? Was one of them coercing the other? Sophie's head spun with possible scenarios, but then the taxi driver said, 'This it, love?'

She was home. Her train of thought rattled away into darkness as she paid the cabbie and walked up the steps to the front door. No dead mice today. It was only two thirty so Daisy would still be at school, despite what Sophie had said to the police.

She unlocked the door and went inside. Guy was on the sofa with his laptop. He glanced up and immediately stood.

'Sophie. What's happened?'

She stood stiffly as he approached, aware she was trembling, and then the tears came, weeks' worth, like rain at the end of a drought, drenching the dry, cracked earth. Guy embraced her and made reassuring noises while she sobbed and let it all out, telling him everything that had happened, all of it, not even sure if she was making sense. But he seemed to understand and when she got to the end he held her tightly and said, 'It's OK, Sophie. It's over.'

She held his face in her hands and searched his eyes. 'Do you think so? Do you really think so?'

He hugged her again. 'It's over.'

She nodded. She wanted to believe him. But she knew he was wrong.

Chapter 36
Day fifty-one, Tuesday, 26 May, 2015

The moment Sophie entered the office, she felt the atmosphere shift. A hush fell over the people around her, the babble of emotional voices she'd heard when she opened the door dropping to a whisper, then silence. But she could read their thoughts.

There she is. There's the one who found the body.

Sophie saw Gisele put her mouth to Carla's ear and Carla looked over at Sophie, shaking her head. Opposite them, a young man whose name Sophie didn't know – a person who Sophie was pretty sure had barely ever spoken to Cassie – burst into tears and rushed towards the exit, almost knocking Sophie over in his haste to get past.

Perhaps she shouldn't have come in. It was half term, the day after the bank holiday, and Guy wanted her to stay at home with him and Daisy. Nothing would have made her happier – some quality time, at last, with her family – but she was still on probation. She didn't qualify for sick pay yet and they couldn't afford for her to lose a day's earnings, let alone a week's. She'd spoken to Tracey on Friday afternoon, who had described the atmosphere in the office: 'They're all talking like she was their best friend. Every time I go into the kitchen I find someone weeping because they've seen the herbal tea Cassie used to drink.' Tracey was barely able to say Cassie's name without getting choked up. Sophie told her she should take off as much time as she needed, but the other woman insisted she was OK.

Sophie had been back to Paddington Green Police Station over the weekend, where she learned that the police had finished interviewing everyone who had been at the event. No one had seen Cassie or anyone else go up to the roof terrace – they had all been too absorbed by the game they were playing – and there was no CCTV on the top floor or in the stairwell. Paterson gave off the air of a deeply frustrated man. Sophie wished she could be privy to what was going on behind the scenes. They would hardly tell her anything. Did the police believe Cassie was pushed? What were they doing about Miranda's disappearance and the arson attack? Paterson would only tell her that they had found traces of kerosene outside Miranda's front door, trodden down the corridor by whoever had set the fire. So they knew it couldn't be Sophie: she had left via the back window.

Sophie told Paterson her theory, that Cassie's accomplice had been at the zombie event, that he or she – though she felt sure it must be a man because of the attack on Josh, and Daisy had said a man took her to the library – had to be the most likely suspect if Cassie had been pushed. Paterson wrote it all down.

'And do you have any ideas about who this accomplice is?' he asked.

Sophie hesitated. There was one person who she kept thinking about. But the idea that it was him, that he was involved in any sort of crime, let alone violent crime – murder, for God's sake – was too incredible. The first time his name popped into her head, she pushed it away. But it kept coming back to her, a niggling sense of unease, lines of logic knitting together.

'Come on,' Paterson urged. 'Spit it out.'

'Simon Falstaff,' she said quietly.

Paterson didn't seem as shocked as she had expected. 'Your manager. What makes you think that?'

'He was the only man at the event who Cassie had regular, close contact with. I thought at one point they might be having an affair.' She described how she had caught Simon with his fly open. 'And he was there the night I got locked in the office. He appeared shortly after Daisy got lost. And he was so hyped up at the zombie event, acting so weird. There was a moment when he was dressed as a zombie, when he was about to attack me, when he said my name. It sounded just like the voice I heard that night in the office. When I was standing outside Franklin's room, before I heard the rest. Someone said my name.'

Goosebumps rippled her flesh.

'Go on,' said Paterson.

'I keep thinking, what if he led me out that door deliberately? He wanted me to find Cassie's body.'

'But why?'

She could feel the walls of the interview room closing in on her. The more she spoke, the more she believed she could be right.

Trust no one, Liam whispered in her ear.

'He wanted to scare me,' she replied. 'Or he wanted me to see what he'd done. What he's capable of.'

He repeated the same question. 'But *why?*'

'I don't know. I honestly don't know.'

Paterson made another note in his pad.

'Are you going to arrest him?' she asked.

'Sophie, we have no evidence it was him. But we'll certainly talk to him again.'

Now, she sat at her desk, wondering what she would do if Simon messaged her, asking her to pop to his office. Would she be able to act normally around him? Tracey had told her he'd returned to work the day after Cassie's death. That had been the main reason she'd returned to work so quickly, why she hadn't gone to the doctor and asked to be signed off.

Because she felt like the truth was within her grasp now. It was like being compelled closer to a flame. She knew there was a good chance she would get burned, but she couldn't stay away.

⌣

'How are you feeling?' Tracey asked her now. She herself had dark circles around her eyes, like she'd had trouble sleeping.

'I'm OK,' she said. 'I mean, I will be OK.'

'Yeah. I get it. And I guess you don't really want to talk about it?' Tracey waited but when no answer came said, 'Do you want a coffee?'

'That would be lovely. Thank you.'

As she passed Sophie's desk, Tracey paused and put her hand on Sophie's shoulder. 'Just the two of us left now.'

Tracey walked away towards the kitchen, leaving Sophie alone at their bank of desks. She noticed that Cassie's computer had already been removed, her pedestal wheeled away, all traces of her gone. She opened her emails and scrolled through, seeing what she'd missed. Mostly work stuff but also an email from Natalie, saying that if anyone wanted to talk to a bereavement counsellor they should contact her. Then there was one from Brian Mortlake which contained the word 'terrible' five times. Poor sod. He'd definitely had a crush on Cassie. If only he'd known what she was really like.

Sophie tapped out a quick reply to Brian, avoiding shattering his rose-tinted view of the dead woman, and opened a spreadsheet, intending to work on the plan for *The Devil's Work*. But she couldn't concentrate. The numbers danced about the screen, the words were blurred at the edges. It didn't help that she still hadn't finished the thing. Hadn't read another page; still only halfway through. It was just so bleak, so awful – the captive, tortured girl. She'd had her own hell to deal with, thank you. What was she doing back here so soon? Why was she here at all? All the hopes she'd had for this job were shattered. It was not so much tainted as poisoned. If this was a relationship, she'd be ending it right now, getting out while she held on to the last shreds of her sanity. Yes, they needed the money, but, Jesus, there had to be better, easier ways of earning a living. They wouldn't end up on the streets. They could sell the flat, move out of London, go and live somewhere cheap. Go back home, to Wolverhampton. Guy would complain, but it would be good for him too, a change of scene, a new start.

And it wasn't just that this job was poisoned. There was another, more urgent reason for her to leave.

Miranda was almost certainly dead. Cassie was gone.

And, though she had no idea why or what was really going on here, she had a sickening feeling she would be next.

This rush of decisiveness, blended with fear, propelled her to her feet. She opened the drawers of her pedestal to take out the scant personal possessions she kept in there, cramming everything into her bag. Tracey, who had long since returned from the kitchen, watched her, confused and concerned.

She hoisted her bag over her shoulder. She was breathing hard.

'Tracey, I just want to say that it's been—'

But Tracey was staring over Sophie's shoulder, eyes widening. Sophie turned.

Franklin Bird stood behind her. He looked dapper in a charcoal suit, his white hair slicked back with hair cream.

'Going out, are you?' he asked.

'I . . .'

'Could I have a word please, Sophie?'

She didn't want to talk to Franklin, or anyone else. She racked her brain for an excuse.

He leaned forward and lowered his voice.

'I know who you are,' he said.

————

She followed Franklin into the lift in a daze, watched him insert a little silver key into a hole beside the button for the top floor, and waited as they were drawn upwards. She followed him to the door she'd pressed her ear against the night she'd been locked in. He unlocked it and they went inside.

It didn't look like any other office in the building. It was more like a study in an old English house, or the lounge of a gentleman's drinking club, lots of dark wood and leather furniture. There was even a fireplace, with a number of trophies – literary prizes – standing proudly on the mantelpiece, and framed book covers around the walls. Among these book covers, a picture stood out: a family photograph of three generations, the grey-haired elders at the rear, children at the front. Franklin stood in the back row, looking about twenty years younger than now, his face stern but proud. And there, easily recognisable despite only being about twelve, was Jasmine, staring at the floor while everyone around her looked directly at the camera. She looked deeply uncomfortable, like she wished she could disappear. The boy beside her, presumably her brother Sebastian, wore a similar unhappy expression. There was no warmth in this family portrait. If this were Sophie's family, she would keep this picture hidden in a drawer.

He gestured for her to sit in one of the armchairs, sitting down opposite her, hands on his knees as he lowered himself onto the cracked leather. He smiled at her, but only with his lips. His eyes contained as little warmth as the portrait. He picked up a glass from the side table and swigged back the clear liquid, ice rattling against his teeth. A gin and tonic he'd left, already in progress. On the side table was a little pile of spent lime wedges. This wasn't his first, then.

'Let's talk about Jasmine, shall we?' he said.

She swallowed, wishing he'd offer her a drink, make it easier for her to speak. 'Did you know? That first day?'

'No. Actually, I didn't. Why didn't you tell me?'

Was this why he had wanted to talk to her, why he was acting so cold? Because he was angry with her for not being open with him?

'I was worried that it might upset you. Being reminded of her, knowing that one of her old friends was working at Jackdaw. And I didn't want you to treat me differently. I wanted you to see me as just another employee.'

He nodded, his eyes remaining fixed on her face. She felt his scrutiny crawling beneath her skin.

Like a cockroach.

'I thought it might have been something like that.'

'How did you find out?'

Franklin didn't answer straight away. He appeared to be gazing into the past, pain flickering around his lips, and Sophie assumed he was thinking about the loss of his granddaughter. It was almost silent here in his office, cut off from the hustle and enterprise downstairs, the traffic so far below that only the occasional car horn was audible. Sophie could sense the gargoyles just outside the window, watching over this room. Guarding it.

She could tell there was something Franklin was itching to say. He took another swig of his G&T.

'She was a bad girl,' Franklin said at last, breaking the silence.

'You mean Jasmine?'

The tip of his tongue darted out to moisten his lips. 'It was clear from when she was only a few months old. She wouldn't sleep, kept her parents awake all night, refused to feed and made her mother – my daughter – sick. Mastitis. Terrible.'

'Well she hardly chose to *make* her sick, did she? She was just a baby. That's normal. I had mastitis when I—'

'Jasmine had it in her from the moment she was born. It was obvious – the way she looked at you. It was in her eyes.'

'What was?'

'The *devil*.'

He glanced up and, seeing Sophie's face, laughed darkly. 'I don't mean it literally, Sophie. I'm a rationalist. I don't believe in God or Satan or any of that claptrap. But there's a bad gene that runs in our family. My grandfather had it. My aunt. My brother. It strikes randomly. And Jasmine had it too. We treated her, thought she'd got past it, that she was able to live a normal life. That's why we let her go to university. A terrible mistake.'

Sophie stared at him. *Treated* her? The shadow of horrible realisation approached her, but before she had time to process it, Franklin said, 'You must have seen it, when you were with her? Come on, answer me.'

For the first time, Sophie felt afraid of the old man. His eyes were black in the dim light of the office. The twinkly-eyed gentleman she'd first met had gone and now Sophie truly understood why Jasmine had spoken so harshly about her grandfather.

'She was rebellious,' she allowed. 'Non-conformist. She and Liam were very self-absorbed. But to say she had a devil in her . . . With all due respect, that's crazy.'

'Crazy? Ha!' His eyes narrowed. 'Did you know what she was going to do?'

'I don't understand. You mean, did I know she was going to disappear with Liam?'

His black eyes rested on her a moment. 'Yes, yes, of course.'

But it seemed very likely this wasn't what he meant. If Sophie had felt uneasy before, now she felt on the verge of panic. Without truly understanding why.

'What did she tell you about me?' he asked, taking a step towards her. Sophie was pierced by a bolt of fear, like an electric shock. He was old, but he had such authority. No, not authority. A malevolent energy. She could see it now. She understood her friend's animosity.

She moved away from him. 'She told me you were controlling. That the two of you didn't get along.'

He studied her, his head tipped slightly. 'And that's all?'

'What else was there to tell?' The words came out cracked, because she knew. With a rush of nausea, she realised that she knew what had happened to Jasmine when she was a child. What this man had done to her. But it would be a grave mistake to give that away.

'I thought she was exaggerating, that it was a teenage rebellion thing,' she said, fighting to keep her voice even. 'But now I can see why she didn't like you.'

He looked amused, continuing to study her. She felt like he was trying to reach into her head. She fought to keep her breathing even, her expression neutral.

'I think it's time you went,' he said, to her great relief. 'You can take the stairs back down. The door isn't locked from this side.'

She hesitated.

'*Go.*'

Confused, reeling from his words, she went over to the door, then stopped, turned back to him. 'You didn't tell me how you found out that I knew Jasmine.'

'Oh, I checked your CV. Put two and two together. You should have told me when we had lunch that first day. But it doesn't matter now. I always find out in the end. I always find out everything.' He smiled, summoning that twinkle from whatever dark place he kept it. 'It's a gift.'

He got up from his chair. 'Perhaps it's best if you left our family, Sophie. I'm sure we can arrange a severance package for you, even though you've only been here for a short time. I'm not sure you fit in.'

He reached past her and opened the door, ushering her out into the chilly corridor.

———

Sophie ran down the stairs, footsteps echoing about her, all the way to the ground floor. She needed to get out, to get some air into her lungs, clear her mind so she could think straight. Work out what it all meant.

Simon.

And what Franklin had said. *We treated her.*

She pushed through the revolving doors and went out on to the street, searching in her bag for a notepad. She was going to get this down on paper. Figure it out. That had always been her way: she never knew what she thought until she'd written it down.

She looked up to see a woman with black hair on the other side of the road, watching her. No, of course she couldn't be. She just happened to be looking this way. She set off, ignoring the woman, not wanting anything to distract her right now, and headed into the courtyard where she'd made the call to Cassie's former manager at Goldfinch, needing space to think, but before she could sit down her phone rang. It was Paterson.

'There's been a development,' Paterson said. 'A stroke of luck. We've got the guy who almost killed you in that fire.'

'What? Who?'

'A guy called Terry Morgan.'

'I've never heard of him.'

'Take a deep breath,' Paterson said. 'You sound like you're about to have an aneurysm.' She did, gulping down air, pacing around the bench in the sunshine. 'He's a thug for hire. If you need some dirty work done, you call Terry. Debt collection. Extortion. Revenge. Destroying evidence. He's a nasty little shit. We arrested him yesterday on a completely different case, intimidating a witness, and he offered us a deal. Said he could tell us about someone who hired him to set fire to a flat, beat up a gay guy . . .'

'He attacked Josh too? Oh, my God.'

'Yes. Apparently, the woman who hired him told Terry to really give Josh a scare. Morgan says—'

'Hang on. A woman?'

'That's right.'

'It must have been Cassie.'

Paterson was quiet for a second. 'Sophie, it wasn't Cassie.'

'How do you know?'

'Because he spoke to this woman yesterday.'

Sophie wasn't sure if her nerves could take much more. 'Who the fuck is she?'

'He doesn't know. That's the way he operates. No names are exchanged so if he gets caught, the client is in the clear. He charges a lot for that privilege. But listen – this is the reason I'm calling you. He'd been hired for a third job. A job involving you.'

Sophie dropped onto the bench, the phone pressed so hard against her ear it hurt.

'Where are you, Sophie?'

'I'm outside my office.'

'OK. You should go back, make sure you're with other people. Terry Morgan was asked to watch you and await further instructions.'

'Watch me?'

'Yes. And, like I said, he was going to be told what to do. He says he thought they wanted him to scare you in some way. But he swears he doesn't know any more details. Don't panic, OK? We have him in custody. It's unlikely that his client, this woman, even knows he's been arrested, but there's a chance they'll try to find someone else to do it. We're doing everything we can to trace the payments Morgan received, looking at the emails he received and so on. We'll find this woman, don't worry.'

'Did he push Cassie off the roof?'

'No. He has a firm alibi for that – he was in Birmingham all day.'

'Have you spoken to Simon?'

'That's in hand. I have to go, Sophie. But take care, OK, and I'll ring you a little later.'

He ended the call. Don't worry? How the hell was she supposed to manage that?

Sophie sat on the bench, shivering in the sunshine. She felt the buildings crowding in on her, tilting forward like they were going to fall and crush her. Her thoughts had been replaced by white noise, a rushing, humming nothingness that filled her head and made her taste blood.

'Are you Sophie Greenwood?'

She jumped and squinted up at the woman before her, her features blurred by light before the clouds shifted. It was the black-haired woman who had been watching Sophie outside Jackdaw. She was in her late forties, petite with light caramel skin, a designer jacket and a beautiful face.

'I'm Mariem Said,' she said. 'Cassandra's mother. I'd like to talk to you.'

Chapter 37
Day fifty-one, Tuesday, 26 May, 2015

Sophie sat opposite Mariem Said in a tea room a little way from the office, certain that this was exactly what Cassie would have looked like if she had lived for another twenty-five years. Mrs Said was a facsimile of her daughter, with a few lines added to her face, more wisdom – and sadness – in her deep brown eyes, her clothes as elegant as those Cassie had worn. Sophie could barely sit still, unable to get the conversations with Paterson and Franklin out of her head. She had wanted to run back to the office, or take a cab home, but Cassie's mum had given her such an imploring, desperate look that Sophie was unable to say no. Besides, this was a safe place, surrounded by people.

'Thank you for agreeing to talk to me,' Mariem said. She had the trace of an accent. Cassie had mentioned that her parents originally came from Tunisia.

'Cassandra spoke very highly of you,' Mariem said. 'She wanted to be just like you.'

Sophie didn't know what to say. Until ten minutes before, she had believed Cassie was at least 50 per cent responsible for everything that had happened. Who was the other woman, the woman who'd hired this thug? She couldn't process it. She forced herself to pay attention to what Mariem was saying.

'She could have walked into a job at her father's firm – she was always very good with figures, just like her dad, and he wanted her to train as an accountant. But Cassandra was a bookworm. All she wanted to do was work in publishing. It caused some friction at home. My husband threatened to stop her allowance, let her try to get by on her publishing salary. But he was always soft where his daughter was concerned.' A little smile. 'She could always twist him around her finger.'

'My husband's the same with our daughter.'

The smile broadened, but Mariem's eyes shimmered with tears. 'They all are.'

The tea arrived and they sat in silence while they poured their drinks and added milk.

'I understand that you found her.'

Sophie nodded.

'That must have been terrible for you.'

'It was.'

Mariem gazed into space and Sophie thought she had drifted into a reverie about her daughter. But then she said, 'I need to find the person who did this. I cannot believe that Cassie would take her own life, or that she would be careless enough to have an accident. She was a very careful girl. I need to know if you saw anything.'

'I've already spoken to the police about this,' Sophie said. 'They must have told you.'

'Yes. Of course. But that detective – I don't trust his abilities.'

'Mrs Said. I think things are happening. Developments they won't tell us about.'

But the other woman wasn't listening. 'I need to know, did Cassie have any enemies at work? People she'd fallen out with? Someone who might have intended her harm?'

Sophie almost laughed. If Mariem had asked her that a few hours ago . . . But even then, how would Sophie have answered? *Yes, I do know who her enemy was. Me.*

Mariem must have misunderstood the confusion that flitted across Sophie's face.

'Perhaps you only saw the good side of my daughter. But she . . . she had an unfortunate habit of getting on the wrong side of people. She wasn't always easy to get along with. People accused her of doing terrible things. She had, well, my husband would never believe it, but I came to believe that Cassie was a little autistic. On that spectrum, as they say. She was never assessed because her father forbade it, and I was frightened to raise the issue. But Cassie didn't always understand other people and they didn't understand her.'

Guilt enveloped Sophie as Cassie's mother went on.

'There was an incident at school. A girl, Cassandra's rival to be head girl, said some dreadful things to my daughter, called her awful racist names, made disgusting remarks about her father having a harem, vile things I do not want to repeat. Of course, no one ever overheard, but Cassandra came home in tears and I eventually forced her to tell me. I persuaded her to report this girl, though she didn't want to. Then this girl committed suicide. A tragedy, but they tried to blame Cassandra and it wasn't her fault.'

'Oh, God.' Sophie put her hand over her lips.

'Yes. And then, her last job . . . Again, Cassandra didn't want to tell me this, why she left when she appeared to love that job so much. But once again I persuaded her to tell me.' Her eyes narrowed. 'Her manager was having an affair with one of the men in their department. This woman – Diana – was married and he was single. I know such things happen a lot, but my daughter got dragged into it.'

'How?'

'Cassandra was friendly with the man, Charlie, and didn't know he was having an affair with her manager. So, after much agonising, she asked him out on a date. He immediately told Diana about it and she went mad, told Cassandra to keep her hands off him. Cassandra was utterly shocked. She stopped talking to Charlie but Diana was still mad at her. She made her life a misery and eventually drove her out. I wanted to sue the company but Cassandra refused. So I tracked down Diana's husband's contact details and sent him an email, telling him all about his wife's sordid little affair. I heard he left her, and then she broke up with her lover who didn't want a full relationship with her.'

Sophie stared at Mariem. She was clearly not a woman to cross. And now Sophie understood why Diana Silver hated Cassie so much.

'Luckily, Cassandra soon landed the job at Jackdaw. But she changed after that incident with Diana. She thought a man was going to be her manager – Simon, she said – but then she found out it was Miranda Singer. She almost didn't take the job. I persuaded her not to be silly, told her that women have to stick together at work, that they weren't all going to be like Diana Silver. But Cassandra was still sceptical. She'd been burned and she didn't trust Miranda. She was convinced Miranda would eventually try to get rid of her too.'

'So that's why she kept a file on her.'

'Sorry?'

'Cassie had a file documenting everything Miranda did wrong.'

Mariem nodded. 'I'm not surprised. I expect she was trying to protect herself.'

'I thought she was probably keeping one on me too.'

'I don't know about that. But lately she was quiet, withdrawn, like she wasn't enjoying her job so much. I wondered if perhaps you were giving her a hard time.'

Sophie thought about how she had accused Cassie of trying to wreck her marriage. Cassie must have thought Sophie was another Diana Silver.

Mariem's phone rang and she answered it, murmuring so Sophie couldn't hear.

'That was the funeral parlour,' she said to her after the call. 'I need to go. I have arrangements to make.'

'I'm so sorry,' Sophie said.

'Yes. I'm sure.' She handed Sophie a business card. 'Please call me so we can continue our talk.'

'But I didn't see anything that day. I don't know anything.'

'You probably know more than you realise, Mrs Greenwood. Please, call me.'

Mariem Said had exactly the same walk as her daughter. Watching her cross the room, Sophie was convinced for a moment that she was seeing Cassie's ghost. And she fought the urge to jump up, to apologise to the dead woman, to tell her that she now believed she had been completely mistaken about her. Everything she had thought to be true had been wrong.

You know more than you realise.

She got up from the table and headed back to the office.

Chapter 38
Day fifty-one, Tuesday, 26 May, 2015

Simon glanced around nervously, worried there might be some-one watching. A nosy neighbour or busybody. He had managed to park the Land Rover directly outside, which was one good thing. It would make it a little easier.

He knocked on the door and waited.

Adrenaline coursed through him. He'd felt on a permanent high since last week, when he'd watched Cassie's arms windmill as she plummeted from the roof terrace. The look on her face! It still made him laugh, still sent the blood to his crotch. That cool, almost emotionless facade shattered at last. It was a waste, though. She was an excellent little worker, not that that mattered anymore, and quite sexy – though he had gone off her a lot when he caught the look of disgust on her face that time she noticed he had his fly undone. And then he'd forgotten to fasten them before Sophie came into the office, and her nose had wrinkled too. Well, fuck them. One of them was dead already and the other one didn't have long left.

He hadn't planned to kill Cassie. It had been fun to watch her wreak havoc, upsetting Sophie and ramping her paranoia up to eleven. Of course, some of it had been part of the plan – like setting up Matt with that fake email and doing everything he could to make Sophie think Cassie was her true enemy in the office. It had been beautifully orchestrated, even if he did say so himself, but Cassie had really run with her unwitting role. The only downside of Sophie's growing obsession with Cassie had been that it had led her to realise something had happened to Miranda. That had been unfortunate, even if Sophie was looking in the wrong direction.

Anyway, it was a shame when Cassie overheard him talking to his beloved on the phone. He had gone up to the roof terrace for a breather when the excitement of the zombie event had got too much, and called her. She'd wanted to know how Sophie was acting, if the madness was building in her – and it was, it was! It was delicious. Yes, she'd gone out of her head when he'd spirited her precious little girl into the library, but she'd recovered with disappointing speed. When she'd got locked in the office after he'd secured the fire exits and crept around with the recording they'd made, re-enacting moments from *The Devil's Work* – that had stayed with her longer. She'd never truly shed it. It was growing in her. And today! Today she was nearly leaping out of her skin at every turn.

He described all this to his beloved, could almost hear her panting at the other end of the line, prompting him to embellish and exaggerate, describing the look of terror on Sophie's face. '*Just like Miranda when I clamped my hands around her throat.*'

And that was when he'd seen Cassie on the roof terrace with him. She'd presumably gone looking for somewhere to escape to, just as he had. When he saw the shock on her face he knew she'd overheard him. He'd acted without thinking, then rushed downstairs to make sure he'd finished her. And there, lo and behold, he encountered Sophie. Perfect timing.

Killing Miranda had been very different. That had also been necessary, but the hours between the discovery of the need for her death and the delivery of it had been an agony. So much sweeter to simply act! Launching Cassie into space! That was what he'd always fantasised killing someone would be like. The joy of it!

It was Franklin who'd killed Miranda, when it came down to it. If the old bastard hadn't sent her out to his second office for those accursed files, she never would have logged on to the computer there and seen the exchange of emails between Simon and his love.

Thankfully, he was able to catch her before she could piece it together sufficiently to tell anyone, the very evening of the day she'd made her discovery. Her face, like Cassie's, had been a picture, when she'd opened the door and found Simon standing there. He'd strangled her right there in the hallway. That was its own pleasure, of course. Her eyes as she'd tried to fight him. If only he hadn't had to wear gloves. Flesh on flesh. He'd updated Miranda's Facebook status straight away, using her phone which he took with him. *I've made a big decision and have decided to follow my heart. This will be my last status update for a while.* Left it there for a few hours so her friends, including those at work, saw it before he deleted her profile.

The awkward part had been disposing of the body, driving it out to the island and weighing it down, dumping her in the Swale. Then having to keep his nerve at work, pretending she'd done a moonlight flit with a Scandinavian. It was remarkable how gullible people were.

Sophie was the only one who'd come close to discovering the truth.

The door, the same door that Simon had superglued those dead mice to, opened, shaking him from his thoughts.

'Can I help you?'

Simon pulled what he hoped was a fearful, anxious face. 'Yes, hello. I'm Simon? Sophie's manager? May I come in? I have something rather urgent to tell you about your wife.'

Sophie's husband had let him in and was closing the door after him, asking what it was about, when Simon drove the syringe home into his thigh.

Guy slapped his hand away, but the plunger had already gone down. The man looked up at him in really quite amusing outrage. 'What do you think you're—' That's as far as he got.

As Guy fell to the floor, the little girl came running out of her bedroom, a Barbie in her hand. She watched her daddy fall and lie still, then looked up at Simon and backed away. 'You're the man,' she said.

'Hello again, Daisy.' He grinned. 'Your mummy asked me to come and get you. Are you going to be a good girl for me?'

Chapter 39
Day fifty-one, Tuesday, 26 May, 2015

Sophie half-ran back to her desk, almost colliding with Gisele, ignoring Tracey's questions about whether she was OK as she rifled madly through her bottom drawer, looking for the manuscript of *The Devil's Work*. It wasn't there. Fuck. Then she remembered. She'd left it at home.

She could go back, but she wanted it now and it would take her an hour to get home. Perhaps she could call Guy, get him to bring it, meet her halfway. But then he would have hundreds of questions and she needed to figure this out herself first.

Simon had a copy, right here, in the office. She sat at her computer and opened Simon's calendar. He had given her access so she could see if he was around when she wanted to arrange a meeting with him. The whole of today was blocked out: *Meetings – External*.

He wasn't here, but that did her no good. His office would be locked.

She called Natalie, cutting her off before she could make small talk or ask how she was doing. 'I left a file in Simon's office and really need to get to it. Can you unlock the door for me?'

Natalie thought about it.

'It's really urgent. Life or death.'

'OK. I'll meet you there in two minutes.'

Sophie beat her there. She breathed deeply, smoothed down her clothes, tried not to look too frantic. She hoisted a smile in place when Natalie came strolling along the corridor. As soon as Natalie opened the door, Sophie pushed through it, eager not to be engaged in conversation about Cassie or anything else.

Natalie waited in the doorway while Sophie scanned the office. Now, where would he have put it? There were huge piles of papers on his desk, books and reports and files. There were two other manuscripts but neither of them was the one she was looking for.

'Can I help?' Natalie asked, coming into the room. She looked around, tutting. 'He's such an untidy bugger.'

Sophie stopped searching for a moment. 'Have you spoken to Simon since what happened?'

'A little.'

'And how does he seem?'

Natalie pulled a face. 'Oh, you know Simon. He's not exactly Mr Sensitive, is he? I'm sure deep down he's affected by what he saw. I expect it will all come out eventually. I know he was fond of Cassie.'

Sophie remembered something. 'At the zombie day, you told me that Simon is spoken for.'

'Yes. Well, so I've heard.'

Sophie's heart was loud in her ears. 'Who is she?'

Natalie checked no one was passing by. 'Nobody knows. Someone he met at our other office.'

'Other office?'

'Oh, yes. It's out of service now that Franklin's back. When he retired a few years ago, he set up an office in his holiday home. I mean, he never really retired at all. Couldn't keep his nose out of things. But during that period, he had Simon and a couple of other people from your department running out there for meetings all the time, because Franklin always took a keen interest in marketing. That's when Simon met her. Some woman Franklin had working as his housekeeper for a time.' She grinned. 'And just like that, we got our new Simon. He started dressing better, wearing cologne. He just had that air about him, you know? The air of someone who's getting laid.'

'Yuk.'

Natalie laughed. 'Exactly.'

'And no one else ever met her?'

'Only Simon ever went out there. Some doubt she really exists. I did ask him about her once, but he begged me not to tell anyone, said that Franklin would go mad if he found out, something about not wanting his staff to fraternise, which seemed a bit daft to me. But Simon was very insistent.'

Sophie was about to ask more when her eyes fell upon the manuscript she was looking for. It was half-buried beneath a pile of *Bookseller* magazines on the table. She grabbed it and hugged it to her chest.

She needed to read through it, check it against what Franklin had said earlier. Because if she was right, she thought she knew who Simon's mysterious girlfriend was. The woman behind everything.

She thanked Natalie and took the manuscript into a little meeting room, closing the door behind her.

She flicked through, recalling a number of passages as she read them, tracing the words with a trembling finger.

He came to visit me again today. He asked me a dozen hypothetical questions. What would you do if you found a wallet containing £50 in the street? Imagine you had a boyfriend who you were obsessed with, and he kissed another woman – how would you feel? I told him

I would hand in the wallet, forgive the woman. I lied. I could tell he didn't believe me.

Sophie read on, moving past the midpoint at which she'd stopped reading.

He told me again today that they feel they may be close to curing the badness inside me. Exorcising the devil. They took me to a room and made me strip and lie on a cold metal table. They tied my wrists and ankles. Grandfather stared down at my naked body, my breasts sliding towards my armpits, and shook his head. Then they turned the hose on me, the icy water, and grandfather stood nearby, reminding me it was all my fault, all my own doing. Because I'm not a good girl.

The character at this point in the book, Sophie now realised, wasn't a child. She was a grown woman. There were two narratives – a girl and a woman – mixed together. And the mysterious 'he' referred to in the first half of the book was now revealed as her grandfather. Sophie read on quickly.

Grandfather wept today. I wept too. He brought me a present, a little stuffed rabbit. He said it wasn't my fault I was bad. It's in my jeans. I didn't understand that. I don't wear jeans. I'm not allowed.

That part was written by a child.

He told me one day, when I've learned to be good, I will inherit a great empire. I will be responsible for making millions of children happy.

A few pages later:

304

Grandfather says it's too late for me now. I will never learn to be a good girl. I will never inherit the empire. He got angry, said that it's all my fault that Sebastian is dead too.

Sebastian? Sophie sat up, her hand flying to her mouth. Good God.

She went back to reading.

I screamed as he came towards me with the needles . . .

Sophie dropped the manuscript and put her head in her hands.

The girl in the book was Jasmine. She'd spoken to Sophie of her brother. Sebastian.

The girl was Jasmine, and her grandfather – her captor, her torturer, bent on driving the devil out of her – was Franklin.

This wasn't a novel. It was Jasmine's memoir, though it had been written like a novel, in a voice that was not really Jasmine's own. Certainly not the way she spoke, anyway. She had chosen to disguise herself.

There were other things, even early in the manuscript, that connected to events that happened at university, subtle things that Sophie hadn't spotted the first time she read it. The mention of needles that made sense of Jasmine's pale face in the tattoo parlour and her refusal to go through with it. The narrator commenting that she shared a name with a Disney princess.

Sophie sat back, running her hands through her hair. Something had happened that last night at university, something that had sent Jasmine back to her prison. But Sophie still couldn't remember what it was. All she knew was that it was connected to Liam and how they had both felt about him.

Jasmine had loved him. And, despite her protests, Sophie had loved him too. There was no point denying it any more.

She'd had crushes before Liam, had been out with a few boys, most notably Kevin, but before she met Liam she had no idea what it felt like to be truly mad for someone. When her friends talked about being in love, of the sickness and elation and despair that came with it – tummies fizzing, hearts pounding and breaking – she couldn't identify with it. Until she met Liam. And then she had experienced the agony without the elation, the pain without the joy. Because he belonged to someone else. And even if he and Jasmine broke up, which they never did, friends' ex-boyfriends were off-limits. It was one of the fundamental, unwritten rules.

Even though Sophie had been able to see his negative qualities – he was pretentious, said cruel things, could be insensitive and vindictive – she couldn't help the way she felt about him. She wanted him to look at her the way he often looked at Jasmine. She craved the feeling of his hands on her skin. She wanted to kiss him. To have him in her bed.

He brought out the weakness in her. And there was nothing she could do about it.

Chapter 40
Friday, 10–Saturday, 11 June, 2000

'David, can I have a quick word?'

They were coming out of the lecture hall, having sat through a talk on Gothic literature, and Sophie took David to one side, suddenly tongue-tied.

'Are you all right?' he asked.

She checked no one could overhear them. 'I was wondering if you could get me some . . . stuff.'

'Stuff?'

'Yeah. You know, I heard that—' She broke off, feeling hideously awkward. 'I heard that you could get—'

'Stuff. Yeah, I might be able to. It depends what you want.'

She dropped her voice to a whisper. 'The fifth letter of the alphabet.'

He laughed, asked her how much she wanted and walked away, still chuckling.

Now it was Saturday night and the Ecstasy pills were in her bag, stuffed at the bottom beneath her hairbrush, a packet of wipes and a small box of condoms. David had brought the pills to her room, where she had fumblingly handed over the cash. 'Have fun. Make sure you drink plenty of water.' He paused before he left the room. 'I assume this is for you and the gruesome twosome?'

She was offended. 'I wish you'd stop being horrible about them.'

'All right, sorry.' He paused, as if deciding whether to say what was on his mind. 'It's pretty obvious that he's got the hots for you.'

'No he hasn't!' Her cheeks burned.

David studied her. 'And you like him too, don't you? Be careful, Sophie. Love triangles can get very messy. I've been there.'

She replayed David's words as she studied herself in the mirror. She kept thinking about the book Liam had tried to give her. Since then, when she had turned down his present, the tension between them had slowly escalated. Often, she would catch him watching her, and she was sure Jasmine was aware of it too, though she never said anything.

Sophie found her thoughts going round and round in a loop. Guilt scratched at her – but she couldn't help the way she felt. She was a terrible friend – except she wasn't going to do anything about it.

So, why, she asked herself now, had she bought this dress? Why was she wearing it for a night out with her best friend and her boyfriend? It was black and flimsy with strappy shoulders and a plunging neckline that showed off the tops of her breasts, and a hemline that displayed what she thought of, in moments of confidence, as her best feature.

She would tell anyone who asked that she was wearing it for herself, because it made her feel sexy, because the weather had turned warm, because she was tired of being the mousy girl who covered herself up as if she should be ashamed of her body. But the truth was, she wanted Liam to look at her. She wanted him to desire her. Even though she would never do anything about it.

She opened the vodka that sat on her desk and did something she would never normally do, taking a big gulp straight from the bottle. She was sick and tired of being inhibited and shy.

Tonight, she was going to have fun.

———

The Student Union building was rammed with sweaty bodies, doormen turning people away because it was at capacity. Sophie threaded her way around the edge of the packed dance floor, aware of boys watching her, taking in her legs, the beads of sweat around her collarbone, staring at her boobs. But she was drunk, the alcohol acting like a suit of armour, and she found she didn't care. Let them look. She was, she reminded herself, having the time of her life.

Jasmine and Liam were seated at a table in the corner, which they had grabbed when a couple who'd been sitting there before had emerged from an hour-long snog and vanished into the night. Sophie placed the beers on the table and slithered onto the stool her friends had been saving for her.

'Cheers!' she said, lifting the neck of the bottle and relishing the way the ice-cold liquid slipped down her throat. She could feel Liam watching her, just as the boys around the dance floor had, and she tried not to imagine him touching her, reminded herself yet again that he was Jasmine's. In fact, Jasmine was being unusually clingy tonight. She wasn't normally into public displays of affection but she kept bending forward to kiss Liam, touching him at every opportunity. She swallowed another mouthful of beer and raised her bottle.

Her words were a little slurred as she said the toast. 'To you guys. You love each other and I love you.'

'And we love you, Sophie,' Liam said. 'Don't we, Jas?'

A half-smile. 'We do.'

Liam had a bottle of vodka in his bag beneath the table and he poured three large measures into plastic tumblers after checking none of the staff were watching. Sophie took another swig of beer and followed it with half her tumbler of vodka.

'When are we going to take the stuff?' she asked.

Jasmine shushed her. 'Not so loud, for fuck's sake.'

'Oops. Sorry. I've heard it's meant to be amazing.'

'Haven't you ever done it before?' Jasmine asked. 'Jesus. Liam, I told you this was a bad idea.'

'No it's not,' Liam said. 'It will be cool for Sophie to lose her virginity with us.'

Jasmine rolled her eyes as Sophie laughed again. Then a look passed between Liam and Jasmine and the other woman took a breath before leaning over and aiming a kiss at Sophie's cheek. Sophie turned her face and kissed Jasmine full on the lips.

'Wow, Jasmine, you look really shocked,' Liam said, laughing.

'Shocked? Don't be ridiculous.' Jasmine grabbed hold of Sophie's face and kissed her back. Her mouth was soft and she tasted of cigarettes.

'Shit,' Liam said and Sophie would have bet anything that he had an erection.

'So,' she said, breaking away from Jasmine and wiping her lips. 'It's ten o'clock. Shall we do it now?'

'Why not?' Jasmine said.

Sophie held her bag on her lap and fished the three tablets out, handing one each to Liam and Jasmine beneath the table. They both popped the pills into their mouths and washed them down with vodka. After a moment's hesitation, in which tabloid headlines about young women dying in nightclubs after taking a single E flashed in her mind, Sophie followed suit.

'Now what?' she said, and Liam laughed again.

'We dance,' he said.

———⌣———

An hour later, Sophie suddenly had to leave the dance floor, exhausted and desperate for water. She wasn't sure the Ecstasy was actually working. She didn't feel elated or happy. She mostly felt simultaneously wired and exhausted.

She queued at the bar, feeling faint, and when she eventually reached the front she asked for a pint of water, which she downed, immediately feeling better. But she needed to perk herself up properly. Confident another couple of drinks would give her a second wind, she ordered three shots of vodka, slamming back the first two and carrying the third with her, drinking it on her way to the ladies.

It was quiet inside the restroom. A pair of women stood by the mirror, reapplying their make-up.

'Did you take anything?' one of them asked her friend.

'No. I was going to get some E but I've heard there's a dodgy batch going round. It's, like, cut with some kind of tranquilliser.'

'Screw that,' said the other girl. 'I'm sticking with booze.'

They left and Sophie found herself on her own, staring in the mirror for the second time that night. Her mascara was smudged and her hair damp. She adjusted her dress and splashed water on her face, desperate to hang on to the buzz she'd felt all evening, fighting the nausea that chewed at her guts. What had those girls said about the dodgy E? She leaned against the basin, her eyes heavy, the room lurching. Someone came in and she forced her eyes open, drunkenly dismissing her fears. The pill she'd taken wasn't dodgy. It was a dud.

She closed her eyes for a second and when she opened them she was certain there was someone standing behind her. A girl with bleached blonde hair. Becky. Sophie whirled around, but there was no one there. Shit, now she was hallucinating.

She splashed more cold water on her face, which cleared her head, went back out into the throng and made her way over to the dance floor, re-joining Jasmine and Liam. The DJ started playing harder house music and soon Sophie felt herself entering a trance, hypnotised by the heavy bass, she and her two friends dancing close together, lost in their own private world. It was as if nobody else here existed, just the three of them, and as the music grew more euphoric and her heartbeat seemed to increase to match the beat, she felt a rush of love for them both, a grin on her face, like a phoenix dancing in the flames.

'Let's get out of here,' Liam breathed into her ear.

She snapped out of her trance and felt his hand in hers, pulling her across the dance floor, Jasmine following. It was warm outside. Sophie experienced a strange jump in time as they crossed the campus. One moment, she was standing outside the Student Union, the next they were leaving the campus. Liam had his arm around her, holding her up. A moment later she was in a taxi. The three of them were pressed together in the back seat, and there were hands on her legs, but she could hardly keep her eyes open and wasn't sure who the hands belonged to. Her last memory was of the taxi depositing them outside Jasmine's house.

The rest was blank.

Chapter 41
Day fifty-one, Tuesday, 26 May, 2015

Sophie remained in the little meeting room for a few minutes, leafing back and forth through the manuscript, trying to work it all out.

If the manuscript told a true story, Jasmine had been holed up in that prison for some time after leaving university, undergoing psychological – and often physical – torture. She struggled to make sense of it. Was Liam there too? There was no mention of him in the book.

Sophie stood up and paced about the room, trying to figure it out.

Had something happened that night, after they got back to Jasmine's, that had sent her back to her prison? From what Sophie had read, that made sense. But had she run back there – or been taken?

Sophie's gut clenched. Had *she* done something to send Jasmine back to that place? Was this, in some way she couldn't remember, her fault?

The lid of the box in which she kept her memories of that night rattled. She wanted to know what had happened – but at the same time she was terrified of finding out.

She picked up the manuscript, turned to the final page. The story ended suddenly, with no resolution. The girl – no, the woman; Jasmine – waiting in her room for her grandfather to appear.

Where had Simon got this manuscript from? Surely there was only one possible answer.

'Oh, my God,' Sophie whispered, talking to her old friend. 'Are you still alive?'

Was the fire on the boat a ruse? Had it been faked by Franklin to make the world think his granddaughter was dead so he could keep her locked up in that place confident that no one would ever look for her?

And if Jasmine was still alive, did that mean that she was behind everything? Sophie knew there had to be a woman involved, because that thug, Terry Morgan, said he'd been hired by a female. Sophie tried to imagine it. Jasmine had been kept locked up by Franklin for all these years. And then . . . and then Simon had come along. If Jasmine's prison was within Franklin's holiday home, where his second office had been based, it made sense that they could have come into contact and struck up a relationship.

If that was the case, then it must mean Liam wasn't around. Was he dead? Had the fire on the boat been real, but only Liam had perished there?

Regardless of Liam's fate, the only explanation that Sophie could come up with involved Simon and her former best friend.

'What did I do to you?' Sophie whispered. 'What did I do?'

The narrative, as twisted as it was, made a sick kind of sense. Sophie had been given the job here so that Jasmine, with Simon's help, could get revenge on her for whatever it was Sophie had done. By making her life a misery. Scaring her, telling Daisy her mummy was going to die, locking her in the office and freaking her out. Attacking Josh to remove her only work friend. Pinning mice to her front door – a creature Jasmine might or might not have used before in an act of vengeance. Leaving cockroaches, which Jasmine knew she was terrified of, in her pedestal.

How did Miranda and Cassie fit in? And why did they have to be killed? Sophie didn't have the answer to that. But she felt certain that Jasmine and Simon had wanted Sophie to know who was tormenting her. That was why they had given her this manuscript.

They wanted her to know how much Jasmine had suffered.

Wanted her to feel guilt.

Did they know she would work it out? Realise the book was by Jasmine? Was that why it was written as a novel, so Sophie wouldn't be able to take it to the police, try to explain how this apparent piece of fiction was in fact an account of true-life horrors?

Were they waiting for her to work it out before they made their final move? The move that involved this thug-for-hire, Terry Morgan?

She sat back, breathing heavily, and looked out at the office. Her colleagues at their desks, heads bent over their computers, getting on with their jobs. They were oblivious to all of this. Only she knew of the darkness that existed at the heart of this place; this company that had been run for years by a man who locked up his granddaughter and tortured her because he believed she had been born bad. How many other members of the family had undergone the same treatment? Jasmine's parents? Franklin's siblings and their offspring?

And did Franklin know about Jasmine and Simon's torment of her? No. He hadn't even known who Sophie was until this week. But the questions he had asked today – it was clear now that he had been probing, trying to find out if she knew what he had done.

Well, she did now.

She needed to talk this through with somebody. After a moment's hesitation, she phoned Guy. If he'd just hear her out, let her walk him through it, maybe he'd work through the logic with her, see if it could possibly add up. She knew he would ask difficult questions, would fixate on her relationship with Jasmine and Liam, but he was her husband. She didn't want to face this on her own anymore.

His phone went straight to voicemail.

She texted him and waited a minute, but he didn't reply. So she tried to call Paterson, but was told he wasn't available at the moment. She left a message, asking him to call her urgently.

Then she picked up the meeting room phone and called Natalie.

'This office,' she said to her the instant she answered, 'the one in Franklin's holiday home. Where is it?'

'On the Isle of Sheppey. Near a place called Queenborough.'

The place Jasmine hadn't wanted Becky to reveal she was from. That had to be the same place she'd been kept when she was a child. That was how Becky had recognised her – Franklin must have allowed Jasmine out occasionally. Taken her for trips down to the harbour. Outside for constitutionals.

'Why are you asking?' Natalie wanted to know, but Sophie put the phone down.

She lay her hand on Jasmine's book. It was maddening that this memoir was fictionalised, that it wouldn't prove what Franklin had done to his granddaughter.

Though if Jasmine was still alive, she could testify.

Sophie was surprised to find that she wasn't angry with Jasmine for what she had done to her. Simon was different, but it wasn't Jasmine's fault, was it? She was fucked up, because of what Franklin did to her. It was his fault. All his fault.

Sophie stood up. She knew what she had to do. Where she had to go.

To get the answers. To apologise for whatever it was she had done to make Jasmine hate her. And persuade her to hand herself in, so she could seek justice against her grandfather, the man who had ruined her life.

Chapter 42
Day fifty-one, Tuesday, 26 May, 2015

Sophie knew that in a few hours' time trains out of London to Kent would be packed with commuters heading home, but right now the train out of St Pancras was half empty. As soon as she boarded she tried to call Guy again, but with no response. It was half term so Daisy wasn't at school today, so she guessed he'd taken her to the park or the supermarket. She wished he'd answer his phone though.

Next, she tried Paterson again, and was once more told that he was out. She left another message, this time telling him she was on her way to Queenborough to visit Franklin Bird's home there. 'Please tell him I really need to talk to him.'

She tried to settle back and enjoy the scenery as the city slipped by and they entered rural Kent. But she was too jumpy, felt like she'd downed a dozen espressos. She fiddled with her phone all the way to Sittingbourne, where she changed onto a train to Sheerness. Sophie had never been to the Isle of Sheppey before, and as the train crossed the bridge over the Swale she thought how odd it was that there was this island so close to London, right next door to it, geographically, that no one she knew had ever visited. It was considered to be something of a backwater. Sophie had never met anyone who came from this place – apart from Becky and, of course, Jasmine.

⌣

When Sophie was with Jasmine and Liam she felt like she had found herself, begun to discover who she really was and who she wanted to be. She no longer felt like the timid, provincial girl from a small city. She no longer felt like a child, a girl struggling to become a woman.

With hindsight, she knew this was typical, something that so many people went through when they left home and started college. She was living through her own *bildungsroman*. But then her two companions on this journey disappeared and she felt abandoned, adrift.

Where had they gone?

The morning after they had gone dancing at the Student Union and taken the pills, Sophie had woken up with a hangover that pinned her to the mattress. She couldn't get back to sleep – her mind was too noisy, like a machine that was falling apart, clanking and crashing inside her skull – but she was unable to drag herself out from beneath the sheets. Eventually, she had managed to get up and found that she was not in her own bed. She was in an unfamiliar room. It took a few blurry minutes for her to work out this was the room of Jasmine's housemate, Helen. Then she caught sight of herself in the mirror. She was still wearing her little black dress, her face a mess of smudged make-up.

She left the room and knocked on Jasmine's door. There was no reply. She pushed it open slowly and found an empty room. It smelled of bleach and there were damp patches on the carpet. But Jasmine and Liam must have gone out.

She called a taxi and went back to halls.

In the shower, she scrubbed herself till her skin was pink. What had happened the night before? She could remember being in the Student Union. She had vague memories of the taxi ride back to Jasmine's, the sensation of hands touching her. She remembered the cab driver's eyes in the mirror. But after that: blankness. Something was stopping her from trying to remember, as if her unconscious mind had taken the memories and locked them in a box while she was sleeping. And she was afraid of what was in that box. She turned cold – despite the heat of the water that pummelled her flesh – when she imagined opening it, revealing what was inside.

She crawled into her own bed and lay there all day, listening to sad music and reading. She stayed there for the whole weekend.

The memories stayed in their newly constructed box.

On Monday morning, she went to a lecture, expecting to see Jasmine. She wasn't there. And she wasn't there the next day either.

Finally, on the Wednesday, Sophie had gone to Jasmine's house. It was a beautiful day, the sun glinting off the sea, summer dresses and shorts pulled from wardrobes across the city. Jasmine's housemate answered the door.

'I haven't seen her,' Helen said. 'When I got back on Monday, she wasn't here.'

'Oh.' That was weird. 'What about Liam?'

'Haven't seen him either.'

'Do you mind if I go up to Jas's room and leave her a note?'

Her room smelled surprisingly clean. The bed was freshly made, though the usual books and CDs and clothes were scattered about the floor. Perhaps they were around but Helen had been out when they were at home and vice versa. But when she suggested this to Helen, she said she'd been here with a cold for the past three days.

They must have gone away. Sophie was a little hurt that they'd gone off again without telling her, but she felt relieved too. She feared them telling her what had happened on Saturday night when they got back here.

But then a week passed and they still didn't return, and she grew worried, unable to concentrate on her final lectures, zoning out in seminars. She sent Jasmine several emails, but received no response. She went round to her house every day. She talked to Liam's other friends. No one had seen nor heard from either of them, but no one seemed that bothered. There was only one week left of term, everyone was demob happy and a lot of students had already finished for the year and gone home. The only other person who seemed anxious was Helen, though this was mainly because she'd received the gas and electric bills and Jasmine owed her £100.

The day before the end of term, Sophie finally went to see the head of the English department, but he wasn't that concerned either.

'It's the end of the year,' he said. 'I expect they decided to finish early. Try not to fret.'

And then it was time for Sophie to go home. She went round to Jasmine's one last time, hoping for a miracle, before embarking on the long journey back to Wolverhampton, forehead resting on the bus window, breath steaming the glass. She had never been lovesick but she imagined it must feel very much like this.

Jasmine didn't contact her over the summer. Sophie sent a few more emails, to both her and Liam, but as the summer wore on the pain faded. She was busy with her part-time job and the different environment meant she didn't hope to see her friends every time she turned a corner. She was sure they would be there when she got back.

But they weren't.

She soon discovered that Liam's parents had reported him missing, as had Jasmine's, that the police had visited the campus during the summer. A week into the new term, a policeman came to see her, asking for details of when she had last seen them, if they had said anything about going away. Sophie asked if the police had spoken to Jasmine's brother, Sebastian, to see if he had heard from his sister. They hadn't, and the police officer gave Sophie the strong impression that they believed the couple had run off together, that they weren't taking their disappearance very seriously. There was no suggestion that they had come to harm. And this was what Sophie believed too. She told the police she had gone back to Jasmine's and that they were gone when she woke up. That was all she could remember.

When the police left, seemingly satisfied, it struck her. Jasmine and Liam had left university. They'd left *her*. And over the coming weeks she went through the stages of grief: denial, anger, depression and, finally, acceptance. She contemplated quitting university herself. Everybody she knew was already in a strong friendship group and she felt lonely and haunted by the absence of her two best friends. On top of that, she had flashes of that lost night, often waking up clutching at the bedsheets in a puddle of sweat, fragments of dreams floating above her like burning paper before they faded and vanished.

But she stuck with it, throwing herself into her studies, gaining a first class degree. And then she moved to London and got a job, met Guy, got married, had Daisy. When Jasmine and Liam were declared dead she had been distraught. She went to both funerals, so dosed up on antidepressants that she floated through them, numb and disengaged. After that, she never talked about them. But for fifteen years – since she woke on the morning after her lost night, the hours she still kept locked tight in her memory box – she had carried a sadness with her. Sadness and guilt. It was like a splinter, buried so deep in her skin that she would never get it out. The impurity, the flaw, would be in her forever.

Perhaps that was why she'd accepted the job at Jackdaw. It would have been so easy to say no. But, subconsciously, she had wanted to confront her memories, face her fears. Force the splinter to the surface. And if Jasmine really was alive, she was going to get her wish.

———————

The train pulled into Queenborough and Sophie disembarked. She had quickly looked it up on Wikipedia on her way here. A small town with around three thousand residents, with high unemployment since most of the manufacturing jobs had vanished. Sheerness, the biggest town on the island, was an important port because it was so close to London and the Thames. It was popular with anglers. There were holiday camps, pebbled beaches and natural beauty spots. But there was no excitement here. It was the kind of place young people fled the moment they got the chance.

She brought up Google Maps on her phone and used it to direct herself through the town towards the harbour. The streets were deserted and Sophie wondered where everybody was. She felt like she'd wandered onto the set of a post-apocalyptic drama where only the seagulls had survived. She passed a few quiet shops and a Chinese takeaway, heading along the side of the creek until she reached the harbour where a number of fishing boats were moored. Most of them had women's names: Sara Jayne and Stella and Tara. There were a few motorboats too, bobbing on the still water. This was where the boat that Jasmine and Liam had supposedly died on had set sail from. Sophie had always thought it was a strange place for them to end up. When she imagined them running away, she pictured them in Ibiza or Thailand, not *this* place.

There were clues in the manuscript. The Jasmine character wrote about flat marshland, a place where the river meets two seas – Queenborough was on the coast of the Swale, a strip of sea, very close to the River Medway and the English Channel.

Sophie checked her phone. Guy still hadn't responded to her texts. When this was all over, she was going to have to tell him the whole story, including everything she had failed to share about her university days. He'd been in a good mood when she left this morning, waiting to talk to Claire about writing for the *Herald* again. Claire had decided that the scandal had blown over now. He was oblivious to Sophie's mood, believing that, with Cassie dead, all Sophie's work problems were behind her. If only he knew.

There was a greasy spoon cafe close to the harbour and Sophie went inside, ordering a mug of coffee.

When the waitress, a middle-aged woman with an apron tied around her waist, brought it to her, Sophie smiled brightly and said, 'I'm looking for Franklin Bird's residence. I wonder if you could tell me where to find it?'

The woman looked Sophie up and down, then marched back to the counter without replying, disappearing into the kitchen.

A minute later a man in his sixties came out and sat at her table. He had ruddy cheeks and a thick thatch of ginger hair. 'I hear you're looking for Mr Bird,' he said in his strong Estuary accent. 'I'm Jack.'

'That's right. Well, his home, anyway.'

'You're a journalist, then. Yeah?' The idea seemed to delight him and Sophie realised that perhaps the Bird family, like many people who own holiday homes and swan into town during the summer, weren't very popular. Maybe he was hoping that Franklin was involved in some sort of scandal. She didn't correct him. 'They live down near Elmley. I'll draw you a map.'

While he did this, Sophie said, 'Have you been here long?'

'What, in this cafe? Donkey's years, love.'

'Did you ever meet Franklin's granddaughter?'

He frowned. 'Yeah. Funny little thing, she was. I remember her from when she was a kid. You'd see them around occasionally, the Birds. She wasn't with them very often, just once or twice.'

'What about as an adult?'

'No. I never heard anything about her until she died on that boat.'

'You remember that?' Sophie asked.

'Never forget it. We've never had anything like that happen here before. It was all anyone talked about for weeks. They never found the bodies, you know.'

'What do you think happened?' she asked.

The man stroked his chin. 'Hard to say. The whole thing was very odd. I mean, where were they going? They weren't fishing and they weren't experienced. I'd never seen either of them down here before. Franklin Bird had only just bought that boat and I don't remember ever seeing him go out on it. The police thought the pair of them had been intending to cross the Channel and I always thought that maybe drugs were involved.' His eyes widened. 'Is that why you're here today? Found something out, have you? About to print a big exposé?' He touched the side of his nose. 'I've heard some odd things about that family. Very odd things.'

'Like what?'

He appeared to have a sudden change of heart. 'Oh, it was probably just gossip.'

'But what was it?' Sophie was aware that it was silent around them, the other patrons attempting to listen in.

'Just stuff about how they treated those kids. Weird stuff. Horrible stuff. If you are doing an exposé on that family, come back and see me.' An oily smile. 'And bring your cheque book.'

He held out the map, which had been drawn on the back of a napkin. 'Here you go.'

She studied it. 'How long will it take me to walk there?'

'Walk?' He laughed. 'Haven't you got a car? You Londoners.' He called across to a man wearing a brown overcoat, greasy hair curling against the collar. 'Oi, Peter. This young lady needs a taxi.'

Peter stood up wearily.

Jack grinned at her. 'Looks like you won't need that map after all.'

———

Peter the taxi driver was taciturn, driving her out of town, following the map he didn't need, first heading inland along the creek, then south, past a grim industrial estate and a patch of wasteland, before they found themselves back in the countryside, road signs pointing towards Elmley Nature Reserve. The landscape was flat, beautiful in a bleak way. Marshland. The occasional grazing sheep. A lone magpie perched on a telephone wire.

Sophie checked her phone again to see if Guy had replied but she'd lost reception. Great. But she couldn't stop now. She had to know if Jasmine was there, if she was still alive.

After a little while they turned onto a quiet country lane, heading past green fields and back towards the water. She spotted their destination.

A large, red-brick house stood on the horizon, half-concealed behind tall oak trees. As they got closer, Sophie saw that the house was ringed by a high fence. The Swale was only fifty feet away and seagulls wheeled overhead. The house looked like it had been here for hundreds of years, frozen in time as the world changed unimaginably around it.

They pulled up outside the gate, beside a black Land Rover.

Sophie couldn't move.

'This is it,' Peter said.

She fumbled in her bag and found a £10 note. He drove off after grudgingly giving up his mobile number so she might call him to retrieve her, should her phone get any reception.

Standing there alone on a muddy patch of ground, she felt sick. Could Jasmine really be here? Alive?

She walked slowly up the front path – overgrown, with weeds poking through cracks in the paving slabs – and found herself standing before the front door. She was surprised how rundown it was. After a moment spent raising her nerve, she knocked on it – and it swung open. For the first time since leaving the office, doubts crept in. Should she really be here, planning to confront two people she believed to be murderers? She could hear Guy's voice telling her she should have waited for the police. But she needed to know if she was right about Jasmine being alive; would welcome the chance to talk to her before the police got hold of her. She wanted to tell her that she knew what she'd endured, that she didn't blame her for anything. She wanted to persuade her to testify against Franklin.

After a long moment of hesitation, she stepped into the entrance hall, which was full of dark wooden bookcases stuffed with leather-bound books.

It was so quiet. Like no one had been here for years. All she could hear was the muffled cries of the gulls that circled above the house.

The silence was oppressive and made her consider running. But something was driving her on, stopping her from fleeing this place. A need to meet her destiny. To put an end to everything that had happened over the past couple of months. No, longer than that – the past fifteen years. Because this story had started a long time ago. She might have been oblivious for much of that time, but now she felt like she had always been heading towards this moment.

'Jasmine?' She called her friend's name, but it stuck in her throat. She tried again, getting a little more volume this time.

The name echoed around the empty space.

She headed towards the door at the end of the hallway. It opened into a sitting room, as quiet and still as a room in a museum. The only signs of recent life were piles of books on the coffee table, all of them with the Jackdaw logo on the spine. She walked through the sitting room and found herself in another large space: an office, with an iMac filling the surface of a desk, a swivel chair, stacks of paper and yet more books. On the wall was a portrait similar to the one Franklin had in his London office, but this one just showed Franklin and his two grandchildren, Jasmine and Sebastian. They were on the lawn outside this house, a summer day, but none of them were smiling. What had happened to Sebastian? With everything else that had been going on, this was the first time she'd wondered this.

Sophie paused. In the manuscript, Jasmine's character had been kept in a bedroom on the top floor and the improvement room was in the basement. She went back out into the hallway and ran up two flights of stairs.

She felt like she was inside Jasmine's manuscript. The bedroom was at the end of the corridor. She approached it and pushed the door open, stepping inside.

There was a single bed pushed up against the wall beneath a small square window that overlooked the marshes. The mattress had been stripped long ago. It bore dark circles, the tell-tale signs of bed-wetting. The walls were bare but there were marks in the wallpaper above the mattress, where someone – Jasmine – had tried to scratch a word into the wall. Sophie peered closely. It was faint but in the sun-washed room it wasn't hard to make out.

Liam.

Sophie stood upright. Had he been here and written his own name?

Then she noticed another word etched into the wall a few inches lower. This one was fainter, but it was clear what it said.

Sorry.

Sophie needed to find Jasmine, talk to her. She was desperate to—

A scraping noise came from downstairs.

Heart hammering, Sophie headed slowly back to the staircase, peering down into the hallway below. She couldn't see anything or anyone. She went slowly down the stairs to the ground floor and listened. She could hear something, sounds of movement, scraping sounds. It was coming from below.

She heard a woman's voice.

Jasmine. She was sure it was Jasmine. Oh, God, she was still alive, she really was still alive. Half of Sophie was screaming at her to get out – Jasmine hates you, she and Simon murdered two people (and where *was* Simon, anyway?) – but it was as if her body was acting on its own, the part of her that needed answers, that craved resolution, sending her over to a door in the wall that, she assumed, must lead to the room below. She opened the door and groped for a light switch. She pressed it. The stairs remained dark.

She hesitated on the top step. Jasmine was down there, she was sure, but now her courage deserted her. She should find a phone, call Paterson, wait for the police to arrive. It would be crazy to go down there.

But before she could turn to leave the stairwell, she was pushed forward, and then she was falling, rolling down the hard wooden stairs and landing in a heap, panting, terrified, at the bottom. Above her the door slammed shut, pitching the stairwell into absolute darkness, and she heard a key turn.

She pushed herself to her feet. Her shoulder and knee throbbed where they had struck the stairs. Her ribs felt bruised. But nothing was broken. Perhaps it would start to hurt more when the adrenaline faded, when she stopped feeling so scared.

If she ever stopped feeling scared.

She reached out and felt wood. Here was the door that, in the manuscript, Jasmine was often led through before undergoing treatment. Sophie had no choice but to grope for and turn the handle.

And as she pushed the door open a male voice from within said, 'Come in, Sophie. Come in.'

Chapter 43
Day fifty-one, Tuesday, 26 May, 2015

Sophie went through and found herself in a room that was as dark as the stairwell she'd come from, the air so damp and cold that she could feel it seeping into her pores, worming its way beneath her skin.

'Hello?' she said.

She could hear breathing on the far side of the room but couldn't see anyone. She had definitely recognised the voice of the person who had told her to come in, which had confirmed her suspicions. But was he alone down here in the dark? What the hell was he doing? And where was Jasmine? It must have been her who had shoved Sophie down the stairs. Oh, God, she'd made a terrible mistake coming here.

'Simon?'

She took a few more steps into the blackness, trying to remain calm. She felt in her pocket for her phone. The screen lit up but, unsurprisingly, she still had no reception. She was about to turn the torch app on when the room was flooded with light.

It burned Sophie's eyes and she screwed them tight.

When she opened them again she saw something that made her cry out, her legs almost giving way.

This was the basement in Jasmine's manuscript. Grey, unpainted walls with patches of mould spreading across them, a concrete floor, fluorescent strip lights above, with the corpses of hundreds of insects showing through.

Everything here was exactly as it had been described. The chair with leather straps. The hose. The metal trolley with various objects lying on it – including a brown leather pouch. The place where Jasmine had been tortured. Where Franklin tried to turn her into a good girl. Sophie knew what was in that pouch. Acupuncture needles. In the book, Jasmine had never spelled out what her grandfather had done with those needles, but Sophie could imagine. Oh, God, could she imagine.

'It's a perfect replica of the original,' Simon said. 'Impressive, isn't it?'

He was sitting on a rickety wooden chair against the far wall. He held a shotgun across his lap and his expression was grim, sweat gathering in beads on his forehead. His whole body appeared as damp as this room.

But it wasn't the sight of Simon that had made Sophie cry out.

Behind him, on the floor, was a thin mattress, half-concealed by shadows. And curled up on the mattress, eyes shut, was a motionless child.

Sophie knew who it was immediately, would have recognised her at any distance, in any crowd, and she headed across the space towards her, footsteps echoing, bouncing off the damp brick walls.

'Daisy! Daisy – sweetheart. It's Mummy. Oh, God, Daisy, please . . .'

Simon lifted the shotgun. 'Back off,' he said.

Sophie halted. All she wanted was to take Daisy in her arms, but the sight of the shotgun pinned her to the spot.

'What have you done to her?' she said, her voice cracking.

Simon shook his head, sweat dripping into his eyes. 'You weren't supposed to come here . . . not yet. We weren't ready.'

'Because you'd arranged for someone to abduct me?'

He raised his eyebrows. 'You know about that?'

She didn't care about that right now. She took another step forward and Simon waved the gun threateningly.

'She's fine, Sophie,' he said. 'Go on, you can touch her. See for yourself.'

She dashed forward and threw herself down before her little girl. Daisy was limp and her skin felt cold, clammy. But she was breathing. Thank God. Oh, thank God. She shook her gently but Daisy didn't stir.

A woman's voice said, 'She's taken some medicine.'

Sophie reeled around, expecting to see Jasmine in the room. But there was no one there, just Simon, who was on his feet now, the shotgun trained on Sophie's back.

'Don't worry, Sophie,' the woman said. 'She'll live. I want her alive for now.'

The voice was coming from a speaker on the wall above the door. There was a red light beside it and, looking closer, Sophie realised it was a camera.

'Jasmine? Is that you?' The voice was distorted by the speaker, echoing in the brick-walled room, so she couldn't tell if it was Jasmine or not.

Laughter filled the room.

'How did you get Daisy?' Sophie demanded, addressing both the camera and Simon. 'Where's Guy?'

'He's dead,' Simon said.

Sophie let go of Daisy for a moment and buried her face in her hands. No, it couldn't be true. It couldn't.

'You didn't really love him anyway,' the woman's voice said. 'Not like you loved Liam.'

Sophie forced herself to get back to her feet. She needed to be strong. For herself but, more importantly, for Daisy. She had to get them out of here.

'Jasmine, it's you, isn't it? I know it's you. I never loved Liam. He was your boyfriend.' A thought struck her. 'Is he still alive too? Is he here?'

Another mirthless laugh. 'No, he's been dead for a long time.'

'He died on that boat?'

'Oh, Sophie. You really don't remember, do you? I thought, all this time, you were pretending. Putting your head in the sand, the happy little ostrich. *I won't think about it; I didn't see it.* But you were there.'

'What? I . . .'

But the walls of the box that she kept her memories in were shaking, threatening to burst open. The lid rattled, her own personal Pandora's Box, all the bad in Sophie's own world pushing, pressing.

'You don't deserve happiness, Sophie. Look at all the *lovely* things that have happened to you since you left university with your *lovely* first class degree. The fulfilling career. A beautiful child. A nice home. Your dream job. And a handsome husband – a man you stole from another woman. Because that's what you do, isn't it? Seduce and steal. Well, now they're *both* gone. And I know you remember that night, don't you? It's all in there, inside that pretty head. Come on, Sophie, let it out. Make yourself remember. You'll feel so much better.'

Sophie knelt on the floor beside the mattress and clutched Daisy's small hand.

She had to take control. Do this on her terms. She had hidden from the truth for too long, unable to face what she'd done. She closed her eyes. The knowledge of what had happened might help her get out of here, somehow, some way. She had to take that chance.

She braced herself and allowed the lid to fly open.

The door of the taxi cab opens and she follows Liam onto the pavement.

'Where's Helen?' Sophie asks, her voice sounding strange in her ears, watery and far away, and Jasmine tells her that her housemate has gone away for the weekend. Jasmine goes into the kitchen to look for something to drink, leaving Sophie alone with Liam.

He smiles at her, puts his arm around her, pulls her close. It feels good. She's so hot but, somehow, he is cool to the touch. She closes her eyes and she's swaying but then Jasmine is back in the room, pouring green liquid into shot glasses and Sophie takes one and downs it, gasping, the liquid burning her chest.

'Absinthe,' Liam says, his arm around Jasmine now. 'Nectar of poets.'

His hair falls over his eye and he grins impishly and even as her head spins Sophie thinks, He's beautiful. So beautiful.

'I have tequila too,' Jasmine says, and she fetches it: a bottle, a couple of limes, salt, and a knife to cut the limes. Why, Sophie wonders, isn't her friend smiling? She tries to hug Jasmine but her knees give way and Jasmine is holding her up, still not smiling, and she says, 'We'd better get you to bed.'

They are upstairs, in Jasmine's room. There's music playing, something ponderous with a heavy bass that drills into her body, shakes her bones. Candles are burning along with incense sticks. Sophie perches on the bed. Liam smokes a cigarette beside her while Jasmine sits cross-legged on the rug, chopping the limes into segments.

Sophie is holding a glass of tequila, salt on the back of her other hand. She doesn't understand what she's meant to be doing.

She drops the glass and the liquid splashes Jasmine.

'For fuck's sake.'

'Hey, chill out,' Liam laughs. 'Some of it got me too. Look, my shirt's all wet. Better take it off.'

He unbuttons it and Sophie can't help but stare at his chest. It's smooth and hairless. Jasmine sits behind him in the flickering candlelight. She is frowning. Sophie tries to say something soothing but her tongue is in a knot. Jasmine is trying to cut the final lime but her hands are shaking and she nicks her thumb. She swears again and sucks the blood, her face so dark, a look in her eyes that Sophie can't read. Suppressed fury. Sadness. Disappointment. Determination. Sophie doesn't understand. They're having a good time, aren't they? The best time of their lives. They're young, crazy, wasted and free. Liam has his shirt off and Sophie tries to say something to Jasmine, something that will comfort her, make her laugh, but the room tilts around her and she can't speak and then . . .

She's lying on her back on the bed.

There's a draught from the window, sea air invading the room, and her bottom half feels cold. She looks down and sees her dress is hitched up around her hips. Liam is sitting beside her on the bed and his hand is on her inner thigh. Jasmine is there too, pulling her top over her head, revealing white flesh. Liam ignores his girlfriend. He is fixated on his hand on Sophie's thigh. He slides it higher and Sophie gasps. She wants this. She's wanted this for so long. She closes her eyes . . .

It's almost dark in the room. A single candle burns. The music drones on, the bass filling her.

Jasmine is on the floor, wearing just her underwear. She is trembling.

Liam is on top of Sophie. She reaches out and feels the cool skin of his back. Feels his lips, soft against hers. Hears him say, 'Are you sure you want to do this?'

Hears herself say, 'Yes.'

She can hardly feel anything. A body pressing down against hers. No pain, but no pleasure. She is numb and she can't move, can't speak. She turns her head and sees Jasmine, still sitting on the floor, watching her. Sophie reaches out but Jasmine remains still. There's something funny about Jasmine's eyes. The candle flame flickers and bends and Sophie sees that Jasmine's cheeks are wet, shining.

Jasmine draws her fingernails across her own cheek and—

There's a gasp from above her. Liam rolls off her, panting, and Sophie slips away, the booze and the drugs and the sex dragging her down into unconsciousness.

It's fully dark in the room when she opens her eyes. There's no weight on her anymore. There's wetness between her legs and she's cold.

She turns her head and sees a blur on the floor in the darkness. Watches until the blur becomes a shape. A body. Two bodies. One lying still, the other moving. Sobbing.

There's a strange smell.

Jasmine's voice comes from far away. 'I need you to help me. I've done something . . .'

Sophie doesn't hear the final words.

———

Sophie hunched over her prone daughter, listening to her breathe, fearing that her own trembling would pass into Daisy's body. She wiped a tear from her cheek, took a deep breath, gathered herself.

She stood and walked over to the camera, ignoring Simon. He wasn't part of this, not really. It was between them. Her and her former best friend.

'You killed him,' she said, staring straight into it.

There was another protracted pause, then a low chuckle.

'Because you were jealous?' Sophie said. 'Because you thought he wanted me instead of you? Is that it? He was yours, Jasmine. He loved you, not me. He chose you. That night was just . . . madness. We were drunk and off our faces. I thought you were into it, that you were going to join in.'

There was no response. Was she still there?

'You were my best friend, Jasmine. I was distraught when you vanished. Yes, I missed him too. But it was you I really missed. It was always you.'

There was still no response.

'But I understand. I've read your book, you know that. I understand what you went through as a child. The awful things your family did to you, here, in this room.'

Sophie paused, imagining Jasmine as a child, locked in this room, suffering, believing she was bad, that she had to be cured. She must have carried that belief with her into adulthood, even when they let her out, allowed her to go to college. The belief that she was rotten inside, not worthy of love. Capable of committing terrible crimes. She had clung to Liam, the first person who, she thought, really cared for and understood her. He was her redemption, her saviour.

But it was impossible for him to live up to her expectations, to give her what she needed. He was barely an adult, a boy discovering the bounties the world holds for a good-looking, charismatic man like him. He probably didn't even think about how much a threesome involving Sophie was going to hurt Jasmine. Because that's exactly what they all knew was going to happen when they got into that taxi, limbs entangled on the back seat. They knew they were going to end up in bed together.

Except Jasmine didn't get into the bed, did she? She watched, writhing in silent agony, as the man who meant everything to her fucked the woman who called herself her best friend.

She had snapped, consumed by anger, a knife already in her hand. She had killed him.

And the call Sophie had heard as she floated in and out of unconsciousness . . .

'You called your grandfather, didn't you? Asked him to come and help you?'

She could imagine it. How a desperate Jasmine, realising the dire trouble she was in, had called Franklin, got him to dispose of Liam's body, clean the room. And then he had brought her back here. Locked her up and forced her to undergo more years of treatment. The bad girl, now a bad woman.

She looked back at Daisy, who was still sleeping. Jasmine hadn't spoken for several minutes.

'And then what?' Sophie said. 'He faked your death because Liam's family kept looking for him? Franklin wanted the world to think you were both dead when only one of you was. Is that right?'

'I always knew you were clever,' Simon said.

Again, she ignored him and continued to address the camera. This was maddening. Why wouldn't Jasmine show herself?

'Your grandfather – he's a monster. You deserve justice. Let me and Daisy go and we can go to the police together, tell them what he did to you. Please, Jasmine. Please.'

There was no response, and a moment later she realised why as the door opened. Sophie took a step back from the camera. The figure on the other side was shrouded in shadows. Then she stepped through the doorway.

'Almost right,' she said, raising the gun and pointing it at Sophie's face.

Sophie was unable to take in what she was seeing.

Who she was seeing.

Chapter 44
Day fifty-one, Tuesday, 26 May, 2015

Sophie took another step back as the woman came into the room and pushed the door closed and locked it behind her. She folded her fist around the key and, in her other hand, held the gun loosely by her side.

Not Jasmine.

Becky.

'Surprised to see me?'

Sophie couldn't speak.

At first glance Becky had barely aged since Sophie had last seen her on that day at college in the coffee shop. She would be thirty-four now, the same age as Sophie. But she still wore her hair in the same style, long and straight, parted at the centre. She was wearing tight black jeans and a figure-hugging black top with black leather boots. She wore short sleeves and, even in the poor light, Sophie could see scars criss-crossing the flesh of Becky's arms, a map of her pain and suffering. There were many more scars than the last time Sophie had seen her.

'I thought . . .'

'You thought you were coming here to find Jasmine. But Jasmine is dead, Sophie. That newspaper report was half true. Jasmine died back in 2002, on that boat. Franklin killed her.'

Sophie felt like she'd been slapped. 'Franklin told you he killed Jasmine?'

Simon, who had remained at the back of the room, came forward, so he stood beside Becky. Sophie glanced over her shoulder. Behind her, against the back wall, Daisy remained unconscious.

'He decided she was untreatable after all,' Becky said. 'But it was really that keeping her alive was too dangerous. This was after he found the memoir she'd been writing in secret, all the things she'd written about him. She had to go. But he made a mistake: he didn't destroy it. There was more in Jasmine's memoir, you know. When I typed it up to give to you, I left parts out. The parts about Liam, what happened after you fucked him. There was a lot in there about you as well. How she found some book that Liam tried to give you, how she was worried that he was going to run off with you. How in her most jealous, paranoid moments she fantasised about leaving cockroaches under your pillow to freak you out.'

Simon was still sweating, despite how cold it was. He was agitated, licking his lips, his eyes darting about. Becky was calm, enjoying herself, but Simon appeared rattled. Perhaps he was the weak link here. Sophie needed to keep them talking while she figured out how to get her and Daisy out of here.

'But why would Franklin tell you all this?' she asked.

'Oh, he told me nothing. But I have ears and eyes. I'm his housekeeper. His fucking little dogsbody.' Becky's eyes narrowed. 'And he treated me like a dog. This house has required quite some keeping from time to time. You wouldn't believe some of the things he's made me do. Or maybe you would believe it. It almost made me feel sorry for Jasmine, seeing what he was like. Knowing what she went through.'

340

Simon went up to Becky and put an arm around her, kissing her cheek, the gun hanging by his side. Becky shuddered, though Sophie couldn't tell if that was caused by the kiss or her memories.

'He should have been more careful. Destroyed Jasmine's manuscript or hidden it better. I guess he thought that even if I found it, no one would believe me – the girl who'd just been let out of the psychiatric hospital, the self-harmer, the fucking loony.'

'That's . . . that's what happened to you after you left university? You were sectioned?'

'Yes.' Becky spat the word. 'My dream of escaping this shithole destroyed. I came back here, back to the hospital where I'd spent half my youth. Little Becky, who won't eat. Stupid Becky, who keeps cutting herself. Bad Becky, who can't fend off the nightmares, the dreams about that place, the dark place where the mice scuttle and gnaw and squeak . . .'

While Becky talked, Sophie's eyes darted around the room, trying to figure out how she was going to get out of here. Daisy was a few feet behind her. To Sophie's left stood the metal trolley. Beyond that, the hose. Could she use any of those objects?

'When Franklin wasn't doing vile things to me,' Becky was saying, 'he wanted me to punish him, tell him he'd been a bad boy. Which was easy enough, believe me.'

'So why did you do it?'

Becky glared at her. 'Money.'

'He paid you? Like a prostitute?'

Simon pointed a finger at Sophie. 'Take that back.'

But Becky waved him away. 'Yes, he paid me. But that was pocket money. I knew I could get a lot more.' She smiled. 'Franklin didn't think I'd have the gumption to video some of the stuff he did to me. None of it illegal, not quite, but enough to make a tabloid editor salivate. Enough to destroy his reputation. With the manuscript revealing what he did to Jasmine and the videos showing what he did to me, I knew he would pay me anything. *Everything*. Don't look so appalled, Sophie. It's your fault. You made me come back here. You stopped me from escaping this island.'

'What? You think I'm responsible for what happened to you at university? What happened to your room?'

'I know you were.'

'No,' Sophie protested. 'It wasn't me! I don't know who did that to your room. I thought it was your boyfriend. Lucas.'

Becky rolled her eyes. 'There's no point lying, Sophie. You're not going to talk your way out of this.' She looked over at Daisy and Sophie came back to life. She stepped to the left, blocking Becky's view of her daughter.

'Don't you dare touch her.'

Simon lifted the nose of the gun. 'Take a step back.'

Sophie hesitated, then did as Simon asked.

On the mattress behind her, Daisy made a little groaning noise and stirred. Sophie immediately moved back towards her, but Becky said, 'Stay where you are.'

'But—'

'Stay where you are!'

Sophie made a placatory gesture and remained still, though her body ached to be close to Daisy, to comfort her when she woke up.

Daisy stirred again, coughing and rolling over on the mattress. Sophie glanced at Simon's gun. Could she get it off him, knock it out of his hand? If she could get to the trolley, perhaps she could shove it into him, knock him off-balance, make him drop the gun, perhaps. But even if they were empty-handed, what could she do? If it was just Becky, she knew she'd stand a good chance. Becky had hatred on her side, but Sophie had something that surely had to be far more powerful: the need to protect her child. Simon's presence made it impossible though, even if she was able to disarm him. He was bigger, stronger. There was no way she could overpower both of them.

She thought about the message she'd left for Paterson, telling him where she was heading. He could be trying to get hold of her right now. Would he and the other police come looking for her? Right now it seemed like their only hope.

'What are you planning to do with us?' she asked Becky.

'You'll see.'

She gestured to Simon, who handed the gun to Becky and moved behind Sophie and grabbed hold of one of her arms, twisting it and making her cry out in pain. He pushed her down into the chair with the straps and pulled one of them over her left forearm, pulling it tight so it dug into her flesh, then fastening it. He did the same with the other arm.

Becky pointed the gun at Daisy.

'It's your turn, Sophie,' Becky said. 'It's time you knew what it feels like to lose *everything*.'

'No, please, please, she's innocent! Please. I'll do anything, Becky.' She struggled, trying to pull her arms free, but the straps were too tight.

A cruel smile spread across Becky's face. 'Do you really think I'd shoot your daughter? Do you think I'm a monster?'

'Oh, thank God, thank God.'

Becky stepped closer, the shotgun beneath her arm, and took Sophie's chin in her hand, forcing Sophie to look up at her.

'It seems to me like Daisy is a spoiled little brat. That she's going to grow up to be just like you. That's why we brought her here, why we set this place up. We're going to treat her, Sophie. *Improve* her. And you're going to watch.'

Sophie screamed at her, a scream of fury and anguish, and Daisy opened her eyes. She sat up and looked around, first at Becky, then Simon, and finally at Sophie.

'Mummy.'

She tried to get up from the mattress, but her legs gave way beneath her and she fell to the hard floor onto her front. Sophie cried out. Becky was shouting too, telling Daisy to stay where she was. But the little girl wouldn't stay still. She scrambled to her feet and lurched towards Sophie, reaching the chair and scrambling onto Sophie's lap.

Simon grabbed hold of Daisy, lifting her up. She fought against him, screaming, 'Mummy! Mummy!' and pounding Simon with her tiny fists, kicking at him.

'Hold her still,' Becky yelled. '*Hold her still.*'

Daisy bit him.

He screamed, a feminine shriek, and dropped her to clutch at his wound, bending over with the pain – towards Sophie. Without thinking, she kicked as hard as she could, her foot connecting with his face. His nose exploded, blood spraying across the concrete and his head snapped up. He twisted as he tried to keep his balance but slipped on his own blood and went down face first, banging his head on the hard floor.

Daisy jumped over him and scrambled back onto Sophie's lap.

Becky didn't appear to know what to do. Half of her wanted to check that Simon was OK – she dipped towards him, then straightened up, pointing the barrel of the shotgun at Sophie and Daisy, who had started screaming again, hurting Sophie's ears.

Becky could shoot them both. But she knew this would fuck up her plan. After all the preparation. Sophie gambled that Becky wouldn't do that.

If only she could get her hands free from this chair.

Wild-eyed, Becky held the gun before her in both hands, pointed straight at her. 'Tell her to get off you!' she screamed.

Sophie shushed her daughter, whose screams subsided, turning into sobs. She kissed the back of her head as Daisy clung to her, hot tears soaking through the fabric of Sophie's top. Sophie lifted her face towards Becky. Despite being trapped, she could feel waves of power rising through her, waves of fury, waves of *madness*, and Becky faltered in the face of it, backed away.

She and Becky stared at each other.

'You need to think, Becky.'

'You need to shut your face.' But the gun was trembling.

'You need to listen. The police are on their way,' Sophie said. 'I spoke to them on the way here. They were at most an hour behind me. They'll be here any moment.'

'You're lying.'

'I'm not. DC Paterson and the others are coming. If you leave now, there's a good chance you can make it. You can run. You can probably find someone in Queenborough who'll give you a ride on their boat, take you across the Channel to Europe. You can start again, Becky. It's time for all this to stop. I know you're not an evil person. You're not, are you?'

A moment of indecision flashed on Becky's face.

'I swear to you I didn't do that to your room,' Sophie said, her voice sounding strange in her own ears. Low, almost like a growl. 'I was the one who came to help you, remember? I felt sorry for you.'

'No. It was all of you. You three planned it together. It said so in Jasmine's book.'

'What?'

'It details how the three of you planned it together. How you had overheard me telling Lucas I was afraid of mice and passed that on to Liam. Then the two of them trashed my room. I bet your job was to be there when I got back, so you could report back to them, tell them how distraught I was.'

'I swear. I didn't know you were afraid of mice. I would never use someone's phobia against them. I would never do *anything* like that. Liam must have told Jasmine he got that information from me but he was lying.'

Becky's gun was still aimed at Sophie's stomach. 'I don't believe you.'

Sophie knew she would never persuade Becky that she was telling the truth. She had no idea why Liam had lied but she didn't have time to dwell on it now. 'Did you do all this because you think I vandalised your room?'

'No! You don't get it, do you? What you did to me at university was the trigger, the incident that sent me back here, back to hospital.'

'Becky,' Sophie said in a gentle voice. 'If that was enough to send you back here, you shouldn't have been at university in the first place. You obviously weren't strong enough. You weren't well enough.'

Becky jabbed the barrel of the gun towards Sophie. 'I *was*. But you shattered all of that. You drove me back here. You destroyed my life.'

There was no point arguing anymore. Sophie could see that Becky had always blamed her, Jasmine and Liam for driving her out of university; she'd had years in psychiatric units to dwell on her bitterness, to nurture and feed it. The manuscript had confirmed that Jasmine and Liam had vandalised her room, but she would never let go of her belief that Sophie was responsible too. That would ruin the narrative she'd created to explain everything bad that had happened to her. A narrative in which Sophie was the only villain available for her to seek vengeance against.

'Becky, whatever you think of me, whatever you think I did, this isn't the right way to make yourself feel better. It's not going to help. You hated being in hospital. Well, if the police catch you, they'll send you straight back. To a high-security psychiatric unit this time. Do you really want that?'

'Becky.'

It was Simon, from his position on the floor. He sounded dazed, his voice thick with blood.

'She's right, sweetheart. Let's go. Get away before the police get here. We can start again, a new life together.'

Becky grimaced. The pressure was getting to her. Sophie could see it. Now it wasn't all going to plan, she didn't know how to cope.

'Go, now,' she said.

Becky lowered the gun. Sophie held her breath.

'No,' Becky said quietly, turning to her. Lip curling. 'I've come this far. You destroyed me.'

She raised the barrel and aimed at Daisy, who continued to cling to Sophie, eyes screwed shut. Sophie swallowed and closed her own eyes. This was it. She had tried. But at least she and Daisy would die together. At least Daisy wouldn't have to endure the *treatment* Becky had planned for her. The torture by another name.

She waited.

Simon said, 'No.'

Sophie opened her eyes to find Simon standing in front of her and Daisy. He was unsteady on his feet, but he was blocking the path of the shotgun shell. Becky was mostly blocked from Sophie's view.

'Get out of the way,' Becky hissed.

'No. This wasn't in the plan. Killing a child.'

'Get out of my fucking way, you pathetic *shit*.' The final word was screamed with venom.

Simon flinched, but he didn't move.

'I'll kill you too,' Becky said, panting. 'You think I love you. You think I love an ugly, fat, limp-dicked nobody like *you*.'

Simon took a step back towards Sophie.

'I know you won't do it,' he said. 'I know you, Becky. Whatever you say, I love you.'

He turned towards Sophie, still shielding her with his body. The lower half of his face was streaked with blood and there were tears in his eyes. He began to unfasten the right buckle.

'Stop!' Becky yelled.

He finished unbuckling the strap and moved to the left.

Becky pulled the trigger.

The noise was unlike anything Sophie had ever heard. It seemed to fill not just the basement but the world itself, before removing even the possibility of sound. Simon had completed his collapse to the floor at their feet in utter silence before Sophie began to hear Daisy's screaming.

Sophie was convinced the shotgun shell had gone through him and struck Daisy, but there was no blood on her. At the same time, she realised, both straps were undone. Becky was staring at Simon's body, blood pumping from the dark hole in his back, a few inches to the right of his spine.

Sophie threw Daisy onto the mattress and leapt to her feet. She launched herself at Becky, punching her in the chest with her fists. Becky fell onto her behind, the shotgun clutched to her midsection. She began to level it but Sophie grabbed the barrel with both hands and wrenched it to the side and down nearly to the floor.

Becky released the weapon with one hand and punched Sophie in the side of the head and Sophie roared, feeling rather than hearing the noise she made as she ripped the shotgun away from her and sent it clattering across the concrete floor. Becky attempted to punch Sophie again, but Sophie ducked so the blow glanced off the edge of her skull, then drove her own elbow into Becky's face and scrambled over to the gun.

She wheeled round with it in her hands and found that Becky was neither charging her nor attempting to seize Daisy, but clutching her own battered face and moaning. Sophie took advantage of the lull to study the shotgun. It seemed enormous to her, and far heavier than she would've imagined. She pressed the butt of it square against her shoulder and made sure she had her finger on the trigger. She had no idea what to do next beyond just squeezing it, but figured that would suffice. And given that Becky had just fired into Simon's back, there seemed little chance of the safety being on.

As though all at once remembering herself, Becky dropped her hands from her face and scrabbled onto her knees.

'Get back!' Sophie yelled, jabbing the gun in her direction. 'Get *back!*'

Becky crouched on the floor, eyes blazing up at her with fury and loathing. Daisy was a few feet behind Sophie on the mattress, seemingly unharmed but still making that terrible noise, staring with horror at the sight of her mother with a weapon in her hands.

'Get up,' Sophie shouted at Becky. 'Unlock that door.'

Becky got slowly to her feet, feeling in her pocket and producing the key she'd used to lock it.

She went over to the door and turned the lock. But she didn't open it immediately. She turned back. 'I'm going to take your advice and leave now, Sophie. But I've waited fifteen years. I can wait a little longer.' She pointed at Daisy. 'You'd better watch her. Never take your eyes off her. Because one day, one day, I'll come back and I'll finish what I've started. And then you'll know, then you'll finally—'

Sophie shot her.

The kick of the shotgun sent her staggering backwards, the blast freshly deafening her. For a nonsensical moment she wondered if she'd somehow shot her own shoulder, but that was just where the gun had been pressed when she'd fired it.

Becky was a pile of bloody clothes and hair at the foot of the stairs. There was no more need for the gun. She placed it on the floor at her feet, then went to her daughter and lifted her into her arms and shushed them both as she rocked her.

Chapter 45
Friday, 26 June, 2015

Sophie sat on the grass while Guy went off to buy ice creams from the van parked outside the playground. Children ran around her, scrambling up the climbing frame, crawling through tunnels, clinging to the roundabout as an enthusiastic dad spun it as fast as it would go. The sun was warm on her face. Last night was the first, since the events on the Isle of Sheppey, when she hadn't dreamed about Becky. In the recurring nightmare, Sophie failed to protect Daisy and Becky shot her as she lay on that dirty, ancient mattress. Then Becky morphed into Jasmine, who told Sophie she'd got exactly what she deserved, before a naked Liam appeared, sitting on the mattress beside Daisy's body, inviting her to come and lie down with him.

Every night, Sophie awoke gasping before running to Daisy's room to check she was still breathing.

Until last night, when she'd slept through. Guy had come into the bedroom with a cup of coffee for her and Sophie had jerked upright, staring around the room, shadows darting towards the walls and vanishing. Shadows shaped like Liam, Jasmine and Becky.

Her new therapist told her she would learn to cope. It would take time, but she would get there. She was keeping a close eye on

Daisy too. The little girl had been suffering from bad dreams as well, just like before, but during the day she acted as if nothing had happened. Sophie knew there was no way Daisy could have experienced all that, seen what she'd seen, without being scarred, even if the scars were hidden for now. She cursed Becky for that. In the meantime, the best she could do for Daisy was ensure she felt safe and loved, that life carried on as normal.

'Mummy, look at me.' Daisy scaled the climbing frame, checking Sophie was watching before heading to the summit. It was hard to believe that a couple of months ago this would have made Sophie anxious. Daisy had been drugged, abducted and threatened by a madwoman with a gun. A climbing frame was nothing.

Sophie noticed a couple of the other mums looking at her. She stared at them and they quickly turned back to their children. This was another after-effect of what had happened. Sophie had been in all the papers and all over the Internet. It was front-page news for days. A perfect story, involving a high-profile member of the establishment in Franklin Bird, murder, a photogenic abducted child and the Gothic horrors of what had happened at the Birds' holiday home. Pictures of the room in which Jasmine had undergone treatment filled the Internet along with the unearthed history of the Bird family.

It had come out too that Jasmine's brother, Sebastian, had hanged himself in the Jackdaw library. He had helped to dispose of Liam's body, was the one who had to cut it up and bury it in the grounds around the house on Sheppey. He had been unable to live with the guilt, the traumatic images that haunted him afterwards. Another death Franklin was responsible for.

'Well, at least he's finally going to pay now,' Guy had said.

Sophie closed her eyes for a moment, thinking about Cassie. Last week, while tidying the flat, Sophie had found her missing notebook buried beneath a pile of magazines. And there was no evidence that Simon had prevented Cassie's email to Skittle from being sent. It was a mistake, that was all. Cassie had been wholly innocent. By being so willing to think badly of her, Sophie had made things easier for Becky and Simon. She'd been complicit in her own suffering.

She watched Daisy descend the climbing frame.

'We almost lost her,' Guy said, as Daisy ambled towards them. And Sophie had thought she'd lost Guy, saying a prayer of thanks every night that Simon and Becky had lied about that. She knew Guy was suffering too, feeling guilty that he had allowed Simon to take him by surprise, coming to the flat and injecting him with a syringe full of Sodium Pentothal before taking Daisy away.

'Let's not talk about it anymore. Not today.'

The sun was warm on her face; it lit up Daisy's hair, casting a halo around her head for a moment. Daisy reached them and jumped onto Guy's lap, reaching over and throwing her arms around Sophie.

'Mummy?' Daisy said, her tone serious, and Sophie held her breath, fearing that Daisy was going to ask something about the lady Mummy had shot, or the man who had told her she was going to die, the man who had taken her away from Daddy. One day she was going to have to explain it all to her daughter. She just didn't feel ready yet.

'Yes, sweetheart?'

'Can I have another ice cream?'

Sophie met DC Paterson in a cafe near her flat.

'How are you doing?' he asked as Sophie sat opposite him. 'I thought you might want an update on where we are.'

She already knew that Franklin was under house arrest, facing a number of charges including conspiring to pervert the course of justice and child cruelty. Jasmine's parents were facing charges too, for complicity in the abuse of their daughter when she was a child. They hadn't known, they claimed, that Jasmine had spent further years in the house on Sheppey. They denied all knowledge about Jasmine's death, but they were willing to testify against the old man for what he had done during Jasmine's childhood. Finally, they were going to stand up to him. Franklin was pleading ill health. Sophie had a horrible feeling it would be decided he was too old and too sick to go to jail.

Simon had survived the shotgun blast to his back, though he'd sustained severe, probably lasting, damage to his intestines and liver and it would be as much as a year before he walked again.

'What's Simon saying now?' Sophie asked.

'Oh, he's quite forthcoming. He's claiming he was under Becky's spell, but that he's now emerging from it and wants to make amends by being cooperative. I think he's just trying to get his sentence reduced. He says that he was so besotted that he would do anything she told him to do. He claims the whole thing, their entire scheme, was her idea.'

Sophie shook her head, though that certainly coincided with her impression of their relationship.

'Have you heard of the expression *folie à deux*?' Paterson asked. 'It's a psychosis shared by two people. Usually you have a primary person, the inducer, who infects – for want of a better word – their partner with their psychosis. Our psychologists think that's what happened in this case. Simon was so smitten with Becky that when she showed him her warped perception of the world and how to achieve happiness, he went along with it.'

Everything that happened to her at work was designed to make her suffer, Paterson said, to weaken her, chip away at her sanity.

The police had found a camera positioned over Sophie's desk, with a powerful zoom. Simon must have watched her log in to Guy's Twitter account and sent the tweet that got him fired. Becky and Simon wanted Sophie to be financially dependent on Jackdaw so she couldn't leave before they had finished with her. Simon even spread that gossip about how she and Guy got together. He admitted to tracking down old colleagues of Sophie's and digging up dirt.

The police had combed through Simon's computer too. He faked the email from Matt to Cassie and got rid of him because he thought he would be a potential ally for her. They got rid of Josh for the same reason, instructing Terry Morgan to scare him so much that he would want to hide away, believing his life was in danger. The only problem Becky and Simon had really faced was when Sophie started trying to find out what really happened to Miranda. They couldn't risk the police combing that flat for DNA so they torched it, knowing it would buy them the extra time they needed.

They also found the recording of Becky acting out passages from *The Devil's Work*, which was what Simon had played the night Sophie was locked in the office. And they had found a video Simon made, using the surveillance camera above Sophie's desk, which showed Sophie's distress when Daisy went missing at work.

Sophie took a mouthful of tea. 'Has he told you why they killed Miranda? Surely they didn't murder her just so there would be a space at the company for me?'

'No. You weren't actually part of their original plan at all. After they found the manuscript Jasmine had left behind, they decided to blackmail Franklin. They were going to tell him that if he didn't give them ten million pounds they would share the manuscript with the world, along with the videos Becky had secretly made, and expose him for, one, what he'd done to Jasmine and, two, his kinky exploitation of a young woman who worked for him. But then Miranda found out what they were planning when Franklin sent her out to

Sheppey to collect some files. She saw an email that Simon had sent to Becky.'

'And they murdered her.'

'Exactly. They were planning to go ahead with the extortion, get the money and leave the country together, start a new life. And then you popped up. If that article about you hadn't appeared online, Becky would never have found you. But, according to Simon, the moment she saw it she became obsessed. She told Simon he had to hire you. They decided to delay their blackmail plan while they had their fun, as Simon phrases it, with you.'

Paterson went on. 'They were planning to contact Franklin after they'd finished with you. They were going to kill you, leave Daisy locked in the basement, and then disappear with Franklin's money. They had a boat waiting in Queenborough Harbour.' He sipped his drink. 'I bet they were pretty shocked when you turned up under your own steam. They'd already grabbed Daisy, but had no idea Terry Morgan was in custody. He was supposed to grab you and take you there that day.'

She let this sink in. Another thing she would have nightmares about: a man grabbing her, bundling her into a car, taking her to that horror house.

'There's one thing I don't understand,' she said eventually. 'Why did Becky and Simon give me Jasmine's book? When I thought Jasmine was behind everything, it made sense. I thought Jasmine wanted me to know what she'd been through. I thought it was her way of reaching out to me.'

Paterson waited for her to continue.

'But it wasn't Jasmine. It was Becky. So why did she and Simon take that risk?'

Paterson's phone beeped. He glanced at the screen, then looked up at her. 'They wanted you to know what was going to happen in their improvement room, so you'd be terrified when you got to the house and they told you what was going to happen to Daisy. They must have thought you wouldn't work out the author was Jasmine, that it was a true story. Not within the timescale, anyway.'

Paterson's phone beeped again. It was clear that he needed to go. But she had one more question. 'Becky told me they left parts out when they typed it up. Did you find the original? When you searched the house?'

'No. Just the copy they gave you. I'm sorry, Sophie. I've really got to go.' He got up from the table, throwing a £10 note down. 'I'll call you, OK?'

Sophie stood. 'Thank you.' On impulse, she hugged him.

He stepped away, a surprised look on his face.

'Look after yourself,' he said. 'And that lovely daughter of yours.'

'I intend to.'

Guy was on his laptop when she got home, Daisy playing with her Barbies in her room. Sophie had bought new ones to replace the tattooed, naked dolls that sometimes appeared in her dreams.

'Claire's harassing me about this article,' he said. 'It's a nightmare.'

She smiled. At least some things were back to normal.

Sophie went into the bedroom and sat on the bed. It still felt strange, not being at work, but she knew she'd never be able to go back to Jackdaw Books, even though a new management team had been put together. Matt had been given his job back and was no doubt chatting to Tracey right now, though probably not flirting in the way he used to.

Sophie was thinking of trying something completely new, possibly starting her own business. She had talked to Josh about it and they had come up with the idea of setting up a small, bespoke design and marketing agency. But what she really wanted to do was fulfil a dream she'd had back when she was a little girl, to write a book like the ones that had inspired her. She had always thought she wasn't good enough, lacked the talent. But now she felt like anything was possible. That she could do anything she put her mind to.

She was so tired, limbs heavy, eyes sore so she lay fully clothed on the bed, intending to nap for no more than an hour. Sunlight danced across her closed eyelids. She couldn't stop thinking about Jasmine. Becky had seemed convinced Jasmine was dead, that Franklin had murdered her. But no body had been found. What if Jasmine had managed to get away, swim ashore, start a new life somewhere else?

Before she could think about it anymore, she was asleep. She dreamed of a phoenix with colourful wings and a tail made of fire, leading her far away across the sea to a foreign land. Jasmine was there and she looked happy. She took Sophie's hand and said, 'I'm free, Sophie. I'm finally free.'

Epilogue

Franklin Bird sat in his study in his home in Belgravia, a gin and tonic in his hand. Plenty of ice. A G&T isn't a G&T if it doesn't crunch. A fire was burning in the hearth, despite the heat outside, and he was sweating, the warmth melting the ice in his drink.

House arrest – how dare they? They called him a torturer, a child abuser, in the newspapers, like he was a common criminal. The miscreants had taken over the legal system. Nobody understood about discipline any more. The world was going to hell and he was glad he wasn't going to be in it for much longer.

He stood and reached up to the bookcase. Lately, there was an aching in his bones that he'd never experienced before, pain in his spine and hips. A throbbing around his ribcage. He ignored it, taking down a large, hardback book, a book that was even older than Franklin, the first book Jackdaw had ever published. *Fantastical Tales for Boys and Girls*.

Except this was not really that book. It had been hollowed out. Inside was the vile screed Jasmine had written in secret. The notepad had made him realise she was incurable, that the rot inside her had gone too deep. Here was the evidence that the treatment, despite all his efforts, had not worked. His attempts to rehabilitate her, to save her from herself, had failed. And then he'd made a rare error, something he cursed himself for. He hadn't destroyed it there and then. He was too fascinated by it. And that loathsome, snooping pair had found and transcribed it before he'd had the sense to bring it here.

He lifted out the notepad and turned to a page near the back. Here, Jasmine had lapsed from the fictional voice she had used to narrate most of the story. This was her real voice. Her confession.

Her condemnation.

When I came out of the blackness I looked down and there he was, lying across my lap, and I said his name, whispered it, then spoke louder, louder still, tried to shake him, but he wouldn't move.

I panicked. I was covered in his blood. It was everywhere. All over my clothes, in my hair, pooling across the floor.

I panicked. I called my grandfather. I called that bastard because who else could help me? Not my weak parents. I couldn't ask Sebastian to do it; he wasn't strong enough either. It had to be the old man.

On the bed, Sophie was still asleep. She had seemed to stir for a moment, while I was on the phone, but her eyes remained shut and I was sure she hadn't seen or heard anything. And I realised: I had to get her out of here, before grandfather arrived. Because how could I convince him Sophie hadn't seen me kill Liam?

I dragged her off the bed, cushioning her fall, and she remained unconscious. I dragged her across the floor and across the hallway into Helen's empty room. Sophie was light, and I was burning with energy that gave me the strength to lift her into Helen's bed.

Grandfather arrived. I was shocked to see he had Sebastian with him. My brother, only seventeen, so innocent. I begged him not to allow Sebastian into the room. I didn't want him to witness what I'd done, but it was too late.

Grandfather looked down at Liam and crouched beside him.

'This is him?' he said. 'This is the boy who drove you to this? Who made you bad again?'

I tried to plead, to defend myself, but how could I? What could I say?

Sebastian crouched by Liam too, and took his wrist between finger and thumb.

'He's alive,' he said.

Grandfather sighed, and picked up a pillow from the bed. He held it over Liam's beautiful face, pressed down. I tried to fight him, but Grandfather ordered Sebastian to hold me back, and my brother was too scared to disobey. At the last moment, Liam's body jerked, and I thought he was going to fight. But then he lay still. Perfectly still. Then Grandfather plucked several hairs from Liam's scalp, slipping them into a compartment in his wallet.

I didn't ask why. I was too busy weeping . . .

Franklin rubbed his eyes. That stupid, stupid girl.

But he had been stupid too. Jasmine had told him her house-mate, Helen, was away. He had failed to ask if there was anyone else in the house. He should have checked. If he'd found Sophie in that other bed, he would have disposed of her too.

She had no idea how lucky she was.

He crossed the room to the window, pushed it open and felt the cool air on his face, then turned and watched it ruffle the fire. Then he walked to the fireplace and threw Jasmine's manuscript into the flames, took a final swig of his G&T, cursing the melted ice, and stepped out onto the balcony. If they thought that he, Franklin Bird, was going to stand trial, risk spending his remaining days among deviants and criminals – the sons of the morally lax, the products of a society that put a child's happiness before all else – they could think again.

Letter from the author

Dear Reader,

I hope you enjoyed *The Devil's Work*. I love hearing from readers and can be contacted in a variety of ways:

Email me at markcity@me.com
Find me on Facebook.com/markedwardsbooks
Follow me on Twitter: @mredwards

Please note, the rest of this letter may contain spoilers, so don't be tempted to peek at it until you've finished the book.

I had a lot of jobs before becoming a full-time writer. In my twenties, I worked in customer services for the Child Support Agency (the most hated organisation in the UK at that time) and a rail company (actually, I think *they* were the most hated). After that, I became an online marketer and worked for a small publishing company for almost ten years.

I would like to point out that none of the characters in this book are based on former colleagues of mine, and Jackdaw Books is nothing like the publisher I worked for. Honest! However, like most people,

I have encountered my fair share of bosses from hell and witnessed enough crazy behaviour to fill a ten-thousand-word epic saga. Gossip, petty tyranny, body odour, all those endless conversations about food – it's all in a day's work. Luckily, none of my co-workers have ever actually tried to murder me or abduct my children.

This novel is dedicated to a man I worked with for several years, Sylvester Stein. Sadly, Sylvester died while I was finishing this book, shortly after his ninety-fifth birthday. He was already in his eighties when I worked with him, still going to work every day, and more creative and innovative than anyone else I have worked with. As well as being a publisher he was a novelist and playwright, an anti-apartheid campaigner who was still winning gold medals for sprinting when I knew him. Apart from working into his eighties, Sylvester was the exact opposite of Franklin Bird in this novel and I owe him a debt of gratitude. You can find out more about Sylvester on Wikipedia.

Finally, I want to thank the many thousands of readers who have bought or borrowed one of my books over the last few years. It's hard to make a living as an author, but I am fortunate enough to be doing just that. Sometimes, when I find myself having conversations with my cat or ordering something from Amazon just so I'll see another human being during the day, I wonder what I'm doing with my life – but then I get an email from a reader telling me how much they enjoy my work, or I read a good review and it makes it all worthwhile.

Plus . . . no more office gossip or co-workers with body odour. That's definitely a bonus.

Thanks again for reading.
Best wishes
Mark Edwards
www.markedwardsauthor.com

Acknowledgements

I owe huge thanks to my editor, David Downing. A good editor acts like a coach, standing trackside and forcing the reluctant athlete to run faster, jump further and try harder. David did all that – and more. He helped get me through the pain barrier and this book would be a much lesser work without him.

Other people who helped towards the end of the process of creating this book were Sophie Missing and Hatty Stiles – thank you both. And as always, a very big thank you goes to Emilie Marneur for her insight, enthusiasm and instincts.

Thanks too to the rest of the team at Thomas & Mercer UK, including Sana Chebaro and Eoin Purcell, along with my brilliant agent, Sam Copeland.

Most of all, though, I want to thank my wife, Sara, who had to live with me while I was writing this book, picking me up from the floor when I was (almost literally) rolling about in despair, listening to me ramble on about the plot for endless hours, and reading and commenting on several early drafts. I know I've been a 'nightmare' – as a character in this novel would say – over the past year. Thank you for not divorcing me!

Several readers' names appear in this book after they won competitions on Facebook: Darren Paterson, Tracey Walsh, Angela Lockwood and Rebeka Venters. Thanks to all of you – and everybody on the Voss & Edwards Facebook page – for your long-term support and cheerleading.

Finally, I want to thank my fellow crime and thriller writers, especially the members of a certain Facebook group that has the same basic rule as *Fight Club*. Crime writers are a wonderfully supportive and friendly bunch. Much, much nicer than the colleagues in this novel.

Free *Short Sharp Shockers* Box Set

Join Mark Edwards' Readers Club and get a free collection of short stories, including *Kissing Games, Consenting Adults* and *Guardian Angel.*

You will also receive exclusive news and regular giveaways.

Get it now at www.markedwardsauthor.com/free

About the Author

Mark Edwards writes psychological thrillers in which scary things happen to ordinary people and is inspired by writers such as Stephen King, Ira Levin, Ruth Rendell and Linwood Barclay.

He is the author of three #1 bestsellers: *Follow You Home* (a finalist in the Goodreads Choice Awards 2015), *The Magpies* and *Because She Loves Me,* along with *What You Wish For* and six novels co-written with Louise Voss. All of his books are inspired by real-life experiences.

Originally from the south coast of England, Mark now lives in the West Midlands with his wife, their three children and a ginger cat.

Mark loves hearing from readers and can be contacted via his website, www.markedwardsauthor.com.